Charles Lindsey

The Life and Times of William Lyon Mackenzie

with an account of the Canadian Rebellion of 1837, and the subsequent frontier

disturbances - Vol. 1

Charles Lindsey

The Life and Times of William Lyon Mackenzie
with an account of the Canadian Rebellion of 1837, and the subsequent frontier disturbances
- Vol. 1

ISBN/EAN: 9783337095604

Printed in Europe, USA, Canada, Australia, Japan

Cover: Foto ©Raphael Reischuk / pixelio.de

More available books at **www.hansebooks.com**

LIFE AND TIMES

OF

WM. LYON MACKENZIE.

WITH AN ACCOUNT OF THE CANADIAN REBELLION
OF 1837, AND THE SUBSEQUENT FRONTIER
DISTURBANCES, CHIEFLY FROM UN-
PUBLISHED DOCUMENTS.

BY

CHARLES LINDSEY.

VOL. I.

TORONTO, C.W.:

P. R. RANDALL, No. 12 TORONTO STREET.

1862.

INTRODUCTION.

A VERY general impression prevails throughout Canada that the late William Lyon Mackenzie had, for some years, been engaged in writing his autobiography; and that, at the time of his death, the work was nearly completed. An examination of his papers showed that such was not the case. He had indeed projected such a work, and arranged much of the material necessary for its construction. The foundation had been dug; but the first stone of the superstructure had not been laid. About his intention, or rather his desire, there can be no doubt. He had made known to all his friends that he had laid out this work for himself; and even his own family were under the impression that he had made considerable progress in its execution. But on examining his papers, I soon discovered that, except detached and scattered memoranda, he had written nothing. Of autobiography, not previously written when some momentary exigency seemed to demand it, or fancy spurred him to put down some striking passage in his life, there was nothing. Beyond this, every thing had to be done by his biographer, if his life was to be written; and such was the public curiosity to learn the connected story of his eventful life, that I was pressed, on all hands, to undertake the work. At great inconvenience, and under a pressure of other exacting literary engagements, I consented.

8

A vast mass of materials was put into my hands. Although it had been subjected to a certain system of arrangement, I did not always readily discover the key to the connection. The general plan of reference was very simple. Take fifty commonplace books numbered, by pages, up to seven thousand, with an index of subjects, and you are furnished the same facility of reference as to a ledger. It is required to find all the available information on any particular subject. Under the proper head in the index, we are directed, let us suppose, to page 6,059. We find a book numbered " 6,001 to 6,062." It will therefore contain the intermediate number required. On opening at the page indicated, we find a number of manuscripts, letters, leaves from pamphlets, and cuttings from periodicals, intermingled with written notes on slips of paper, cut to the exact size necessary to contain the observations noted. All these papers are left loose for facility of removal.

So far all is plain sailing. Deficiencies, I soon found, had to be supplied; and I was sometimes puzzled to see the connection of documents lying entombed between the same pages. One subject runs into another; and to exhaust the available information on any one point, an endless number of references and comparisons had to be made. Some twenty years of newspaper files had to be carefully read. To give an idea of the mass of materials with which I had to deal, it will suffice to say that the Navy Island correspondence alone, occupying a single page of one of fifty-five common-place books—and there is a second series with a second index—would make a large printed volume.

These facts are characteristic of the methodical habits of the man whose life is, however imperfectly, delineated in this work.

Full of the fiery energy of the Celtic race; impetuous and daring; standing in the front rank of party combatants, in times and in a country where hard knocks were given and taken, it was the fate of Mr. Mackenzie to have many relentless enemies. If I had undertaken to refute all the calumnies of which he was the subject, and to correct all the false statements made to his injury, this biography would have taken a controversial form, which must have rendered it less acceptable to a large class of readers. The plan I have followed has been to tell the story of his life as I find it, without much reference to what friends or enemies, biased one way or the other, may have said under the excitement of events that have now passed into the great ocean of history. [There were some few cases in which it was necessary to clear up disputed questions, over which men still continue to differ.

The striking want of moral courage in many who were engaged with Mackenzie in the unfortunate and ill-advised insurrection, in Upper Canada, in 1837, led them to attempt to throw the odium of an enterprise that had failed in its direct object entirely upon him. Men, of whose complicity in that affair the clearest evidence exists, cravenly deny all knowledge of it. Mackenzie never shrank from his share of the responsibility. He lived to see and admit the error of the movement, and to express deep regret for the part he had taken. But an enterprise which cannot be justified, and the engaging in which involved him in ruin, was in the end advantageous to the country. Much of the liberty Canada has enjoyed, since 1840, and more of the wonderful progress she has made, are due to the changes which the insurrection was the chief agent in producing. Unless those changes had been made—unless a responsible government especially had been established—Canada would ere now either have been lost to the British Crown; or, ruled by the sword, it would have been stunted in its growth, its population poor, discontented, and ready to seek the protection of another power. The amelioration which the political institutions of Canada have undergone would probably have come in time, if there had been no insurrection; but it would not have come so soon; and there is no reason to suppose that the Province would yet have reached its present stage of advancement.

Being several thousands of miles distant when the insurrection and the frontier troubles took place, and having never been in

Canada till several years after, I lay under the disadvantage of not having any personal recollection of what occurred in those stirring times. But considering the stores of materials and the sources of information at my command, perhaps this is no great loss; certainly it will be more than compensated by the impartiality with which an unconcerned spectator can pass in review the events of that troubled period.

In the private documents in my possession, containing the secret history of the frontier movements, I found much that had never seen the light; including projects of invasion and insurrection, of which the public has never had more than the vaguest notions. The use I have made of these documents will, I presume, not be regarded as unwarranted.

I first saw Mr. Mackenzie, in 1849, when he came from New York to Canada, on a visit. Our differences of opinion on the politics of Canada during the last ten years have been notorious. Still I knew his real views perhaps better than any one else. In private he never concealed his hand to me, during the whole of that time. By the hour, when no third person was present, he would speak with great earnestness and animation on the claims of justice, the odiousness of oppression, and the foulness of corruption. The offer of office under the Government was more than once obliquely—once, I think, directly—made to him after his return to Canada, and it always threw him into a fit of passion. He received it as an attempt to destroy his independence or to shackle his freedom of action. A thousand times I have heard him protest that he would rather die of starvation than descend to any meanness, or be guilty of any act that would deprive him of that title to an unpurchasable Patriot, which he deemed the best heritage he could bequeath to his children.

CONTENTS.

7

8 CONTENTS.

LIFE

WILLIAM LYON MACKENZIE.

CHAPTER I.

General Remarks—Mackenzie's Parents—His Birth—School Days—Youth—
Characteristic Incidents—Religious Instruction imposed by his Mother—
The Books he read.

FEW men who have led a life of great mental acti
vity long survive the abandonment of their accustomed
habit of labor. Nor was it different with Mr. Mackenzie
When he resigned his seat in the Legislative Assembly,
in 1858, few of his colleagues were equal to the endurance he underwent. It was no uncommon thing for
him to burn the midnight oil till streaks of gray were
visible in the eastern horizon. He would do this three
or four nights in the week. He could jump as high,
and run as fast, as the youngest and the most athletic
member of the House. Every one thought there were
still left many years of wear in his slender but wiry
frame; but the seeds of mortality had been already sown
in his system. As a steam engine of disproportionate
size shakes to pieces the too frail vessel in which it is

11

placed, his ponderous brain, overworked with long years of mental toil, wore out the bodily frame. Nor did the brain itself escape the penalty of over-exertion. Loss of memory was the first symptom of the brain-softening thus superinduced. Violent pains in the head, accompanied by the refusal of the stomach to perform its accustomed functions, followed. For the last two years of his life, he failed more rapidly than his most intimate friends were able to realize. In his declining health, pecuniary embarrassments threw a gloom over the latter days of his existence. Whether he was himself aware of the extent to which his health had failed, that the iron frame was so far shaken and debilitated as it was, it is impossible to say. His tenacity of life would probably prevent him from admitting to himself the true state of the case; and though he often spoke of the decline of his strength, he generally did so by way of inquiry and with a view of eliciting the opinion of others on the subject. It was a point on which he was morbidly sensitive; and the last time he was out, before being confined to his death-bed, he inquired anxiously of one of his daughters whether people remarked that he was failing. When he did so, he drew himself up in a more erect posture and walked with a show of unwonted firmness, as if desirous to disprove an impression that he dreaded. Relying on the extraordinary strength of his constitution, he promised himself, in his moments of flickering hope, many years of life. But at length he became weary of battling the world, and was anxious to lie down to rest.

The public probably fancied that the Homestead

subscription had given him some degree of ease in his worldly circumstances; but the truth was that beyond the house in which he lived and died, the product was very little, and when that little was exhausted, he found himself without an income. It is doubtful whether the paper he published, *The Weekly Message*, ever yielded any profit; and he was finally compelled to abandon its publication. After this, he lived on borrowed money, obtained at usurious rates, upon the endorsement of political friends. When at last, he had to battle with despair, he ceased to desire to prolong the painful endurance of life. One day he remarked to some members of his family, that though he would not destroy the life that God had given him—that he had no right to do so—he cared not how soon it might please the Author of existence to take back the life that he had given. He died heart-broken with disappointment, as much as of brain-softening; died because he no longer knew where to find the means of existence, and because his proud spirit forbade him to beg. From his most intimate friends, who might have helped him, he concealed the embarrassments of his pecuniary position.

Such were the causes of the death of this extraordinary man, whose powers of agitation, at one period of his life, gave him an almost absolute command over the masses in his adopted country. When he had ceased to be able to speak or write, he seemed much concerned for his family; and placed the hand of the mother of his children in mine, as if to commend her to my protection. It seemed his last hope and his last wish.

In writing his biography, it will be my duty, as far as convenient, to allow him to tell his own tale; and where opinions must be expressed, it will be my aim to make them judicial and just, though I may not conceive that he was always right, either in act or opinion. In this spirit and with these feelings, I begin this tale of shipwrecked hopes and overwhelming disappointments.

Under the head " Mackenzie,"* I find among Mr. Mackenzie's papers several slips of memoranda, going over a long story of pedigrees. On reading them my curiosity was excited to see whether he was going to give point to the recital by tracing his own descent from some of the ennobled members of his family name; but the conclusion somewhat brusquely excluded any claim of this kind. According to what was long the orthodox method of writing history, he derived the Mackenzies from Noah; but with this difference, that, instead of pretending to complete the chain, he made a safe assumption of the fact.

Mr. Mackenzie's parents were married at Dundee on the 8th of May, 1794, by the Rev. Mr. Macewen.†

---

* " This ancient family," writes Mr. Mackenzie, " traces its descent from the House of Gerald, Ireland, (whence sprung some of the noble families of Leinster, Desmond, etc.,) a member of which and his followers settled in Scotland about 1261, and was created Baron of Kintail. His name was Curlinus Fitzgerald, First Baron of Kintail. He married a daughter of Walter, High Steward of Scotland; was succeeded by his son Kenneth; who again was succeeded by a son of the same name, Third Baron of Kintail, called in Gaelic, Kenneth Mackenneth, which in English was pronounced Mackenzie Mackainzie; and hence (says Burke's peerage) arose all the families of Mackenzie, in Scotland."

† The following entry is copied from an old family Bible:

Daniel Mackenzie and Elizabeth Mackenzie, both natives of Kirkmichael, Perthshire, Scotland, were married at Dundee, by the Rev. Mr. Macewen, on the 8th of May, 1794.

Of this marriage William Lyon Mackenzie, the object of this biography, was the sole issue. He was born at Springfield, Dundee, Scotland, on the 12th of March, 1795;* and his father died when the child was only twenty-seven days old.† His death was brought on by a cold contracted at a dancing party; and during his illness, which lasted only a few days, he suffered severely from a violent pain in the head. The knowledge of this circumstance caused the son, throughout his life, to dread the severe pains in the head with which he was occasionally afflicted, at long intervals, and generally after great and long continued mental exertion. What he had dreaded all his life came upon him before his death. For several weeks he complained of increasing and almost constant pains in the head. At all times, when they occurred, they had been extremely violent; and in his last illness, but chiefly before he took to his bed, or had ceased to struggle against the disease, they were the cause of intense suffering. The discrepancy between the ages of his parents was great; his father being only twenty-eight years old when he died; while his mother had seen forty-five summers when her only child was born.

His mother, by the death of her husband, who left

* William Lyon Mackenzie, born at Springfield, Dundee, Forfarshire, Scotland, March 12th, 1795. Baptized on the 29th by the Rev. Mr. Macewen, Seceder Minister.—*Entry in Family Bible.*

† Daniel Mackenzie died at Dundee on the 9th of April, 1795, leaving only one child, William Lyon, then twenty-seven days old.—*Entry in Family Bible.*

behind him no property of any account, became to a
great extent dependent upon her relatives, of whom
she had several in the Highlands; and she sometimes
lived with one and sometimes with another. Some
of them were poor, others well to do; and if it be
presumed that she gave the largest share of her patronage to the latter, the former were probably not
missed in their turn. At the same time she always
managed, by some ingenuity of industry, to keep a
humble home over the heads of herself and her boy.
Her constitutional temperament always kept her busy,
let her be where she might; her high nervous organization rendering inaction difficult to her, except towards the close of her life. In this respect, there
was a remarkable resemblance between herself and
her son; and from her, it may safely be affirmed, he
derived the leading mental characteristics that distinguished him through life.

She was so small in stature as to be considerably
below the average size of her sex. In complexion
she was a brunette; her hair was dark-brown, till
whitened by age, and at ninety it was as abundant as
ever, and always long. Her dark eyes were sharp
and piercing, though generally quiet; but when she
was in anger, which did not often occur, they flashed
out such gleams of fire as might well appall an antagonist. Her features, corresponding with her size,
were small; and the prominence of her cheek-bones
gave unmistakable indications of her Celtic origin. The
small mouth and the thin, compressed lips, in harmony with the whole features, told of that unconquer-
able will which she transmitted to her son. The fore-

head was broad and high, and the face seldom relaxed into perfect placidity; there were always on the surface indications of the working of the volcanic feelings within. The subduing influences of religion kept her strong nature under control, and gave her features whatever degree of repose they ordinarily wore.

Her strong religious bias made her an incessant reader of the Scriptures and such religious books as were current among the Seceders. With this kind of literature she early imbued the mind of her son; and, it would not be difficult to show, the impressions thus formed were never wholly effaced. Though of Highland origin, she spoke Gaelic but rarely, it would seem, for she never imparted more than a very slight knowledge of it to her son. She cherished some plausible superstitions, firmly believing that a Mackenzie never died without warning of the coming event being given by some invisible messenger in a strange, unearthly sound, and had a strong suspicion that fairies were something more than myths. The strongest reciprocal affection existed between her and her son, at whose house she spent the last seventeen years of her life, having followed him to Canada, in company with Mr. J. Lesslie, in 1822, and died at Rochester, N. Y., in 1839, while her son was a state prisoner, in Monroe county jail, under sentence for a breach of the neutrality laws of the United States. She had attained the mature age of ninety years, a fact which goes to show that it was through her that Mr. Mackenzie inherited a physical frame capable of extraordinary endurance, as well as his natural mental endowments.

2

Daniel Mackenzie, father of the subject of this bio
graphy, is described as a man of dark complexion; and
his grandfather Colin Mackenzie, used to bear the cog-
nomon of "Colin Dhu," or black Colin. Daniel learned
weaving in all its branches; but entering into an unprofitable commercial speculation, he was reduced to keeping a few looms for the manufacture of "green cloth."

But Mr. Mackenzie may here be allowed to tell his
own tale of his ancestry. In June, 1824, just when
he had entered on his editorial career, he was called
upon to meet the charge of disloyalty; and his defence, which is in his happiest mood, shows how much
better were his early compositions when youth was
fresh and hope beat high, than those of his later days,
when the pangs of disappointment had fastened upon
his soul, and the great aims of his life had miscarried.

"My ancestors too stuck fast to the legitimate race of
kings, and though professing a different religion, joined
Charles Stuart, whom (barring his faith) almost all
Scotland considered as its rightful sovereign. Colin
Mackenzie, my paternal grandsire, was a farmer under
the Earl of Airly in Glenshee, in the highlands of
Perthshire; he, at the command of his chieftain, willingly joined the Stuart standard, in the famous 1745,
as a volunteer. My mother's father, also named Colin
Mackenzie, and from the same glen, had the honor to
bear a commission from the Prince, and served as an
officer in the Highland army. Both my ancestors
fought for the royal descendant of their native kings;
and after the fatal battle of Culloden, my grandfather
accompanied his unfortunate prince to the low countries, and was abroad with him on the continent, fol-

lowing his adverse fortunes for years. He returned at length; married, in his native glen, my grandmother, Elizabeth Spalding, a daughter of Mr. Spalding, of Ashintully castle, and my aged mother was the youngest but two of ten children, the fruit of that marriage. The marriage of my parents was not productive of lasting happiness; my father, Daniel Mackenzie, returned to Scotland from Carlisle, where he had been to learn the craft of Rob Roy's cousin, Deacon Jarvie of the Saltmarket, Glasgow, or in other words, the weaving business, took sickness, became blind, and in the second year of his marriage with my mother died, being in his twenty-eighth or twenty-ninth year. I was only three weeks old at his death; my mother took upon herself those vows which our Church prescribes as needful at baptism, and was left to struggle with misfortune, a poor widow, in want and in distress. It is among the earliest of my recollections, that I lay in bed one morning during the grievous famine in Britain, in 1800-1, while my poor mother took from our large Kist (which is an article of furniture of a sort only to be found among the Scotch and Irish) the handsome plaid of the tartan of our clan, which in early life her own hands had spun, and went and sold it for a trifle, to obtain for us a little coarse barley meal, whereof to make our scanty breakfast; and of another time during the same famine, that she left me at home crying from want and hunger, and for (I think) 8s. sold a handsome and hitherto carefully preserved priest-gray coat of my father's to get us a little food. How the mechanics and laborers contrived to exist during these times, is what I cannot tell; my recollections of this period are faint and indistinct. Well may I love the poor, greatly may I esteem the humble and the lowly, for poverty and adversity were my nurses, and in youth were want and misery my familiar friends; even now it yields a sweet satisfaction to my soul, that I can claim kindred with the obscure cottar, and the humble laborer, of my native, ever honored, ever loved Scotland.

> "'Long may thy hardy sons of rustic toil
> Be blest with health, and peace, and sweet content!'"

"My mother feared God, and he did not forget nor forsake her: never in my early years can I recollect that divine worship was neglected in our little family, when health permitted; never did she in family prayer forget to implore that He, who doeth all things well, would establish in righteousness the throne of our monarch, setting wise and able counsellors around it. A few of my relations were well to do, but many of them were poor farmers and mechanics, (it is true my mother could claim kindred with some of the first families in Scotland; but who that is great and wealthy, can sit down to count kindred with the poor?) yet amongst these poor husbandmen, as well as among their ministers, were religion and loyalty held in as due regard, as they had been by their ancestors in the olden time. Was it from the precept—was it from the example of such a mother and such relations, that I was to imbibe that disloyalty, democracy, falsehood, and deception, with which my writ-

ings are by the government editor* charged? Surely
not. If I had followed the example shown me by my
surviving parent, I had done well; but as I grew up
I became careless, and neglected public and private
devotion. Plainly can I trace from this period, the
commencement of these errors of the head, and of
the heart, which have since embittered my cup, and
strewed my path with thorns, where at my age I
might naturally have expected to pluck roses.

"Earnestly did my mother desire me to honor my
heavenly King, to remember my Creator in the days
of my youth, and I at this distant day have much
greater cause to regret the little attention I then paid
to her well meant admonitions in that respect, than to
take blame to myself for either thinking or speaking
disrespectfully of our anointed sovereign. The celebrated traveller, my namesake, Sir Alexander Mackenzie, died on the same month on which I was born,
and just a quarter of a century thereafter. I came
into existence the 12th of March, 1795; he left the
world the same date, 1820; he was no kinsman of
mine, but he was a Mackenzie, and if I can spread
the fame of *The Advocate*† to regions as far west as to
where he travelled, I shall be very well satisfied,
whether Sir Thomas gets his copy or not."

His first school-teacher was Mr. Kinnear, of Dundee, who was master of a parish school. One of his
school-mates,‡ from whom I have sought information,

---

* Mr. Charles Fothergill, editor of the Upper Canada *Gazette*, then published
in Toronto, and King's Printer. The *Gazette*, like the *Moniteur* of Paris, had
an official and a non-official side.

† The name of the first newspaper he published.

‡ Mrs. Reid, of Rochester, N. Y.

describes him as a "bright boy, with yellow hair, wearing a blue short coat with yellow buttons." The school-house, large and well lighted, had previously been a Catholic chapel. The stone basin, placed in a niche in the wall, which had formerly been a repository of "holy water," was now converted into a seat of punishment, called the "holy cup." Though very small when he first entered, Willie, as he was called, was generally at the head of his class. His progress in arithmetic, particularly, was very rapid. He was often asked to assist other boys in the solution of problems which baffled their skill; and while he rendered this service, he would pin papers or draw grotesque faces, with chalk, on their coat backs. "He was ever ready," says my informant, "to help the girls, particularly if they were good looking." Even then his power of declamation was considerable, and on one occasion the school was made a scene of uproar and confusion, on his account; the scholars shouting at the top of their voices and hissing at the master. The thing happened in this wise.

One day he went into the master's closet, donned the fool's cap, and with the long leather taws tied a canvass sack round his shoulders, and then, with birch in hand, he took his seat on the "holy cup," to the great amusement both of the boys and girls. While thus seated, making grotesque faces and speechifying, in walked the dominie, a man six feet eight and proportionably stout, just when the mirth was at its height. Though boiling over with rage, Mr. Kinnear could hardly escape the contagion of the general laughter. When angry, his face was any thing but prepossessing. Little Willie saw the danger and attempted to escape; but he came back at the demand of the angry voice of the excited dominie. The crime of going into the sacred apartment of the master must be visited with condign punishment. Willie's hand being held out was touched with a small brush, dipped in whitening, made from "calmstone," and then struck with the taws twelve times, till his face was all spotted over. Then he was conducted back to the holy cup. This exhibition excited the indignation of the larger boys, who hissed and shouted, till a scene of perfect confusion was created, in the midst of which some, who were particularly conspicuous in their demonstrations, were seized by the indignant dominie, and imprisoned in a small room; by which means peace was restored. Willie was ordered to go to the master's house next day; whence, after being detained a few minutes, he returned with his face as radiant as ever. When the dominie's back was turned, he made such grimaces as he alone could make. Young Mackenzie's overpowering sense of the ridiculous, which on this occasion he tried to excite in others, adhered to him through life. After leaving Mr. Kinnear's school, he went to that of Mr. Adie; but how long he spent there cannot be ascertained.

At the age of ten years, some difficulty occurring between him and his mother, he resolved to leave home, and set up on his own account. For this purpose he induced some other boys, of about his own age, to accompany him to the Grampian Hills, among which he had often been taken, and where, in a small castle which was visible from Dundee, and of which

they intended to take possession, they made the ro-
mantic resolve of leading the life of hermits. They
never reached the length of the castle, however,
and after strolling about a few days, during part of
which they were terribly frightened at the supposed
proximity of fairies, they were glad to trudge their
way back to the town, half famished. This incident
is characteristic, and might have been regarded as
prophetic; for the juvenile brain that planned such
enterprises would not be likely to be restrained, in
after life, where daring is required. In it we see the
same impatience of restraint that impelled Captain
John Smith, best known by his association with Poca-
hontas, to sell his books and satchel, when a mere
urchin, with a determination to steal away to sea.

It is probable that the difficulty between young
Lyon and his mother, which led to this escapade, arose
out of the long reading tasks which it was her custom to impose upon him. He was in this way thoroughly drilled in the Westminster Catechism and
Confession of Faith; he got the Psalms and large portions of the Bible by rote, and was early initiated
into " Baxter's Call to the Unconverted," and several
similar works. When one of these tasks had been
given him, his mother used to confine him closely till
it had been mastered. That he sometimes felt these
reading tasks to be irksome is known from his own
statements; and his idea, in mature life, was that the
thing had been overdone. This early exercise of the
memory, it may be reasonably assumed, tended to
give to that faculty the strength which in after life
was a source of astonishment to many. Perhaps,

however, those who did not know Mr. Mackenzie's personal habits often attributed to his unaided memory much that was the result of reference to those stores of information which he never ceased to collect, and which were so arranged as to admit of easy access at any moment. It would be a mistake to suppose that the large amount of religious reading he was compelled, at an early age, to go through gave him a distaste for that kind of literature. On the contrary, what had been imposed as a task seems to have become, in time, a pleasure, if we may judge by the list of theological works which he voluntarily read between the ages of eleven and twenty-four years. He has left in his own hand-writing a list of "some of the books read, between the years 1806 and 1819, by W. L. Mackenzie,"* in which are fifty-four works under the head of "Divinity," one hundred and sixty-eight on History and Biography, fifty-two of Travels and Voyages, thirty-eight on Geography and Topography, eighty-five on Poetical and Dramatic Literature, forty-one on Education, fifty-one on Arts, Science, and Agriculture, one hundred and sixteen Miscellaneous, and three hundred and fifty-two Novels; making, in all, nine hundred and fifty-eight volumes, in thirteen years. One year he read over two hundred volumes. Here the list ends, and it may be taken for granted Mr. Mackenzie's reading of books became less after 1824, when he got immersed in politics, and

---

* See Appendix A. The number of books read was thus distributed over the different years:—In 1806-7, 89 vols.; 1808-9, 204 vols.; 1810, 79 vols.; 1811, 52 vols.; 1812-13, 61 vols.; 1814-15, 198 vols.; 1816, 48 vols.; 1817, 68 vols.; 1818, 49 vols.; 1819, 88 vols.; 1820, 27 vols.

4

had a newspaper to conduct. It is not often that the world is enabled to see, at a glance, the stores of information by which the mind of a remarkable man has been enriched and modified; and it is peculiarly fortunate that a catalogue has been preserved, in this case. With his tenacious memory, Mr. Mackenzie must have been enabled to draw, from time to time, upon these stores, during the rest of his life. The works are confined almost exclusively to the English language; and the truth is, that he had only an imperfect knowledge of any other. Otherwise there is little reason to object to the want of variety, and there does not appear to be any reason why they should have given any undue bias to the mind. Of a tendency to scepticism, of which he was accused in the latter part of his life—with what justice will hereafter be seen—there is, in the works which must have tended to give a cast to his mind, an almost entire absence.

In whatever occupations young Mackenzie was engaged, from the period of his leaving school to his coming to Canada, the facts already stated show that he was constantly storing his mind with varied information. His mother used to tell how, when a little boy, he would read till after midnight—different books it may be presumed from those in which his daily tasks were set—till she thought "the laddie would read himsel' out o' his judgment."

In early youth, politics already possessed a charm for him; the Dundee, Perth, and Cupar *Advertiser*, the first newspaper he ever read, serving to gratify this inclination. But he was soon admitted to a

wider range of political literature; for he was introduced to the Dundee news-room, at so early a period
of life that he was for years after its youngest
member.

The adventurous life of a sailor had, at one time,
strong fascinations for him. His own account of this
boyish fancy runs: "When a little fellow at school, I
had at one time a strong inclination for the sea, and
used after school-hours, or between them, to accompany some of my playmates to the pier, and wager
marbles which of us could soonest double the cap,
pass the double cross-trees, and turn this vessel's
vane. I well remember that I won more marbles
than I lost in this way; and when I went on board
the venerable ship, tight and in good condition as she
still remains, and had fairly recognized my old acquaintance, I felt a mingled sensation of pain and
pleasure, at the recollection of the past."* His ven-
turesome habits, when a boy, once nearly lost him his
life. With a courage above his skill, he plunged into
the waters of the Tay, making an effort to swim, and
sank twice before he was rescued.

* This was in 1833, when he revisited his native town.

CHAPTER II.

Young Mackenzie is employed in a Draper's shop—Then in the Counting
House of Mr. Gray, of Dundee—Meets Dr. Chalmers before he had emerged
from obscurity—Starts business at Alyth, near Dundee, when under age,
and fails—Goes to England—Certificate of the Minister and Session Clerk
of Alyth—Becomes Clerk to the Kennett and Avon Canal Company in England—Seeks employment in London—The resolution to go to Canada—
First visits France.

FOR a short time after leaving school, and when he
must have been a mere boy, he was put into Mr.
Henry Tulloch's draper's shop, High Street, Dundee;
but disliking the situation, he did not long remain
there ; probably only a few months.

He afterwards became an indentured clerk in the
counting house of Gray, a wood merchant, in a large
way of business, in Dundee. Mr. Mackenzie's papers
relating to the early part of his life were, with
others, placed with some friend in the country, at the
time of the rebellion ; but the custodians, of what
might be dangerous documents, got alarmed on the
execution of Lount and Matthews for high treason,
and they committed the papers to the flames. It becomes more difficult, for this reason, to fix dates with
precision at this period of his life. Of Mr. Gray,
Mr. Mackenzie was in the habit of speaking in the
highest terms. In a letter, dated Dundas, March 16,

1850, he said: "Mr. Gray, an excellent man, was one of my earliest and best friends. I was then a clerk in his counting room, under indenture for a term of years, and well remember going over occasionally to his brother-in-law's, at Kilmany, in Fife, where I first saw Dr. Chalmers, then about thirty years old, and living in comparative obscurity. He appears to have been deeply impressed, while at Kilmany, with the benefits conferred upon society by the religious instruction of youth at Sunday Schools. Chalmers was no ordinary man, but truly great and good." It was probably while in the counting house of Mr. Gray that Mr. Mackenzie acquired that knowledge of the mysteries of accounts, which afterwards made his services of considerable value as Chairman of the Committee of Public Accounts, in the Legislative Assembly of Canada, and which has enabled him to render important service in the Welland Canal investigation, and on other occasions, when financial mysteries had to be solved.

At an early age, apparently when he was about nineteen, he went into business for himself at Alyth, some twenty miles from Dundee, setting up a general store, such as is kept in country places, in connection with a circulating library. He remained here for three years, when the result of inexperience assumed the shape of a business failure. His creditors were all honorably paid after he had acquired the necessary means in Canada, at the distance of some years.

It was about the middle of May, 1817, when he left Alyth; and he soon afterwards went to England. The time when he went to Alyth and when he left is fixed by a certificate, signed by the minister and the clerk of session at that place, written shortly before his departure for Canada:

"ALYTH, *March* 30, 1820.

"That the bearer, Lyon Mackenzie, resided in this Parish about three years preceding Whitsunday, eighteen hundred and seventeen, when he removed from this Parish, without anything known to us, at his removal hence, to prevent him from being admitted into any Christian Society, or partaking of Church privileges, is attested by

" WM. RAMSAY, Minister.

" EDW. PATERSON, Session Clerk."

Young Mackenzie afterwards, leaving his native Scotland, crossed to the South of the Tweed; where at one time we find him filling the situation of Clerk to the Kennett and Avon Canal Company,* at another

---

* The following summons proves him to have been in the employment of this Company in October, 1818; which was eighteen months before he sailed for Canada.

WILTSHIRE, } *To all Constables, Tythingmen, and others, His Majesty's Officers*
TO WIT.   } *of the Peace in and for the said County, whom these may concern,*
           } *any or either of them.*

THESE are in His Majesty's Name, to will and require you, on Sight hereof, to summon David Slowly, Captain of the boat No. 6, Euclid Shaw, of Bath, owner, personally to be and appear before me, and such other of his Majesty's Justices of the Peace for the said County of Wilts as shall be present at the Town Hall in Devizes, in the said County, on Tuesday, the Tenth day of November next, at eleven of the clock in the forenoon, to answer to what is and shall be on His Majesty's Behalf objected against him by *William Lyon Mackenzie, Clerk to the Kennett and Avon Canal Company,* for having, on the third of October instant, offended against the eleventh article of the said Company's Bye-Laws, by carrying shafts and poles constructed contrary to the same. And you are to attend at the time and place above appointed for the appearance of the said parties, and to make return of this precept and of the execution hereof.

Herein fail not at your perils. Given under my Hand and Seal, the tenth day of October, in the fifty-eighth year of the reign of our Sovereign Lord

time in London; and he used to relate that he was for a short time in the employ of Earl Lonsdale, as a clerk. In the autumn before he left for Canada, our future emigrant was in London, where he appears to have been either without employment or not to have been so satisfactorily engaged as to preclude the desire of a change. A correspondence took place between him and a Mr. Wm. Dunsford, who held an office in a Canal Company's office, at Swindon, Wiltshire. There was a question of the Company establishing a Gauging Dock; and if this was done, Mr. Mackenzie was to be recommended for an office in connection with it. The Committee of Directors, with whom the decision would rest, was not to meet till December, 1819; and whatever was the result at which they arrrived, Mr. Mackenzie was destined to cross the Atlantic and become a resident of Canada next Spring. Mr. Dunsford, in October, writes in a friendly, if not very encouraging tone,* and adds a postscript, asking to borrow the for-

GEORGE the Third, by the Grace of God of the United Kingdom of Great Britain and Ireland King, and in the year of our Lord, 1818.

HENRY BAYNSTON.

* CANAL OFFICE, SWINDON, October 18, 1819.

SIR:—I received your letter of the 15th yesterday, and am sorry you have not succeeded in making an arrangement with the K. & A. Co., to allow us the use of their Tables. I do not expect that Mr. Thomas will communicate with me on the subject. The very *liberal* ideas of that gentleman as to the neighboring Canals, as you represented them to me, forbid the hope of such an accommodation.

I therefore look forward to the time when the Companies for whom I am concerned will be able to set on foot an establishment of their own for the purpose, and it shall not be my fault if this is delayed a moment after the necessary means can be procured; but you are aware that such a thing cannot be effected in a moment, and that before the expenditure of at least £700 or £800

mula of certain gauging tables belonging to Mr. Mackenzie.

That he was probably without employment, and was certainly in search of an occupation, in October, 1819, appears from Mr. Dunsford's letter; and as he conceived he had not met with fair usage, it is probable that it was not long after this time when he resolved to sail for Canada the next Spring. He appears then to have only just left Swindon and the Kennett and Avon Canal Company; for Mr. Dunsford, at that date, mentions the failure of Mr. Mackenzie's attempt to effect a certain arrangement with his employers to allow their Gauging Tables to be used by another Company. This occurrence must have been of recent date; and it is probable that Mr. Dunsford replied as soon as he learned from Mr. Mackenzie the result of the application, which may be presumed to have been made before the latter left the service of the Canal Company.

can be resolved upon, the Committee will require time for deliberation. Their next meeting is not till the middle of December, and until that time, all that I can say is, that in the event of their determining on a Gauging establishment, I should not hesitate to recommend you to their notice, being perfectly satisfied of your competency for the business, and not doubting the testimonials you could bring to your character. I will further add that the salary you expect would not be objected to, together with a comfortable house for your residence. Under these circumstances, it appears to me that you had better not omit *any* favorable appointment that may offer for your settlement; but should you not be better provided, in the event of our building a Gauging Dock, upon your favoring me with your future address when convenient, I will not fail to remember you; and wishing you the success you appear to deserve, and better usage than you say you have had,

I remain your obedient servant,

WILLIAM DUNSFORD.

If you feel no objection to sending me the formula of your Gauging Tables, I should be obliged, as it would assist me in explaining the system to our Committees better than my memory will serve.

The idea of going to Canada is said to have been first suggested to Mr. Mackenzie by Mr. Edward Lesslie, of Dundee. He was elated at the prospect which the New World held out to him, and gave expression to his hilarity in a demonstrative manner.

Before starting for Canada, he visited France. The date of this visit cannot now be fixed with certainty; but it was probably in November or December, 1819.

He confesses to having, a little before this time, plunged into the vortex of dissipation and contracted a fondness for play. But all at once, he abandoned the dangerous path on which he had entered, and after the age of twenty-one never played a game at cards. A more temperate man than he was, for the rest of his life, it would have been impossible to find.

5

CHAPTER III.

Sails for Canada in the Psyche—Personal Appearance—Is connected with the
Lachine Canal Survey—Enters into the Book and Drug Business in York—
Afterwards in Dundas—The Partnership with Lesslie Dissolved—Starts a
separate business in Dundas—Removes to Queenstown—Abandons Mercantile
Business for Politics—The First Office that he is Elected to is that of School
Trustee.

IN April, 1820, there was among the passengers of
the Psyche, bound for Canada, and commanded by
Captain Thomas Erskine, a young man just turned
twenty-five years of age, born of poor Scottish parents; whose mother, widowed in his infancy, had
sometimes been at a loss to find the plainest food for
his nourishment; a young man who had been a clerk
in a counting house, at Dundee; who had tried mercantile business on his own account, in a small Scottish market town, and failed; who had held a clerk-
ship under a company and a nobleman in England;
who, without having enjoyed any other advantage of
education than the parochial and secondary schools of
Dundee offered, had a mind well stored with varied
information which he had devoured with the appetite
of a literary glutton; who was so little known that
his departure from his dear native soil excited no
public interest or attention. Yet was it fated that this
young man should change the destiny of the country

to which the good ship Psyche was bearing him. He
was of slight build and scarcely of medium height,
being only five feet six inches in stature. His massive
head, high and broad in the frontal region and well
rounded, looked too large for the slight wiry frame it
surmounted. He was already bald from the effects of
a fever. His keen, restless, piercing blue eye, which
threatened to read your most interior thoughts, and
the ceaseless and expressive activity of his fingers,
which unconsciously opened and closed, betrayed a
temperament that could not brook inaction. The chin
was long and rather broad; and the firm-set mouth
indicated a will which, however it might be baffled
and thwarted, could not be subdued. The lips, firmly
pressed together, constantly undulated in a mass,
moving all that part of the face which lies below the
nostrils; with this motion the twinkling of the eyes
seemed to keep time, and gave an appearance of
unrest to the whole countenance. The deep dimples
in the cheeks, exaggerating the protuberance of the
cheek bones, were connected by a strongly marked
sunken line which shot up to about half the height of
the nose, and left a slight ridge which ran at right
angles with the upper part of the cheek bone. The
centre of the nose at the base protruded a rounded
point below the orifice of the nostrils. The deep-set
eyes were overarched by massive brows, which threw
the forehead a little out of its perpendicularity, and
which alone gave it the least receding angle. This
assemblage of features will at once be seen to have
been striking and characteristic. They were almost
constantly animated by a flow of spirit which put the

rest of the passengers in good humor; for the hope
of youth deceptively painted with its roseate views that
future which, to the young Dundee emigrant, was to
be beset with so many difficulties, bestrewed with thorns,
and watered with tears of blood.

After his arrival in Canada, Mr. Mackenzie was for a
short time employed in connection with the survey of
the Lachine Canal; but it could only have been a few
weeks, for in the course of the summer he entered into
business in York, as the present city of Toronto was then
called. "My first occupation," he has left it on record,
"in York was mercantile. I had the profits of one part
of the establishment in this town, which was resigned
when I went into partnership in trade,"* in Dundas.
In York, Mr. John Lesslie and he were in the book and
drug business; the profits of the books going to Mr.
Lesslie, and that of the drugs to Mr. Mackenzie. It
was found, I believe, that physic for the body was in
greater demand than garniture for the mind; and the
question arose of finding another place at which to
establish a second business, in which Mr. Mackenzie
and Mr. John Lesslie were to be partners. The business in York was afterwards conducted for the exclusive benefit of the remaining partner. Kingston was
thought of, but Mr. Mackenzie did not like the place,
and Dundas was selected. Here he conducted the business of the partnership for fifteen or sixteen months;
during which time, I have heard him say, a clear
cash profit of £100 a month was made. In a printed
poster, I find the firm styled "Mackenzie and Lesslie,
Druggists, and Dealers in Hardware, Cutlery, Jewelry;

* *Colonial Advocate*, January 21, 1828.

Toys, Carpenter's Tools, Nails, Groceries, Confections, Dye-Stuffs, Paints, &c., at the Circulating Library, Dundas." The partnership was dissolved, by mutual consent, in the early part of 1823. A division of the partnership effects was made; and, in papers which have been preserved, Mr. Mackenzie appears as a purchaser from the firm of Mackenzie & Lesslie to the amount of £686 19s 3½d. The goods included in this purchase were as miscellaneous as can well be imagined; and they were destined to form the nucleus of a separate business to be carried on by Mr. Mackenzie. The invoice is headed, " Dundas, U. C., 24th February, 1823. William Lyon Mackenzie bought of Mackenzie & Lesslie;" and its completion bears date, " Dundas, March 20th, 1823." Below this date, at the bottom of the figures, is a memorandum of agreement of purchase and sale:

" We agree that the above is a correct, true, and proper invoice, in the items and in the amount; the same being six hundred and eighty-six pounds nineteen shillings and three pence ½ curr'y.

"WM. L. MACKENZIE,   JOHN LESSLIE."

With this stock a separate business was commenced; but it was not long continued, for in the autumn of the same year Mr. Mackenzie removed to Queenstown, and there opened a general store. Before leaving Dundas, he sold to Mr. Lesslie one of the buildings he had erected at that place, but retained a storehouse. At Queenstown, he resided only a year; and before the expiration of that time, he had abandoned commerce for politics; and as a journalist, made the first step in the eventful career which opens with this period of his life. The stock of miscellaneous goods was disposed of to a store-keeper in the country; and thus the business was closed without resorting to the tedious practice of selling off in detail.

While living in Dundas, Mr. Mackenzie was married. This event took place on the 1st of July, 1822, at Montreal. Miss Isabel Baxter, his bride, may be said to have been a native of the same town as himself; for she was born at Dundee and he at Springfield, a suburb of the same place. Though they both were at the same school together, when young, they had ceased to be able to recognize one another when they met at Quebec. The marriage took place within three weeks from the first interview: a circumstance that accords with the general impulsive nature of his character. Of this union the issue was thirteen children: three boys and ten girls; six of whom are now living: four daughters and two sons. Five died in infancy: one at thirteen years, and one at thirty-two.

Up to this time, Mr. Mackenzie had not held any other office in Canada than that of School Trustee; and he confessed that even that mark of public confidence inspired him with pride. He and Mr. Thorburn were elected to that office, at the same time, at Queenstown. Speaking of this occurrence, he says: "The first newspaper I ever issued was a protest against binding down our projected university to the dogmas of any sect: whether of Oxford, Edinburgh, Rome, or Moscow." Never was prophecy more literally fulfilled than that of his regarding the effects of giving a sectarian character to a university which had not yet come into existence.

CHAPTER IV.

Mr. Mackenzie's Reasons for going into Politics—Condition of Canada in 1820
—Moderation of the Political Principles with which he set out—Most of the
Reforms he advocated Carried—On some subjects Public Opinion went
far beyond his Starting Point—State of the Press in Upper Canada, in
1826—A Union of all the North American Provinces—General Election,
of which the Result was Unfavorable to the Executive—A Scene in Court—
Mackenzie on Judge Boulton.

WHEN Mr. Mackenzie abandoned trade for politics,
he was doing well, and had done well ever since he
commenced business. A perseverance in the career
on which he had entered four years before would
have led to wealth. In the first number of *The Colonial Advocate*, published at Queenstown, on the 18th
May, 1824, he describes himself as being "as independent as editors can well be;" and this evidently had
reference to his pecuniary position, for he adds, "We
are not in want, neither are we rich." The step which
he had now taken was one of the most important in his
whole career, since it involved every thing that followed. Why did he take it? Fortunately the answer can be given in his own words. In a letter written to a friend while he was in the United States, he
says :—

"When you and your father knew me first, in
1820, I was a young man connected with trade in

York and Dundas. The prudent, judicious, and very profitable manner in which I conducted, alone, the partnership concerns of a large trading establishment, at the head of Lake Ontario, surely afforded satisfactory evidence that I had no occasion to leave my private pursuits for the stormy sea of politics, with a view to the improvement of my pecuniary prospects. When I did so, and assumed, as the westernmost journalist in the British dominions on the continent of America, the office of a public censor, I had no personal enemies, but was on friendly terms with many of the men whom since then I have steadily opposed. I never interfered in the public concerns of the colony, in the most remote degree, until the day in which I issued twelve hundred copies of a newspaper, without having asked or received a single subscriber. In that number I stated my sentiments, and the objects I had in view fully and frankly. I had long seen the country in the hands of a few shrewd, crafty, covetous men, under whose management one of the most lovely and desirable sections of America remained a comparative desert. The most obvious public improvements were stayed; dissension was created among classes; citizens were banished and imprisoned in defiance of all law; the people had been long forbidden, under severe pains and penalties, from meeting anywhere to petition for justice; large estates were wrested from their owners in utter contempt of even the forms of the courts; the Church of England, the adherents of which were few, monopolized as much of the lands of the colony as all the religious houses and dignitaries of the Roman Catholic Church had had the control of in Scotland at the era of the Reformation; other sects were treated with contempt and scarcely tolerated; a sordid band of land-jobbers grasped the soil as their patrimony, and with a few leading officials, who divided the public revenue among themselves, formed 'the family compact,' and were the avowed enemies of common schools, of civil and religious liberty, of all legislative or other checks to their own will. Other men had opposed, and been converted by them. At nine-and-twenty I might have united with them, but chose rather to join the oppressed, nor have I ever regretted that choice, or wavered from the object of my early pursuit. So far as I or any other professed reformer was concerned in inviting citizens of this Union to interfere in Canadian affairs, there was culpable error. So far as any of us, at any time, may have supposed that the cause of freedom would be advanced by adding the Canadas to this Confederation, we were under the merest delusion."

This picture of Upper Canada, in 1820, may be highly colored; but in the general outlines, repulsive as they are, there is too much truth. The limner lived to see a change of system in Canada; and after he had had a more than theoretical experience of Democracy in the United States—having resided there for several years—he warns Canadians not to be misled by the delusion that the cause of liberty would be advanced by uniting these Provinces to the American Republic. When we come to see at what price he purchased the experience, which entitled him to express such an opinion, the value of this admonition

6

cannot fail to be enhanced in the estimation of all un-prejudiced judges.

In some respects, the condition of the Province, in 1820, was worse than Mr. Mackenzie described it. He dealt only with its political condition; but the ab-sence of demand for employment made wretched those who depended solely upon their labor for subsistence. When Lord A. Hamilton suggested, in the House of Commons, April 28th, 1820, that an emigration to the North American colonies would be the most effectual means of relieving distress at home, the Chancellor of the Exchequer replied, that the emigrants who had re-cently gone there, " so far from finding increased means of subsistence, had experienced a want of employment fully equal to that which existed in the most distressed manufacturing districts of this country. The North American Provinces of Great Britain had been so overloaded with emigrants, that the government of Canada had made the strongest remonstrances to the government of this country on the subject."

Public meetings, the actors in which had been de-puted to represent any portion of the elections, were illegal; and every thing in the shape of a convention was held to be seditious. Any new comer, who had not been six months in the Province, was liable to be banished, not for any thing he had done, but upon a mere suspicion that he was "about to endeavor to alienate the minds of his Majesty's subjects of this Province from his person or government." Under the sedition act of 1804, which armed the government with this authority, Mr. Robert Gourlay, a Scotchman of respectable antecedents and shattered nerves, was sen-

tenced to banishment, and afterwards imprisoned for refusing to obey the order. The shock was too much for
his acute organization; and the imprisonment before
trial—the fourth he had to undergo—deprived him of
his reason. On the verdict being pronounced—guilty
of refusing to leave the country—he asked one of the
jurymen whether it was for sedition that he had been
tried. The object of the convention, which was held at
York in 1818, was to arrange for sending commissioners
to England, to bring before the Imperial authorities the
condition of the Province, with a view to its amelioration. Col. Beardsley of Hamilton, the chairman, was
tried by court martial, and deprived of his commission.
Among the delegates, there were many who had shown
their attachment to their sovereign during the war of
1812. The lands to which they were entitled, as
bounty, were withheld from them, on account of their
presence at that assemblage. A very difficult and
irritating question arose, of the state of the naturalization laws, as they affected persons of British birth,
who had remained in the United States till after 1783,
and then came to settle in the Province. Of the Post-
office revenue, no account was given; and in return for
high rates of postage the service was very indifferently performed.

With what opinions did the future leader of an insurrection, which it cost so many millions of dollars
to quell, set out? Was he a fierce Democrat, who had
resolved with malice prepense to do all in his power
to overthrow those monarchical institutions which had
suffered gross abuse at the hands of those to whom
their working had been confided? No prospectus

having gone forth as an *avant courrier* of *The Colonial Advocate*, the first number of the journal, which was in 8vo. form, was devoted chiefly to an exposition of the principles of the editor. The range of topics embraced was wide, and the tone of discussion, free from the bitterness that marked his later writings, was frank. A Calvinist in religion, proclaiming his belief in the Westminster Confession of Faith, and a Liberal in politics, yet was Mr. Mackenzie, at that time, no advocate of the voluntary principle. On the contrary, he lauded the British government for making a landed endowment of the Protestant Clergy, in the Provinces, and was shocked at the report that, in 1812, voluntaryism had robbed three millions of people of all means of religious ordinances. " In no part of the Constitution of the Canadas," he said, " is the wisdom of the British Legislature more apparent than in its setting apart a portion of the country, while yet it remained a wilderness, for the support of religion." Mr. Mackenzie credited Lord Melville, when Mr. Dundas, with having been the first adviser of this measure ; but this is a mistake, for the Archbishop of Canterbury had previously interested himself in the matter, and Col. Simcoe had pronounced in favor of a church establishment, in Canada, as a means of upholding a distinction of ranks, and lessening the weight of democratic influence. Mr. Mackenzie compared the setting apart of one seventh of the public lands for religious purposes to a like dedication in the time of the Christians. But he objected that the revenues were monopolized by one church, to which only a fraction of the population

belonged. The envy of the non-recipient denominations made the favored church of England unpopular.
Though this distribution of the revenues was mani-
festly in accordance with the law creating the Reserves, the alteration of that law, if it should not
meet the wishes of the people, had been contemplated
and provided for by its framers. By this argument,
Mr. Mackenzie was easily conducted to the conclusion, "that Catholic and Protestant, Episcopalian and
Presbyterian, Methodist and Baptist, Quaker and
Tunker, deserve to share alike in the income of
these lands;" and he expressed a hope that a law
would be enacted, "by which the ministers of every
body of professing Christians, being British subjects,
shall receive equal benefits from these Clergy Reserves." But this was not to be; for agitation, or the
question, was to be directed to the abrogation, not the
equal division, of these reservations.

On this question, the conservative character of Mr.
Mackenzie's opinions was found to be out of harmony
with the general sentiment, as it gradually unfolded
itself, and his own opinions changed. He could not
have retained these views, and maintained his popularity. Besides, as the subject was more discussed, he
saw reason to change them. On another question—
that of establishing a Provincial University—he contended for a principle, the adoption of which would
have caused a great deal of subsequent difficulty.
Cordially seconding the proposal of Dr. Strachan, to
establish such an institution, he predicted that it
would attract but few students, and not answer the
purpose for which it was required, "if tied down by

tests and oaths to support particular dogmas." This warning was unheeded, and for the reasons he had given, the university had to be turned upside down a quarter of a century afterwards, having in the meantime produced a minimum quantity of good fruit.

The Executive Government, the Legislative Council, the Bench, the Bar, the Church, all came in for a a share of attention. Governor Maitland was disadvantageously compared to De Witt Clinton, of the State of New York. The members of the Executive, apparently for no sound reason, were described as "foreigners." The Legislative Council, a majority of whose members held offices under the crown, and were even pluralists in a small way, were represented as being "always selected from the tools of servile power." The dependent position of the Judges, being removable at the pleasure of the Executive, was lamented. As for the Church, which claimed to be the established religion of the country, its ministers were declared to be not of that class who endure persecution for conscience' sake. The Bar was admitted to have four righteous members, and might, therefore, be considered to be in a hopeful condition. But the standard to which its members were expected to attain was no common one. Lawyers were expected at all times to be ready, without fee or other reward than the approval of a good conscience, to plead the cause of the unfortunate poor.

In so many words, the young journalist volunteered a disclaimer, by way of anticipation, of being a Radical Reformer. He had joined no Spafield mobs. He had never benefited by the harangues of Hunt, Cob-

bett, or Watson. He was not even chargeable with
being a follower of Gourlay, who had already rendered himself odious to the ruling faction. With
none of these sins was Mr. Mackenzie chargeable.
And though he was a warm reformer, he "never
wished to see British America an appendage of the
American Union." American liberty was good, but
British liberty was better. From the Americans we
might learn something of the art of agriculture; but
of government nothing. Yet our own system of cross-
purposes required reformation. The proposed Union
Bill of 1818 had been rightly rejected, and the only
desirable union was one of all the British American
colonies. The first existing law against which Mr.
Mackenzie directed his pen, after that which gave the
Church of England the entire proceeds of the Clergy
Reserves, was that upholding the right of primogeniture.

Such are the views promulgated by the young journalist at the outset of his career. Yet, moderate and
even conservative as they were, on many points, an
organ of the official party suggested that he should be
banished the Province, and the whole edition—which
it would not have been easy to collect after it had once
been distributed through the country—seized. We
look upon them now as being for the most part moderate and rational; and where the majority of the
present generation of Canadians will differ from him
is that, on the Clergy Reserves question, he did not
hold the voluntary view. At that time, he would
have denounced secularization as a monstrous piece
of sacrilege. The views which he expressed in refer-

ence to a Provincial University, before it had been brought into existence, afterwards came in the shape of a reform, the fruit of a long and bitter controversy. Members of the Legislature no longer hold subordinate offices, much less are they pluralists. The judges hold their offices for life, and are not removable at the pleasure of the Executive. The Executive Council can only be composed of such men as can obtain the favor of a legislative majority. The Church of England, having no exclusive privileges, and making no pretensions to dominancy, no longer excite jealousy, envy, or hatred. All the Provinces of British America have not yet been united under one government, it is true; but the question of uniting them never before occupied the same degree of attention. The right of primogeniture has been abolished, and intestate estates are equally distributed among the children. The mode of administering the government has been so revolutionized as to be equivalent to a complete change of system. The game of cross-purposes, of which Mr. Mackenzie complained, is no longer played between the two branches of the Legislature, or between the popular branch and the Executive. In making the Legislative Council elective—saving the rights of life-members already appointed—we have gone a step beyond what Mr. Mackenzie dreamed of in 1824, and which he would probably, at that time, have opposed as a radical departure from the British system of government.

Something new under the sun had appeared in the newspaper world of Upper Canada. To official gazettes containing a little news, and semi-official sheets,

which had an intense admiration of the ruling oligarchy, little York had previously been accustomed.
To newspaper criticism the Executive had not been
inured; and it was determined that the audacity of
the new journal should be rebuked. In spite of all
his protestations, Mr. Mackenzie was called upon to
defend himself against an imputation of disloyalty;
and, judging from his reply, he appears to have felt
this as one of the most galling and at the same time
one of the most untrue accusations that could have
been made against him. A Mackenzie disloyal! In
the annals of the whole clan no record of so unnatural
a monster could be found. On the 10th of June, Mr.
Mackenzie replied at great length. A part of this
reply has already been given, in the way of family
history; and the more material parts of the remainder
must not be omitted:

"Had Mr. Fothergill not been pleased to accuse me
in plain terms of democracy, disloyalty, and foul play,
I should not have devoted so much of this number to
party argument. It is necessary for me, however,
when my good name is so unexpectedly and rudely
assailed, in the first place, to deny, in plain and positive terms, such a charge; it will then accord with my
duty, as well as with my inclination, to inquire how
far he or any man is entitled, from any observations
of mine to advance such statements as appear in the
official papers of the 27th ult. and 3d instant.

"I consider it the bounden duty of every man who
conducts a public newspaper, to endeavor to regulate
his own conduct in private life, so as that the observations he may publicly make on the words and ac-

tions of others, may not lose their weight and influence on being contrasted with his own behavior,
whether as the head of a family or as an individual
member of society. Were I a native of the village
in which I now write, or of the district in which it is
situated, the whole of my past life could be fairly referred to, as a refutation, or as a corroboration of what
he has urged against me ; but as that is not the
case, this being only the fifth year of my residence in
Canada, I must refer to that residence, and to such
other circumstances as I may consider best calculated
to do away the injurious impression that will be raised
in the minds of those that do not know me, and who
may therefore be unjustly biassed by his erroneous
statements. I will, in the first instance, refer to every
page of the four numbers of *The Advocate*, now before the public ; I may ask every impartial reader,
nay, I may even ask Mr. Robinson* himself, (that
is, if he has any judgment in such matters,) whether
they do not, in every line, speak the language of a free
and independent British subject? I may ask whether
I have not endeavored, by every just means, to dis-
courage the unprofitable, unsocial system of the local
governments, so detrimental to British and Colonial
interests, and which has been productive of so much
misery to these Colonies ? Whether I have not endeavored to inculcate in all my readers, that godlike
maxim of the illustrious British patriot, Charles James
Fox, that 'that government alone is strong that has
the hearts of the people.' It is true, my loyalty has not
descended so low as to degenerate into a base, fawning,

* Then Attorney General, now Chief Justice of the Court of Queen's Bench.

cringing servility. I may honor my sovereign surely,
and remember the ruler of my people with the respect
that is due unto his name and rank, without allowing
my deportment to be equally respectful and humble to
His Majesty's butcher or his baker, his barber or his
tailor! If I were reduced to poverty and distress, and
were unable to work for my bread, I would cheerfully
submit without repining at the Divine Providence, and
ask an alms from my fellow-creatures, as a temporary
sustenance to this tabernacle of clay, until in due time
I were called home; but I feel that not to gain the
wealth of the Indies, could I now cringe to the fun-
guses that I have beheld in this country, and who are
more numerous and more pestilential in the town of
York, than the marshes and quagmires with which it
is environed.

" It may be proper that I should for this once add
a few other reasons, why disloyalty can never enter
my breast; even the name I bear has in all ages proved
talismanic, an insurmountable barrier. There are
many persons in this very colony who have known me
from infancy, so that what I may say can there or
here easily be proved or disproved if it should ever
become of consequence enough to deserve investigation. If Mr. Fothergill can find that any one who
bears the name which from both parents I inherit, if
he can find only one Mackenzie, and they are a very
extensive clan, whether a relation of mine or otherwise, whether of patrician, or (as he terms me) of
plebeian birth, who has ever deserted or proved disloyal to his Sovereign in the hour of danger, even I
will allow that he had the shadow of a reason for his

false and slanderous imputations; but if in this re-
search he fails, I hope, that for the sake of truth and
justice, for the honor of the Canadian press, for the sake
of the respectability of that official journal of which he
has the management, if not for mine who never
wronged him, that he will instantly retract a charge,
which, to say the least of it, is as foolish and groundless, as the observations he has connected with it are
vain and futile. Only think of the consequences which
might result from owing allegiance to a foreign government; think that in a few short weeks, or it may be
years, one might be called on, upon the sanctity of an
oath, to wage war against all that from childhood upwards he had held most dear : to go forth in battle
array against the heritage of his ancestors, his kindred, his friends, and his acquaintances ; to become in-
strumental in the subjugation by fire and sword to
foreigners, of the fields, the cities, the mausoleums of
his forefathers—aye perhaps in the heat of battle it
might be his lot to plunge the deadly blade into the
breast of a father, or a brother, or an only child.
Surely this picture is not overcharged. In our days
it stands on record as having been verified."

There is no reason, not even in the subsequent history of Mr. Mackenzie, to doubt the sincerity with
which those protestations were made. Years after he
went so far, in a letter to Lord Dalhousie, Governor-in-
Chief, as to suggest the possible return to their allegiance to England of the United States, if it were
once understood that the full rights of British subjects were to be conferred upon the colonies. And he
constantly raised a warning voice to show the danger

of a persistent refusal to give to colonists the full en-
joyment of those rights. His nature had evidently
to undergo a great change before he could become a
leader of insurrection. Mr. Fothergill* does not appear to have shown any disposition to prolong the
personal contest he had provoked; and he afterwards
became an advocate in the Legislature of the man he
had at first made a personal antagonist. In December, 1826, we find him moving—any member then
had the initiation of the money votes—in the Legislative Assembly, that a small sum be paid to Mr.
Mackenzie for the reports of the debates he had published. As affording a picture of the state of the
press of Upper Canada, at that time, and as throwing
light on this period of the life of the subject of this
biography, an extract from the speech is worth reading:

"Mr. Fothergill intended to move for a sum to be
paid to the editor of *The Advocate*. That paper had
during the session endeavored to give an accurate
account of their proceedings. Many of their resolutions, bills, reports of committees, and petitions of a
public nature, had been first printed in *The Advocate*,
for the advantage of their constituents, as also the
speeches pro and con on several important questions;
Mr. Mackenzie had made great exertions—established.
the only newspaper on an imperial sheet, and that too
without any increase in the price of his journal, ever
printed or published within the colony. He had last
fall, in addition to his former establishment, purchased,

---

* Mr. Fothergill was an English gentleman, born in Yorkshire, and well
educated. He brought considerable means with him to Canada; but they
were all dissipated many years before his death.

at great expense, a new patent cast iron press—the
first ever seen here, also new founts of types. He had
been led to believe that this additional supply of materials would be free by virtue of the bill of last session passed both houses, but was disappointed; and
instead of relief, found that new and heavy duties were
laid on another material article in his trade—paper.
His extended circulation subjects him to a more than
ordinary share of that tax felt by all printers in some
degree, namely, the payment of newspaper postages
quarterly in advance, rigidly enforced from those who
send the papers away, and irrecoverable whether they
arrive at their destination or not. And if they do arrive there, he (Mr. F.) could tell, for he had had
experience as a printer, that in proportion as a paper
became popular, and therefore more extensively
ordered for the country, in like proportion did the
proprietor become embarrassed. The readers were
scattered over a vast country, thinly populated, and
the returns were very long in coming back—often
never; this should induce the house to pay a better
price for the papers they saw fit to receive from printers; and no one in the colony suffered more from
extensive credits than Mr. Mackenzie, whose impression of six or seven hundred went chiefly to the country by various conveyances. He (Mr. F.) was credibly
informed that, in order to induce inquiry in England as
well as here, *The Advocate* had been sent free to persons
in Canada since its commencement, as many as nine or
ten thousand copies, and that since the session opened,
eighty or ninety copies had been weekly forwarded free,
to British members of parliament, by the mail. This

would help to draw attention in the proper quarter to our country. It was plain that newspapers which assumed anything like independence in their principles or feelings were, in Upper Canada, totally excluded from benefiting by any advertising over which the government had control. He thought the newspapers furnished, and bills, resolutions, &c., reported by the editor of *The Advocate*, were fully as useful to the country, and as deserving of payment from the funds of the people, as were the proclamations for which the Kingston *Chronicle* received £45 last year from the casual revenues of the crown."

The motion for granting Mr. Mackenzie £37 16s. was carried; but the Lieutenant Governor struck the item out of the contingencies, and it was not paid. Mr. Fothergill, having had experience of newspaper publishing, was no indifferent judge of the difficulties he described. The payment in advance, by the publishers, of postage on all the papers they sent out in a year for every weekly paper, must have been next to a prohibition of newspapers altogether; and we may be sure that they were regarded with no friendly eye by the government. While postage was exacted on Canadian newspapers in advance of their transmission, United States papers were allowed to come into the Province without being prepaid; an anomaly characterized by Mr. Mackenzie as a premium upon democratic principles, and a not ineffectual method of revolutionizing opinion in the Canadas.

A union of all the British-American colonies had few earlier advocates than Mr. Mackenzie. In a

letter to Mr. Canning, dated June 10, 1824, he touches
on this question.

QUEENSTOWN, U. C., *June* 10, 1824.

* * * A union of all the colonies, with a government
suitably poised and modelled, so as to have under its
eye the resources of our whole territory, and having
the means in its power to administer impartial justice
in all its bounds, to no one part at the expense of
another, would require few boons from Britain, and
would advance her interests much more in a few years,
than the bare right of possession of a barren, unculti-
vated wilderness of lake and forest, with some three
or four inhabitants to the square mile, can do in centuries. A colonial marine can only be created by a
foreign trade, aided by free and beneficial institutions;
these indeed would create it, as if by the wand of an
enchanter. If that marine is not brought into being;
if that trade, foreign and domestic, continues much
longer shackled by supreme neglect, and by seven
inferior sets of legislative bodies, reigning like so many
petty kings during the Saxon heptarchy, England
may yet have cause to rue the day, when she neglected
to raise that only barrier, or counterpoise to republican
power, which could in the end have best guarded and
maintained her interests.   *   *   *   *   *

British members of parliament and political writers,
who talk of giving the Colonies complete independence
now, either know not that our population and resources would prove very insufficient to preserve our
freedom, were it menaced, or else they desire to see
the sway of England's most formidable rival extended

over the whole of the vast regions of the North American continent. I have the honor to remain, Sir,
Your obedient, humble servant,
W. L. MACKENZIE.

To THE RIGHT HON. GEORGE CANNING.

Nor was this a mere casual expression of opinion. On the 14th December, 1826, we find in his journal the following testimony to his continued advocacy of this measure, under the head of " A Confederation of the British North American Colonies :"

" Right glad should we be, indeed, if the confidential information received by *The Albion* should prove correct. We have written much and often, advocating an effective united government for the colonies, in the bonds of amity and relationship with England, we have sent hundreds of copies of our journal to Europe to distinguished persons, with that project specially marked and noted, but were always afraid that the idea would be treated as ' an idle chimera,' even by the wisest and ablest of British statesmen. It would, however, be the best and safest policy ; for England can continue to hold Cabotia* only by the ties of friendship, amity, and mutual advantages—ties which, with the divine blessing, would be greatly strengthened, were the talent, the resources, the enterprise of all the colonies fully brought into action in a liberal, enlightened, and united general government."

* A word derived from the discoverer Cabot, and one which has been regarded as the best designation for the whole of British North America. While Nova Scotia, or New Brunswick, would not like to sink her individuality as part of Canada, she would not object to be part of Cabotia. Canadians, however, would object to change the name of their country.

8

The mode in which Mr. Mackenzie proposed to bring about this change was this :

" Let an Act be passed in the British Parliament calling a convention of all the colonies, and let a British nobleman or gentleman of competent knowledge preside, as representing His Majesty, at that convention; let representatives from each section of British America, chosen by the people and in proportion to the population, compose that convention ; let the outlines of a constitution be drawn up by this confederation of the talents .and wisdom of His Majesty's American subjects, and sent home for the consideration of the Imperial Parliament; let the convention be dissolved, and Great Britain will then know what her colonies want, what they require, and it will be for the British Legislature to alter or amend such constitution, so that justice may be done to all parties, and the interests of neither sacrificed."*

Some years before the colonial department had had this union under consideration, and, in 1822, Mr. Robinson, afterwards Chief Justice of the Court of Queen's Bench, at the request of the Imperial authorities, gave his opinions at length on a plan of union that had been proposed.† He thought he saw many advantages in such a union ; but the Imperial government appear to have entertained a fear that it would lead to the colonies combining against the mother country. Mr. (afterwards Sir John) Robinson did not share those fears. The question attracted some attention in Nova Scotia about the same time, and Mr.

* *Colonial Advocate,* June 24, 1824.
† *Canada and the Canada Bill,* by John Beverly Robinson, Esq., 1840.

Halliburton wrote a pamphlet in which it was advocated.

Soon after Mr. Mackenzie had entered on the career of a journalist a general election came on. It was held in July. The poll was kept open a week in those times. The result, a majority opposed to the Executive, might have been contributed to by Mr. Mackenzie's efforts, though there is no reason to believe that it was much affected by his writings, since he had issued only a few numbers of his paper. There had been a great change in the *personnel* of the House. Only sixteen members of the previous Assembly had been re-elected; there were twenty-six new members; from Essex the return was short by one member; the whole number being forty-five.* In the new House the government was destined to

* In the following list of members, those whose names are in italics, held seats in the previous House:—

RETURN OF MEMBERS FOR THE NINTH PROVINCIAL PARLIAMENT OF UPPER CANADA.—Granville—*Jonas Jones* and Hamilton Walker. Glengary—Alexander McDonnell and Duncan Cameron. Stormont—*Archibald McLean* and *Philip Vankoughnet.* Norfolk—*Francis L. Walsh* and Duncan McCall. Prince Edward—*James Wilson* and *Paul Peterson.* Hastings—*Reuben White* and Thomas Coleman. Kent—*James Gordon.* Northumberland—Zaccheus Burnham and James Lyons. [Mr. Lyons was unseated by a committee and Mr. Ewengo declared the sitting member.] Frontenac—Hugh C. Thomson and James Atkinson. Middlesex—John Rolph and John Matthews. Prescott and Russel—Donald McDonald. Lanark—*William Morris.* Oxford—*Thomas Hornor* and Charles Ingersoll. Lincoln—Bartholomew C. Beardsley, *John Clark,* John J. Lefferty, and *Robert Randall.* Leeds—*Charles Jones* and David Jones. Essex—Alexander Wilkins. Wentworth—*John Willson* and *George Hamilton.* Carlton—George Thew Borke. Halton—Richard Beasley and William Scollick. Lennox and Addington—Marshall S. Bidwell and Peter Perry. Durham—George Strange Boulton. York and Simcoe—William Thompson and Ely Playter. Dundas—John Chrysler. Town of York—*John Beverly Robinson.* Town of Niagara—Edward McBride. Town of Kingston—John Cumming.

be confronted by large majorities, even on their own measures—the Alien Bill, for instance—but the principle of executive responsibility was not acknowledged, and no question of ministerial resignation ever followed a defeat.

Prior to the meeting of the new Legislature, there arose a government prosecution, on which much popular feeling was excited; and when the case had come for a jury, Mr. Mackenzie showed more feeling at the demeanor of the judge than, from his writings, he appears to have previously displayed. Mr. Whitehead, the customs collector, at Port Hope, had commenced a prosecution against Mr. Wm. Mackintosh, the owner of the *Minerva Ann*, for an infraction of the revenue laws, in neglecting to report her arrival. The fact was admitted, but the public feeling ran strongly in favor of the defendant, the offence being looked upon as merely nominal. The jury, probably sharing the common feeling, found a verdict for the defendant; and they were about to give their reasons for doing so, when the court interposed an objection to the irregularity of such a course. Mr. Justice Boulton told the jury that their verdict was "contrary alike to the law and the evidence." The Solicitor-General, (son of the judge,) who was conducting the case for the crown, proposed that the record should be read to the jury, whom he wished to reconsider their verdict. Mr. Washburn, on behalf of the defendant, attempted to reply, when a scene, the reverse of creditable, occurred. The judge having peremistorily ordered Mr. Washburn to sit down,

"Mr. Washburn said, I wish to know from your

Lordship, whether I am to be allowed to reply to Mr. Solicitor General's arguments or not?

"Mr. Justice Boulton—Sit down! Sir, I say—sit down! It is indecent for you to interrupt the Court.

"Mr. Washburn again attempted to speak.

"Mr. Justice Boulton—Sit down! Sir,—Sit down! or I'll—I'll—Mr. Sheriff, take this fellow out of Court!

"Mr. Washburn—My Lord! I must and will be heard. Your Lordship informed me that I should have liberty to reply. I am standing here in defence of a client who has committed his case to my hands. I have a duty to perform to him, which is paramount to every other consideration. I will not desert him now; nor can I be driven to abandon him by any man. I therefore request once more to know, before I sit down, whether I shall be allowed to reply?

" Mr. Justice Boulton—Sit down! Sir. Mr. Sheriff —Mr. Sheriff, take this man out of Court!"*

The sheriff, probably making allowance for the warmth of the judge, did not attempt to obey the order. After the judge had again addressed the jury at great length, they retired a second time, and brought in a special verdict in writing, amounting, in effect, to precisely the same as the first. Again the judge remonstrated ; but the foreman of the jury cut the matter short by informing his lordship, that he should prefer to starve to death rather than alter his verdict.

On this proceeding, Mr. Mackenzie commented with greater indignation than he had shown on any pre-vious occasion:

* The *Report* is taken from the York *Observer*, a government paper.

"Were I at this moment immured in a dungeon, and denied the privileges of the lowest hind that breathes the vital air, and crawls along, I would not exchange places with our high born ruler, surrounded by such men as he now delights to honor; no! I would spurn—I would loathe the very idea of such a prostration. I am the son of an humble, obscure mechanic, bred in the lap of poverty; but not to inherit the noble blood which flows in his veins—not to possess the ancestral grandeur that surrounds his name—not to wear the star that adorns his breast, nor the honorable orders that mark his valor—no! not for worlds would I exchange situations with him, surrounded by men whose whole career is like 'vanity tossed to and fro of them that seek death.'

"If a judge can bully a jury into submission to his dictation, though expressly contrary to their own solemn verdict; if a Solicitor for the Crown can trample under foot the dearest rights of Britons; if a government, emanating from England, can cherish such a corrupt, such a detestable star-chamber crew—then the days of the infamous Scroggs and Jeffries are returned upon us; and we may lament for ourselves, for our wives and for our children, that the British Constitution is, in Canada, a phantom to delude to destruction, instead of being the day-star of our dearest liberties."

This was followed by an appeal to the new Legislature, to address the Governor General to dismiss from his presence and counsels the politicians by whom he was then advised, including "the whole of the Boulton race, root and branch."

CHAPTER V.

Removal to York, the Seat of the Upper Canada Government—Reporting and Publishing Legislative Debates—Newspapers and Postage—The Foundation of Brock's Monument raised to fish up an obnoxious Newspaper—Parliament House at York Burnt—A Hospital turned into a Legislative Building —Meeting of the New House—The Government in a Minority—An Irresponsible Government—Temporary Resolve (not carried out) to return to Dundas—Kissing and Government Printing go by Favor—Journey to Kingston—A Singular Character—Feeling towards the "Yankees"—The Perils of Plain Speaking—Dismissal of a King's Printer—Mr. Mackenzie resolves to abandon Politics and publish a Literary Journal—His Ideal of a Patriot.

As the Legislative session approached, Mr. Mackenzie saw reasons for removing his establishment to York, then the seat of the government for Upper Canada. A paper published at Queenstown must necessarily reproduce stale accounts of the Legislative proceedings. It was doubtful whether any newspaper, which had then been published in Upper Canada, had repaid the proprietor the cost of its production. Any publisher who sent a thousand sheets through the post-office must pay $800 a year postage, quarterly in advance. Though some of the other settlements were well supplied with post-offices, there were none at all on the South-western frontier, from Chippewa, by Fort Erie, to the mouth of the Grand River. The three thousand settlers in Dumfries and Waterloo had to travel from sixteen to forty miles before they reached a post-office. Postmasters received nothing for distributing newspapers, and were accordingly careless about their delivery. Other modes of distribution were occasionally resorted to by publishers to avoid the heavy postal tax. Mr. Mackenzie, at one time, thought of publishing the Legislative debates in a quarto sheet, without comment; but he must have left his own impulsive temperament out of the account if he fancied he could become a silent recorder of other men's opinions.

Since 1821, Francis Collins had furnished the principal reports of the Legislative debates; but it is in evidence that, up to 1827, the operation of publishing them had never been remunerative. Mr. Mackenzie's 'political enemies and rivals in the press, maliciously circulated the story, that he had removed to York under a promise from a majority of the members of the new House, that he should be guaranteed the printing of the bills and the laws; to which he replied that he would feel much more obliged if they would speedily improve an important department of internal economy of the Province—the post-office—than if they gave him all the jobs in their gift for a century to come. The new House paid a reporter £100 for reporting during the session; the reports to be delivered to the papers for publication, unless the Committee on Printing should exercise the arbitrary discretion of refusing to allow any particular report to be printed. While these reports were permitted to be published in *The Observer*, they refused to allow them to appear in *The Advocate*. After this, Mr. Rolph and Mr.

Beardsley asked to have their names struck from off the Printing Committee. Beardsley is reported to have voted for the exclusion of *The Advocate*. Mr. C. Jones, Mr. A. McLean, and Mr. Beardsley must divide the honor of the act among them. It was they who assumed the power of suppressing the reports altogether at pleasure. The question came up in the House, and although there was no decision upon it, the exclusion was not long maintained. The spite against that journal was carried to great lengths. After the ceremony of re-interring the remains of General Brock, at Queenstown Heights, on the thirteenth of September, 1824, some person, in the absence of Mr. Mackenzie, put into a hole in the rock, at the foundation of the monument, a bottle which he had filled with coins and newspapers, and among which was a single number of *The Advocate*. When the fact became known to the authorities, the foundation was ordered to be torn up and the obnoxious paper taken out, that the ghost of the immortal warrior might not be disturbed by its presence, and the structure not be rendered insecure.

Combining a book store with publishing, Mr. Mackenzie once entertained the idea of relying principally on the printing of books, and issuing a political sheet occasionally. *The Advocate* had not indeed appeared with strict regularity; only twenty numbers having been published in six calendar months. Some numbers had, after several weeks, been reprinted, and others continued to be asked for after they could be supplied. The last number of *The Advocate*, published in Queenstown, bears date, November 18, 1824; and
9

the first number printed in York appeared on the twenty-fifth of the same month. In January, 1825, its circulation was stated at eight hundred and thirty. At Christmas, 1824, the northern wing of the Legislative buildings, situated on the site of the present Toronto jail, was accidentally burnt down; and as the new House was to meet on the 11th of January, 1825, there was not much time to find new quarters for the Legislature. No time was lost in putting the new, now the old and abandoned, hospital, into order for that purpose.

The first trial of party strength, if such the election of Speaker could be considered, seemed to indicate a pretty well balanced House, the vote being twenty-one against nineteen;* but upon other questions the government minority shrunk to much smaller dimensions. Mr. Willson of Wentworth had become the successor of Mr. Sherwood in the Speaker's chair. The Liberals were in ecstasies. "The result of this election," said Mr. Mackenzie, "will gladden the heart and sweeten the cup of many a Canadian peasant in the midst of his toil." The advantage of such a victory must, however, be very small, under a condition of things which permitted the advisers of the sovereign's representative to keep their places in spite of a permanently hostile legislative majority. Not only were

* Vote of the House of Assembly, at the election of Mr. John Willson, as Speaker :

  Yeas.—Messrs. Rolph, Ingersoll, Matthews, McCall, Horner, Beasley, Beardsley, McBride, Clark, Randall, Lefferty, Scollick, Hamilton, Playter, Thompson, Thomson, Lyons, Peterson, Perry, Bidwell, and Walsh.—21.

  Nays.—Messrs. Att'y General, Atkinson, White, Coleman, Burnham, Boulton, Gordon, Wilkinson, 3 Jones's, McDonell, Macdonald, VanKoughnett, McLean, Morris, Chrysler, Cameron, and Walker.—19.

ministers not responsible to the House; they did not admit that they had any collective responsibility at all. The Attorney General (Robinson) said, in his place in the House, "he was at a loss to know what the learned member from Middlesex (Mr. Rolph) meant by a prime minister and a cabinet; there was no cabinet: he sat in that house to deliver his opinions on his own responsibility: he was under no out-door influence whatever." All eyes were turned towards the Lieutenant Governor; and as there was no responsible ministry to stand between him and public censure, the authority of the crown which he represented could not fail to be weakened by the criticism of executive acts. The new House was described by Mr. Mackenzie as being chiefly composed of men who appeared to act from principle, and were indefatigable in the discharge of their duties. In committee of the whole, the Speaker entered into the debates with as much freedom as any other member.

Before he had been in York five months, Mr. Mackenzie formed a fleeting resolution to leave it, and return to Dundas. He had, while there, become much attached to the people. If his paper found a less number of readers there than at York, the prospect was rather consolatory than otherwise, since he would have fared better if the number of his patrons had been diminished by five hundred.* Mr. Mackenzie's friends had urged him not to carry this resolution into effect; but it was taken, and was not, as he per-

* A collector whom he had sent into the country with $1,400 of newspaper accounts, collected in eleven weeks only £42 13s 10d, from which £15 was deducted for personal expenses. To obtain this much the collector walked 1200 miles.

suaded himself, to be shaken. His friends—we are
not told who they were—rejoined: "If you remain,
you may next year get the Legislative printing." He
had offered to print of the laws one thousand copies
for less than £100—the King's printer having received
over £900 for the same work in the previous year
—and failed to obtain the contract. "Business shall
be dull with me," he said, "if at any future day
I condescend to take those measures to obtain the
work of a legislative body, which I find to be the sure
means of success in York." For whatever reason, he
changed his resolution to return to Dundas, and remained at the seat of government.

In March, Mr. Mackenzie went to Kingston, where
some of his wife's relatives lived; "a journey of nearly
four hundred miles, on some of the worst roads that
human foot ever trod, and in an inclement season of
the year." The villages of Port Hope and Cobourg,
which, five years before, had contained some half a
dozen houses each, were now rapidly increasing post-
towns. At Kingston, he found that foreigners were
not allowed to visit the Royal Navy Yard, the English Dock Yard customs being observed. He obtained
a visiting pass from Captain Barrie, the acting Commissioner. He could not help expressing a hope that
the boastful Yankees might be taught civility.

"I went on board the great ship St. Lawrence, and
although none of your warlike sort of people, except
in a quiet way and upon paper, I do hope that if she
is ever again put in commission, she will give these
noisy brethren of ours on the other side the lake such
a broadside as they may remember; so that at the peace

which will be thereafter, I may hear less of their glorious and uninterrupted line of victories by sea and
land—General Hull's campaign to the contrary notwithstanding."

Near Port Hope, he met an innkeeper, whose description is singular enough to deserve preservation:

"An innkeeper of eccentric manners resides at the
'Bull Tavern,' near Port Hope. I never miss calling
on him when I go that way; indeed our acquaintance
is of five years' standing, for I remember when he
first pitched his tent where now stands the hospitable
caravansary of 'John Bull.'

"The name of mine host is Mr. Thomas Turner
Orton, and he is far above the ordinary cast of inn-
keepers, inasmuch as he is a linguist, a polemic, and
a political economist of no mean celebrity. When
the stage stopped at the 'John Bull,' Mr. Orton was
busily engaged reading the Hebrew Bible, with the
aid of a Lexicon, and he, much to my edification, condescended to instruct me in the difference between a
Lexicon with and without points. I believe the
learned Parkhurst himself could not have given a
clearer definition. While we rested, I learnt from
him, that Mrs. Thomas Turner Orton, his lady, had
been bred along with the royal family of France. As
also that the Lieut. Governor had made him an offer of
the U. C. *Gazette*, that he is an adept at the French
language, that he had long been intimate with his late
Majesty of Sweden, (Gustavus,) and on the most familiar terms with the King of Denmark. Mr. Orton
was formerly, as we are informed by the London Di-
rectory for 1814, a 'Ship-owner and General Commis-

sion Agent, Orton's Terrace, Commercial Road,' Lon
don; and it was, when a prisoner of war, that this
intimacy with the predecessor of Bernadotte had its
commencement."

At the end of a year after its commencement, forty-
three numbers of the newspaper had appeared. The
subscribers, who were accounted with at the rate of
fifty-two numbers for a year, were warned that they
must not expect any greater regularity in future. The
attention which even a weekly newspaper required,
put an end to the devouring of large numbers of
books, to which, Mr. Mackenzie was previously ad-
dicted. "Much of my past life," he said, "has been
spent in reading; to this the last twelve months form
an exception, as in that time I have scarcely had an
opportunity to open a volume." One year's experience had taught him that "the editor in Canada, who, in
the state the Province was then in, will attempt freely
to hazard an opinion on the merits and demerits of
public men, woe be to him! By the implied consent
of king, lords, and commons he is doomed to speedy
shipwreck, unless a merciful providence should open
his eyes in time, and his good genius prompt him 'to
hurl press and types to the bottom of Lake Ontario.'"

The time was rapidly approaching, when, in his
own case, the evil genius of his enemies was to perform this service for him, and literally throw his types
into a bay of Lake Ontario.

From the 16th June to the 18th December, 1825,
there was a cessation of the publication of *The Advocate*. In about eleven months, fifty-one numbers had
been issued; but the intermissions, of which no notice

was given, did not conduce to the success of the journal. The readers desired to receive it regularly every
week, and the preparation requisite for a compliance
with their desire necessitated a breathing spell. After
that was over, Little York was promised a newspaper
equal in dimensions to the more noted of the New
York sheets. Unexpected delays, however, prevented
its appearance till more than a month after the legislative session had commenced. The experiment must
have been a hazardous one in a country where the
population was scattered over a very wide extent of
territory, and numbered only 157,541; not much more ✓
than the united populations of Montreal and Toronto
at present.

The one paper circulating among this population,
which yielded a certain profit, was the *Upper Canada
Gazette.* It became necessary for Mr. Mackenzie to
notice a story that he had been offered the editorship
of the official paper in reversion. He showed the ab-
surdity of the supposition that such an offer could be
made to him who had opposed nearly all the measures
of the government. At the same time, he thought he
could make it very interesting, in a few weeks, if it
were under his control; and while he should certainly
accept the offer, if made, he should regard him that
made it with the greatest possible contempt. Mr.
Fothergill, the editor of the official paper, had a per-
verse habit of speaking his mind very bluntly in his
capacity as legislator; and when there was a rumor
of his intended removal, Mr. Mackenzie said he
had too good an opinion of the Lieutenant Governor
to think that he would attempt to injure Mr. Fother-

gill for having spoken in the Legislature as became
the scion of an ancient and honorable family and a
free-born Englishman. Mr. Fothergill had joined the
extreme Liberals, on the Alien question, contending
that all Americans then in the country ought to have
the full rights of British subjects conferred upon them
by statute; and he had moved strong resolutions on
the back of an inquiry into the mysteries of the Post-
office revenue, taking the ground that it was contrary
to the Constitutional Act to withhold from the Legislature an account of this revenue, or to deprive it of
the right of appropriating it. He had also moved an
address on the Land-granting Department—always a
tender subject; and in those days persons who obtained free grants of land thought it a monstrous
hardship to be obliged to pay the official fees, making
more contortions of feature over the transaction than
a settler makes now in paying his two dollars per
acre. By taking this course, he had assisted to produce those numerous defeats which had fallen, one
after another, with such irritating effect upon the
government. A man who did this could not long
continue a special favorite of the government in those
times; but that Mr. Mackenzie was ever thought of
in connection with the editorship of the non-official part
of the official *Gazette* is out of the question. The ink of
Mr. Fothergill's reported speech on the Post-office question was scarcely dry when he was dismissed from the situation of King's Printer. He had not abused his trust
by turning the paper with the conduct of which he was
charged against the government, but he had ventured
to confront a gross abuse in the Legislative Assembly.

That was his crime, and of that crime he paid the penalty. The office of King's Printer, in Lower as well as in Upper Canada, was held at the pleasure of the Governor, and the incumbent might be dismissed without any cause being assigned. None was assigned in this case. Mr. Fothergill had no warning, and the event appears to have come somewhat unexpectedly upon him, though he could not have been ignorant of rumors that were in everybody's mouth. It was no doubt inconvenient to have a King's Printer, who, even in his legislative capacity, opposed himself to the government; but the fault lay in the system which permitted the incumbent of such an office to hold a seat in the Legislature. The union of judicial and legislative powers in the hands of one person was a still greater evil; and though it might have been productive of far worse results, it was permitted to exist long after the period of which we are now writing.*

Free speech met small encouragement at the hands of the Executive. Francis Collins, who had been the official reporter of the Legislature for five years, in an evil hour, in 1825, commenced the publication of a

---

* There still were reasons why the government and their dismissed servant should deal somewhat tenderly with one another. Mr. Fothergill explained the matter of his dismissal in an address to his constituents; and though he hinted that there were men in the public service who had built palaces without any visible means of accomplishing such a feat, he could not assert, he remarked, that undue influence had been exercised in the administration of justice, or that "improper persons had been exalted into guardians of the prerogative, Legislative councillors, arbitrers between the King and the people." The sarcasm was well calculated to produce effect in vulnerable places; and it was of no consequence if the general public did not understand it. A bond for £360, to cover the amount of his overdrafts on the treasury, was not taken into account in his settlement with the government. If he was a patriot, his persecutors were not without a spark of generosity.

10

newspaper, the *Canadian Freeman*, and in that year the Lieutenant Governor cut off his remuneration. He exhausted his means in the vain effort to report the debates at his own cost, and found himself embarrassed with debt; Mr. Mackenzie seldom or never printed Collins' reports, in the sessions of 1825–6; sometimes he dropped into the House and took a few notes on his own account, but generally this service was performed by some one else.

About six weeks before his printing office was destroyed by a mob, Mr. Mackenzie drew a contrast between the life of an editor, in those days, and that of a farmer; in which a vast balance of advantages appeared in favor of the latter. The perpetuity of task-work involved in the conduct of even a weekly paper was felt to be such a drag that he became appalled at it; and for the moment he resolved to have done with politics and political newspapers. He would by this means release himself from a galling dependence on sottish printers, reduce his expenses with the size of his paper, and manage to have at least the Sundays to himself. Having drawn a dreary picture of editorial existence, in 1826, on six-sevenths of the week, he added:

"Such is his life for six days in the week all the year round; and how think you is the seventh disposed of? If I would speak for myself I might truly say, that I am often so wearied and fatigued with the toils of the working days as to be perfectly unable to enjoy the rest provided by a kind Providence on the Christian Sabbath. That instead of being fit to attend church, read the Scriptures, or in any way engage in the duties of divine appointment, I am glad to lay me down on my bed or on a sofa, as a temporary relief from the effects of incessant toil."

Henceforth his paper should be a Journal of Agriculture, Manufactures, and Commerce; politics should have no place in it:

"I will carry it on as a literary and scientific work, will enrich its pages with the discoveries of eminent men, and the improvements of distinguished artists; but from thenceforth nothing of a political or controversial character shall be allowed to appear in the Journal of Agriculture, Manufactures, and Commerce. By diminishing its size the expense and trouble attending it will be greatly lessened, and truly I shall be as well satisfied to employ my people generally at book work, which is a more easy employment, and can be increased or let alone at pleasure. I shall then be freed from a toilsome and irksome dependence, and if I lose thereby all political influence over the minds of the people, I shall gain in exchange, what is to me of far greater importance, a more extensive command of my own time. I must endeavor to set apart a day and a paper wherein to review my past labors; it is good to take a look at the past, as well as to endeavor to rend asunder the veil which enshrouds futurity.

> "'Till youth's delirious dream is o'er,
> Sanguine with hope we look before,
>   The future good to find.
> In age, when error charms no more,
>   For bliss we look behind.'"

How long this resolution was kept—whether one or two days—cannot be determined; but the next number of his journal, which took the folio shape, was chiefly filled with a long review of the politics of the Upper Province. He gave an account of the effect of his two years' journalistic campaign; claiming to have largely assisted in producing a party revolution. Men were astonished at the temerity of his plain speaking; for, since Gourlay's banishment, the prudent had learned to put a bridle on their tongues. Timid lookers-on predicted, in their astonishment and with bated breath, that the fate of Gourlay would soon fall on Mackenzie and silence his criticisms. Nearly the whole press of the country was on his back; but in spite of the rushing torrent of abuse he kept the even tenor of his way, avoiding personalities as much as possible. In the number of the 4th of May, 1826, he drew an excellent picture of a patriot;* and there is no doubt that he had tried to realize the description in his own person.

After the issue of two numbers, the quarto form was abandoned, and the broad sheet resumed. But the

---

* A patriot is none of your raving railing, ranting, accusing radicals-nor is he one of your idle, stall-fed, greasy, good for nothing sinecurists, or pluralists; he is in deed and in truth a friend to his country. He studies the laws and institutions of his nation, that he may improve others; endeavors rather to cultivate the acquaintance of, and shew a correct example to the better informed classes; he associates only with those whose private conduct is in unison with their public professions. Is not a mob hunter, nor a lecturer of the multitude; desires rather the secret approbation of the enlightened few than the ephemeral popularity of the many. If he is a member of Parliament he looks carefully into the merits of the question and votes consistently with his conscience, whether with or against the ministry. He is neither a place hunter, nor a sinecure hunter. He promises his constituents very little, but tries to perform a great deal. Finally he is among the last of men who would countenance political 'gamblers and black legs;' but a wise, manly, and vigilant administration is his delight."

resolution to abandon political disquisitions—probably
the impulse of temporary dejection or despair—was,
like the proposed removal to Dundas, given up, apparently almost as soon as formed. At all times,
during his life, Mr. Mackenzie was subject to great
elation at a brightening prospect, and to corresponding depression in other circumstances. Two weeks
after the contemplated change in his journal, he announced that it would be placed under the editorial
direction of some one else; and there was an attempt
to carry out the idea that this had been done, but it
appears to have been only an excusable devise for
keeping the personality of the editor out of view.

CHAPTER VI.

Destruction of *The Colonial Advocate* Printing Office by an Official Mob—Who threw the First Stone—Mr. (afterwards Chief Justice) Macaulay publishes Mr. Mackenzie's Private Correspondence with him—The Type Rioters cast in Civil Damages—Illness of some of the Jurors while locked up—Mr. Fitzgibbon collects the Amount of the Damages among the Officials and their Friends—Whether the Damages were Exemplary or Excessive—Sparring between a Judge and the Attorney-General—Francis Collins Iudicted for Four Libels—He Retaliates and causes the Type Rioters to be Proceeded against Criminally—Their Conviction—Henry John Boulton and James E. Small tried for Murder, arising out of a Fatal Duel—The Official Party procure a Presentment against Mr. Mackenzie for Libel.

ONE fine summer evening, to wit, the 8th June, 1826, a genteel mob, composed of persons closely con-nected with the ruling faction, walked into the office of *The Colonial Advocate*, at York, and in accordance with a preconcerted plan set about the destruction of types and press. Three pages of the paper in type on the composing-stones, with a "form" of the Jour-nals of the House, were broken up, and the face of the letter battered. Some of the type was then thrown into the bay, to which the printing-office was contigu-ous; some of it was scattered on the floor of the office; more of it in the yard and in the adjacent garden of Mr. George Munro. The composing-stone was thrown on the floor. A new cast-iron patent lever-press was broken. "Nothing was left standing," said an eye-witness, "not a thing." This scene took place in broad daylight, and it was said that one or two magistrates, who could not help witnessing it, never made the least attempt to put a stop to the outrage. The valiant type destroyers, who chose for the execution of their enterprise a day when Mr. Mackenzie was absent from the city, were most of them closely connected with the official party, which was then in a hopeless minority in the Legislature, and had recently been exasperated by a succession of defeats.

Mr. Baby, Inspector-General, was represented on the occasion by two sons, Charles and Raymond, students-at-law. Mr. Henry Sherwood, son of Mr. Justice Sherwood, gave his personal assistance. Mr. Sherwood, while yet a law student, held the office of Clerk of Assize. Mr. Lyons, confidential secretary of Lieutenant-Governor Maitland, was there to perform his part. To save appearances, Sir Perigrine found it necessary to dismiss Lyons from his confidential situation; but he soon afterwards rewarded him with the more lucrative office of Register of the Niagara District. Mr. Samuel Peters Jarvis, son-in-law of a late Chief Justice of the Court of Queen's Bench, performed his part, and found his reward in the appointment to an Indian Commissionership, where he became a defaulter to a large amount. Charles Richardson, a student-at-law in the office of the Attorney General and Commissioner for taking affidavits, showed his zeal for the cause of his official friends, and received in requital the office of Clerk of the Peace for the Niagara District. James King, another Clerk of Assize and student-at-law in Solicitor General Boul-

ton's office, did not hesitate to give his active assistance. Mr. Charles Heward, son of Colonel Heward,
Auditor General of Land Patents, and Clerk of the
Peace, and Peter Macdougall, a merchant or shop-
keeper in York and an intimate friend of Inspector
General Baby, complete the list of eight against whom
the evidence was sufficiently strong for conviction.
The whole number of persons concerned in the destruction of *The Advocate* office was fifteen.

The accompanying plan will assist in the comprehension of the affair. The original names of the
streets have been retained on the plan; but it should
be explained that what is there set down as Post-office
is now Caroline Street; and that the block between
Caroline and George Streets is divided by Frederick
Street, which runs north and south. Mr. Mackenzie's
house and printing office, which were joined together,
stood on the corner of what are now Caroline and
Palace Streets. The house had been the residence of
one of the early governors of the Province; and was
accidentally destroyed by fire four or five years ago.
The audacity of the rioters and the open connivance
of leading officials, who witnessed the scene with satisfaction, form an instructive comment on the state of
society in the Family Compact of the little town of
York, in the year of grace, 1826.

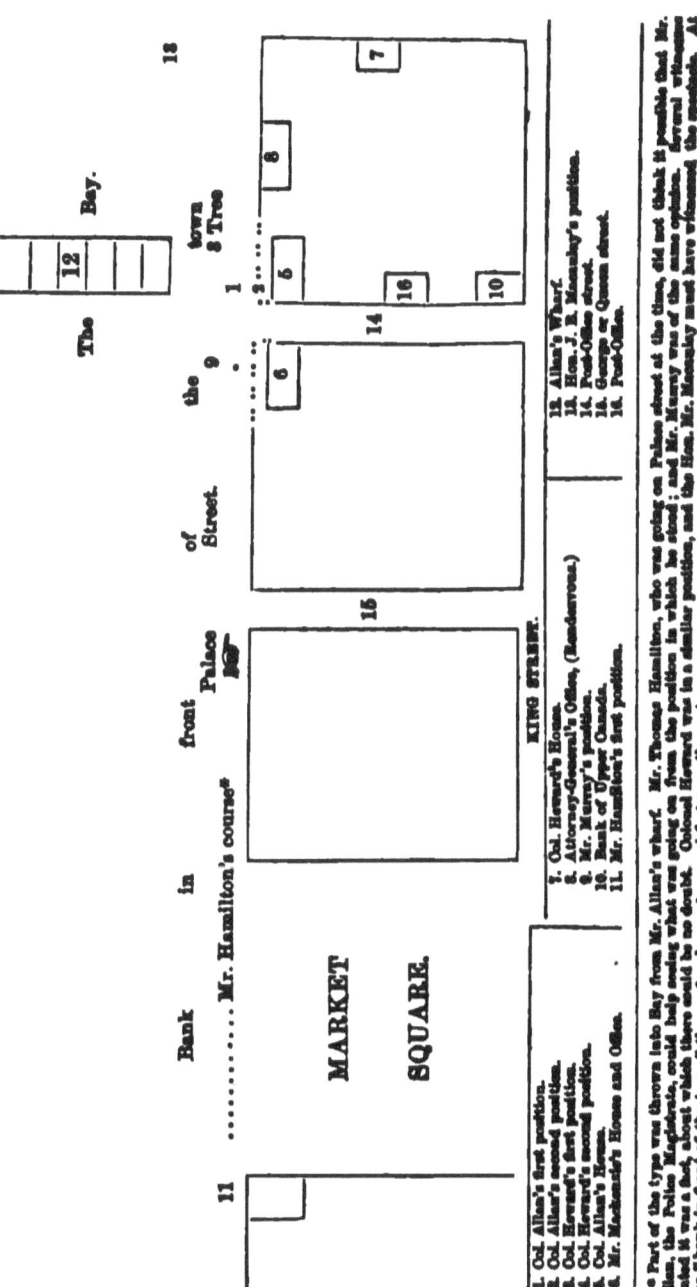

It is difficult to believe that a band of young men, subordinate officials and sons and relatives of the official party, planned the destruction of the printing office of an obnoxious journal in secret, and executed it without the knowledge of any of their superiors. Lyons miscalculated, it is true, if he thought he had adopted the road to immediate promotion; for whatever secret pleasure the members of the government might derive from the outrage, a British governor could not protect in a confidential, one who had been directly concerned in it. But what he could do, and did do, with indecent haste, was afterwards to reward with lucrative official positions not only Lyons, but also others who had taken part in the outrage. After it became certain that a conviction would be obtained, and a criminal prosecution might be instituted, a very business-like offer was made to pay the actual damages, much in the same way as one who had accidentally broken a sheet of plate glass while passing by a shop on a public street, might do:

"MY DEAR SIR:—The gentlemen prosecuted for a trespass upon *The Advocate* Press, so far from entertaining a desire to do an irreparable injury to the property of the concern, went openly to the office without any attempt at concealment, and aware at the time of the responsibility they would incur. An offer of indemnity to the actual extent of the injury would have been tendered immediately, had less clamor been raised and less exertion been used to prejudice the public mind.

"The real cause of the step is well known to all; it

is not to be ascribed to any malice—political feeling—
or private animosity; the personal calumnies of the
latter *Advocates* point out sufficiently the true and
only motives that prompted it; and I have now to
offer to pay at once the full value of the damage occasioned to the press and types, to be determined by
indifferent and competent judges selected for that
purpose. Will you inform me how far your client is
disposed to meet this proposal?

"This advance is in conformity with the original intention, and must not be attributed to any desire to
withdraw the matter from the consideration of a Jury
of the country, should your client prefer that course;
but in that event, it is to be hoped no further attempts
will be used by him or his friends to prejudice the
cause now pending, nor any future complaints be
made of a reluctance or hesitation to compensate, voluntarily, a damage merely pecuniary, although provoked by repeated assaults upon private character and
feeling not susceptible of any adequate redress.

"I am, very truly yours,
"J. B. MACAULAY."

"J. E. SMALL, Esq.

If the party who committed the violence had from
the first intended to pay the damage they had done,
in the deliberate business-like way indicated by Mr.
Macaulay, it is surprising that some of them—not
perhaps any of those finally cast in damages—should
have absconded, to evade the consequences of their
crime; but it is possible that they feared a criminal
prosecution, and left their solicitor and friend, who
had himself offered more provocation to criticism than

any of them, to make a bargain that would save them from the jail. It seems possible that a criminal prosecution was at one time thought of; for I find that the Bidwells advised Mr. Mackenzie not to proceed in that way. The press-destroying mob were probably surprised at the indignation their achievement excited in the public mind; and in the beginning they endeavored to stem the torrent by issuing two placards in justification. But Mr. Mackenzie had been guilty of no aggression to turn the tide of public feeling against him, and the experiment failed. It was not till after this that the above offer was made. The first proposal not being listened to, a second was made through the same medium:

"6th *July*, 1826.

"My Dear Sir:—My friends do not seem inclined to make any higher proposals than follows, and which are dictated in a conviction that they fully meet the justice of Mr. Mackenzie's claim—the real extent of which they are by no means ignorant of, or unable to prove:

"They will (receiving the press and appurtenances) be willing to pay £200 for them. This sum is considered not only the value of the whole material of the establishment, but amply sufficient to cover any contingencies also; with respect to further compensation there would be no objection to add £100 more; in all £300 to end the matter.

"Or they will agree to £200 as above stated, and leave any excess to the decision of indifferent persons —or they will leave the whole to indifferent and competent referees as at first suggested.

"If your client can meet this in any way so as to terminate the controversy, I shall be very glad; if not, I fear the law must take its course.

"I am, very truly yours,

"J. B. MACAULAY."

"J. E. SMALL, Esq.

This second proposal met the same fate as the first; and indeed, if there had been no object in making an example of the perpetrators of an outrage that reflected disgrace on all concerned, the amount offered as compensation was ridiculously inadequate. But Mr. Mackenzie refused any amicable settlement with Mr. Macaulay's clients and friends; and there was nothing left but to send the case to trial, and let a jury, upon the hearing of the evidence, award equitable, and, if they thought fit, exemplary damages.

Mr. Macaulay, in the first letter, in which he proposed a settlement of the matter, assumes that the outrage was caused by " the personal calumnies of the latter *Advocates;*" and it becomes necessary to see where the aggression commenced, and what degree of provocation the independent journalist had given to the official party, by whose satellites the work of destruction had been done. Nothing is plainer, on an examination of the facts, than that, until violently provoked, Mr. Mackenzie had been exceedingly sparing of personalities, and from the first he had been anxious to avoid them altogether. In one of the earliest numbers of his journal, he said: "When I am reduced to personalities, I will bring *The Advocate* to a close." To the personal abuse of the government papers he made no personal reply; confining him-

self to complaining, in the spirit of injury, of the
wrong he suffered. Of these Mr. Carey's *Observer* appears to have been, up to this time, the greatest of-
fender. Between the personal and political character
of the actors with whom he had to deal, Mr. Mackenzie observed a proper distinction. Of Governor Maitland he said, "that he was religious, humane, and
peaceable; and if his administration had hitherto produced little good to the country, it may not be his
fault, but the fault of those about him who abused his
confidence." Mr. J. B. Macaulay (afterwards Chief
Justice of the Court of Common Pleas) he described—
and he did it from a sense of duty—as a gentleman
evincing "so much honor, probity, just feeling, and
disinterested good will," as generated in the publicist's
mind, "a greater degree of respect and esteem for the
profession in general than we had before entertained."
He expressed a desire to see his friend replace Mr.
Justice Boulton on the Bench. Upon this latter
functionary he had been, at first, playfully sarcastic,
comparing him to Sir Matthew Hale, and latterly
severe, as we have seen in the case of the *Minerva Ann*
trial; but it will not be denied that the judge had
fairly laid himself open to criticism. While opposing
the Attorney General of the day, (afterwards Chief
Justice Sir J. B. Robinson,) he did ample justice to
his talents and his personal character:

"Mr. Robinson has risen in my estimation, in regard to abilities, from what I have seen of him during this session; indeed, there are not a few of his
remarks which I have listened to with pleasure; and
some of the propositions he has made in Parliament,

the road bill especially, (with a few modifications,) have my entire approbation. As a private gentleman, as a lawyer, and as a law officer, he stands as high in the estimation of the country as any professional man in it. As a counsellor of state to the Emperor of Russia, or Napoleon Bonaparte, he might have figured to advantage; but his principles will, if not softened down, for ever unfit him for a transatlantic popular assembly. He advocates those doctrines with singular force, the repugnance to which un-colonized the thirteen United States; and every taunt which he utters against our republican neighbors, tells in account against the interests of Great Britain, so far as they are united with this colony. It is evident that Mr. Robinson has not been long enough in the school of adversity to learn wisdom and discretion. He is a very young man, and I do hope and trust, that when the heat and violence of party spirit abate within him, he will yet prove a bright and lasting ornament to the land which gave him birth, and that the powers of his mind will be exerted to promote the happiness and welfare of all classes of his fellow subjects."

And again: "I would wish Mr. Robinson out of Parliament or out of place; and his former political career none condemned more boldly than I did. I have seen him this session without disguise; I have watched his movements, his looks, his language, and his actions; and, I will confess it, I reproached myself for having used him at one time too harshly."

Mr. Mackenzie had been severe upon Mr. Jonas Jones, but that gentleman had first set the example of using harsh terms. He had said in reply to a

very able speech in the House of Assembly, on the
Alien question, that the member, (Dr. Rolph,) who
made it, had a "vile democratic heart, and ought to
be sent out of the Province." If an appeal to the
Sedition Act could silence an opponent, why take the
trouble to refute his arguments? He had, moreover,
used threats of personal violence against Mr. Mackenzie, and was, of course, open to severe retaliation.
In the Legislative Assembly he had called Mr. Hamilton, the member for Wentworth, a "fellow," when a
scene followed on which it was necessary to drop the
curtain to hide it from the vulgar gaze of the public.
Considering these circumstances in mitigation, it must
be confessed that the criticisms upon Mr. Jones scarcely
exceeded the bounds of merited and justifiable severity.
To Mr. Henry John Boulton, Mr. Mackenzie had declared an absence of personal dislike in criticizing
his public acts. Considering Dr. Rolph too severe in
his strictures on the government, he had opposed him
on that account, and a personal estrangement had
been the consequence.

Such is the manner in which Mr. Mackenzie had
treated his political opponents during the two years
he had controlled a political journal; and it may
easily be conceived how slender was the pretext, on
the ground of provocation, for the destruction of his
printing-office. I do not say that he had never applied to his opponents language of severity, but I do
say that he was not the aggressor; that under the
greatest provocations he had avoided personalities;
and that, at the worst, he had not proceeded to any
thing like the extremity to which his assailants had

gone; and this not for the want of materials* to work upon.

In the meanwhile, how were his political adversaries bearing themselves towards Mr. Mackenzie? The Hon. J. B. Macaulay had gone to the unwarrantable length of violating the seal of secresy, and publishing private letters addressed to him by Mr. Mackenzie; though there was not in the conduct of the latter the shadow of excuse for this outrage. Mr. Macaulay was now a member of the Executive Council, and Mr. Mackenzie, who had previously praised him, had hinted that he was not an independent as formerly; but this was in a private letter. The cause of the quarrel was utterly contemptible, and Mr. Macaulay showed to great disadvantage in it. A disagreement had taken place between the Rev. Dr. Strachan, then Rector of York, and one John Fenton, who had officiated as clerk under the rector. Mr. Mackenzie, being in Niagara, learned that Mr. Radcliffe had received a letter from Mr. Fenton, in which the latter stated his intention to publish a pamphlet on the state of the congregation in York. Meanwhile Mr. Fenton was reinstated in his position. Accordingly, a paragraph was inserted in *The Advocate*, which certainly left the impression that a fear of the threatened pamphlet had led to the reinstatement of Fenton,† with an increased

* In *The Advocate* of May 4, 1826, he said:—" What a place Little York is for scandal ! Nothing can equal it! Had we set apart but one number, and used our usual diligence to embody the tales current of the vulgar great, with whose residence this place is honored, we could have set the good people, our neighbors and friends, at pulling caps; aye, even in time of church service. But we left the quartering of the arms of our York nobility to more friendly hands, pursuing the even tenor of our way."

† The paragraph was in these words:—" CLERK OF THE CHURCH—*A New Era !*—Mr. Fenton, as it is said, having announced a forthcoming pamphlet

12

salary.   It is possible that the insinuation was not
just; and yet this could not be said, if there were
no mistake about the alleged facts on which it was
founded.   It was not denied that Mr. Fenton had
been reinstated, but it was alleged that his salary
was increased; and Mr. Mackenzie certainly had what
seemed to be good authority for stating that the publication of a pamphlet had been announced.   This
was the only statement in dispute, and if it was not
proved, it certainly was not disproved.   Mr. Radcliffe
might have been asked to write a note, stating that
he had not received such a letter from Mr. Fenton,
and that would have settled the matter.   Mr. Macaulay was one of the church-wardens, and after
the lapse of three weeks he wrote to deny the statement that a pamphlet had been threatened, and that
Mr. Fenton's reinstatement carried with it any increase of salary.   Mr. Macaulay's letter was sent to
The Advocate for publication, and after it was in type
he wrote to recall it, not because the matter had assumed a new shape, but because Mr. Fenton had written a denial of that part of the paragraph which
related to the pamphlet.   Mr. Mackenzie refused to
cancel the letter to which Mr. Macaulay had appended, not his own signature, but the *nomme de plume*
of "A Church-warden," on account of the offensive
attitude the writer had assumed towards the editor;*

upon the state of the York congregation, the doctor made him new advances,
and he has actually been reinstated as clerk of our Episcopal Church, with an
additional salary.   'Tis a good thing to be in the secret!"

   * The paragraph is in these words:—"Had the church-warden confined his
remarks to his fellow functionary 'the clerk,' we would most readily have
distributed the types of his letter yesterday, as he requested.   But the tone he
has seen fit to assume towards ourselves is not to be borne.   There was a time

and the few lines in which Mr. Mackenzie explained his refusal to comply with the request of a person, who he thought had forfeited all claim to his indulgence, contains the whole extent of the provocation he gave to Mr. Macaulay. Clever men often do very foolish things in a passion; and Mr. Macaulay must have been in an uncontrollable rage before he brought himself to publish the private letters addressed to him by Mr. Mackenzie, on the subject of the Fenton affair, and to make jeering remarks in reference to Mr. Mackenzie's mother, an aged woman of seventy-five years. But he did not stop here; he sent the manuscript into which he had condensed his rage to Mr. Mackenzie, with an offer to pay him for its publication in *The Advocate;* a paper which he declared his intention to do all in his power to crush. One of his advertise- ments, a little less libellous than the rest, would have been published; but the money being demanded in ad- vance, Mr. Macaulay refused to redeem his promise, and pretended to have a right to insist on its publica- tion without the payment he had at first offered. He taunted Mr. Mackenzie with his poverty, and with what he called "changing his trade," and advised him to "try to deserve the charity" of the public a little bet- ter than previously, if he expected to support his mo- ther and his family by the publication of a newspaper;

when we looked upon *that church-warden* as one that would become the most open, manly, and independent of his class, but it has gone by. We prized his talents, his abilities, and his judgment by far too high; and the tenor of his railing accusation against us will show the Province that he has not improved the style of his compositions since he left off studying Byron. The church- warden, who is not one of our subscribers, will find to-morrow that even to him we shall not meanly truckle, nor shall we to any man, although the black- est poverty should be, on earth, our reward."

as if it were asking charity to publish a public journal, at the usual price, and a crime for a man to support a mother,* who was too aged and too helpless to support herself. Without even mentioning him by name, Mackenzie had described Mr. Macaulay as a man whom he had ceased to look upon as possessing manly independence; and in return this member of the government claimed as a right to have published in *The Advocate* letters containing gross personal abuse of its editor and ridicule of his aged mother. To these letters he had not the manliness to append his name; if he had, he was aware that their virulence would not have prevented their publication, for in that case the writer would have placed himself, as well as his antagonist, upon trial before the public; and every one who read them, in connection with the comments they must have provoked, would have been able to judge of the spirit in which they were conceived and the justice of their contents. The right to compel the editor to publish anonymous communications, which Mr. Macaulay had claimed, was wholly without foundation; and as for courtesy to such a correspondent it was out of the question. But it is useless to reason upon the acts of a man who had permitted passion so completely to get the mastery over his judgment.

* This piece of insolence was founded on the following passage in a private letter addressed by Mr. Mackenzie to Mr. Macaulay:—"As to the motives and character of my journal, let its unexampled circulation among the better classes in the colony speak for me. As to the result—I feel that I mean to do right—I am well satisfied that I am doing good, and though I have to struggle with a slender capital and a government who make the public advertising subservient to other purposes than that of giving general information of the thing advertised, I am as well pleased and as contented to struggle along through life as free as the air on the Scottish mountains; yea, and more so than the most

It is far from my desire to rekindle animosities that have long since died out, and the recollection of which is only preserved from oblivion by a few scattered documents and the shadowy memory of the observing men of those times who still survive; but in this biography it is necessary that the history of an act of gross violence be faithfully given. I have gone into the provocation offered by Mr. Macaulay at length, because it was in reply to a pamphlet, in which he embodied all this venom, that Mr. Mackenzie told some stories about certain members of the Family Compact that he never would have put into print if he had not been provoked beyond endurance. If in striking back, a few blows fell upon Mr. Macaulay's official associates, who had not joined openly in the provocation, Mr. Mackenzie exceeded the bounds of strict retaliatory justice; it must be remembered that the connection between all the sections of the Family Compact was very close, and that when the last word of defiance has been hurled at a man he is not to be bound by a very rigid etiquette, if he finds it necessary to "carry the war into Africa." But the reply, calmly

voluptuous courtier can be, even in his most joyous hours. If I am enabled to maintain my old mother, my wife and family, and keep out of the hands of the law for debt, I care not for wealth, and should as willingly leave this earthly scene not worth a groat as if I were worth thousands. I one day thought I should have wished to have seen you member of the Legislature for York, and that you would have become a useful and truly independent representative of the people. It was not to be, however. I greatly mistook your views, which, situated as you now are, are not likely to become more liberal."

Mr. Macaulay, in commenting on this, sneered at what he called the "printing business," and asked why Mr. Mackenzie left his "former honest calling," as if a profession in which a man speaks his own free thoughts is not just as respectable as that of the man who hires out his wits and his eloquence in defence of every species of criminal who can pay his fee.

viewed at this distant day, so far as it affected Macaulay, appears mild and playful beside the savagery
of the unprovoked attack ; I say unprovoked, because
it does not exceed the bounds of fair or ordinary criticism to tell a political opponent that you have ceased
to see in him a person possessed of manly independence. At the same time it must be confessed that
some of Macaulay's friends came in for knocks which
there is no public evidence of their having merited at
Mr. Mackenzie's hands ; and it would have been better
if he had confined the punishment, he was well entitled to inflict, to the man who alone had raised a
hand (except through the medium of the convenient
instruments of their will) to strike him down.

Macaulay's libel did not produce the effect intended.
The object, it is plain enough, was to provoke Mr.
Mackenzie into the use of language for which he
might be prosecuted, and either banished, like Gourlay, or shut up in a prison. But Mackenzie was too
wary to be caught in this clumsy trap; and his reply,
instead of retorting rage for rage, was playfully sarcastic and keenly incisive. The dialogue form was
adopted ; the speakers being a congress of fifteen contributors to The Advocate, who purported to have assembled in the Blue Parlor of Mr. McDonnell, of
Glengary, at York. Patrick Swift, nephew of the immortal Dean, who had inherited a share of his uncle's
sarcasm, was a prominent actor, and infused his playful spirit into the other contributors. Over a huge
bowl of punch, toasts are drunk, tales told, songs sung,
and politics discussed. Judging from the spirit of these
proceedings, Mr. Patrick Swift and his coadjutors were

intent on copying the style of his uncle and their pro-
totype: ·

> "From the planet of my birth,
> I encounter vice with mirth ;
> Wicked ministers of state
> I can easier scorn than hate;
> And I find it answers right:
> Scorn torments them more than spite."

"Lawyer Macaulay" was "the knight of the rueful
countenance ;" and it was hinted by one of the wits
that even he had family reasons for not scoffing at
persons for "changing their trade." When one of
the company was asked for a song, he excused himself
by saying, "Macaulay's screech-owl notes are the
music of the spheres compared to my singing ;" and
so he claimed the privilege of telling a story instead.
Among the stories told was one of a person who got
a grant of land for his mother, many years after her
death, and twelve hundred acres for an unborn child;
and a document, apparently genuine, was produced,
showing that an honorable personage desired to locate
two hundred acres on Burlington Bay, and the surveyor was instructed that the distinguished name
must not appear on the plan. One of the speakers
added, by way of explanation, that the two hundred
acre limit produced a block of some thousands, which
the honorable recipient sold to great advantage. By
virtue of his official position, this personage made large
grants of land to himself, and appointed himself
puisne judge, receiving an additional salary of £500
for the performance of scarcely any duties. This had
no reference to Macaulay, though about half the ten-
columns' dialogue was devoted to him, much of which

consists of a sharp refutation of statements published in the Macaulay pamphlet, most of which were either too absurd or too malignant to deserve an answer at all. Mr. Macaulay could not have made a worse se- lection of the time he chose for attempting to strike Mr. Mackenzie down. The latter seriously contem- plated retiring from political discussions, and pru- dence might have suggested that he should be allowed to depart in peace.

Mr. Mackenzie's enemies were furious. He had stung them to the quick; but he had dealt with matters to which it would not be desirable to give additional notoriety by making them subjects of prosecution. Truth might, legally speaking, be a libel, but there are unpleasant truths, which, though it be illegal to tell, cannot 'well be made a ground of action. Juries might be obstinate and refuse to convict a writer, who, after unbearable provocation, had been stung into telling unpleasant facts, a little dressed up, or exaggerated though they may have been, to give effect to their narration. It was clear that Mackenzie could not be banished for sedition. He could not even be tried under the Sedition Act, having been some years in the Province; and he had neither spoken nor published any thing of a seditious nature. What then remained? The sole resource of violence; and violence was used: the office of *The Advocate* was de- stroyed by a mob, consisting of persons who bore sus- piciously close relations to the government.

The trial came off at York, in the then new but now disused Court-house, in 1826. The defendants had elected to have a special jury; and on the ninth of

October, it had been struck at the office of the Deputy Sheriff, in presence of Messrs. Small and Macaulay, attorneys for the plaintiff and defendant respectively. On the day of trial, only eleven of the special jurors appearing, the deficiency was made up from the petty jury list. Of the twelve jurors* who were to try the case, nine resided in the country, and only three in York. Chief Justice Campbell was the presiding judge; and by his side sat, as associate judges, the Hon. William Allan and Mr. Alexander McDonnell. Both sides were well provided with able counsel. For the plaintiff appeared the younger Bidwell and Messrs. Stewart and Small; for the defendants, Macaulay and Hagerman. Every inch of standing room in the Court-house was occupied by spectators, eager to witness a trial which had prospectively excited universal public interest. Many witnesses testified to the destruction of the printing office, and proved that the eight defendants were engaged in it. It was shown that the Hon. Mr. Allan, who played the part of associate judge on the trial, had been in conversation with Col. Heward, whose son was among the desperadoes, at a point where they must have witnessed the whole scene. Though they were both magistrates, neither of them attempted to remonstrate with the defendants, nor to induce them to desist. The defendants called no witnesses; and Mr. Hagerman, in addressing the jury on their behalf, assailed

* Their names were:—Robert Rutherford, of York, foreman; Ezra Annis, of Whitby; James Hogg, Milford Mills; David Buyer, Markham; Valentine Fisher, Vaughan; Robert Johnson, Scarboro; Joseph Tomlinson, Markham; Peter Secor, Markham; Edward Wright, York; Joel Beman, George street; George Shaw, York.

13

The Advocate; but he did not venture to read the objectionable matter to the jury. Without a tittle of evidence to support his assertion, and in the teeth of well known facts, he stated that Mr. Mackenzie had left York at the time his printing materials were de- stroyed, to evade the payment of his debts. The trial lasted two days, which were days of great anxiety for the plaintiff; "because," as he himself stated, "great expense had been incurred, and I knew that if by any means a verdict should be delayed, or no verdict re- turned, the consequences would to me be ruinous in the extreme."

For a long time, it seemed very unlikely that the jury would agree. At an inclement season of the year, they were put between the sweating walls of a newly plastered room, the air of which was raw and unpleasant, where they remained for thirty-two hours. Some of them were far advanced in years, and three were ill. Mr. Jacob Boyer, a German by birth, was so bad as to require medical assistance; and Dr. McCague being sent for, bled the enduring juror. Boyer said he was prepared to make a pillow of his great coat, and endure another day of that close cold room, if necessary. The evidence was clear to his mind, and he would not be starved into giving a ver- dict against his convictions. During all this time, va- rious amounts of damages had been discussed. Sums varying from £2,000 to £150 had found favor with different jurors; but the real difficulty was with one man—a George Shaw—who tried to starve his fellow jurors into compliance with a verdict, giving £150 damages; but finding this impracticable, he at last gave way. Mr. Rutherford, the foreman, named £625 and costs, and the amount was agreed to by all the jurors. Referring to the result of the trial, soon after, Mr. Mackenzie said: "That verdict re-established on a permanent footing *The Advocate* Press, because it enabled me to perform my engagements without disposing of my real property; and although it has several times been my wish to retire from the active duties of the press into the quiet paths of private life, I have had a presentiment that I should yet be able to evince my gratitude to the country which, in my utmost need, rescued me from utter ruin and destruction."

Shortly after the trial, the amount of the verdict was paid by Mr. Macaulay to Mr. Mackenzie's attorney. The money was raised by subscription; the political friends of the press-destroyers feeling in duty bound to bear harmless the eight volunteers who had performed the rough task of attempting to silence, by an act of violence, an obnoxious newspaper. Col. Fitzgibbon, laboring under an irrepressible sense of duty towards the kid-gloved "roughs," took round the hat. Unhappily, no list of the contributors is obtainable; though it is believed the officials of the. day were not backward in assisting to indemnify the defendants in the type riot trial, for the adverse verdict of an impartial jury. No mark of approbation could well be more sincere than this; and it is a question whether the voluntary accomplices after the fact were wholly ignorant that the outrage had been planned before they knew that it was put into execution. Col. Fitzgibbon was already a Colonel of Militia, Deputy Adjutant General, and Justice of the Peace. But such

services as his were not deemed to be requited by such
paltry appointments, and he was therefore appointed
Chief Clerk to the Legislative Assembly.

· There remained the question of a criminal prosecution. Mr. Mackenzie, being called before the grand
jury, declined to make any complaint; and the question was raised by some of the journals, whether it was
not the duty of the Attorney General to take proceedings criminally against the press rioters. The counsel
for the defendants gave as the reason why the Attorney General had not proceeded by criminal information, that it would have brought on him the censure
of having desired to prevent the plaintiff obtaining
damages in a civil action; as if the one proceeding in
any way precluded the other. When afterwards,
in April, 1828, the Attorney General prosecuted
Francis Collins of the *Freeman* criminally for libels
upon himself, he appeared to be considerably embarrassed at the novelty of the proceeding he had initiated;
and a remark he made led to a singular piece of
fencing between himself and Judge Willis, between
whom there was very little good feeling. On the
Attorney General remarking that, during the ten years
he had had the office of Crown Lawyer, he had uniformly abstained from instituting criminal proceedings
unless upon complaint made; the judge remarked
that this was proof that his practice had been uniformly
wrong. The Attorney General, nettled at the reproof,
said he believed he knew his duty as well as any judge
on the Bench; an assertion which drew from the judge
the caustic rejoinder: "That may be; but you have
neglected it." The Attorney General then assured his

lordship that he should continue to follow the practice he had hitherto pursued; when the latter informed him that, in that case, it would be his duty to report such conduct to the British Government, and that while he sat in the Chief Justice's seat, it was his place to state to the Crown officers their duty, and theirs to perform it.

It became afterwards a common complaint with Mr. Mackenzie's political friends and business rivals, that the damages obtained were in excess of the actual loss. It is possible that this may have been the case; for he himself became convinced, after the office was reestablished, that he had at first overestimated the loss. But it was not upon his representations that the amount of the verdict was determined; and as Mr. Bidwell had insisted strongly on the necessity of exemplary damages being given, it is possible that the jury did not altogether overlook this hint. But such pretences, as afterwards found persons to utter them, that "the loss was not fifty dollars," were too evidently charged with malice to be entitled to the least consideration.

But though Mr. Mackenzie refused to ask the grand jury to initiate criminal proceedings against the rioters, the matter was not allowed to rest. Francis Collins, having been proceeded against criminally, by the Attorney General, for four libels,* in April

* Mr. Mackenzie, objecting, in his journal, to the composition of the grand jury as unfair, showed himself possessed of that sort of power which moves the masses into action. A short extract will serve as a sample:

" Wherever the seat of justice is open to corruption, there ought the sentinel of liberty, 'a free press,' to alarm the country; it should 'cry aloud and spare not.' And if the day should ever come upon us in this favored land, when men in power, forgetful of the public good, and mindful only of their private gain, shall desire to intimidate the public journals and to harass their pro-

1828, retaliated upon the party of his accusers. On information laid by him, seven of the defendants who had been cast in civil damages for the destruction of *The Advocate* office, were tried for riot. Raymond Baby was not among them. This proceeding being of a retaliatory nature, and taken against the wishes of Mr. Mackenzie, was not looked on with much favor; and though the defendants were found guilty, they were let off with nominal damages.

But Collins did not stop here. He procured informations against Henry John Boulton and Jas. E. Small, for murder, arising out of their connection with a duel, in which Mr. John Ridout, son of the Surveyor General, had been shot by Mr. Samuel Peters Jarvis. Mr. Jarvis was not included in the indictment, having been previously tried and acquitted. When on the 12th of April, the grand jury brought the "true bill" into court, Col. Adamson, the foreman, was greatly embarrassed. Mr. Justice Willis, though he could have had no personal sympathy for one of the accused,* shed tears. Mr. Boulton, who filled the high

prietors on frivolous or imaginary charges of libel and sedition—let the people look to it. Their last, their best, their sure, and only safeguard from dark oppression and misrule is about to be butchered in the public streets. Their lives, their fortunes, their religion, and the quiet of their domestic hearths, are menaced. The walls of the citadel begin to crumble, the strong tower of freedom totters at its base. Again we say, danger is at hand, LET THE PEOPLE LOOK TO IT."

* Judge Willis afterwards expressed a contemptible opinion of the Solicitor General's legal qualifications; referring to a statute, "in order," as he said, "that it may be seen what reliance is to be placed on the opinion of Mr. Solicitor General Boulton." Dr. Baldwin stated before a Committee of the House of Assembly, June 28th, 1828, "I cannot help thinking that he (Judge Willis) was rather more lenient in his charge upon the indictments of Mr. Boulton, Mr. Jarvis, and the type rioters, than the occasion required."

position of Solicitor General, lost his usual sprightli-
ness of manner, and sat silent and thoughtful beside
Attorney General Robinson. A pin might have been
heard fall in the crowded court-room. When the
thirteen jurors had made their presentment, the colleague of the accused Solicitor General rose by his
side, and said he should frame the indictment against
Messrs. Boulton and Small, as accessories of Jarvis in
the fatal duel. The Court made no remark. Judge
Sherwood had been sent for; but when he came,
he retired into the grand jury room instead of taking
his seat on the bench beside the Chief Justice.

Mr. George Ridout, the advocate of Collins, came
into court, and moved that the name of Col. Fitzgibbon be struck off the list of grand jurors, on the
ground that, having protected the type rioters, he was
not a proper person to be on the grand jury. Had
he not been there, Mr. Ridout contended, the true
bills against Collins would not have been presented.
He read a letter written by Col. Fitzgibbon, on the
type riot, to show that his objection was well founded.
The Attorney General objected, and the court reserved
its decision.

The trial for murder lasted two days, and was pro-
tracted the first night two and a half hours beyond
midnight. "The candles, untrimmed," wrote Mackenzie, "yielded a faint and glimmering light upon
the judgment seat; the presiding minister of justice
in his long black robe, was supported by the associate judges and surrounded by the officers of the court."
There was a dense mass of human beings in the court,
all still and attentive listeners "to a tale of misery, of

horrors and of woe, such as mortal man has seldom heard." The defendants were acquitted; and the judge expressed a desire that the proceedings might not be published at length, but only the result stated; a wish that seems to have met a general compliance on the part of the press.

Though the trial of Collins was not proceeded with, the government paper announced that it had not been abandoned; and it came on at the next assizes.

Nor had the end of judicial retaliations yet been reached. Mr. Mackenzie was not to escape. And yet he deserved some consideration at the hands of the official party. When called as a witness in the type riot prosecution, which he had refused to originate, he said he had no desire to prosecute the rioters against whom civil damages had been obtained; and he expressed a hope that they would receive only nominal punishment. His suggestion had been acted upon. But all this did not avail, at a time when Collins was proceeded against for four libels in Upper Canada, and Mr. Neilson for an equal number in Lower Canada. It was not Mr. Mackenzie's fault that the old duel case had been raked up; but one of the crown officers had been put upon his trial' at the instance of another editor; and why should Mr. Mackenzie escape when crown officers were in question? Accordingly, on the 17th of April, the grand jury made a presentment against the editor of *The Colonial Advocate*, for an alleged libel* published in that paper on the 3d of that month.

* The following is the paragraph charged as libellous:
 " VALUABLE REPORT ON THE CONDUCT OF THE CROWN LAWYERS.—Always

Being in Court when the presentment was made, Mr. Mackenzie went to the Attorney General, and told him that he should be ready to proceed with his defence next day. The zeal of the grand jury appears not to have been readily seconded; for when Mr. Mackenzie applied personally to the Court to recommend the crown lawyers to bring the charges to trial, the Attorney General refused to proceed with an indictment. On the night after the presentment was made, the defendant collected a long list of very miscellaneous authorities,* by the aid of which he felt con-

anxious to inform our readers of the most important proceedings of the Colonial Legislature, we hasten to direct their attention to the report of a select committee of the House of Assembly on the petition of Mr. Forsyth, of Niagara Falls, loudly complaining of the conduct of the crown officers, and of a defective and partial administration of justice. The report speaks a language not to be misunderstood, and we trust that a perusal of it will serve to stir up the dormant energies of the wholesome part of the population, and induce them to exert themselves manfully to clear the House of Assembly next election, of the Attorney General, Speaker Willson, Jonas, David and Charles Jones, Messrs. Burnham, Coleman, Scollick, Gordon, McDonell, Beasley, Clark, McLean, Vankoughnet, and the whole of that ominous nest of unclean birds which have so long lain close under the wings of a spendthrift Executive, and (politically to speak) actually preyed upon the very vitals of the country they ought to have loved, cherished, and protected. No wonder it is that Parliament should find its energies all but paralyzed, when such an accumulation of corrupt materials is left UNSWEPT WITH THE BESOM OF THE PEOPLE'S WRATH from out of these halls they have so long and so shamefully 'defiled with their abominations.' "

* "Blackstone's Commentaries; A file of the Advocate, from 1 to 150; A few choice selections from the U. E. Loyalist; Journals of Assembly, 1820, 1825, 1826, and 1827; Burnett's History of his own Times; A speech of John Horne Tooke; The Bible; The Book of Common Prayer; Edinburgh Review, 1811, article on 'The Liberty of the Press;' Gourlay's Statistics, 8 vols.; Simpson's Plea for Religion; Swift's Works, a volume containing 'The Drapier,' &c.; The Roman Missal; The Alien Question Unmasked; Earl Stanhope's Rights of Juries; A volume of Erskine's Speeches; Dr. Towers on Libel; Hone's three Trials; The Black Book, or Corruption Unmasked; Selections cut out of files of the Times, Globe and Traveller, and Courier, London daily papers,

14

fident he should be able to make out his case. His
own account of his preparation for a forensic display,
in self-defence, may here be given:

"I carried into Court, tied up in a large bundle
[of books] with striped tape, and having placed them
before me on the barristers' table, began to arrange
them after a very imposing legal fashion, having by
me my memoranda of references, by which, as to an
index, I could refer to the newspaper, book, or paper
wanted, and bring forward the proofs or arguments on
any subject connected with the matters set forth in
the alleged libel, in a moment of time. By a little
exertion over night, but far more by anticipation at
former periods, I had before me a collection of materials fit and relevant for my purpose; and had I been
allowed to go into the merits of the case, it would have
defied all the Attorney Generals in British America to
have furnished an opposing argument equally solid,
strong, and convincing. I had carefully consulted
both the law and the practice. I had, in fact, done all
that man could do to give the judges and crown lawyers such a dose as would have cured their itching for
state prosecutions on alleged political libels for a long
time to come."

by myself, and reserved for a case of libel, as fair specimens of the style of political discussion in use by the respectable London periodical press; Babylon
the Great; Junius; Peter Watson's Trial; Dr. Strachan's Pamphlet and
Chart; Trial of J. A. Williams for a libel on the Durham Clergy; and selections cut out of Parliamentary speeches, published in the U. E. Loyalist. These
with Mr. Stanton's ' Yankee Doodle Committee Report on Captain Mathews ;'
' The Rejected Addresses ;' Cobbett on the Freedom of the Press; The Freeman, containing Peter McPhail's effort at the York Independence meeting,
and several other documents.'

Instead of being put upon his trial for the alleged political libel, Mr. Mackenzie had to give security to the amount of £200, that he would answer the charge at the next assizes; a delay of which he thought himself well entitled to complain.

CHAPTER VII.

An Event that lessens the Popular Faith in the Impartial Administration of
Justice—Removal of Judge Willis by the Local Executive—The Cause of
the Difficulty—He is falsely accused of Displaying. Temper in Court—
A wordy Duello between Judges Sherwood and Willis—Leading Members
of the Bar side with Judge Willis in the Legal Dispute—Decision of the
Privy Council Unfavorable to Judge Willis—Collins convicted of Libel on
the Attorney General, fined £50, and sentenced to a year's imprisonment—
Worse Offenders of another Political Stripe overlooked—The Fine paid by
Subscription—A Committee of the House desire to interrogate Judge Sherwood about his Direction in the Collins' Case—He refuses to have his Judicial Conduct inquired into, but gives the Information to the Executive—
The Assembly denounce his Direction; but the Privy Council pronounce it
all right—The Libel Prosecution against Mr. Mackenzie abandoned—Murder of one Knowlan, a Powerful Bully, by Charles French—The latter, a
Witness in the Type Riot, is Executed.

BEFORE the trials for libel could come on, an event
occurred, in the removal of Judge Willis, which was
not calculated to inspire the defendants with confidence in the impartial administration of justice. If
the local Executive suspended a judge, because his in-
terpretation of the law did not accord with their views,
the power of the Executive in political prosecutions
could not but be regarded as a source of danger to
public liberty. Mr. Willis had only received his appointment on the eleventh of October, 1827; and on
the sixth of the following June, he was suspended
until the pleasure of His Majesty's Imperial Govern-

ment should be known. We have seen that, far from bending to the influence of power, he had undertaken to teach the Attorney General his duty. In the Hilary term of Michaelmas, then past, Mr. Justice Willis had taken his seat on the bench beside Chief Justice Campbell and Mr. Justice Sherwood; and differences of opinion on points of great legal importance had arisen among them. Before the following Easter term, the Chief Justice had obtained leave of absence; and the differences of opinion between the two remaining judges, Willis and Sherwood, were carried to such a length as to excite public attention. Under these circumstances, Judge Willis directed his special attention to the Constitution of the Court; and he found that the statute creating this tribunal provided " that His Majesty's Chief Justice, together with two puisne judges, shall preside in the said Court." Considering the Court illegally constituted without three judges, he refused to sit with Mr. Justice Sherwood for his only colleague, when, according to his reading of the law, there ought to be another. Sometime before Trinity' term, it came to the knowledge of the Provincial Government that Mr. Justice Willis had come to this conclusion. When the opportunity presented itself, he delivered his opinion at length on the subject. Having dealt with the question of what was required, under the Provincial statute, to constitute a legal Court of King's Bench, he touched upon the cause of the legal inefficiency of that tribunal. The Chief Justice had obtained leave of absence; but he had obtained it from the Lieutenant-Governor alone, while Mr. Willis contended that the consent of the Governor in Council was necessary.

The opponents of Mr. Justice Willis accused him of showing temper in the delivery of his opinion; but the accusation, when sifted, was found to be groundless. A Committee of the House of Assembly, of which Dr. Baldwin was Chairman, reported that they had "particularly inquired into this matter," and came to the conclusion, "that to the public eye and ear, the manner and language of Mr. Justice Willis, on the occasion of so expressing his opinion on the Bench, relative to the defective state of the Court, in no respect departed from the gravity and dignity becoming him as a judge; and peculiar malevolence alone could represent it otherwise." The evidence fully bore out this statement. "When Mr. Justice Willis delivered his opinion," Mr. Carey* told the Committee, "his conduct was dignified and honorable."

When Mr. Justice Willis had concluded his opinion, an unseemly spectacle took place. Mr. Justice Sherwood ordered the clerk to adjourn the Court. Mr. Willis replied that it was impossible to adjourn what did not exist. There was no legal Court. Mr. Sherwood rejoined: "You have given your opinion; I have a right to mine, and I shall order the Court to be adjourned." "He spoke," says Mr. Carey, "apparently under great irritation." Mr. Willis bowed and withdrew, the clerk obeying the order of the remaining judge.

The difficulty that had occurred between Mr. Jus-

---

* Mr. Carey was editor of the *York Observer*, and had long been a firm supporter of the government; but at this time he was wavering in his allegiance.

tice Willis and Attorney General Robinson, on a previous occasion, was also made a subject of inquiry before the Parliamentary Committee; and Mr. Carey, in his evidence, stated that so far as manner was concerned, the only thing to complain of in the judge, was his too great lenity in presence of the treatment he received.

Dr. Baldwin, Mr. Robert Baldwin, and Mr. John Rolph, practising barristers, entered a protest against the legality of the Court, when it had been constituted with two judges; giving at length their reasons for agreeing with Judge Willis, that in order to a legal constitution of the Court, there must be three judges. A petition, which the Duke of Wellington thought deserved no particular notice, bearing the signatures of thousands of Upper Canadians, in favor of the independence of the judiciary, and sustaining the position of Judge Willis, was sent to the King and the two Houses of Parliament. The law point was finally decided by the Privy Council adversely to the views of Mr. Justice Willis, whose removal was thereupon ratified by the Imperial Government.

It was now certain that the juries who might try the libel cases, would not bo directed by Mr. Justice Willis, but by some one whose affinity to the prosecutors was undoubted. Soon after this time, Mr. James Stephens, then counsel to the Colonial Office, told a Committee of the House of Commons, that "throughout the colonies a body of gentlemen are acting as judges, who, however accomplished in other respects, are totally destitute of legal education." If, in addition to this they were also mere dependents of the

Executive, the case must be much worse. Soon after the commencement of the York assizes, which opened on the 12th October, 1828, the libel prose-cutions against Collins came on. Of that upon the Attorney General, he was found guilty, and sentenced by Mr. Hagerman—who had temporarily gone upon the Bench, leaving the Kingston collector-ship of customs to take care of itself—to be imprisoned for twelve months in the York jail, and pay a fine of £50. The libel consisted of imputing "native malignancy" to the Attorney General, and stigmatizing, as "an open and palpable falsehood," a statement made by that functionary in open court.*

It is not necessary to raise the question whether such libels as this ought to have been met by a criminal prosecution. But if it was the duty of the Attorney General to prosecute Collins, it was also his duty to

* Collins was a man of uncouth exterior, but was possessed of considerable ability. When Dr. Horne, in whose office he was a printer, gave up the publication of the *Upper Canada Gazette*, Collins applied for the post of King's Printer, and was told in reply, that the office " would be given to none but a gentleman." Being disappointed in the attempt to dispose of his services to the government, he some time afterwards commenced the publication of an opposition paper, a very slight acquaintance with which will convince any one that in spite of his natural ability he sometimes mistook coarseness for strength of language. He was an excellent reporter, and for several years acted officially in that capacity, as the servant of the House. It was not his habit to write his articles. He put them into type as he composed them. He had the strange vanity of boasting his descent from royal personages, and was naturally laughed at for his pains. When he was incarcerated for libel, Mr. Mackenzie did all he could to secure his release, a service which he repaid with the blackest ingratitude and the coarsest abuse. From sheer business jealousy the *Freeman* had at all times been excessively abusive of Mr. Mackenzie, a coin in which the latter never stooped to repay him. But, with all his faults—and who is faultless?—Collins must be admitted to have done good in his day. He died of cholera, in 1834, when Mr. Mackenzie held the position of first Mayor of Toronto.

prosecute others, connected with the government press, who had used fully as great a latitude of expression. One of these writers* had signalized several members of the Legislative Assembly as "besotted fools," actuated by no other feeling than malice, to gratify which they pay no regard to truth or decency. Addressing a single member, the same writer informed him, "There are no bounds to your malice;" and the whole House was described as an "intolerable nuisance." "The poison of your malignant disposition," also made use of, was an expression fully as offensive as "native malignancy." If it was the duty of the Attorney General to prosecute for the use of such language, he was bound to perform that duty impartially, and was not entitled, in fairness, to single out opponents for victims, while the offences of political friends were overlooked.

A public subscription was raised to pay the amount of the fine; public meetings were held and committees formed to take the case of Collins into consideration. To a petition for his release, the Lieutenant-Governor, Sir John Colborne, who had but recently arrived in the Province, replied, through Assistant-Secretary McMahon, that he respected the liberty of the press very much, but that he had an equal respect for trial by jury; and that the danger of interfering with their decisions must be very great, unless when they are clearly illegal. This was on the 8th November, and ten days later Mr. Collins's petition for a remission of the sentence elicited a direct negative, through Mr. Secretary Mudge, who was instructed to add, that

* *Kingston Chronicle.*

15

at the expiration of his term of imprisonment, "any application you may decide to make will be taken into consideration upon the facts alleged in your statement," which, at this distant day, reads very much like a mockery of the prisoner's misery. At a later period the House of Assembly interposed in behalf of Collins, but they failed to change the determination of the Executive to keep him in close confinement for the whole of the prescribed term of his sentence. Sir John thought himself entitled to snub the House for their interference, by expressing extreme regret at the course they had taken. He forgot that the Sovereign whom he represented is the fountain of mercy, and thought only of his obligation to carry a rigorous and cruel sentence into effect.

The Assembly's committee called upon Mr. Justice Sherwood to give evidence in the case on which he had presided, but he refused, rightly most persons will now think, to have his judicial conduct inquired into by a committee of the House, and did not answer the questions put to him. A judge is necessarily liable to impeachment for improper conduct, but not to account either to the Sovereign or to Parliament for any particular judgment he may have given. But if the House of Assembly was wrong in demanding to know from Judge Sherwood the grounds on which his judgment was based, and he was right in refusing to answer, he was wrong in giving to the Executive government, as he afterwards did, the information he had refused to the House.* Mr. Hagerman, who

---

* The Legislative Assembly pronounced Mr. Justice Sherwood's charge "an unwarrantable deviation from the matter of record, and a forced construction

was acting as judge at this time, was also called before the committee, but he refused to answer the
questions put to him, on the ground that they impeached the conduct of a brother judge. The Legislative Assembly having denounced the conduct of the
judges, and the matter having been made a subject
of complaint in a petition to the Imperial authorities,
the case came before the law-officers of the crown, in
England, for their opinion thereon. They reported
that they saw nothing objectionable in the direction
of the judge or the verdict of the jury.

The threatened prosecution of Mr. Mackenzie for
an alleged political libel had been kept suspended
over his head for nearly a whole year, when a day
was fixed by the Attorney General to strike a special
jury, which had been demanded by Mr. Mackenzie,
when he found that the list of petty jurors had not been
returned to the crown office as usual. Mr. Sullivan
having unsuccessfully applied for the list, on behalf
of Mr. Mackenzie, went to Sheriff Jarvis to inquire
the cause; when he was informed that Mr. Justice
Sherwood had directed him not to return the list as
usual. For some reason, however, the Executive re-

of language, contrary to the ends of fair and dispassionate justice." They also
resolved that "Mr. Justice Hagerman one of the persons alleged on the record
to be libelled, refused to receive the verdict first tendered by the jury, viz:
'Guilty of libel against the Attorney General only,' with which direction the
jury complied, whereby the defendant was made to appear on record guilty
of charges of which the jury had acquitted him, and whereby false grounds
were afforded upon the record for an oppressive or unwarrantable sentence."
"Mr. Hagerman," it was further declared, "did concern himself with Mr.
Justice Sherwood in measuring the punishment of defendant; thereby, without necessity for it, violating the rule that a man shall not be judge in his own
case."

solved to abandon the prosecution, and two days before the date fixed for the striking of the special jury, the Attorney General addressed a note to Mr. Sullivan stating the conclusion that had been arrived at.

The alleged libel, of which the prosecution was thus abandoned, was purely political. It was neither more nor less than a recommendation to certain constituencies to change their representatives at the then next ensuing general election ; and expressed in language that must be admitted to have been very strong, but also very general, why this should be done. " The besom of the people's wrath" may be an alarming figure of speech ; but after all it is only a figure. Connected with a general election, it ceases to wear a terrific aspect, and becomes a mere question of defeating certain supporters in the Legislative Assembly of the ruling minority. The report of a committee of the House, on which the paragraph was founded, contained more serious accusations than the alleged libel itself. The committee, of which Mr. Beardsley was chairman, reported, among other things, " that some of the most daring outrages against the peace of the community have passed unprosecuted, and that the persons guilty have, from their connections in high life, been promoted to the most important offices of honor, trust, and emolument, in the local government." Surely this more than justified a recommendation, however strong the language in which it was conveyed, that the supporters of such a state of things should be rejected by the people, at the next general election. It was certainly a wise resolution to abandon the pro-

secution, whatever may have been the cause* that
led the government to its adoption.

About two years after the type riot, a tragical event,
which bore some relation to it, took place. Charles
French, who was in Mr. Mackenzie's employ, as printer in 1826, and was one of the principal witnesses on the trial, became a marked man. He tried
to keep the rioters out of the office, and was a principal agent in their conviction. At this time, there
lived in York an Irish laborer, of the name of Knowlan, a stalwart and pestiferous bully, standing considerably over six feet high, and possessing great
muscular power. Accustomed to carry a pair of short
iron tongs concealed about his clothes, to attack persons in the street, and insult them at the door of the
theatre, he was the terror of the place. As savage as
a gorilla and twice as vicious, Knowlan was the man
who undertook to execute vengeance upon Charles
French. During the winter of 1827-8, French had
fallen into habits of dissipation, and got accustomed

---

* Mr. Mackenzie, writing of the result at the time, says:—"We can only
conjecture the cause for this new and judicious procedure. 1st. We should
think that Sir John Colborne would be ill inclined to administer to the
legacy of prosecutions bequeathed to him by his predecessor. 2d. That
there were very poor hopes of success, in the present state of public opinion, as must have been evident from the facts that the alleged libeller had,
after giving the libel the greatest possible circulation, after presentment, been
returned to the Assembly for the county where he resided, and where the offensive libellous matter had been previously published. 3d. That the country is
disgusted with the cruel and vindictive punishment awarded to the editor of
the *Freeman*. 4th. That the libel is *true* and not *false*, as stated in the indictment. 5th. That the committee of the Commons of England had deprecated
this sort of prosecutions. 6th. That the people's representatives, in Parliament
assembled, had addressed the throne on the injustice and the partiality hitherto
pursued in libel cases, and pointed out to His Majesty its bad effects."

to divide the late hours of the night between the dram-shop—of which there were sixty in a town of less than two thousand inhabitants—and the theatre. He occasionally took a subordinate part among the actors. Remaining out very late one evening, and returning flushed with liquor, French met Mr. Mackenzie's remonstrance with abuse, and was dismissed, in consequence, from his employment, on the 6th of May, 1828. About a fortnight after, he was seized upon one night by the bully Knowlan, who, in answer to an inquiry from Mr. Charles Baker, said he was going to carry him to the river and drown him. In releasing his victim, whom he had hoisted upon his shoulder, Knowlan threatened, with an oath, that he " would settle him yet." On the 4th of June, Knowlan was at the militia training, where he assaulted a constable, and was to have been brought up next day for the offence. But death intervened. Knowlan was at the theatre that night, with his tongs, as usual. When the play was about half over, in an insulting manner he went up to French, and taking out his tongs, he was heard to swear that he would measure them over the head of French and those of two or three other persons, if he only had them outside the theatre. French, who was of a naturally mild disposition when sane and sober, was subject to violent fits of insanity; and liquor, when too freely taken, produced the most terrible effect upon him. He had been drinking, and became excited by the menace of Knowlan, aggravated as it was, by a hideous contortion of his brows, and recalling, as it must, the threat which Knowlan had made against his life, a fortnight before. Besides,

French was suffering from a pain in the breast, occasioned by a blow from the ruffian, some time before.
It was while listening to "Tom and Jerry, or Life in
London," that French became alarmed at Knowlan's
threats. He mentioned the circumstance to one William Gedd, saying he felt his life in danger, and was
without any means of defence. A person named Gos-
ling, a boon companion of French, hearing of this,
went to one Wm. D. Forest, and asked to borrow from
him a pistol that was in his possession. French, being
called out of the theatre, was informed by Forest, that,
though he had but one pistol, and that a borrowed
one, he would let him have it. It was loaded with
ball. French returned to the theatre, but left before
the farce was over, and took more drink. About midnight, when he and three companions were returning
from drinking at Howard's, they met Knowlan walking a little behind some of his associates. French
having spoken to him, Knowlan asked with an oath,
why he was standing there? He approached towards
French, and raised his hand, as French supposed, to
fulfil his threat, when the latter fired the pistol, and
shot Knowlan through the liver. Knowlan died
eighteen hours after he received the wound; and
French was found guilty of murder and sentenced to
be hanged. The trial took place on the 17th of October, and the execution was to follow in three days.
In a few hours, a petition for the mitigation of punishment, was signed by eleven hundred persons; it
was taken to the Lieutenant-Governor, at Stamford;
but the only result was a respite till the 23d, six days

after the trial, when the sentence of death was carried into effect.

In a statement made by French, in his last moments, he reproached himself with the reflection, that, "had I attended to the oft-repeated advice of my friends, especially my dear mother and Mr. Mackenzie, and avoided bad company and drinking, I should not now be here; but I would not attend, and now I have to suffer."

CHAPTER VIII.

Effect of the Destruction of the Advocate Printing Office contrary to the Expectations of its Perpetrators—Pecuniary Embarrassments—Fever brought
on by Anxiety and Vexation—Herculean Feats by the Midnight Lamp—
Tableau of an overworked Newspaper Editor—Haunted by Ague—Sickness and Death in the Family—Robert Randall; his Influence on Mr. Mackenzie—Acting in Concert with Mackenzie and others, Randall goes to
England with Petitions on the Alien Question—The Pocket Test of Patriotism—Letters to Earl Dalhousie—Statement of the Alien Question—British
Subjects made Aliens by the mere Act of Passing through a Foreign Country—Difficulty of the Question; Its final Settlement—Mr. Mackenzie's
Faith in Appeals to the Colonial Office.

VIOLENCE is a blindfolded demon, more likely to
defeat its own objects than to attain them. The means
taken to crush a public journal, obnoxious to the
ruling faction, proved the cause of its resuscitation and
firm establishment. At the very time when the press
was broken and the type thrown into the bay, the last
number of *The Advocate* had been issued. The fact
was not known to Mr. Mackenzie's enemies, or they
might not have smote the lion that was supposed by
its own keeper to be dead, and thus recalled its suspended energies to life and action. The publication, burthened as it was with a postal tax payable in advance,
and addressing itself to a small scattered community,
had never repaid the expenditure necessary to sustain
it. What means its proprietor had made in trade
16

were soon dissipated on the literary speculation. Between *matériel*, and debts, and losses, the publisher had been brought to a dead stand, and was unable to make further way. In winding up the mercantile business, many debts had been left uncollected and were still unpaid. What between purchasing land and building, buying printing materials and carrying on an unprofitable publication, he had gone beyond the compass of his available capital. He was threatened with prosecution for debt. In May, 1826, he was offered a loan of money that would have relieved him; but it was only for three months, and he could not assure himself of his ability to repay it in that time. His property, real and personal, was worth twice the amount of his debts; but he was embarrassed for ready money; threatened with *capias* by one creditor, and thoroughly disheartened. From these embarrassments he resolved to free himself. With the consent of Mr. Tannahill, his principal creditor, Mr. Mackenzie went to Lewiston, in order to prevent the accumulation of law costs, till his affairs could be settled. To have continued the paper another year, even if money could have been raised, would have been absolute ruin. From Lewiston he wrote, on the 27th of May, to Mr. Cawthra, at York, proposing to place the whole of his property into the hands of three trustees to be sold; and after the claims of his creditors had been satisfied, the balance to be handed over to him. "The place at Dundas," he wrote, "you could quickly dispose of; and that place is the one I am least willing to give away; but let it go for what it may fetch." His enemies afterwards pretended that he had gone to Lewiston for the purpose of defrauding his creditors; but this calumny is sufficiently disproved by his letter to Mr. Cawthra, and by the fact that, while there, he voluntarily granted a cognovit covering the amount of the whole of the claims against him by his creditors. This was done three days before the destruction of the printing office; and consequently before any new reason had arisen for his immediate return to York. After it was all over, the creditor, by whom he had been threatened with *capias*, confessed, in writing, "I have not done by you as I would have wished."

Besides, his health was broken; and he had some time before been thrown into a fever by the vexation he had suffered. His eldest daughter had died, and another member of his family was ill. Under these circumstances, it is not surprising that he should have sighed for that repose which journalism had interrupted in the first instance, and of which it still continued to prevent the return. But while he loved repose, he had not been able to resist the excitement of the semi-public life of the journalist, who already dreamed of the overthrow of an administration and the reform of the oligarchical system then in operation. He who repiningly compared his own toils to the quiet life of the farmer would sit up whole nights, laboring assiduously to accomplish political ends. Though he could be a child among his children, and was never so happy as when he joined in their play, he would frequently sit up for two consecutive nights, at the patient but exhausting labor of the pen. And if the pen be more powerful than the sword, it is also, in the hands of the overworked journalist, more dan-

gerous to himself than is the active use of the sword
to the soldier. A fevered pulse, an aching head, and
all the long train of horrors resulting from a disordered
stomach, are his portion. With him life is little else
than endurance. The strongest nerves become un-
strung, and the most powerful frame gives way. Mr.
Mackenzie was blessed with a constitution, such as
not one man in ten thousand possesses. It has been
said of Lord Brougham, that he has been known to
work for six days and six nights without ever going
to bed. At a later period of his life, this extraordinary feat Mr. Mackenzie actually performed. On
the occasion of these long vigils, when drowsiness
came on, he would have water poured upon his
head, and, thus roused up, take a fresh start. When
overtaxed nature could no longer be resisted he would
sleep a few minutes in his chair, then, waking, would
walk round his room a few times and recommence his
never-ending task. It is, or used to be, thought a
great feat for a man to walk a thousand miles in a
thousand hours. The overworked journalist has his
mile to walk every hour of his life, and when he
comes to the end he is in his grave! He goes there,
too, much before his appointed time; or, if all things
be appointed, it is his lot, by a violent wear of the
constitution, to carve out for himself an early sepul-
chre. The sixty-seven years that he lived carried
Mr. Mackenzie almost to the allotted limit of human
existence, but if his marvelously strong constitution had
had fair-play, there must have been fully twenty years
more wear in it. But after all, the wonder is that he
lived so long, when his mode of life and what he was

called upon to endure are considered. Soon after his arrival in Canada, he took ague in Kingston; it went with him to Dundas, and appeared with greater intensity after his arrival in Toronto, then called York. To the last, he was subject to that modification of it which is known as "dumb ague." He was subject, at infrequent intervals, to terrible pains in the head— one of the well-known symptoms of over-mental exertion. Of the time previous to the destruction of his printing office, he has left it on record: "My health had for three or four months been in the most precarious state, and much sickness in my family had depressed my spirits beyond any thing I had ever felt or endured before." In Queenstown he lost his eldest daughter, born at Dundas, at the age of eleven months; and in York, near the close of 1824, his second child, born at Queenstown; also a daughter, died of small-pox. One of the competing newspapers showed its sympathy by hinting that the infected neighborhood of the rival's house and office had better be avoided. And the suggestion was not unheeded; for such was the terror of small-pox in those days, that while it was in the house the only stranger or neighbor who crossed the threshold was the elder Mr. David Patteson, an ironmonger at York, whose deeply scarred face was his best security against the danger of infection. The condition of his own health, as well as domestic and pecuniary reasons, made Mr. Mackenzie desirous that his connection with the press should cease.

At the time of the destruction of his type and press, Mr. Mackenzie had a contract for printing the journals of the Legislative Assembly, at the rate of about

six dollars, a page; but whatever profits were made
out of other printing were swallowed up by the newspaper, or scattered over the country in the shape of
doubtful debts. Besides, he was constantly printing
for gratuitous distribution political squibs, in various
shapes and forms; an operation which did not tend
to improve the state of his exchequer.

It often happens that the influence of one individual
upon another, at a critical period of his life, shapes
and moulds his destiny. Was Mr. Mackenzie subject to any such influence? Perhaps this question
cannot be satisfactorily answered. While living at
Queenstown, he became acquainted with Mr. Robert
Randal, a Virginian by birth, (and a near relative of
John Randolph, of Roanoke,) who had come to this
Province as a permanent settler, and was then living
at Chippewa. Randal was a politician, and it is
probable that his influence on Mr. Mackenzie first led
him into politics. The proof is not clear; but Mrs.
Mackenzie is of that opinion. Randal was a man
who, with a keen eye to the future, selected land at
different places where future towns were certain to
spring up. He was entangled in law suits, involving
property to a very large amount; and in one way or
another was cruelly victimized. His lawyers played
him false, and the officers of the law conspired to defraud him. He, became involved in pecuniary embarrassments, and was charged with perjury for
swearing to a qualification which, based on a long list
of properties the ownership of some of which litigation had rendered doubtful, was declared to be bad.
Mr. Mackenzie took his part; they continued to be

firm friends, and when ~~Randall~~ died he bequeathed a share of his property to the man who had in some sort been his protector. The connection produced its effect upon Mr. Mackenzie for life. Long before Randall's death, Mackenzie had embraced his quarrels, and made them his own. They were afterwards to become his inheritance; and they were well calculated to assist in embittering the existence of one of his keen susceptibility.

In the spring of 1827, Mackenzie raised the question of sending to England an agent to plead with the British Government the cause of the American-born aliens, in Canada. A petition, said to have been signed by fifteen thousand persons, was ready to be carried to England. A central committee, charged with the protection of the rights of the aliens, met at Mr. Mackenzie's house, and he acted as its confidential secretary. Mr. Fothergill, who had taken the popular side on the Alien question, and been dismissed from the office of King's printer, desired the mission. The central committee offered it to Dr. Rolph, who declined acceptance. The question was then between Fothergill and Randall; Mackenzie, favoring the appointment of the latter, carried his point. Randall was in the position of the persons whose cause he had to plead. On behalf of the committee, the delegate's instructions were drawn up by Mr. Mackenzie; and the committee having advanced a sum for his expenses,* part of which had

* Mackenzie makes "Tom Moore, jr.," say :—"Among the numerous petitions against the Alien Bill, we observed one from the head of the lake, signed at Flambro' west, by upwards of 100 individuals, owning property equal to at least $200,000 value. Among this opulent portion of the people we are credibly informed that a sum equal to $20 was raised in aid of a mission to England.

been raised by subscription, Randall set off for London, in the month of March.

In order to smooth the way for the delegate in England, Mr. Mackenzie addressed letters to the Earl of Dalhousie, Governor-in-chief, surcharged with expressions of loyalty, and recommending colonial representation in the Imperial Parliament. It is worthy of note that the first of these letters contains several extracts from American authorities predicting a dissolution of the Federal Union. After giving these extracts, the writer asks: "And is this the government, and are these the people whose alliance and intimacy we ought to court instead of those of England? No, my lord; their constitutional theory is defective, and their practice necessarily inconsistent. Their government wants consolidation; let us take warning by their example." Mr. Mackenzie afterwards expressed the opinion that these letters, taken as a guarantee for the loyalty of the opposition, materially assisted Randall's exertions in England. A few weeks later, he was writing about the "glorious opportunity of England to recover her most ancient and valuable colonies by simply giving the remaining Provinces a voice in her national councils."

There were in the Province a large number of per-

That is to say, they gave a shilling apiece, or a ten-thousandth part to save the rest!

> "To keep the cause of liberty
> In Italy afloat,
> Illustrious Bennet's generous hand
> Subscribed a one pound note!
>
> To keep the cause of liberty
> In Canada from falling,
> The patriots about Dundas
> Gave each a Dublin shilling!"

sons, who, though born in British Colonies, had, by the progress of events, and the effect of laws resulting from those events, lost the legal quality and privileges of British subjects. All who were born in the old American Colonies, and had continued to live there till after the peace of 1783, became, on the 3d of September of that year, by the Treaty of Independence, citizens of the United States. They, therefore, by that fact, ceased to be British subjects. Both American and English law courts agreed as to the effect of the treaty upon the nationality of those who resided in the United States, at the peace of 1783. Of those who came to Canada, after that date, many had adhered to the British standard through the revolutionary war; but among these immigrants there were doubtless many others who had not.

The laws relating to aliens were stretched so as to cover a class of persons they could never have been intended to affect. A person born in England, or Ireland, or Scotland, who came to Canada through the United States, was held to have lost the character of a British subject on the way, and to be incapable of exercising the elective franchise till he had been seven years in the country; as if the mere touch of United States soil had the magic power to divest an Englishman of his nationality, the reintegration of which was only to be obtained by a seven years' probation. Robert Gourlay, a Scotchman by birth, was charged under the Sedition Act with not having been six months in the country, nor taken the oath of allegiance.

Persons who had made immense sacrifices by adhering to the British standard during the revolution-

17

ary war, lost, in some cases, large amounts of property, in consequence of their inability to inherit as British subjects. The case of Elizabeth Ludlow, niece of a Chief Justice of New Brunswick, had just been de- cided adversely in the English courts, on the ground that her father had resided in the United States, after the Treaty of Independence was ratified ; and though the whole family had made great sacrifices for the British cause, she was declared incapable of inheriting the property in dispute. A large number of Amer- icans, whose ancestors had taken sides—some one, some the other—in that contest, were then residents in the Province. Most of them were possessors of land ; and their rights were never challenged or brought in ques- tion till after the close of the war of 1812, when, under the presidency of Sir Gordon Drummond, a proclamation was issued with the view of putting a stop to the immigration of American citizens into Ca- nada. The effect of a possible political propagandism, exercised through the medium of these immigrants, appears to have been feared. It is doubtful, however, whether this proclamation had legal ground to rest upon. Lieutenant Governor Gore, who succeeded Sir Gordon, thought it had not, and that Americans were entitled still, not only to come and settle in Canada, but also to receive such modified naturalization as the English laws had sanctioned. By a British statute passed in 1790, a seven years' residence, the taking of the oath of allegiance and the sacrament of the Lord's Supper, according to the usages of the Protestant Church, and observing other formalities, all aliens who came to the colonies could acquire the rights of

British subjects, with certain reservations. But they could not become members of the Privy Council or of Parliament;* they were incapacitated from holding any position of trust, civil or military, in the United Kingdom or Ireland; and they could not accept of any grant of land from the crown. The provisions of this statute were hardly ever complied with by alien emigrants from the United States. No distinction was made or could be made between the absconding debtor who had fled from the United States to defraud his creditors, and the loyalist, who, adhering to the fortunes of the British crown during the revolutionary war, had not left that country till after the peace of 1783, when, in spite of himself, the treaty made him an American citizen. Men whose industry had cleared the country of forests, who had carried civilization into the wilds of the west, and assisted to repel invasion, found themselves aliens, without any legal security for their property.

Whatever might be the effect of a narrow or rigid construction of the Alien Law upon these persons, they had not hitherto received the treatment of aliens. They had received grants of land from the crown and devised real property ; some of them had held offices of trust in the militia, and spilt their blood in defence of the country, in which they were now to be denied the rights of citizens, except upon conditions which they regarded as degrading. It was not to be expected that a man who had fought beside the gallant Brock would feel complimented if asked to take

* In May, 1826, an Imperial Act was passed to render naturalized foreigners capable of sitting in the Legislature of Upper Canada.

the oath of allegiance. The recent decision of the Court of King's Bench, in England, in the Ludlow case, created uneasiness, alarm, and indignation. After much correspondence with the Lieutenant Governors on the subject, the Imperial Government sent instructions to Sir Perigrine Maitland to cause a bill to be introduced into the Legislature, by which all the rights of British subjects could be conferred upon the aliens in the Province. The bill passed the Legislative Council, whose members owed their nomination to the crown, in the session of 1826; and when it was sent down to the Assembly, it met an equal amount of opposition and support, on two several divisions. The House was equally divided for a whole week; and the bill, after being five times negatived by the casting vote of the Speaker, was at length irregularly passed. Though the division of numbers was so long equal, the majority of the members who spoke opposed those provisions which required all persons, placed in the category of aliens by the recent judicial decision, to remedy their former neglect by complying with certain prescribed formalities; a residence of seven years and the taking of the oath of allegiance being necessary to confer on them those rights which many of them had from the first, exercised without question. Whatever may have been the merits or demerits of this measure, it is proper to quote the declaration of Mr. Wilmot Horton, then under-Secretary of State for the Colonies, that the " Lieutenant Governor and Legislative Council of Upper Canada cannot be considered responsible for those parts of the present bill which have excited the most earnest opposition. Lord Bathurst's

instructions to the Lieutenant-Governor, founded, as
they were, upon his Lordship's impression that the
measure proposed would be satisfactory, were peremp-
tory, and left the local Governor no discretion on the
subject." At the same time, it is pretty certain that
Lord Bathurst's impression must have been derived
from the official information he received from Canada.
The Imperial Government showed by their subsequent
action that they were anxious to do what would give
full satisfaction to the people, whose rights were in
question.

Mr. Bidwell, whose father when elected for Lennox
and Addington, in 1822, had been declared ineligible
to take his seat in the Legislative Assembly, on account of his being an alien, proposed as an alternative measure to declare all Americans then in the
Province entitled to all the rights of British subjects.
The real hardship was in confounding two distinct
classes: persons who were born British subjects, or
whose fathers had been born British subjects, and who,
so far from having done any thing to forfeit that character, had throughout been true to their allegiance,
with others who had come to the Province not from
political choice, but because they found emigration
convenient, or thought it would be profitable. Among
the latter there were some who were anxious to enjoy
all the rights of British subjects without taking the
oath of allegiance, and who considered it a glorious
diversion to cross the frontier line to enjoy the demonstrations that take place on the anniversary of
American independence. If it was desirable that
these persons should submit to a formal act of natur-

alization, it was impossible to distinguish between them and others, who, having been born British subjects, had never desired to relinquish their allegiance And here arose the real difficulty of the case.

The bill passed by the Legislature was of that nature which rendered necessary its reservation for the signification of the Royal pleasure. To prevent the Royal assent being given to it, Randal had been selected to bear the petition of some thousands of the persons whom it affected. His success was complete. The committee from whom he received his instructions consisted of Messrs. Jesse Ketchum, Alexander Burnside, Joseph Shepherd, and Thomas Stoyell. Messrs. Hume and Warburton rendered him every assistance in their power, and Lord Goderich showed the most anxious desire to meet the wishes of the petitioners. Another bill, framed in conformity with the Royal instructions, which Mr. Randal's exertions had procured, was introduced, into the Upper Canada Assembly, by Mr. Bidwell, a prominent member of the opposition. It invested with the quality of British subjects all residents of the Province who had received grants of land from the crown, or held public office, as well as their children and remote descendants; all settled residents who had taken up their abode before the year 1820, their descendants to have the right to inherit in case the parents were dead; all persons resident in the Province on the 1st March, 1828, on taking the oath of allegiance after seven years' residence in some part of His Majesty's dominions. If these persons had resided seven years in the Province, they would at the age of nineteen be entitled to take the oath of allegiance at any time within three years. It was also provided that no person of the age of sixteen, on the 26th of May, 1826, should be debarred from inheriting property on account of its descent from an alien, and any person claiming to hold property on account of those nearer akin, being aliens, must have had actual possession and made improvements on the property before that date; a contract for the sale of property so held to be valid, if there had been no adverse possession.

The bill passed the Assembly with only such feeble opposition as the official party and their friends ventured to offer in the way of amendments. Their chagrin appears to have been shared by the Lieutenant Governor, who, in his reply to the Assembly's address informing him that they had passed the bill, petulantly threatened to tell the Colonial Secretary that it was precisely such a measure as the House had rejected in the second session of that Parliament. The House, without any such direct reference to the Lieutenant Governor as would have been unparliamentary, flatly denied this statement in the first of a series of resolutions, in which reasons for rejecting the Alien Bill in the second session were given. These resolutions, eight in number, were severally carried against the government by about two to one; and it became the duty of the Lieutenant Governor to transmit them to England. It was, no doubt, true that the bill passed was some modification of the simple declaratory measure with which the opposition had proposed to cover the whole case in the preceding session. The compromise, for such it must be called, was probably the best that could have been devised. It shared the fate of all compromises, in meeting the opposition of a few extreme persons. The Legislative Councils altered the preamble, and amended the bill so as to prevent it repealing any statute then in force. The Legislative Assembly, after a little grumbling on the part of two or three members, accepted the amendments unanimously.

The appeal so successfully made to the Imperial Government, was suggested by Mr. Mackenzie; and it was he who got up the Committee, which decided to send an agent. He drew up Randal's instructions, and caused him to be selected in preference to another.

It often happens that some particular event produces upon the minds of even clever men impressions which, though not altogether well grounded, they never get rid of as long as they live. The success of Randal's mission to England had this effect upon Mr. Mackenzie; for, ever after, except a few years about the period of the rebellion, he believed in the specific of an appeal to the Imperial Government. His own subsequent visit to the Colonial office, and the success he met, confirmed an opinion which he cherished to the day of his death. Appeal from the oligarchy to the justice of the Imperial Government seemed at one time the only hope of the colonists, until the local Excutive could be made responsible to the popular branch of the Legislature; but after the change wrought by the introduction of responsible government, Mr. Mackenzie failed to make sufficient allowance for the new state of things.

CHAPTER IX.

Mr. Mackenzie conceives the idea of Publishing a Daily Paper in Montreal
—"Printer to the Hon. House of Assembly"—Not a Sure Partisan—His
Estimate of the Intelligence of the Assembly in 1827—Irresponsible Government—Union of Legislative and Judicial Functions—Colonial Representation in the Imperial Parliament.

IN May, 1827, Mr. Mackenzie visited Montreal,
with a view of ascertaining, from the information he
could collect on the spot, whether it would be advisable
to commence the publication of a daily paper there.
An examination of the ground convinced him that the
speculation would not answer commercially; and he
returned to York, resolving not to enter on the doubtful experiment.* From the 25th of January, 1827, to
the 10th of January, 1828, the imprint of *The Colonial*

---

* A few months afterwards—November, 1827—he gave an account of the
Periodical Press of Montreal. The *Herald* printing office was then the most considerable in the British Colonies. There were, besides, the Montreal *Gazette*
and *Herald*, the *Courant*, the *Canadian Spectator*, *La Minerve*, with very limited
circulations—many farmers both in Upper and Lower Canada then receiving
their intelligence of current events from oral information—the *Christian Sentinel*, a church of England journal, circulating six hundred copies a week.
The *Quarterly Review* had recently died for want of support; and a new Colonial Magazine had obtained twenty-one subscribers. The Quebec *Gazette* was
the only paper in Lower Canada distinguished for the attention it paid to commercial affairs. Mr. Mackenzie described it as occupying, in Canada, the position that the *Times* occupied in England, as the organ of the most respectable
class of the population. A wonderful revolution in journalism has taken place
since then.

18

Advocate described the paper as being "Printed and Published by W. L. Mackenzie, Printer to the Hon., the House of Assembly of Upper Canada." The contract was for the whole of the printing required by the House; and so low was the price that it does not appear to have been profitable. He preferred a claim for £25 extra, on account of the unusual expedition required by the House;* and although the extra sum he had paid to printers was larger than this, the claim was refused.

At no time does Mr. Mackenzie appear to have been a very strong partisan. Not that his views and position were not decided. He was strongly opposed

* In a letter to Mr. H. C. Thompson, of the Printing Committee, dated January 15, 1828, Mr. Mackenzie said:

"Last session, Mr. Carey received for work done to the Legislative Council nearly at the rate of 3s. 3d., and for work done for the Assembly 3s.; Mr. Stanton received 3s. for some, and 4s. from the government for the rest, and offered to do more for 2s. I had some at 3s., some at 1s. 8d., and some at 1s. per one thousand ems. Such a system is surely absurd and unjust. It is not my intention to ask for one farthing more than my one shilling contract; if the House are anxious to get their work done at an **fair price, and to give nobody but your brother-in-law (Mr. Stanton, the King's Printer) even journeyman's wages, I will not selfishly complain—but I wish very much their "saving fit" would become more general in its operation. There is a law . maxim which runs thus: '*Lex neminem cogit ad impossibilia*'—the law compels no man to perform impossibilities;—and upon this principle I claimed the other £25 only, not of additional price, but for double allowance made and promised my people to get forward expeditiously with the accumulated printing of the House, at hours when they should have been in bed. This claim was supported by three affidavits, setting forth the fact that such extra work had been done, and that without working almost continually, all the hands in the office (ten or eleven) could not have done the printing in time—for we were often obliged to leave off one job and begin a second, or even a third, in order to meet the new orders of the clerk." The letter concluded with an offer to do the sessional work of the House for 1828, at twenty cents per one thousand ems composition. He also suggested a division of the work at fair prices; and this suggestion was acted upon, three printers being included.

to the ruling minority; but he was very far from having unbounded confidence in the majority of the Assembly. Of the leaders of the opposition, Messrs. Rolph and Bidwell, he sometimes spoke in sharp terms of condemnation; showing that he was under no sort of party control or leadership. When reminded by one of his own political friends in the House that certain petitions laid before the Legislature were not privileged communications; that an action for libel would lie, if they contained what the law regarded as libellous matter, and were reprinted in a newspaper; his reply was, that he intended to publish both the petitions in question in the next number of his paper, a promise which was faithfully kept.

Before the commencement of 1828, Mr. Mackenzie was a declared candidate for a seat in the next House of Assembly; and it.is not impossible that he already aimed at attaining to the leadership himself. Speaking of this House as a body, in a letter to Earl Dalhousie, he said: "Many of these Legislators are qualified to sign their names; but as to framing and carrying through a bill on any subject whatever, the half of them wisely never attempted such a herculean task." And in the same letter, he expressed undisguised contempt for the whole sham of Colonial Legislatures then in vogue. "I have long been satisfied," he said, "that if the North American Colonies were rid of these inferior and subordinate Legislatures, which are and must ever be insufficient for the purposes for which they were intended; and allowed, instead, a due weight in both branches of the British Parliament, it would prove the foundation of their permanent and true happiness." The difficulty was that these representative assemblies were mocked with a semblance of that legislative power, with the substantial possession of which they were never endowed. Even the Reformers had only an imperfect conception of the true remedy. The ministry might be subjected to a succession of defeats in the Legislative Assembly without raising a question of resignation; and the liberal journals very seldom undertook to deal with the question of ministerial responsibility. Mr. Mackenzie was the "advocate of such a change in the mode of administering the government as would give the people an effectual control over the actions of their representatives, and through them over the actions of the Executive."* Most of those who essayed to effect reforms, contented themselves with encountering abuses in detail; a mode of warfare which left untouched a radically defective system of administration.

When we look back upon the system that existed, the mind is filled with astonishment that it should have enjoyed such comparative immunity from attack. A party triumph at the polls carried hardly any of the advantages of victory into the Legislature. The members of the Executive belonged to the minority. The majority might pass bills in the Assembly; but, unless they pleased the ruling party, they were rejected by the crown-nominated chamber. There was no general separation of legislative and judicial func-

---

* *Advocate*, January 10, 1828.—These sentiments he claimed to have enunciated in the first number of his paper; but if so, the utterance was not very distinct.

tions; and when the Assembly, in 1826, addressed the
Imperial Government to remove the Chief Justice
from the sphere of politics, the answer was that the
Lieutenant-Governor had profited greatly by his advice, and that there was nothing in the circumstances
of the colony to render a change of system desirable.
The Judiciary and the members of the Executive received their appointments and the greater part of their
pay from revenues belonging to England, on which
they were largely dependent. When the House presented an address to the King, praying that the
bounty lands which had been withheld from those
officers of the militia who attended a convention on the
grievances of the colony in 1818, Governor Maitland,
by the command of His Majesty, replied, that when
they expressed "deep contrition" for presuming to ask
for a redress of grievances, the lands would be granted
to these erring militia-men of 1812. The system re-
acted upon itself; the bad advice sent by irresponsible
ministers from this side came back across the Atlantic
matured into the commands of the Sovereign; and the
name and the authority of England suffered, while
the real culprits escaped the merited punishment of
ejection from office by the votes of a majority of the
people's representatives.

It is not surprising, under these circumstances, that
a scheme so impracticable as Colonial representation
in the Imperial Parliament should have been turned
to, in despair, by Mr. Mackenzie. A union of the
colonies, which he had often advocated, would have
necessitated a change of system if it was to be an ef-

fective remedy for the glaring defects of administration which then existed.

In the commencement of 1828, while advocating a responsible Executive, Mr. Mackenzie disclaimed all "intention or desire to assist in cutting any colony adrift from its parent state." He confesses, however, that his proposal for representation in the Imperial Parliament had not met universal reprobation. The ruling faction desired to have things their own way; and so comfortable were existing arrangements that they were afraid of the effects of a change. The people were unfortunately becoming suspicious of the external influence that sustained the oligarchy; and were wisely disinclined to listen to a scheme of representation in a distant Parliament, where their feeble voice must have been drowned in the clangor of over six hundred representatives.

CHAPTER X.

Mackenzie becomes a Candidate for the Legislative Assembly—" Parliament-ary Black List"—Improvement in his Pecuniary Circumstances—His Elec-tion—Complexion of the New House—Mr. (afterwards Sir) Allan McNab is declared Guilty of a Breach of Privilege, and on motion of Mackenzie sent to Jail—Mr. J. H. Boulton Reprimanded for a like offence—Mr. Mackenzie, as Chairman of a Committee on the Post-office, recommends that the De-partment be placed under Provincial Control—His action as Chairman on Privileges—The Chaplain of the House—The Government Pecuniarily Inde-pendent of the Assembly—The Public Debt and overdue Debentures unpaid —Mackenzie contends that all the Provincial Revenues should be placed under the Control of the Legislature—Resolutions on the State of the Province—Sir J. Colborne does not meet the Expectations formed by him —Specimen of Mackenzie's Oratorical Powers.

HAVING once resolved to seek a seat in the Legis-lature of his adopted country, Mr. Mackenzie waited for no deputations to solicit him to become a candi-date; he submitted his claims to no clique of election managers, and heeded not their voluntary resolves. Months before the election was to take place, he issued an address* to the electors of the County of York, not

* "TO THE ELECTORS OF THE COUNTY OF YORK.—*Gentlemen*:—I have the honor to inform you that it is my intention to come forward as a candidate at the next Election of Members to serve for your County in the Provincial Parliament; and I most respectfully solicit your votes and support.

"I have no end in view but the well being of the people at large—no ambi-tion to serve but that of contributing to the happiness and prosperity of our common country. The influence and authority with which you may invest me, shall always be directed, according to the best of my judgment, for the

very prolific in promises; containing nothing that would make more than a very meagre modern "platform;" yet it was sufficient to satisfy the people to whom it was addressed.

Mr. James E. Small was not connected with the government; but he belonged to one of the "old families" of York. He had been Mr. Mackenzie's solici-

general good; and it will be my care to uphold your rights to the utmost of my power, with that firmness, moderation, and perseverance, which become the representative of a free people.

"If honored with your suffrages, it will be alike my duty and my pleasure to watch over the local interests of this great county, and to promote every public improvement and useful undertaking, which shall be found conducive to your prosperity and the general welfare.

"I have ever been opposed to ecclesiastical domination ; it is at enmity with the free spirit of Christianity; and nations which have bowed to its yoke, are become the dark abodes of ignorance and superstition, oppression, and misery.

"That corrupt, powerful, and long endured influence which has hitherto interfered with your rights and liberties, can only be overthrown by your unanimity and zeal. An independent House of Assembly, to Upper Canada, would be inestimable.

"I have been a careful observer of the conduct of the people's representatives in the Colonial Assemblies; I have seen men in whom was placed the utmost confidence, fall from their integrity and betray their sacred trust; men, too, who had entered upon their legislative duties with the best intentions towards the people, and who evinced for a time a firm determination to support their rights. But there are others who continue to maintain and uphold the interests of their country, unshaken and undismayed; who consider it their highest honor to persevere in a faithful discharge of their public duties, and eagerly strive to deserve the good will, the affection, and the confidence of their fellow subjects.

"Among this latter class I am desirous of being numbered; and, unless I shall be found deserting the cause of the people, I trust that the people will never desert me.

"Accept my sincere thanks for the abundant proofs of kindness and confidence, and for the liberal assurance of support, with which you have honored me, and believe me,

"Gentlemen, Your faithful and humble servant,

"W. L. MACKENZIE."

YORK, *December* 17*th*, 1827.

tor, in the famous type case; but he was astonished at the temerity of his late client in venturing unasked to declare himself a candidate for the representation of the most populous county in Upper Canada. It so happened that Mr. Small was to be a candidate for the same county. He called upon the presumptuous editor of *The Advocate*, to give him some advice about this York election. He dwelt on the folly of a person in Mr. Mackenzie's position attempting to oppose one whose long residence and family influence would be more than sufficient to secure his return. These arguments neither convinced Mr. Mackenzie nor changed his determination. He had declared himself a candidate, and a candidate he would be.

The election managers took the case of the county of York into their keeping. On the 4th of February, 1828, a committee, delegated by a public meeting held at Newmarket, tried to ballot Mr. Mackenzie out of the field. Nine votes were cast for Mr. Small, and only three for Mackenzie; while of the other candidates Mr. William Roe got fifty-seven, and Mr. Jessie Ketchum forty-one. Had not Mr. Small told him how it would be? But he was not to be got rid of in this scientific manner, and he announced:

"I have attended two public meetings, but it is not my intention to go to any more until I meet the people at the hustings—it is a needless waste of time,—and benefits nobody but the tavern-keeper. If I go into the Legislature, it must be in my own way, or not at all. For I mean to break through all the old established usages, to keep no open houses, administer to the wants of no publican, hire no vehicles to trundle
19

freemen to the hustings to serve themselves, nor to court the favor of those leading men who have so powerfully influenced former elections. I will not lessen my own resources for maintaining independence, by spending at the outset, as was done by others four years ago, a sum sufficient to maintain my large household for a twelvemonth; but if I shall become one of the stewards of the Province, I hope I shall be found not only faithful, but also fully competent to discharge the duties of a representative in such a way as ought to secure for me the confidence of an intelligent community."

Virtuous resolves are good; but election expenses are not easily brought under control, and no power on earth is strong enough to put them down entirely. Mr. Mackenzie's first election cost £500.

Opposed by the administration and its organs, from political reasons, Mr. Mackenzie's candidature was contested even by professed liberal journals, from a business jealousy that derived its venom from the circumstance of his own paper having a circulation larger than any rival in Upper Canada. Assailed by every newspaper in York, except his own; libelled in pamphlets, and slandered in posters, he pursued the even tenor of his way, and managed to find time for the preparation of electioneering documents, calculated to influence not merely the county of York, but the whole Province. His "Legislative Black List," early commenced and assiduously kept up, contained a short commentary on the divisions that had taken place during the two previous Provincial Parliaments, on prominent and important questions. The publication was commenced on the 29th May, and the Provincial Parliament was not dissolved till the 24th July. Compared with electioneering documents of the present day, whether in Canada or the States, " The Black List" was mild and moderate. In republishing Mr. Small's election address, he simply appended to it, within brackets, " Printed at the Government office." The effect of this new mode of election warfare was visible when the time for counting votes came. Mr. Jonas Jones, whose public career and conduct probably presented as few points on which admiration could find a resting place as any other Colonial politician of his time, was defeated by Mr. Buell, in Leeds. The Attorney General was re-elected by a majority of only seventeen. Mr. G. S. Boulton, brother of the Solicitor General, was rejected by the county of Durham; and several other similar results were visible at the close of the contest.

By this time, Mr. Mackenzie's pecuniary circumstances had greatly improved. In a letter, written previous to the election, he gives us some information on this point:

" By an unwearied application to business, I am now again an unincumbered freeholder of Upper Canada, to more than thrice the amount required by law, as a parliamentary qualification, besides being possessed of nearly as much more lands, with good bonds for deeds. I have also a valuable personal property, including a business which nothing but the actual knowledge of the election of a bad parliament, in aid of the present corrupt administration, would induce me to quit. Being therefore easy in my circumstances, entirely freed from the terrors of litigation, prosperous in my business, in good health, and owing very few debts, I have applied to the people of the most populous county in Upper Canada, for the highest honor in their gift, the surest token of their esteem and confidence."

The result showed that Mr. Small had miscalculated the relative influence of himself and his opponent.

The first session, in which Mr. Mackenzie had a seat in the Legislative Assembly, opened inauspiciously for the advisers by whom Sir John Colborne was surrounded. Having been convened on the 8th January, 1829, it soon gave proof of its hostility to the administration. The vote on the speakership, which stood twenty-one for Mr. Willson, the late Speaker, and twenty-four for Mr. Bidwell, did not at all indicate the strength of parties; for, while Mr. Willson received the support of the Government, the division showed that he still retained many friends among the opposition. The address in reply to the speech from the throne, founded on resolutions framed by Dr. Rolph, and containing the strongest expressions of a want of confidence in the advisers of the Lieutenant Governor,* was carried with the nearest possible

---

* "For the insurance of those most important objects, we, His Majesty's most faithful Commons, confiding in the candor of your Excellency, and in your readiness to recognize us as constitutional advisers of the crown, do humbly pray your Excellency against the injurious policy hitherto pursued by the Provincial administration ; and, although we at present see *your Excellency unhappily surrounded by the same advisers as have so deeply wounded the feelings and injured the best interests of the country,* yet in the interval of any necessary change, we entertain an anxious belief that, under the auspices of your Excellency, the administration of justice will rise above suspicion ; the wishes and interests of the people be properly respected ; the constitutional rights and independence

approach to unanimity: thirty-seven against one.* In these days an unanimous vote of censure on the Governor's advisers produced no change of ministry. The Assembly complained of the Government, when they ought to have struck a blow at the system which rendered it possible for a party, who could command only a small minority in the popular branch of the Legislature to continue their grasp upon the reins of power.

Such was the House in which Mr. Mackenzie first held a seat; such the practice of the Government, when he first entered public life.

During this session an event occurred that brought him into collision with two members of the Legislature, who were afterwards active in his expulsion from the House, upon pretexts that were wholly inadequate to form anything like a justification. The new Governor, Sir John Colborne, had been exhibited in effigy at Hamilton, and a rumor had found currency that there was a conspiracy to liberate Collins from jail by force. Whatever connection these two subjects may have had, they were jointly referred to a special committee of inquiry. Mr. Gurnett had

of the Legislature be held inviolable ; the prerogative and patronage of His Most Gracious Majesty be exercised for the happiness of his people and the honor of his crown, and the revenues of the colony be, hereafter, sacredly devoted to the many and urgent objects of public improvement, after making provision for the public service upon the basis of that economy which is suited to the exigencies of the country and the condition of its inhabitants."

* The following is the list of members:—Messrs. McDonald, Fraser, McLean, Blacklock, Shaver, Brouse, Longley, Henderson, Kilborn, Buell, Morris, Thomson, Dalton, Bethune, Radenhurst, Bidwell, Perry, Lockwood, Samson, Peterson, James Wilson, Lyons, Ewings, Smith, Ketchum, Mackenzie, Cawthra, Matthews, John Rolph, Robinson, George Rolph, Hopkins, Randal, Lefferry, Terry, Woodruff, John Willson, Hamilton, Dickson, McCall, Baldwin, Hornor, Malcolm, Wilkinson, Baby, McMartin, Bercsy, and Fothergill.

stated in his newspaper* that the intention of certain petitioners for the release of Collins was to liberate him by force, if necessary. On the 29th January, Dr. Rolph moved that Mr. Gurnett be brought to the bar of the House to be interrogated touching this statement. When he came he refused to answer, on the ground that his evidence would implicate himself. Mr. (now Sir) Allan McNab was also among the witnesses called. He was then young and not indisposed to have the House take some action against him that might give him a chance of becoming a member of the next Assembly; so he refused to answer the questions put to him. On motion of Dr. Baldwin, he was declared guilty of a high breach and contempt of the privileges of the House. Being taken into the custody of the Sergeant-at-arms, and brought a prisoner to the bar of the House, he complained of having been tried and convicted without a hearing. His defence was not satisfactory to the House, and he was, on motion of Mr. Mackenzie, committed to York jail, under the warrant of the Speaker, during the pleasure of the House. Mr. McNab is said not to have looked upon this inconvenience as a disservice; but he would hardly consider himself bound to be grateful for it. Mr. Solicitor General Boulton was also called as a witness. He, too, thought himself entitled to refuse to answer the questions of the committee, and for this contempt and breach of privilege was let off with a reprimand from Mr. Speaker Bidwell.† Mr. Macken-

* *The Gore Gazette.*

† The history of England does not furnish a single instance of a witness persisting in refusing, like Mr. McNab and Solicitor General Boulton, to answer questions put by a committee of the House of Commons. There is, there-

zie would not have been more lenient to him than to
Mr. McNab, and the Solicitor General was not of a
nature to forget or forgive. Besides, he harbored
contempt, not knowing that it produces its like, and
afterwards failed to find in the vocabulary words to
express the strength of that feeling towards Mr. Mackenzie.

No sooner had Mr. Mackenzie got into the Legislative Assembly than he became one of its most active
members. He commenced as he ended, by asking for
information, and probing to the bottom questions of
great public interest. In the committee room he
made his mark, during the first session, not less dis-
tinctly than in the House. As chairman of the select
committee to inquire into the state of the Post-office
department, in Upper Canada, he drew up a comprehensive report, replete with the most valuable information and suggestions. The mail service was mise-
rably performed ; and matters were so managed as to
leave a considerable surplus profit, which failed to
find its way into the Provincial exchequer. Not a
mile of new post road could be opened, or a single
Post-office established, without the authority of the
Postmaster General, in England, who was necessarily
destitute of the minute local information necessary for
the correct determination of such questions. The
postage on a letter between England and Canada
ranged from five shillings to seven shillings and six
pence. The tri-weekly mail between Montreal and
the present city of Toronto was slowly dragged over

fore, no precedent for the punishment that should be accorded for this contempt and novel species of breach of privilege.

roads that were all but impassable; and it was a standing wonder how the mail carriers were enabled to
perform their duties westward. Mr. Mackenzie recommended, as the beginning of all efficient reform,
that the department should be placed under the control of the local authorities. He also laid it down as
a principle that no attempt should be made to draw
a revenue from the Post-office; but that the entire re-
ceipts should be devoted to the securing of additional
postal facilities. In case the department came under
local control, he recommended the retention of Mr.
Stayner, then Deputy Postmaster General, on the
ground that he had shown himself fully equal to
the discharge of the duties. Complaints had been
made, in previous sessions, that the colonists were
taxed without their consent, through the Post-office
department, and that the surplus revenue was never
accounted for; a complaint which had been met by
Attorney General Robinson by a reference to Dr.
Franklin, who was said not to have regarded postage
in the light of taxation. Inquiries had been made;
but until now no bold and comprehensive remedy was
proposed. Here, as on so many other questions, Mr.
Mackenzie was in advance of his cotemporaries and of
the times. The remedy he suggested, of placing the
department under local control, came before the
end of another generation; but if it had come sooner,
the Province would have been the gainer.

Nor was this the only committee of which Mr.
Mackenzie was chairman. In that capacity he made
a report on the privileges of the House and the conduct of returning officers at the recent election. Dr.

Powell, a previous clerk of the House, had been dismissed by the government, without reference to that branch of the Legislature whose servant he was, and his successor had been appointed in the same way. The House had silently acquiesced in the appointment of Mr. Fitzgibbon thus made, some years before; but Mr. Mackenzie was not willing to consecrate a principle that entrenched on the privileges of the body of which he had become a member. At the previous election, some returning officers had made charges of doubtful legality against the candidates. Of that nature was the item for their own services; while the cost of stationery and printing incident to the election was legally charged against candidates. So was the remuneration of the poll clerk. Mr. Mackenzie reported these facts to the House, without indicating a specific remedy; but he afterwards carried, on a vote of twenty-seven against five, a resolution that the chief clerk, with the approbation of the Speaker, should appoint the subordinate officers of the House, except the Sergeant-at-arms and any others appointed under the existing law.

He endeavored to bring the clerks of the Crown up to their duty; and for this purpose carried an address calling the attention of the government to the fact that the census returns, required to be made annually under the Assessment Act, were frequently neglected by these functionaries, and making suggestions for preventing the omission.

During this session Mr. Mackenzie carried various other motions and addresses to the government. On nearly every vote he was sustained by immense ma-

jorities. When certain powerful interests were interfered with, his success was not so marked; and on a
few occasions he failed to obtain a majority. In those
days, the Legislative Assembly counted a chaplain
among its servants; and in accordance with the attempt, which had not yet been abandoned, to give the
Church of England a position of ascendancy in Upper
Canada, he was a member of that Church. On a
vote of eighteen against fourteen, Mr. Mackenzie carried a resolution which struck at this exclusiveness,
by declaring that, during the remainder of the session,
the clergy of the town, generally, be invited to officiate, in turn, as chaplain, and their service be paid
out of the contingent fund. But the bill repealing
the clause of a statute then existing, which provided
for the payment of a fixed salary to the chaplain, was
rejected by the Legislative Council. When he asked
the members to pay the postage of their own letters,
if they exceeded a certain weight, he failed of success.

Upon most of the propositions he offered to the acceptance of the House, Mr. Mackenzie carried overwhelming majorities with him. But the Government
was so fenced in that it could exist in the face of any
amount of opposition. This session it was entirely
independent of the House for the means of carrying
on the government. No money grant was asked; and
the House was officially informed that it would not
be expected to trouble itself with the matter. The
Crown revenue, which came into its hands, under an
Imperial statute of 1774 (Geo. III. cap. 88), sufficed to
defray the expenses of the government and of the ad-

ministration of justice.* And any bills passed by the House, which did not meet the sanction of the government, could be easily disposed of in the Legislative Council. The public debt, amounting to £112,166 13s. 4d.,† might have been supposed to require special attention, for there were £32,000 of overdue debentures unpaid.

With this responsibility, the Province was spoken of as being "overwhelmed with a great public debt;" and if its embarrassment is to be held as a criterion, it must be admitted that this debt was a greater burthen than some $60,000,000 is at present; though we now look at the amount of the debt in 1829 as utterly contemptible. Mr. Mackenzie's idea was, that a rigid course of economy should be pursued till the whole of the debt was paid off. In the course of this session, he brought before the House a series of thirty-one resolutions—a moderate number compared with the celebrated ninety-two of Lower Canada—on the state of the Province. He therein took a position far in

* This was generally the case—the government was financially independent of the House; and the money votes for public improvements were, under the vicious system then in vogue, just as liable to be initiated by members of the opposition as by the government. In Lower Canada, the Legislature contested the right of the government to appropriate the Crown revenue. The Crown revenue, in that Province, was not sufficient to defray the expense of the government; and when application was made to the House to supply the deficiency, the whole question of revenue and expenditure was brought into discussion. There had previously been complaints that the Post-office revenue was not under the control of the House; and Mr. Mackenzie was among the first to suggest that all the revenue raised in the Province ought to be appropriated by the local Legislature.

† The public debt had been contracted for the following purposes: Militia pensions, £11,666 18s. 4d.; Kettle Creek Harbor, £8,000; Burlington Canal, £12,500; Welland Canal, £75,000; public service for the year 1824, £10,000.

advance of the times. Contending for that right of local self-government, of which the constitution—substantially the same which united Canada now possesses—contained the guarantee, he asserted the right of the House to control the entire revenue arising within the Province; complained that money voted for the civil service had been applied to the pensioning of individuals in sums of from £1,000 to £500 a year; denounced the favors shown to a particular church, pensions—in a rather wholesale way it must be admitted,—monopolies, and *ex-officio* and criminal prosecutions, at the instance of the Crown, for political libels. The necessity of making the Canadian judges independent was asserted, in opposition to opinions expressed in high quarters in England. The unlimited power of sheriffs, holding office during pleasure, was declared to be dangerous to public liberty; especially as the office was often filled by persons of neither weight nor responsibility. The patronage exercised by the Crown or its agent, the Lieutenant Governor, in the Province, was asserted to be at variance with sound policy and good government. Though the importance of Canada to England, as a nursery for her seamen, and as a country consuming a larger quantity of British goods in proportion to the population, was insisted on, it was alleged that the discontents arising from the abuse of power were among the causes that led to the invasion of the Province in the war of 1812; the losses suffered from the war, by the most active friends of the British power, falling most heavily on the Niagara District, ought, it was contended, to be made good out of the territorial revenue of the Crown,* instead of being left unliquidated or allowed to fall on a poor province. The appointment of an accredited agent at the seat of the Imperial Government, was declared to be desirable. The resolutions constituted a budget of grievances, most of which have not only been redressed, but forgotten. The resolutions were not without blemishes; the chief of which consisted of the advocacy of the protective system; a fault very common in those times, when free trade had not become fashionable, and when the chief organs of English opinion asserted that sufficient favor was not shown to the productions of Canada. So little does even the popular branch of the Legislature appear to have been conscious of the justice and necessity of many of the principles asserted in several of these resolutions, that they were not pressed on the House for adoption. So far was Mr. Mackenzie in advance of his contemporaries.

The arrival in the Province of Sir John Colborne, in the capacity of Lieutenant Governor, had been hailed as the sure promise of a new era. Before the close of the session, during which an Executive Council, which found itself in a permanent minority in the popular branch of the Legislature, had been kept in office,† the illusion had vanished. Mr. Mackenzie, who had been elated by hopes which were destined

* The war losses compensation was a constant subject of discussion for some twenty years after the war was over. In many cases exorbitant claims were probably made; and this was one cause of the delay in settling them. Another difficulty was about the funds out of which they were to be paid.

† The following is a correct list of the names of those members who formed the Executive Council, the dates of the mandamuses, and the time

not to be realized, now uttered complaints where he had before been disposed to bestow praise. He had gone into the Legislature with a desire to point out and, if possible, remedy what he believed to be great abuses in the Government. Of his speeches during the first session, he took the trouble to preserve but few. The first speech he publicly delivered, of which I find any record, was made before the "Constitutional Society of Upper Canada," in March, 1828. It gave a premonition of that power of swaying the masses, which he was afterwards to wield with so much effect.* The speech was made in oppo-

when each of them were sworn into office; one of whom had held office for a period of thirty-seven years:

NAMES.	DATES OF MANDA-MUSES.	WHEN SWORN IN.
James Baby.	5th May, 1794.	9th July, 1792.
John Strachan	25th July, 1817.	12th February, 1818.
William Campbell . .		20th October, 1825.
James B. Macaulay. . .	5th May, 1825.	27th June, 1826.
Peter Robinson . . .	5th July, 1827.	6th February, 1828.
George H. Markland . .	6th July, 1827.	6th February, 1828.

* This speech was made in opposition to a proposal to elect Francis Collins a member of the Society; and as it is the first of his I find on record, it may not be amiss to give an extract: "I have been accused, sir, of enmity and disaffection to this government; but the charge was as unjust as it was foolish. I have lent my feeble energies to the cause of truth; and would desire to see men at the helm of affairs who would call out and foster the latent genius of our people; who would patronize, protect, cherish, and multiply among us seminaries of useful learning, and become the distinguished friends of science, the arts, domestic manufactures, and great public improvements, whose ambition would be to add to the sum of human happiness, to enlighten the mind of the benighted peasant, and call even from the recesses of the forest and the wilderness of Canada to Senate and Assembly men whose patent of nobility would bear the impress of their Maker's image, and who would forget personal aggrandizement in the nobler and better purpose of promoting the public good. . . . Sir, I wish to live in peace with all men, before God and the world. I envy no man, nor have I any revenge to gratify. The tomb will soon, very soon, cover these limbs of mine; and the dust of death will bury in oblivion

sition to a proposal to elect Francis Collins a member of the Society.

the recollection of political triumphs and political reverses. . . . I have suffered years to elapse before I undertook even to defend myself against the sweeping denunciations of a being who delighted to trample upon truth and justice, and to hold me up to the people as a traitor to the true interests, happiness, and glory of my adopted country. I come at length to the facts on which my objection rests." Mr. Mackenzie seldom replied to personal abuse; and he refused to receive or read the productions of the "Kennel Presses," as he called the journals that pursued him with slander. Speaking of them towards the close of 1829, he said: "These vehicles continue, week after week, to vomit up calumny with the force and effect of so many forty shrew-power steam engines. It is of no use to try to shame them, they have no sense of shame." And a week or two later, he again noticed the "Kennel Presses," in these words: "We stated lately the titles of some six or seven provincial vehicles of news, which we had declined to receive, read, or exchange with. To that list has been since added, *the York Observer*. We positively do not want to have served up to us, almost daily, an endless farrago of nonsensical jargon and abuse. Those who admire the eloquence of a scolding woman will stay and hear her hold forth ; those who do not, will maintain a proper distance from her bell-clapper. Although desirous to take rank among the latter class, we must concede the fact, that a female shrew or a male scold will, each of them, have their own way ; there is no stopping them."

CHAPTER XI.

Visit to the United States—Admires Cameronian Preaching and Scottish Psalmody—Letter to the *National Gazette*—Comparisons between the States and Canada—A Charge of Disloyalty met—Mr. R. Baldwin elected to the Assembly, but does not take his Seat—Action for Libel, growing out of this Election, brought by Mr. Small against Mr. Mackenzie—The Legislative Session of 1830—The House Unanimous in demanding a Change of Administration—The Lieutenant Governor sends a Contemptuous Reply—Mackenzie proposes to send a Commissioner to England to lay the state of the Province before the Imperial Government—Is Chairman of the Committee on Banking—The Government hold one-fourth of the Shares in a Bank—The Chaplain Question—Revenue—Libel Laws—Disgraceful State of Prisons—Placemen in the Legislative Council—The Canal Era—Financial Jugglery—Effect of the Canals on the Price of Produce.

ENGLISHMEN travelling in the United States may be divided into two classes: enthusiastic admirers or critical objectors. British subjects of all ranks and conditions have been found in each class. Young and inexperienced persons, who are willing to accept appearance for reality, were most likely to become the admirers of American institutions. Nothing short of a fixed residence in the States, for some years, would cure these persons of their predilections. The ardent temperament of Mr. Mackenzie was well calculated to betray him into admiration with specious appearance, the real value of which could only be detected by years of observation.

In the spring of 1829 he visited New York, Washington, Philadelphia, and other places in the United States, with a disposition to view every thing he saw there in *couleur de rose;* adding brilliancy to the hues and tints by hideous contrasts. The alarming sound of a threatened dissolution, of the Union even then fell upon his ears; he could detect in them nothing but the complaints of disappointed faction. He, however, learned something of the American character which he did not know before, and his mind was taken back to the Alien question. In one of his letters, written on the 14th May, he confessed: "I have never yet seen an American who would prefer another system of government to his own: local circumstances may cause him to emigrate, but an American is, in his heart, an American still;* and the more I see of this country the better I can account for the objections made by persons in office, in Canada, to the admis-

* It was evidently not Mr. Mackenzie's intention to say this in dispraise of the Americans, for he noticed with disapprobation the following versified and offensive expression of the same idea in *The Upper Canada Courier:*—

"I turn my lay, a feeble lay, I fear,
To those small men who've just departed here,
And meet for legislation once a-year.
But let me say, before my bark I launch,
I sing the lower, not the higher branch.
First—who's their head? A man of solid sense,
A *Mr. Bidwell,* saving of his pence.
By birth a Yankee—what can you expect
From Democrats with British honors decked?
Though they may crouch and cringe to you, and pray,
Their natal feeling ne'er will wear away.
And e'en when cherished far above the rest,
Still rankling venom works within their breast.
Still they'll contend that happiness or bliss
Is not 'beneath a Government like this.'"

21

sion of its citizens to naturalization among us." A
Scotsman "in feeling and principle," he looked upon
the United States as an asylum for the oppressed of
all countries, in spite of that slavery which was ".the
worst and darkest blot on its escutcheon."

Two things, mentioned in his letters from New York,
serve to show that the influence of the principles
which had been instilled into him from his earliest
days had not been effaced in the rude collision with the
outer world. "In the afternoon," he writes, "I went
to hear Dr. McLeod, a steadfast Presbyterian of the
old school; the genuine Cameronian, and a good
preacher. There the old and solemn tunes of our
fathers have not yet made way for ballad rhymes;
there the single line of old Scottish Psalmody is given
out by the preacher in truly national style; there the
discourse is divided and subdivided into heads and ob-
serves in true covenanting fashion. I felt more at
home in this church, the members of which are either
Scotch, or generally from the north of Ireland, than
I have often done while listening to the splendid eloquence of much more popular orators." The other
instance is to be found in a reference to Tom Paine, of
whom he says: "Had he had sense enough to remain
contented with his ample share of fame as the author
of 'The Rights of Man,' and 'Common Sense,' without interfering with revealed religion, he would at
this day have probably stood next to Washington and
Franklin, as a promoter of the glorious revolution
which gave freedom to America."

When Mackenzie republished some of Paine's political works, political malice ascribed to him a participa-

tion in the skeptical opinions expressed by the author in some other works. On the injustice of an imputation made on such grounds, and upon such a pretext, there cannot be two opinions.

While on his visit to the United States, Mr. Mackenzie wrote a long letter, on the political condition of Canada, to the editor of the *National Gazette*. The authorship was not avowed, and though various conjectures were hazarded on the subject, it is difficult to see how it could have been a question at all. The letter bore the strongest internal evidence of its authorship, and was besides little more than an amplification of the thirty-one resolutions he had brought before the Legislature in the previous session. The principal points in the letter, that were not urged in the resolutions, were an elective Legislative Council, which, like so many other changes which found in him an early advocate, has since been effected, and an elective Governor, which nobody now asks for. He regarded the Legislative Council as serving in some sort as a shield to the Lieutenant Governor, by relieving the Executive of a responsibility which it must otherwise often have assumed. But as its members owed their appointment to the Crown, and most of them were office-holders of one grade or another, the instrument did not conceal the hand that had used it.

The contrasts made between the government of Canada, as then administered, and that of Washington, could hardly be otherwise than of dangerous tendency. An English statesman might make them with impunity; but if a Canadian followed his example, his motives would not fail to be impugned. So it was

with Mr. Mackenzie, who claimed to be, in English
politics, neither more nor less than a Whig. These
contrasts obtruded themselves by the propinquity of
the two countries; and there is no reason to suppose
that in Mr. Mackenzie's case, they, at this time, implied any disloyalty to England.*

---

* Attached to one of the letters which Mr. Mackenzie addressed to the Earl
of Dalhousie, in May, 1827, is a manuscript note: "I was for England in 1820,
1824, 1827, 1833, 1834; but 1836-7 choked off my loyalty." As the general
election of 1831 approached, the misrepresentations of the object of Mr. Mackenzie's mission to the United States continued to be repeated with increased
virulence and rancor. He met them by the publication of the following letter:

Department of State, }
Washington, July 28, 1830. }

"Sir:—Your letter of the first of this month to the Secretary, on the subject of an article which appeared some time ago in the columns of the *New
York Courier and Enquirer,* and has since been re-published in other public
journals, both of Canada and the United States, with additional innuendoes
and particulars, was received on the 19th inst. at this office, during his absence;
but I lost no time in communicating its contents to him. The object of the
article or articles referred to, is, to indicate a visit to the United States and to
its capital during the last summer, as connected with some revolutionary movement in the Canadas, in relation to which your agency was employed with the
Federal Government; and you call upon the Secretary, in his official capacity,
positively and decidedly to contradict it.

"I have, accordingly, just received a letter from Mr. Van Buren, the Secretary, dated at Albany, the 23d of this month, expressly authorizing me to deny
all knowledge of or belief, on his part, in the designs imputed to you, as I now
have the honor of doing, and to state, moreover, that he has not the smallest
ground for believing that your visit had anything political for its object. He
directs me also to add, that if the President were not likewise absent from the
seat of Government, he is well persuaded he would readily concur in the declaration which I have thus had the honor of making in his behalf.

"I am, Sir, respectfully,
"Your obedient servant,
"DANIEL BRENT, Chief Clerk.

"William L. Mackenzie, Esq., *York, Upper Canada.*"

The narrative would be incomplete if it were not added that the late Mr.
George Gurnett, as publisher of the *Upper Canada Courier,* was active in cir-

THE CANADIAN REBELLION. 165

During the parliamentary recess, a vacancy having
occurred in the representation of York, by the appointment of Attorney General Robinson to the Chief
Justiceship of the Court of King's Bench, the vacant
seat was contested between Mr. Robert Baldwin, whose
father was then a member of the House, and Mr.
James E. Small. Mr. Mackenzie supported the former, who obtained ninety-two votes against fifty-one
given to his opponent ;* and after the election was
over, the journalist felt himself entitled to counsel the
successful candidate not to carry into the Legislature
the habits of the advocate.

The day before the election commenced, Mr. Mackenzie printed charges against Mr. Small, that were
afterwards made the subject of an action for libel.
The matter complained of as libellous, consisted of
statements made by Mr. James Hogg, of Milford Mills,
and Mr. Daniel McDougal, affecting the reputation
of Mr. Small, as Solicitor, in a case in which they
were concerned, one as plaintiff, the other as defendant.

Taking the House of Assembly for our guide, it

culating these accusations. Of the latter, Mr. William Wallace, formerly a
partner of Mr. Gurnett, wrote from Richmond, Virginia, September 1, 1830,
that while living there, "he (Mr. Gurnett) renounced his allegiance to all po-
tentates, and particularly to the King of Great Britain, as is recorded in our
Court." Mr. Gurnett afterwards became Clerk of the Peace for the county of
York, and Police Magistrate of Toronto. He died in the fall of last year.

* The House declared the election null and void upon a point of privilege.
The Governor had assumed the responsibility of issuing the writ, contrary, it
was said, to the privileges of the House, who had the right to adjudge the
seat vacant, and order the speaker to issue a writ for a new election. The Governor yielded the point; causing the great seal to be affixed to the writ issued
by the House. Mr. Baldwin was re-elected.

would be difficult to imagine a government administered in more direct defiance of the public will than
that of Canada, in 1830. The Legislative session opened
on the 8th of January; and in the address in reply to
the speech of the Lieutenant Governor, the House
was unanimous in demanding the dismissal of the Executive Council. "We feel unabated solicitude," said
the representatives of the people, "about the administration of public justice, and entertain a settled conviction that the continuance about your Excellency of
those advisers, who, from the unhappy policy they
have pursued in the late administration, have long,
deservedly, lost the confidence of the country, is highly
inexpedient, and calculated seriously to weaken the
expectations of the people from the impartial and disinterested justice of His Majesty's Government." The
House was unanimous in desiring the removal of the
advisers of the Lieutenant Governor; but a discussion
arose upon the proper method of accomplishing that object. Mr. Fothergill suggested impeachment; but there
were two objections to such a procedure. Impeachment must proceed upon a specific crime; but here it
was a question of non-confidence. And before whom
could the impeachment be tried? The Legislative
Council might be asked to adjudicate upon the case;
but, as Dr. Rolph remarked, that would be to ask the
son to try the father. Mr. Mackenzie hit upon the
true remedy. "I would," he said, "candidly inform
His Majesty's ministers that they do wrong to encourage and support in authority an organized body of
men in direct opposition to the wishes of the people
of the country." If there was any hope of making

the wishes of the House prevail, it was by an appeal to England. The Lieutenant Governor had, in the previous session, been appealed to by an almost unanimous vote of the House, to remove his advisers; but he had felt himself at liberty to ignore the wishes of the people's representatives. On a direct vote of a want of confidence, the government had, in the previous session, been able to muster one vote out of thirty-eight; now their solitary supporter had deserted them. By the personal favor of the Governor, they were still retained in office. Mr. Mackenzie's proposition to send a commissioner or commissioners to England, to lay before the Imperial authorities the state of the colony, looked to an efficient remedy, and if acted upon, might have led to the result which the whole House desired to produce.

The Lieutenant Governor received the address of the House with a curtness that reveals a petulant sullenness bordering on insult: "I return you my thanks for your address," was all he condescended to say. That it might not appear invidious, he used the same formula in receiving the echo address of the Legislative Council.

No member of the House had the same knowledge of financial matters, revenue, banking, and currency, as Mr. Mackenzie. There were more finished scholars and more brilliant, though not more powerful, orators than he; but in his knowledge of the mysteries of accounts he was unrivalled. At the commencement of the session, he concluded an able speech on the currency, by moving for a committee of inquiry. Of this committee he was chairman; and in that capacity made an elaborate report* on banking and currency. One of the results of the inquiry was the passage of an Act (Geo. IV. cap. 6) introduced by Mr. Mackenzie, declaring that such British coins as were depreciated more than one twenty-fifth of their weight, should not be a legal tender. There was much room for amendment in the principles on which the banks were established. One fourth of the stock of the Bank of Upper Canada was held by the government,

* "The system of banking," said the report, "in most general use in the United States, and which may with propriety be termed 'the American Banking system,' is carried on by Joint Stock Companies, in which the stockholders are authorized to issue notes to a certain extent beyond the amount of their capital; while their persons are privileged from paying the debts of the institution, in the event of a failure of its funds to meet its engagements." On this system, which had found its way into Canada, Mr. Mackenzie was anxious that no more banks should be chartered; but in case the House resolved upon that course, he recommended the following precautions, as likely to afford some security to the bill-holders: "First, That a refusal to redeem their paper should amount to a dissolution of their charter. Second, That the dividends be made out of the actual *bona fide* profits only. Third, That stock should not be received in pledge for discounts. Fourth, That stockholders, resident within the district in which any bank is situated, should not vote by proxy. Fifth, That either branch of the Legislature should have the power to appoint proper persons to ascertain the solvency of the bank, or detect mismanagement, if they should see fit to institute an inquiry. Sixth, And it should be stipulated, that any act of the Legislature, prohibiting the circulation of bills under five dollars, shall not be considered an infringement of the charter. Seventh, The book or books of the company, in which the transfer of stock shall be registered, and the books containing the names of the stockholders, shall be open to the examination of every stockholder in business hours, for thirty days previous to any election of directors. Eighth, Full, true, and particular statements should be periodically required, after a form to be determined on, and which will exhibit to the country the actual condition of the bank to be chartered." To fourteen different questions put to them by Mr. Mackenzie, the officers of the Bank of Upper Canada refused to reply; but it does not appear that any of them were committed for contempt. Such a thing had never occurred in the Parliamentary history of England; but the bank officers here had the bad precedent of the Solicitor General, who was also their solicitor, for their guide.

and the stockholders were only responsible for the amount of their shares.

The Provincial government had, as we have seen, assumed the appointment of a chaplain to the Legislative Assembly. Mr. Mackenzie took up the question as one of privilege; and proposed to resolve that the House refuse to receive the Rev. Dr. Phillips as its chaplain; but that, instead, the ministers of the different denominations of York be requested to officiate during the session as chaplains, under such arrangements as may be made by the Speaker. But Mr. Mackenzie treated the question as something more than one of privilege; as a part of a system which gave a positive dominancy to a particular denomination. Resolutions embodying these views received the assent of the House.

He moved an address for detailed accounts of the different branches of the public revenue; introduced a bill—which passed unanimously at its final stage— providing that the publication of truth, unless with malicious intent, should not be a libel; and that the defendant in an action for libel should be entitled to plead truth in justification and produce his proofs. Another bill he introduced for the support of the poor, lame, blind, and persons deprived of their reason. The libel bill was rejected by the Legislative Council, in company with over forty others.

As chairman of a committee, Mr. Mackenzie brought to light some disgraceful facts bearing upon the conditions of the Provincial prisons. Into an underground cell of the York jail, three female lunatics were stowed; one of whom had become deranged by

22

the desertion of her husband. They were lodged in lock-up cribs, on straw; two in one crib, and the third in another. The stench of their insalubrious dungeon, where they were confined in strait jackets, was complained of by the prisoners above. The bed clothes of some of the prisoners were not washed for six or eight months together. The atmosphere was in the last degree pestilential, and the food insufficient. An idle apprentice and a person charged with murder associated in the same room; which necessarily became a school of vice for the less hardened.

As in the previous session of 1829, Mr. Mackenzie brought forward resolutions, directed against the practice of filling the Legislative Council with dependent place-men; but they were not pressed on either occasion. If this point had been pressed by the House, which showed an inexplicable backwardness in dealing with it, there is reason to believe that it would have been conceded by the Imperial Government.*

---

* In a dispatch, addressed by Sir George Murray, then Colonial Secretary, to Sir James Kemp, Governor of Lower Canada, Sept. 29, 1829, and also "virtually" addressed to Sir John Colborne, as he was officially advised, the following passage on the subject of the Legislative and Executive Councils occurs:

"The constitution of the Legislative and Executive Councils is another subject which has undergone considerable discussion, but upon which His Majesty's Government must suspend their opinion until I shall have received some authentic information from your Excellency. You will, therefore, have the goodness to report to me, whether it would be expedient to make any alteration in the general constitution of those bodies, and especially how far it would be desirable to introduce a larger proportion of members not holding offices at the pleasure of the Crown; and if it should be considered desirable, how far it may be practicable to find a sufficient number of persons of respectability of this description." Under these circumstances an immense power was placed in the hands of the Governors.

The canal era preceded that of railroads. In 1824,
not a single effort of a practical nature had been made
to improve the inland navigation of the Province.
In 1830, the Rideau had been completed. A vessel
of eighty-four tons burthen had, in the previous November, passed through the Welland. The Burlington and the Desjardins canals were far advanced towards completion. Mr. Mackenzie, who had been a
warm advocate of internal improvements, obtained a
committee, in the session of 1830, to inquire into the
management and expenditure of the Welland Canal
Company. The whole thing had so much the appearance of a financial juggle—the original estimates of
£15,000 to £23,000 having been followed by an expenditure of over £273,000*—that curiosity must
have been much excited to know by what legerdemain
the different steps in the financial scheme had succeeded one another.† Mr. Mackenzie fully appreci-

* This canal has now cost £1,727,922 5s. 8d.

† The original estimates were only for a canal that would pass vessels of
forty tons burthen. The company's capital was originally limited to £40,000.
The government was empowered to take the work at the end of thirty years,
on paying the company twenty-five per cent premium on the outlay. The estimates were made in 1824 ; and in April, 1828, an act was passed increasing
the capital stock to £200,000. The Province subscribed for £25,000 of the
stock, in 1825 ; and next year it loaned to the company £25,000, at interest, for
three years. In 1827, this loan was converted into stocks, by a very close
vote, twenty against eighteen. In 1826, the Legislature had been told that
the work would be completed by the spring of 1827, at a cost of £20,000 less
than the company's capital. When 1827 came, the usual story about unfore-
seen circumstances was told ; and by 1830, it was admitted that the whole expenditure would be £800,000. Although Lower Canada had only a remote
interest in the work, her Legislature came forward, in 1827, with a subscription of £25,000 to the stock. Next year, Mr. Merritt visited England, and
obtained from the British Government a loan of £50,000, in security for which
authority was afterwards given to assign the whole work. He also sold some

ated the effects of these internal improvements upon
the price of produce. " Instead of 1s. 10½d. to 2s. 6d. a
bushel for the superior wheat of this fertile Province,"
he said, in May 1830, " paid too often to the farmer in
goods at double their value, we now find the miller
and the merchant eagerly purchasing grain at 5s., and,
in some places, even at 6s. currency per sixty pounds."
As a commercial speculation the work was not destined to pay the stockholders ; but the Province,
which became the proprietor of the canal, has been
amply repaid by the increased value given to its produce. A more striking example of this fact than that
given by Mr. Mackenzie need not be desired. So well
satisfied was he with the result of the internal improvements, so far made, that he declared, " I would
cheerfully consent to involve the Province in debt, in
conjunction with Lower Canada, in order to improve
the St. Lawrence to the ocean." Lower Canada had
taken the lead by making an appropriation for the
survey of the St. Lawrence above Montreal.

shares elsewhere.   In 1830, stockholders in New York had paid in £72,000 ;
in Lower Canada, £12,825 ; and in Upper Canada only £2,462, exclusive of
the Legislative subscription.

CHAPTER XII.

The Small Libel Suit—Mackenzie Pleads his own Cause and Succeeds—Din of the Electoral Battle—Responsible Government—Canada compared with other Countries—Rules for Elections—A subdued Black List—The Opposition to Mackenzie's Re-election—The Principles on which he Successfully Appealed to the People—The Politics of Bank Discounts—Success of the Official Party in the Election.

In writing the biography of one who had many enemies in the public period of his life, while some of his cotemporaries are still living, it is impossible to avoid the revival of recollections that will give pain, or cause offence. But the duty of the impartial biographer is plain. While it should be his study not to inflict needless wounds upon the feelings of the living, the author is not at liberty to omit prominent facts which are essential to the elucidation of his subject. It is my aim, in dealing with events that may revive unpleasant recollections in the minds of some of the actors, to present the facts in the spirit of impartial history, free from rancor or animosity.

When Mr. James Edward Small appealed to the electors of York, in 1828, to select him instead of Mr. Mackenzie, a story affecting his professional reputation was circulated to his disadvantage. Every one loves to find some other cause for his want of success than the relative merits of himself and his opponent;

and Mr. Small alleged that he had lost the election by the circulation of a statement affecting his professional integrity. He stated, on the hustings, his intention to prosecute. Mr. Mackenzie was not the author or retailer of the alleged slander. Mr. George Ridout, Mr. Small's brother-in-law, canvassed Mr. James Hogg, of Milford Mills, for his vote. The miller replied that he could not vote for a man who had cheated or defrauded him out of forty or fifty dollars. Mr. Hogg was prosecuted for slander. He was not permitted to justify, or produce evidence in support of the accusation. The jury gave Mr. Small fifty pounds damages. The costs swelled the amount to £78 19s.

The story had been told by Hogg for Mr. Mackenzie's benefit—at least that was the effect, though it was probably not the intention—and he, in turn, repeated it, on the strength of the evidence in the Hogg trial, for the benefit of Mr. Baldwin. Mr. Mackenzie was prosecuted, too, but with a very different result. The alleged libel bore date November 25, 1829. The evidence in the former trial, which formed the staple of the second alleged libel, showed that one Daniel McDougal held a note against Hogg for £3 13s., " payable in liquor at the market price." The liquor had not been taken, and the question was whether the note could be collected. Mr. McDougal called to consult Mr. Small on the matter. The lawyer gave an opinion that the note, if sued in the Court of King's Bench, could be collected. Mr. McDougal left the note with Mr. Small, but alleged that he ordered him not to sue or make costs upon it, and that he made a

second visit to the lawyer to .repeat these instructions. The note was sued, and the costs reached
£12. Mr. McDougal further stated that he brought
Mr. Small before the Court of Requests to compel him
to pay over the amount of the verdict, but that defendant pleading his privilege as a barrister, McDougal had to pay the costs, and was kept out of his
money still longer. Mr. Mackenzie, in publishing
this statement, reflected upon Mr. Small for taking
advantage of the monstrous maxim, "the greater the
truth the greater the libel," arguing that the proper
way for a man to wipe a stain from his reputation
was "not by £50 verdicts, but by producing and admitting all the facts, but utterly disproving the charge
made against him."* The alleged libel was an argument upon statements sworn to in a suit for slander,
and so far from being charged with malignity, it contained such admissions as this: "I myself have had
some dealings with Mr. Small, and although I looked
carefully into his conduct towards me, I am happy to
testify that I found him just and honorable in his
dealings." It must be confessed that, if the evidence
of Daniel McDougal could be relied upon, Mr. Small
had taken advantage of a legal maxim that has since
ceased to disgrace the laws of England.

---

* Judge Hagerman told the jury that if they believed that Hogg had used
the words complained of, they must find a verdict for Small; that great scandal had been occasioned to the detriment of Small, by the unwarrantable conduct of Mr. Hogg; that a lawyer's reputation was of the utmost importance to
him in his profession; that the jury must discard McDougal's evidence, showing the cause of Hogg's using these expressions, since it was inadmissible; that
McDougal ought to have been stopped sooner; and he concluded by directing
them to give a verdict for the plaintiff.

Such was the alleged libel, which came to trial on the 8th of April, 1830. A special jury had been struck, at the instance of Mr. Small. Messrs. Baldwin and Sullivan were solicitors for Mr. Mackenzie; and at one time it was his intention that they should act as his advocates, at the trial; but he finally resolved to be his own advocate. Mr. Draper appeared for Small. The trial lasted from half past nine in the morning to the same hour at night. Four hours out of the twelve were taken up by Mr. Mackenzie's address to the jury. During the whole time, the court-house was densely crowded. Mr. Justice Sherwood presided; and Mr. Mackenzie has commended his impartiality on the occasion. The Chief Justice and the Hon. Mr. Allan took seats beside the presiding judge. The jury,* who remained out all night, gave a verdict for the defendant; and they are said to have debated among themselves whether it was not competent for them to award damages to Mr. Mackenzie for the annoyance of a frivolous prosecution.

The verdict was set aside by the Court above, on the ground that the witnesses had been permitted to say too much in the way of justification. But Mr. Small, far from thinking it desirable to push this seeming advantage, was willing to let the matter rest where it was—the costs having been thrown on the defendant—but Mr. Mackenzie desired to fight the contest to its natural close. With that view, he offered a special plea in justification; but the judges,

* Their names, Messrs. Joseph Wixon, Pickering; Jas. Pearson, Whitchurch; Stilwell Wilson, John Chew, and Thos. Bell, of York; Wm. Cornell, Scarboro'; John Dalziel, Vaughan; Christian Recsor, Markham; Joseph Sylvester, Vaughan, and John Austin, of Toronto.

on application of Mr. Small, put off the new trial till the spring of 1831. A general election was to take place in the interim ; and it was destined that the new trial was to be indefinitely postponed, Mr. Small remaining satisfied with his first defeat.

After the close of the session of 1830, the belief seems to have generally prevailed that the Executive government would dissolve a House which had been unanimous in asking the Lieutenant Governor to dismiss his advisers. The death of the King, George IV., settled all doubts that might have existed on this head. But before the intelligence of this event reached Upper Canada, the battle cry of party had been raised, in anticipation of a dissolution of the new House. In the month of July, Mr. Mackenzie addressed a series of very long letters to Sir John Colborne, Lieutenant Governor, apparently intended to influence the constituencies. Several columns of the first letter were devoted to a complaint founded on the accusations brought by the government press against the loyalty of the Legislative Assembly, and abuse of its members.* These attacks followed closely upon the pub-

* The Upper Canada *Courier*, published by the late Mr. Gurnett, described the House, as a "tyrant gang whose hatred is levelled at all loyal subjects;" the Speaker, as "a treacherous plotter," whose face and form were "spiteful and bitter as the venomed asp;" whose heart was "the home of every evil passion," and whose "looks betray the mawkish hypocrite."

"———Mouthpiece of a tyrant gang, (the House of Assembly,)
Whose hatred is levelled at all loyal subjects.
Poor abject creature, of a rebel race,
I scorn thy brief and undeserved authority."

And again :

"A thing like him (the Speaker) will only breed contempt,
And cause our House to prove a scene of riot,
23

lication of a despatch from Sir George Murray, Colonial Secretary, to Sir James Kemp, Lieutenant Governor of Lower Canada, in which the Imperial Minister inculcated "the necessity of cultivating a spirit of
conciliation towards the House of Assembly ;" plainly
showing the feelings of the British government on the
subject. After collecting a long list of accusations
against the dominant party in the Assembly, Mr.
Mackenzie met them by quoting the remark of a
" celebrated politician," that, " by this means, like the
husband who uses his wife ill from suspicion, you
may in time convert your suspicions into reality."
But before he had completed the series, he met the
charge of disloyalty brought against the Legislative
Assembly and the party it more particularly represented, in direct terms. " The people of this Province,"
he said, " neither desire to break up their ancient connection with Great Britain, nor are they anxious to
become members of the North American Confederation ; all they want is a cheap, frugal, domestic government, to be exercised for their benefit and controlled
by their own fixed land-marks ; they seek a system by
which to insure justice, protect property, establish

Uproar, and noise. A theatre for spouting
Disgusting trash and scurvy billingsgate,
The scoff and scorn of all who witness it.

"Devoid of dignity, address, and manners,
He seems a thing unworthy to preside
O'er doating fools who loiter at camp meetings,
To hear old women prate in mawkish phrases.

"Out upon them (the House of Assembly) ; shouldst thou choose him
(Mr. Bidwell) Speaker,
Thou'lt prove thyselves a base and shameless faction,
Disgraceful both to government and people."

domestic tranquillity, and afford a reasonable prospect that civil and religious liberty will be perpetuated, and the safety and happiness of society effected." It was one of Mr. Mackenzie's complaints, that the members of the Executive government were not responsible to the people of Canada, through their representatives; and that there was no way of bringing them to account for their conduct. When the election contest approached more nearly he put forward responsible government as a principal of vital importance. As a needful reform, he placed it on a level with the necessity of purging the Legislative Council of the sworn creatures and dependents of the Executive, who comprised the great majority. Of Upper Canada politicians, we are entitled to place Mr. Mackenzie among the very earliest advocates of responsible government.* It is doubtless true that others afterwards made the attainment of this principle of administration more of a specialty than he did; for where abuses grew up with rank luxuriance, he could

* In September, 1830, he put forth the following programme, and afterwards frequently repeated its publication:

"To insure good government, with the aid of a faithful people, the following five things are essential:

"1. The entire control of the whole Provincial revenues are required to be vested in the Legislature—the territorial and hereditary revenues excepted.

"2. The independence of the judges; or their removal to take place, only upon a joint address of the two Houses, and their appointment from among men who have not embarked in the political business of the Province.

"3. A reform in the Legislative Council, which is now an assembly chiefly composed of persons wholly or partly dependent upon the Executive government for their support.

"4. An administration or Executive government responsible to the Province for its conduct.

"5. Equal rights to each religious denomination, and an exclusion of every sect from a participation in temporal power."

not help pausing to cut them down in detail. The independence of the judiciary, for which he persistently
contended, has, like responsible government, long
since been attained; and indeed, the somewhat-fanci-
ful idea of making judges only of persons who have
never dabbled in the muddy waters of colonial politics is the only change which he put prominently forward, in 1830, that has not now been long in the enjoy-
ment of Canadians.

His letters to Sir John Colborne are not free from
remarks to which a general consent would not now be
given. In drawing up an indictment, containing a
hundred counts against the administration, the constitution was not always spared; but the system of administration, then pursued, would now find no supporters in this Province; and if we were obliged to
believe that it was constitutional to sustain in power
a ministry condemned by the unanimous voice of
the people's representatives, the necessity for constitutional reform would be universally insisted on. If
the British government and even the British constitution came in for a share of condemnation, it must
be remembered that the oligarchical system, which
reduced the popular branch of the Legislature to a
nullity, was sustained by the Imperial Government;
and that the Reform Bill of Lord John Russell had
not yet been passed.

The letters to the Lieutenant Governor were immediately followed by *"An appeal to the people of Upper
Canada from the judgments of British and Colonial Governments."* This "Appeal" was one of the mildest
productions Mr. Mackenzie ever wrote. Free from

personalities, it consisted entirely of an appeal to the reason and the better feelings of the people. But no description would convey so good an idea of it as a few extracts; and for that reason I resort to the latter method. Addressing the farmers of the country, he shows his love for Canada by comparing it with other countries:

"A kind Providence hath cast your lot in a highly favored land, where, blessed with luxuriant harvests and a healthful climate, you are enabled to look back without regret upon the opulent nations of Europe, where the unbounded wealth of one class, and the degrading poverty of another, afford melancholy proofs of the tyranny which prevails in their governments. Compare your situation with that of Russia, an empire embracing one half of the habitable globe, the population of which are slaves attached to the soil, and transferable to any purchaser; or with Germany, Italy, Portugal, and Spain, where human beings are born and die under the same degrading vassalage. Traverse the wide world and what will you find? In one place, a privation of liberty; in another, incapacity to make use of its possession; here, ignorance, vice, and political misrule; there, an immense number of your fellow men, forced from their peaceful homes and occupations 'to fight battles in the issue of which they have no interest, to increase a domain in the possession of which they can have no share.' Contrast their situation with yours, and let the peaceful plains, the fertile valleys of Canada, your homes, the homes of your wives and children, be still more dear to you. Agriculture, the most innocent, happy, and important of all human pursuits, is your chief employment; your farms are your own; you have obtained a competence, seek therewith to be content.

> "'Contentment, rosy, dimpled maid,
>   Thou brightest daughter of the sky,
>   Why dost thou to the hut repair,
>   And from the gilded palace fly?
>   I've traced thee on the peasant's cheek;
>   I've marked thee in the milkmaid's smile;
>   I've heard thee loudly laugh and speak,
>   Amid the sons of noonday toil;
>   Yet in the circles of the great,
>   Where fortune's gifts are all combined,
>   I've sought thee early, sought thee late,
>   And ne'er thy lovely form could find.
>   Since then from wealth and pomp you flee,
>   I ask but competence and thee!'"

The plea of poverty—which is very liable to lead to corruption—as an excuse for not attending the poll, he met by saying:—"Poor, indeed, in soul or in substance must that farmer or mechanic be, who, being in health, cannot, in two or four years, spare time for one day's journey to the hustings to express an opinion by his vote, concerning the persons chosen to watch over the public welfare." Far from having any desire to change the monarchical for a republican form of government, he said:—"It is not a change in the form of government which will remove any difficulties or grievances under which you labor;" and so little did he flatter the people, that he told them "The grand panacea is self-reformation." He went further: "Beware," he said, "of electioneering sycophants! for if they flatter you, they will assuredly flatter power after you elect them." Never were truer words spoken, or more necessary advice given. Of the further rules he gave for the selection of representatives, the following are not worthless specimens:

"If you find a lawyer who has tried to fill his neighborhood with litigation—who is more famed for gaining causes than for scrupulous virtue in accepting their management, he is 'a minister of municipal litigation, and the fomenter of village vexation,'—avoid him. But wherever a lawyer can be found among you, worthy of the high vocation whereto he has been called—learned, industrious, and faithful—less anxious for the fees of office than for the peace of society—always willing to embark in the most perilous duties of his profession, the protection of property, personal rights, domestic peace, and parental authority, entreat him to come forward as a candidate; elect him with acclamation; he will surely maintain your rights, and stand as a sentinel upon the watch-tower of Freedom, to warn you of approaching danger.* Men whose conduct, in their private dealings with their fellows, has been found to be regulated by covetous, unchristian, selfish principles, will be sure to make dishonest and unprincipled legislators; for how can he who takes daily advantage of the necessities or the follies of his brother, be a lover of mankind, benevolent, and kind? Mind not his boasted patriotism, nor his exclamations against existing abuses; for there is guile in his heart and deceit on his lips."

Against the votes of members during the late Parliament, there was much less to be said, from Mr.

---

* There is reason to believe that, in giving this description, Mr. Mackenzie had Dr. Rolph in his mind; for he had previously spoken of him in nearly equivalent terms.

Mackenzie's point of view than against those of their immediate predecessors. The *Black List*—a running commentary upon prominent votes—was therefore meagre and comparatively feeble.

Mr. Mackenzie's re-election for York was opposed by nearly every newspaper in the country; and the few that did not oppose, remained silent. Some carried the virulence of personal abuse to an extent that caused him to complain of injustice; but he would neither condescend to reply nor to meet his assailants with their own weapons. He would not reply, " because," as he said, " he thinks that his conduct, during his political career of seven years, has sufficiently enabled the people to judge of the value which ought to be attached to such productions." The county of York returned two members; and of the four candidates on this occasion, two represented the opposition, and two the official party. On the liberal interest stood Mr. Mackenzie and Mr. Jesse Ketchum; opposed to them were Mr. Simon Washburn and Mr. Thorne. So far did Mr. Mackenzie carry his sense of fairness that he publicly announced that he would " abstain from using the press as a medium of injuring, in the public estimation," whoever might be opposed to him as candidates; an English-like love of honor and fair-play that might be copied to advantage in the present day. " He was," he said, " anxious to gain his election, more as a triumph of principle, than as a personal gratification. He will, therefore, neither keep open houses, bring voters to the hustings, nor in any way treat, entertain, or recompense any electors, either before, at, or after the polling. His return (should he be elected) must be the deliberate result of public opinion alone, opposed, as it would be, to the powerful influence of the local government, the dominant priesthood, the provincial bank, and every human being who profits by the present irresponsible system."* On this ground he put the contest; and the result † justified his confident anticipations.

The new House‡ met on the 7th of January, 1831.

* Shortly before the election came on, Mr. Mackenzie had given "Reasons," occupying four newspaper columns, "why the farmers and mechanics should keep a sharp look-out upon the Bank [of Upper Canada] and its managers." These reasons were based upon the refusal of the officers of the Bank, in the previous session, to answer the inquiries on numerous points of a parliamentary committee; on the statement, in evidence of Mr. R. Baldwin, that notes had been discounted and refused discount from political reasons; on the palpable defects which then existed in the charter, defects which were such as even then no economist or good business man in Europe would have thought of defending. In order to exclude Mr. Mackenzie from the last annual meeting proxies had been refused.

† The result of the polling was: For Ketchum, 616; Mackenzie, 570; Washburn, 425; Thorne, 243.

‡ The following are members returned with the places they represented:

Glengary.—Alex. McMartin and Alexander Fraser.

Stormont.—Archd. McLean and P. Vankoughnet.

Dundas.—John Cook and Peter Shaver.

Grenville.—Richard D. Fraser and Edward Jessup.

Leeds.—William Buell, jr. and Matt. M. Howard.

Brockville.—Henry Jones.

Carleton.—John Bower Lewis.

Lanark.—William Morris.

Frontenac.—Hugh C. Thomson and John Campbell.

Kingston, (Town).—Christopher A. Hagerman.

Hastings.—Reuben White and Jas. H. Samson.

Lennox and Addington.—Marshall S. Bidwell and Peter Perry.

Northumberland.—James Lyon and Archibald McDonald.

Durham.—John Brown and George S. Boulton.

York, (Town). — William Botsford Jarvis.

York, (County).—Jesse Ketchum and William L. Mackenzie.

Simcoe.—William B. Robinson.

Middlesex. — Mahlon Burwell and Roswell Mount.

Norfolk.—Duncan McCall and Wm. Willson.

24

No previous Assembly had committed half as many
follies as the one that now met for the first time was
to perpetrate.

Oxford.—Chas. Ingersoll and Chas. Duncombe.

Kent.—William Berczy.

Essex.—William Elliott and Jean B. Magon.

Wentworth.—John Willson and Allan N. McNab.

Halton.—Wm. Chisholm and James Crooks.

Niagara, (Town).— Henry J. Boulton.

Lincoln.—Robt. Randal, John Clark, William Crooks, and Bartholomew C. Beardsley.

Haldimand.—John Brant.

CHAPTER XIII.

Meeting of the New House—The Official Party elect Mr. McLean Speaker—
The Chaplain and State Church Question—Cause of the Party Revolution—
'Power of the Purse—State of the Representation—Mackenzie obtains a Committee upon it—Officials and Dependants on the Executive in the House—
Grants of Public Lands to Members of the House—Cheering in the Galleries
of the Assembly—Permanent Civil List first Granted—Mackenzie inquires
into the Public Expenditure, and becomes a Thorn in the Side of the Official
Party—Bank Mysteries made Public—Unsuccessful Attempt to expel Mackenzie for distributing Copies of the Journals of the House at his own expense—Mr. McNab tries to pay off the Grudge of his previous Imprisonment—Scheme of Representative Reform—Undue Influence of the Executive on the Legislative Council—Mackenzie starts an Agitation for Responsible Government and other Reforms—Petitions to the Imperial Authorities
—Journey to Quebec—Shipwrecked in the Ice of the St. Lawrence.

THE first trial of party strength, in the new House,
showed that the majority had passed to the official
side. It was then the habit of the Upper Canada Assembly, as it is now that of United Canada, to change
the Speaker with every revolution of party. The re-
election of Mr. Bidwell, by the new House, was out
of the question; and Mr. Archibald McLean became
his successor, on a vote of twenty-six against fourteen. He was the first native Canadian elected to the
chair of the Upper Canada Assembly. His father
had emigrated from Argyleshire, Scotland; and the
son had, in previous local parliaments, allied himself
with the Official or Family Compact party. Person-

ally, he was not obnoxious, even to the opposition ; and his pleasing address was much in his favor. But his election indicated a complete change in the politics of the House; and the party now dominant in both branches of the Legislature, as well as in the government, was subject to no check whatever. The way in which it abused its power, will hereafter be seen.

Early in the session, Mr. Mackenzie brought forward a resolution re-affirming the right of the House to appoint its own chaplain, and denying that the Executive government had been entrusted with the power to prescribe the religious duties, exercises, or ceremonies of the House, or to incorporate with the tenets of any particular sect the institutions of the country. In Lower Canada, where the majority of the population, and of the Legislative Assembly, was Roman Catholic, the House had no chaplain. But this was not necessarily the result of the denominational complexion of the population ; for Upper Canada was the only British American Province where the government undertook to appoint a chaplain to the Legislative Assembly. Even in Nova Scotia, where the Church of England was fully established, the popular branch of the Legislature claimed and exercised the right of appointing its own chaplain. The legal establishment of the Church of England in Canada was contested ; and it was chiefly as a protest against the assumption that it occupied such a position, that Mr. Mackenzie brought up this question, session after session. If the Church of England was not securely established, as a State Church, it had made some not unsuccessful efforts at dominancy. It claimed a seventh of all the granted lands in the Province. It had obtained control of the University of King's College, at York; and it had obtruded a chaplain on an unwilling House of Assembly. In the temper of the new House, no decision could be got upon the question raised by Mr. Mackenzie. It was superseded by a motion, brought forward by ex-Speaker Willson, "that the question be not now put." Mr. Mackenzie then moved that a request be presented to the ministers of the different denominations, in York, to say prayers in the House, during the session, under such arrangements as the Speaker might make; but a large majority of the members—about three-fourths—refused to entertain the question, and the subject was referred to a committee, consisting of Messrs. McNab, Willson, and Samson. In the course of the debate, Solicitor General Hagerman threatened the House with "confusion," and that "an end would be put to their proceedings," if they ventured to oppose the wishes of the Lieutenant Governor. Attorney General Boulton compared the assumption of the House, of the right to appoint its own chaplain, with the right of the assassin who shoots down a man in the street—the exercise of mere brute force. And the House accepted the argument, and bowed before the menace.

It was already evident that Mr. Mackenzie had lost in the new House the influence he had exercised in that which the Executive—unable to find in it a single friend in need—had caused to be dissolved. Instead of praying for a removal of the ministry, as on the previous occasion, the Address of the House was a mere echo of the speech with which the Lieutenant Governor had opened the session.

It is impossible to note the change in the character of the House produced by the election of 1830, without inquiring to what possible causes so extraordinary a party revolution was attributable. The enigma seems to be not wholly incapable of solution. The opposition to the Executive, in the previous House, had gone far to abolish all party lines. Very few members, who served from 1828 to 1830, had any serious political sins to answer for, in respect to that period. The purse-strings were held by the Executive. Holding the crown revenues independent of the Legislature, it could wield the influence which money gives; and, in a young colony, poor and struggling, this was necessarily considerable. The state of the representation was, in some respects, worse than that in the unreformed House of Commons. The session was not very old when Mr. Mackenzie moved for a committee of inquiry on the subject. When he rose to address the House, a collector of customs sat at his elbow, and another of these officers was contesting the election of a member who held office under the Executive during pleasure; while the Speaker whom he addressed held the office of Clerk of the Crown in the district where he lived. In England, a postmaster could not vote for a candidate seeking a seat in the unreformed Parliament; half a dozen postmasters held seats in the Upper Canada Assembly. There were, besides, office-holders of almost every grade: a Sheriff, Inspectors of still and tavern licenses, County Registers, and Commissioners of Customs. If any one is innocent enough to suppose that this crowd of officials could make independent representatives, a recollection of the fate of Mr. Fothergill will serve to undeceive him. Mr. Fothergill had been dismissed from the office of King's Printer, on account of the independent position he had taken in the House. Capt. Matthews, of the Royal Navy, had been temporarily deprived of his pension, through the complaints of spies, who made it a subject of serious complaint against him that, when he had indulged too freely in wine at dinner, he had thoughtlessly or imprudently called on the orchestra to give "Yankee Doodle," in the little theatre of York. Mr. Mackenzie, with his colleague for York and the member for Lanark, represented a larger number of people than fifteen other members. There was more than one member whose whole constituency did not number over twenty or thirty votes. The county of York, which had two representatives, contained more people than Hastings, Dundas, Haldimand, Niagara, and Brockville. A majority of the whole House represented less than a third of the population; and if property were taken into account as a basis of representation, the matter would be still worse. Members of this House and its predecessor had obtained grants of crown lands, over which the Executive and not the Legislature held control, to the extent of from five hundred to two thousand acres,* on simply paying the fees exacted by the officials. With great force Mr. Mackenzie urged these facts, for the most part discreditable, as a reason for

---

* These grants were probably legal. The objection was to the system which permitted of abuse.

inquiring into the state of the representation. On a vote of twenty-eight against eleven the House granted the committee; and after two attempts on the part of the officials and their friends to break the force of the conclusion arrived at, Mr. Mackenzie got a committee of his own nomination, consisting of Messrs. Shaver, Howard, Buell, Lyons, and himself.

Even when his speeches did not move the House, they sometimes caused the galleries to respond with involuntary cheers. One instance of his forcible way of putting things will show the secret power that brought these dangerous responses from beyond the bar. Mr. Burwell had proposed to grant a life pension to the widow of one of the leading public officers, when Mr. Mackenzie opposed the proposition in these terms :—

" He objected to the introduction of a pension list of this kind, because if it were admitted that the lady of one public functionary had a right to a pension, it would follow that others had the same right, and gentlemen holding lucrative situations would depend on the public and squander more profusely their ample incomes. A man came from Scotland with a most excellent character, expended all he had to bring himself, a wife, and large family to these shores; had Lord Bathurst's letter in his pocket deluding him with the hopes of a grant of land, found it a deception, and went back into the bush upon a reserve to combat ill health, poverty, and disappointment. The Lieutenant Governor and Council would do nothing for this poor man ; his wife, separated from her friends, pined and died; her husband had a few hours before

come to inform him, with tears in his eyes, that she
had been that very day coffined. Was it to be borne
that while respectable emigrants were thus made the
sport of a faction in the colony as pitiless as death
itself, that the rich, the wealthy, the opulent, they who
had obtained and doubtless well deserved thousands
of acres of public lands and thousands of pounds of
public money, should now, at the eleventh hour, come
forward and seek pensions out of the hard earnings of
British emigrants?—and that where British settlers
with empty pockets were told to buy land at its highest price and pay with interest for leave to live in
a wilderness, ladies of fortune and high connection
should receive pensions out of the public bounty? It
might be fashionable in Britain, but was quite unfit
for Canada."

The utterance of these words was followed by clap-
ping of hands and cheering in the galleries, which
produced a motion ordering that strangers should be
required to withdraw. The ebullition of feeling appeared to have been uncontrollable, and after a discussion on the subject, in secret session, the public
was re-admitted.

During this occasion a permanent Civil List of
£6,500 was granted. £8,000 had been asked from
the House, by the Imperial Government, which, at
this time, surrendered its interest in certain duties,
estimated at £11,500 a year, levied under Imperial
statute, and which had previously been applied to the
support of the civil government. The Civil List granted
in return for these revenues provided for the salaries
of the Governor, the Judges of the Court of Queen's

25

Bench, the Attorney and the Solicitor General, five Executive Councillors, and the Clerk of the Executive Council.* The revenue now ceded had recently made the Executive independent, in money matters, of the House; and as there was no other means of making the advisers of the representative of the Crown responsible to the Legislature, the granting of a permanent Civil List was looked upon, by the Reform party, as another means of perpetuating that immunity from control, which the Executive enjoyed, and which was the source of so many evils. There was no reason to expect that the Legislature would long have remained satisfied to permit these revenues to be disposed of without its sanction; for, though they were raised under Imperial statute, they were paid by the Province, and were in their nature essentially local. The Legislative Assembly, if armed with the power of annually voting the salaries of the members of the government, might, Mr. Mackenzie and those who acted with him thought, have some control over them. If the government had been responsible to the Legislature, this ground of opposition to what received the name of the "Everlasting Salaries Bill," would, in all probability, not have been taken, because the object which the opposition sought to accomplish would have been more effectually obtained by other means. The vote upon the question was a strictly party vote, and it is very certain that, under the conditions of go-

---

* The salaries were: Lieutenant Governor, £2,000 sterling; Judges of the Court of King's Bench, altogether, £3,300 sterling; Attorney and Solicitor General, £500 sterling, each; Five Executive Councillors, £500 sterling, each; Clerk of the Executive Council, £200 sterling.

vernment which then obtained, no permanent Civil
List would have been granted either by the preceding or the subsequent House of Assembly. Under
other circumstances—in the presence of a responsible
government—the Liberals would probably not have
opposed the granting of a permanent Civil List; but
under a system which deprived the Assembly of all
control over the advisers of the Lieutenant Governor,
they can hardly be blamed for seeking to enforce Executive responsibility by the only means that seemed to
be in their power.

It had already become evident that, even in the
present House, Mr. Mackenzie would frequently get
his own way, and that he would give no end of trouble to the official party. He brought forward motions which the House, in spite of its adverse composition, did not venture to reject, and they were sometimes accepted without opposition. He had carried a
motion of inquiry into the fees, salaries, pensions, and
rewards paid out of that portion of the revenue which
was not at the disposal of the Legislature, as well as
a motion for a return of all sums, paid out of the same
source, to religious denominations. He had made
strong efforts to effect a reform in the very defective
system of banking which then prevailed. The friends
of bank mystery had been obliged to give way, and
allow regular returns of the state of the Bank of Upper Canada to be made. Attorney General Boulton,
who was solicitor for the bank, held out against the
requirement of publicity as long as he could, but he
had to give way. On this subject Mr. Mackenzie did
not carry his motion, but he compelled those who

opposed him to yield much of what he contended for.

If a member, who gave the official party so much trouble could be got rid of, how smoothly things might be expected to glide along in the House, as at present constituted! Could a vote of expulsion not be carried? To this question an attempt was made to give a practical answer. Previous to the general election, Mr. Mackenzie had distributed, at his own expense, several copies of the journals of the House, unaccompanied by comment, and precisely in the shape in which they were printed by the House. The declared object of the distribution was to give the voters, in different places, the means of referring to the official record of the votes and proceedings of the House, in order that they might be able to trace every vote, motion, and resolution of their late representatives, and to ascertain when they were absent and when present; whether their votes were acceptable or not. It appears that it had been decided at a private party meeting, at which several of the leading officials are said to have been present, that this should be treated as a breach of privilege, and be made the ground of a motion to expel the member guilty of it. For this purpose, the aid of a committee of inquiry was obtained: consisting of Attorney General Boulton, Messrs. McNab, Willson, Samson, and Wm. Robinson. Mr. McNab was selected as the minister of vengeance; and it may be presumed that he performed his task *con amore*, since he had an old grudge to settle with the member, on whose motion he had, in a previous session, been sent to prison for refusing to answer the inquiries of a committee of the House. Mr. McNab based his complaint chiefly upon the fact that the journals had been distributed without the appendix. If the appendix had gone too, he owned "that he should not so readily have made up his mind on the question of privilege." The idea he attempted to convey was, that the journals alone gave a partial view of the proceedings of the House; but this pretence was wholly groundless. All the votes and proceedings of the House are contained in the journals. The motion was in these words: "That it having appeared upon the report of the select committee, to whom was referred the resolution of this House, and the report of the Clerk on the subject of printing the journals, that William Lyon Mackenzie, Printer, of this town, who was employed to print the said journals, had abused the trust reposed in him by publishing portions of the said journals, and distributing the same for political purposes, among individuals not entitled to copies thereof; thereby committing a breach of the privileges of this House." The Solicitor General made no hesitation in denouncing the circulation of the journals as "altogether disgraceful, and a high breach of the privileges of the House." He deemed it monstrous to circulate them, "without the consent or approbation of the House," and for the shameful purpose of letting the constituencies know how their members had voted. The Attorney General said the question was whether, for this "bad purpose, any portion of the journals of the House could be published;" and he answered it by unhesitatingly declaring his "opinion, as a lawyer, that such a publication was a breach of Parliamentary privileges, whether done with an evil intent, or for a praiseworthy purpose." He attempted to make the British constitution responsible for the folly his party were attempting to perpetrate. "He had been suffering much from indisposition all day; but he felt it to be his duty to stop in his place and vindicate those privileges which ought to be dear to every man who loved, as he did, the British constitution." The spirit of the dominant party of the day is fairly shown by this style of pleading. Technically speaking, there may be little doubt of the correctness of Mr. Boulton's Parliamentary law; but nobody knew better than he, that the rule which forbids any one to publish the proceedings of the House, without authority, was violated every day; and that its violation was looked upon, not as a crime to be punished, but a public benefit and a general convenience. Mr. Dalton had, in the previous session, published portions of the proceedings of the House in his journal;* and if Mr. Mackenzie was liable to be punished, so was he. Every newspaper publisher was equally guilty.

Mr. Mackenzie had a clear appreciation of the effect which such an ill-advised movement would produce on the public mind. "If," he said, "the object of this resolution is to do me injury, it is but another proof of the incapacity and folly of the advisers of this government, who could not have better displayed their weakness of intellect and unfitness for office, than by bringing me before the public as a guilty person, on an accusation, against which the whole country, from

* *The Patriot.*

one end to the other, will cry out, 'Shame!' Of what
am I accused? Why, Mr. Speaker, I have committed
the high crime and misdemeanor of distributing, before a general election, at my own private expense,
one hundred and sixty-eight copies of the public official journals of this House, without note or comment,
and after the Clerk had corrected the proofs, in order
(as the circular letter I sent with them declares) that
the freeholders in every district might have in their
own hands the best possible means of judging of the
fitness or unfitness of honorable members again to
represent their feelings and interests; and in order
that means might be at hand to refute the slanders
of those who would desire to mislead the public by
anonymous placards, handbills, and idle gossip, in
favor of one candidate to the prejudice of another."
" Were this motion to carry," he said in another part
of his defence, "we should find that we had privileges
contrary to precedent, contrary to usage; privileges,
of which no popular legislative body, until now, ever
heard or dreamed; privileges, which set common sense
and human reason at defiance. If I have done wrong,
every newspaper editor in London, in Lower Canada,
and in this Province, is deserving of punishment."

Nothing could be plainer than that the charge on
which it was sought to justify the motion for expulsion was a mere pretext. For if the publication of
the proceedings of the House, and worse still, as was
alleged, of a portion of those proceedings, was an offence which that body, in vindication of its privileges,
was bound to punish, proceedings ought to have been
taken against every newspaper publisher. It was not

the member but the publisher of the journals who was alleged to have offended in this instance; and why should the member be punished for what the publisher had done, while every other newspaper proprietor, who was obnoxious to the same charge, was to go scot free? These considerations must have flashed upon the House; and in spite of its subserviency to the administration, and in spite of the desire to get rid of Mr. Mackenzie's active opposition by removing his presence from the House, a majority, fearing the effect of the proceeding upon the constituencies, shrank from sustaining Mr. McNab's motion. The vote stood fifteen against twenty; the names of the Attorney General and the Solicitor General figuring in the minority.

Baffled for the time, but resolved not to forego their purpose of getting rid of a troublesome opponent, a new pretext was soon invented. It was pretended that Mr. Mackenzie, the journalist, had printed a libel upon the House. But for libel the law had provided severe remedies, and placed the accused at the great disadvantage of not being able to plead in justification that the alleged libel was true. To the law of the land, the accused journalist was amenable; and might have been put upon his trial, either civilly or criminally.* But this would not have answered the purpose of Mr. Mackenzie's assailants; which was to rid the House of his presence and his opposition.

* I do not, of course, intend to deny the constitutional right of the House to punish for libels upon itself. But the power is one that requires to be exercised with great caution; and assuredly it should not be abused by making it a pretext for the expulsion of a member, who is found troublesome to the dominant party.

Before the time came for the second motion for expulsion, the House had entered on another session; and in the interval Mr. Mackenzie was far from having done any thing to conciliate the dominant faction. On the 16th of March, 1831, the committee on the state of the representation, of which he was chairman, reported. It condemned the practice of crowding the House with placemen; showed that the Legislative Council had repeatedly thrown out bills for allowing the same indemnity to members for towns as was paid to those for country counties—ten shillings a day, without any allowance for travelling expenses—recommended the modification of that provision of the law which gave a representative to every town having one thousand inhabitants, so as to include a portion of the adjoining country sufficient to give the constituency four thousand inhabitants; an approach to the equalization of constituencies, in other cases, was recommended in detail. Some of the suggestions have since been carried into effect. The report is entirely free from that quackery which consists of the iteration of what is readily accepted as a principle, but which without some modification does not admit of practical application. It was shown that the Executive had exerted undue influence on placemen who held seats in the Legislative Council; and compelled them to change their tone and vote in direct opposition to their convictions previously expressed in their places. A few had had spirit enough to protest; but submission had been the rule.

The Legislative recess was of less than ordinary length; the Provincial Parliament, prorogued on the

26

16th of March, having been again convened on the
17th of November, 1831. But the period had been
long enough for Mr. Mackenzie to arouse an agitation
which shook Upper Canada throughout its whole extent. Nothing like it had ever before been witnessed
in the Upper Province. In the middle of July, he
issued, in temperate language, a call for public meetings, to appeal to the King and the Imperial Parliament against the abuses of power by the local authorities. He did not mistrust the justice or the good
intentions of the Sovereign. On the contrary, he
showed the people that there were substantial reasons
for believing in the good intentions of the King towards the Province. " If," he said, in a public address, " you can agree upon general principles to be
maintained by the agents you may appoint in London,
I am well satisfied that his Majesty's government will
exert its utmost powers to fulfil your just and reasonable requests ; your King's noble efforts on behalf of
your brethren in England, Ireland, and Scotland, are
an earnest that you have in him a firm and powerful
friend." In these public meetings, York led off; and
was followed by responsive movements throughout the
Province. Mr. Mackenzie was personally present at
many of the meetings, and even in such places as
Brockville and Cornwall he carried every thing as he
wished. Each petition adopted by those meetings was
an echo of the other ; and many appear to have been
exact copies of one another. To produce a certified
copy of the proceedings of the York meeting was sure to
obtain assent to what it had done. A demand for a responsible government found a place in these petitions.

The King was asked " to cause the same constitutional principle which has called your present ministers to office to be fully recognized and uniformly acted upon in Upper Canada; so that we may see only those who possess the confidence of the people composing the Executive Council of your Majesty's representative." Representative reform—which then occupied so much attention in England—was demanded. The control of all the revenue raised in the Province was asked to be placed in the Legislative Assembly;* the disposal of the public lands to be regulated by law; the secularization of the Clergy Reserves; the establishment of municipal councils which should have the control of local assessments; the abolition of exclusive privileges conferred upon particular religious denominations; law reform; provision for impeaching public servants who betray their trust; the exclusion of judges and ministers of the gospel from the Executive Council and the Legislature; the abolition of the right of primogeniture: these items completed the list of those grievances, of which redress was asked. Some of the copies varied a little from the original formula; in substance the different petitions presented but little variation.

Of these petitions Mr. Mackenzie afterwards became the bearer to England. The aggregate number of signatures appended to them was over twenty-four

---

* In respect to Lower Canada this principle had already been conceded. Lord Howiek had stated in the Imperial Parliament, on the 11th of April previous, that "the government of Canada would be asked to surrender to the Provincial Assembly, the whole of the disputed revenue; but at the same time he would ask of them a moderate provision for the salaries of the governor and judges;" a civil list, in fact, to be granted every seven years.

thousand, five hundred. In spite of counter petitions numerously signed, Mr. Mackenzie's mission, as we shall see, was far from being barren of results.

During the spring of 1831, Mr. Mackenzie made a journey to Quebec, to pay a visit to some of the leading politicians of Lower Canada. He took passage at Montreal, in the steamer Waterloo, for Quebec. While on her way down, the vessel was wrecked. early on the morning of the 13th April, opposite St. Nicholas, and the passengers had a narrow escape for their lives. The vessel went down in deep water. The accident arose from the supposition that the ice-bridge at Cap Rouge had given way, and left the channel clear. It was the general wish of the passengers that the vessel should proceed, and the captain acted upon it. Mr. Mackenzie wrote an account of the occurrence, dated — " Malhot's Hotel, Quebec, April 13, 1831.

" When off Dechambault, one of the company's pilots came on board and said he had certain information that the ice at Cap Rouge had gone down and left the channel clear. Towards night, Mr. Lyman, of the house of Hedge & Lyman, Montreal, expressed to me some doubts as to the danger of our situation, but I confess I had no fears whatever, but believed that by midnight, at least, we would be off the wharf here. About twenty miles above this city, however, we came near to the great body of ice with which the channel is choked up, and the master and pilot judged it prudent to turn about and anchor in what was considered a safe place several miles up the river. Late in the night we cast anchor in clear, smooth water;

the Lady having previously anchored not far above us. We neither saw nor dreamt of the bay of ice that afterwards bore down upon us with the ebb of the tide. The passengers and the crew numbered, perhaps, upwards of fifty persons, five or six being women, one with a child only nine weeks old. There were about fourteen in the upper cabin with me, and the wife of Mr. Collins, an Englishman, from Oxford, occupied the ladies' cabin below ours. By eleven the passengers were all in bed, except Mr. Lalanne, of Montreal, and myself. At midnight Mr. L—— also retired, and I sat above another hour reading a book that interested me. Mr. Lyman had only lain down with his clothes on, such were his just apprehensions. I took the candle about one in the morning, went round the vessel; found all well; no appearance of storm or danger; I then stripped, went to bed, and fell fast asleep. At two o'clock Mr. Lyman and other passengers awaked me, said we were in danger, that the ice had come down upon us and was driving us among the ice above Cap Rouge, where in all probability, we should be lost. The ice made a dreadful din, but I confess I apprehended nothing, so went asleep again, and was again awaked. We had dragged one anchor, and lost the other, and had drifted into the midst of the ice. The vessel had become unmanageable. The efforts of the crew to back her out were useless, the cables being in the ice. For three hours before the wreck several passengers had declared their conviction that we would all go to the bottom, but I lay still in my berth and listened to their arguments *pro* and *con* until half-past five. In a moment. as it were, a

vast mass of ice came down upon her with a tremen-
dous force; the engine instantly stopped, and in less
than a minute she filled. I jumped up in my shirt,
caught hold of my trowsers and overshoes, and was
soon on a large cake of ice on which they had hauled
the ship's boat and a bark canoe. The passengers had
all previously gone upon the ice, and were stepping
from island to island, or rather from hill to hill, and
from valley to valley of ice, endeavoring to make the
shore, which was about a mile distant. Capt. Perry,
his mate, and some of his people remained with the
boat, near to the wreck, which at that time had been
left by all, it being supposed that she would suddenly
be engulphed by reason of the very heavy cargo and
the weight of her engine. After helping to haul the
boat a little farther on· the ice, I went close to the
steamer, observed that the water ceased to make as at
first, and returning to Capt. Perry took his advice as
to the chance I had of going down if I returned for
my clothes and baggage. He thought I might venture, and in a moment I was on board; got my watch
and pocket-book from under my pillow; seized hold
of my saddle-bags, valise, great coat, and other
clothes, and·without hat or boots made for the land.
It was a difficult task, but I was last, and the track
of the feet of others often guided me when I could
see no one. The tide was then making, and the
water in several places gushed up through the rent
and rotten ice as if it would forever stop my progress. In one hole I was nearly up to the neck in
water, and as my overshoes would not stay on my
feet, I added them to my luggage, of which I was

heartily tired. At length I came up with Mr. Lyman and a poor woman who had almost given in and was weeping bitterly. Mr. L——'s leg had been broken during the Montreal Tailors' Riot of last summer, by a stone thrown by a tailor, and he found walking very difficult. I kept company with him and the woman until by the good providence of God and the wonderful bridge of ice he had that morning provided for us his humble creatures, we all got safe to land at the village of St. Nicholas, the property of Sir John Caldwell, about sixteen miles above this city. I was quite hoarse with cold, and very much fatigued, for no other passenger had ventured to stop for his baggage. Seeing, however, from the shore that the vessel was still above water, and correctly judging that she was supported by the ice that had got under her wings, the passengers offered rewards to the Canadian peasants to bring baggage ashore. With their efficient aid, the assistance of Mr. Sutton, a most hospitable and friendly man who resides in the seigniorial house at St. Nicholas; the advice of the parish priest, Mr. Dufresne, who took an active, lively interest on behalf of the wrecked; and of the captain, mate, and seamen, (all of whom I admired for their coolness and deliberation,) nearly all of the upper cabin furniture, and bedding, the most of the passengers' baggage, and the boat's books and papers were saved. Among the rest of the odds and ends my hat and boots made their appearance, the latter well soaked in water. * * *

"I must not omit to state that the sterling honesty of the Canadians in humble life never appeared to me in a fairer light than in their transactions of the morn-

ing of the shipwreck. Not one pin's value of property did the humblest of their peasants or peasants'
boys attempt to secrete or claim. No! It was de-
lightful to see the little fellows one by one come up
to Mr. Sutton's with their loads and lay them down
among the baggage, without even claiming praise for
their exertions. Had some of our legislators, who
made invidious comparisons between the Upper and
Lower Canadas last winter in the Assembly been with
me to see the benevolent creatures exert themselves
on our behalf, they would certainly have felt ashamed
of their censures."

There is one incident connected with the landing
of the passengers, not mentioned in this letter, which
Mr. Mackenzie often related. The poor woman whom
he overtook, in company with Mr. Lyman, was unable to jump from one piece of Ice to another, or
was afraid to venture. Mr. Mackenzie threw himself across the breach, and she walked over upon his
body!

208

Fac simile of a Gold Medal presented to Mr. William Lyon Mackenzie by his constituents, on his re-election, after his first expulsion from the Legislative Assembly of Upper Canada.

CHAPTER XIV.

First Expulsion of Mr. Mackenzie from the House for an alleged Libel and Breach of Privilege—His Defence—Partial Character of the Proceedings against him—Libels on the previous House complimented by the Lieutenant Governor—Mackenzie's Defence voted an Aggravation of his Offence—The House refuses to inquire whether any one else has Libelled them during the Session—Libellous Language of the Crown Officers—The Feeling excited by these Proceedings—Petitioners go in a body to the Government House—Fears of the Government shown by Military Preparations—The Expelled Member carried triumphantly through the Streets, amid the Acclamations of the Populace—Public Meeting resolve to present the Expelled Member with a Gold Medal in Approbation of his Political Career—His Re-election —His Opponent gets One Vote—Gold Medal and Chain Presented.

In the last session, the attempted expulsion of Mr. Mackenzie had failed. The pretext adduced to excuse the proposal was so flimsy and untenable that a majority of the House shrank from committing themselves to it. A new crime had been invented, and a new pretext found. Before it was a breach of privilege, for distributing the journals of the House; now it was a libel, constituting a breach of privilege. The House met on the 17th November, 1831, and on the 6th December Mr. Mackenzie's first expulsion was proposed. The proceedings were initiated by a flourish about the privileges of Parliament; the intention

27

being to justify an outrage which it was proposed to
perpetrate in their name. The ball was opened by
Mr. John Wilson, a late Speaker of the House, supported by Mr. Burwell, against whose motion to create
a pension, in the previous session, Mr. Mackenzie had
roused an uncontrollable feeling in the galleries. This
preliminary motion affirmed, "that the privileges of
Parliament were established for the support and
maintenance of the independent and fearless discharge
of its high functions, and that it is to the uncompromising assertion and maintenance of these privileges in
the earliest periods of English history, that we are
chiefly indebted for the free institutions which have
been transmitted to us by our ancestors." Mr. Bidwell, seconded by Mr. Perry, with a view of showing
the animus of the proceedings, moved in amendment
that so much of the journals as related to the previous
attempt at expulsion be read; but in a House of forty
members he was beaten by a majority of ten. Mr.
Bidwell returned to the charge, proposing to amend
the resolution so as to give credit to "a free
press, in modern and enlightened times, notwithstanding the many different attempts to destroy its
liberty," a share in the preservation of the free institutions transmitted to us by our ancestors. This
amendment being rejected, on a vote of twenty-four
against sixteen, another amendment, embodying an
extract from the *Colonial Advocate* of the 24th November, 1831, and another of the 1st December, was
moved. It had for sponsors Mr. Samson and Mr.
Thomson, the latter of whom was proprietor of the
Kingston *Herald*, a paper opposed in politics to Mr.

Mackenzie.* The first of these articles was a mere summary of the proceedings of the House on the sub-

* The amendment was as follows:—"That an article published in the newspaper called the *Colonial Advocate*, of date the 24th of November, 1831, in the following words:

"'STATE OF THE COLONY.—The people of this Province will probably be able to form a tolerably fair estimate of the manner in which their petitions on public affairs are likely to be treated in the Representative branch of the Legislature, when they learn the manner in which the first of the series has been disposed of. The petition of the people of Vaughan, unanimously agreed upon at their town-meeting, and signed by the chairman, secretary, and from two to three hundred freeholders and other inhabitants, was the first presented to the House; and after it had been read and had lain two days on the table, Mr. Mackenzie, a representative of the people from whom it came, moved that it should be referred to a committee of five members, viz: Mr. Ketchum, the other member for the county in which the petition was voted, and Messrs Buell, Perry, and Shaver, with the mover, as a matter of course. Mr. Thomson, of Frontenac, the editor of the Kingston *Herald*, who had previously expressed great bitterness against the petitioners and their petition, in the public journals, immediately rose and objected to referring the petition to its friends, and allowing them to consider of and introduce any measures desired by the petitioners, and which they might consider expedient, to the notice of the Legislature. We told the people of York last July, that this would be the result of any application to the Assembly; and therefore the more earnestly requesting them to unite in addressing the King's Government, as by this means distinct propositions could be submitted to a new Assembly, called, as in England, on the Reform Bill. We now urge all those entrusted with the general petitions to the King and House of Assembly, to send them to York, by mail, on the earliest possible day, in order that the former be forwarded to London, and the latter submitted to the Assembly, now in session. We learn that Chief Justice Robinson's successor in the law business, Mr. Draper, either has gone off this week to London, or is now about to set off, to oppose the general petitions, and advocate the interests of the Executive faction here, with His Majesty's Government. They take the utmost pains to conceal their weakness in the estimation of the country, and one of their ablest assistants leaves his own private business and prospects, to watch the signs of the times at home. Mr. Thomson's amendment, already spoken of, was a resolution, 'that the petition of the people of Vaughan, with all other petitions relating to the same subject, be referred to a select committee of seven members, to be chosen at twelve o'clock to-morrow.' The Attorney General characterized the petitions as, 'the expression of a few people,' 'a few individuals,' 'mere casual meetings,' 'he happened to have seen some of these meetings, but a few respectable

ples of greater severity of denunciation. At the distance of less than a quarter of a century, we look back with amazement at the paltry passions and narrow judgment that could construe these articles into libels on the House, constituting a breach of privilege, for which nothing less than ignominious expulsion of the author would be a fitting or adequate punishment.

When the charge had been put into a tangible shape, the accused member was asked to avow or disavow the authorship of the alleged libels. He promptly accepted the responsibility of the articles, both as author and publisher. The Speaker, being appealed to, decided that Mr. Mackenzie had a right to be heard in his own defence. The latter then proceeded to address the House; but before he had concluded, an adjournment took place. Next day, Mr. Bidwell moved for a committee to inquire whether any libels had been published on the House during the session. The motion was declared to be out of order. The Speaker also announced that he had given an erroneous decision, on the previous day, in giving the accused the right of self-defence. But Mr. Mackenzie was allowed to proceed. He denied the jurisdiction of the House, in prosecutions for libel; they could not, he argued, be a fit tribunal in a case where they would occupy the impossible position of complainant, judge, and jury. If they complained of libel, they could address the Lieutenant Governor to order the

Province, as to the proceedings and motives of their representatives; and is, therefore, a breach of the privileges of this House. And W. L. Mackenzie, having avowed the authorship of the said articles, be now called upon for his defence."

crown officers to institute legal proceedings.* Upon the charge brought against him, he was entitled to, and he demanded, a legal trial before a jury of his country.

So much did Mr. Mackenzie urge against the judicial fairness of the proceeding. It must be admitted, however, the strongest point he made was not by the use of arguments which tended to question the competency of the tribunal; but in demonstrating the partial and one-sided nature of the proceedings.† He was not the only member of the House who published a newspaper; and others had, in speaking of the proceedings of the Assembly, used much harsher language than he had. But the truth was, one party was permitted any latitude of language, in dealing with their opponents. This had been apparent in the prosecution of Collins, and the menaced proceedings against Mackenzie, while the newspaper organs of the official party were left undisturbed in their carnival of unmeasured abuse of opponents. It was the policy of tying the hands of your antagonist, and then setting your fiercest hounds upon him.

The Lieutenant Governor, whose nod would have been sufficient to quash these proceedings in a House swarming with placemen and dependents on the Executive, had received "with much pleasure," a petition from certain "gentlemen," residing in the county of Durham, in which the previous House was spoken of as "a band of factious demagogues, whose acts per-

* This was done in the case of Wilkes, whose expulsion was not pronounced until it was found that he had absconded.

† See Appendix B.

. ceptibly tend to disorganize society, to subvert legitimate authority, and to alienate men's minds from constitutional government." And in another part of the
document thus graciously received, the Assembly was
described as being composed of " unprincipled and
designing men ;" deluders " under the dark mantle of
specious patriotism."

So far as related to the decision of the House, it
was to no purpose that Mr. Mackenzie exposed the
gross partiality of these discreditable proceedings.
The majority had marked their victim, and no argument that could be used would induce them to forego
the sacrifice.

At half past five o'clock on the evening of the 9th
of December, Mr. Mackenzie, having closed his defence, retired from the House, leaving the majority to
act unembarrassed by his presence. No vote was
taken that night. Next day, Mr. Perry, seconded by
Mr. Cook, moved that the order of the day on the
question of privilege be discharged. He obtained but
fifteen votes against twenty-seven. This was the third
division on the proceedings, and it was in complete
harmony with the two which had taken place before
Mr. Mackenzie had made his defence. Attorney General Boulton, who seems to have feared that Mr. Mackenzie would renew his defence, moved to amend Mr.
Samson's resolution by striking out the order for hearing the accused in his defence ; and it was carried by the
same party majority that had voted down Mr. Perry's
amendment. On the same day, the House acting
as accuser, judge, and jury, declared Mr. Mackenzie
guilty of libel. The vote was precisely the same as

on the two previous divisions—twenty-seven against fifteen—a fact which shows, in the strongest light, how incapable was this partisan tribunal of deciding fairly upon a question of libel. By a party vote Mr. Mackenzie's guilt had been pronounced; by a party vote he was to be expelled.

On the 12th December—Sunday having intervened since the last proceedings on the subject—on motion of Mr. Samson, seconded by Mr. McNab, the House declared the defence of Mr. Mackenzie to be a gross aggravation of the charge brought against him, and that "he was guilty of a high breach of the privileges of this House."* They refused to strike a committee to

---

* "MONDAY, *December* 12, 1831.

"Mr. Samson, seconded by Mr. McNab, moves, That it be resolved that William Lyon Mackenzie, Esq., a member of this House, having avowed himself the author of the articles published in the newspaper, called the *Colonial Advocate*, mentioned in the resolution of this House on Saturday last—which articles are grossly false, scandalous, and defamatory—and having been heard in his place in defence of the same, has by the whole tenor of such defence flagrantly aggravated the charge brought against him, and is therefore guilty of a high breach of the privileges of this House. [The word 'therefore' was afterwards struck out.]

"In amendment, Mr. Perry, seconded by Mr. Lyons, moves, that after the word Resolved, in the original, the whole be expunged, and the following words inserted: 'That as this House has allowed many other publications to pass without punishment or censure, reflecting on the character and motives of its members for many years past, and as addresses to the head of the Provincial government for the time being have been published in the *Official Gazette*, containing such reflections with answers of His Excellency, the then Lieutenant Governor, expressing his thanks for such addresses, and as this House has, by the resolution adopted on Saturday last, asserted its privileges, and shown its determination hereafter to take notice of such offensive publications, it is not expedient to take any further notice of the said libels published in the *Colonial Advocate*."

"On which the House divided.

"YEAS—Messrs. Beardsley, Bidwell, Buell, Campbell, Clark, Cook, Howard, Ketchum, Lyons, McCall, Perry, Randal, Roblin, and Shaver—14.

28

inquire whether any other libels upon them had been published since the commencement of the session.

" NAYS—Messrs. Attorney General, Berczy, Burwell, Boulton, Brown, Duncombe, Elliott, Fraser A., Fraser R., Ingersoll, Jones, Lewis, McNab, McMartin, Maçon, Morris, Mount, Robinson, Samson, Shade, Solicitor General, Thomson, Vankoughnet, Warren, Werden, and Wilson W.—26.

Then the question was taken on that resolution, whether Mr. Mackenzie's defence was an additional offence; and the twenty-six members who had voted against Messrs. Perry and Lyons' amendment, as above stated, voted that it was. The fourteen who had voted for Messrs. P. & L.'s amendment voted that it was not. Question carried—found guilty of the defence by a majority of twelve.

" Mr. Samson, seconded by Mr. Asa Werden, moved that it be resolved, that William Lyon Mackenzie, Esq., be expelled this House.

" In amendment, Mr. Perry, seconded by Mr. Lyons, moves, that after the word ' moves,' in the original, the whole be expunged, and the following inserted: ' That this House having fully asserted its privileges by resolving some particular remarks contained in the *Colonial Advocate* of the 24th of November and of the 1st of December, reflecting on the proceedings of this Assembly, and some of its members, to be a libel, and a high breach of the privileges of this House, it is expedient to appoint a Committee of Privilege to inquire and report to this House what other, if any, libels have been published against the proceedings of this House, or any of its members, since the commencement of this present session, and that Messrs. Attorney General, Berczy, Duncombe, Beardsley, and Ketchum do compose said committee.'

" On which the House divided.

" YEAS—Beardsley, Bidwell, Buell, Campbell, Clark, Cook, Howard, Ketchum, Lyons, McCall, Perry, Randal, Roblin, Shaver—14.

" NAYS—Attorney General, Berczy, Boulton, Brown, Burwell, Duncombe, Elliott, Fraser A., Fraser R., Ingersoll, Jones, Lewis, McMartin, McNab, Maçon, Morris, Mount, Robinson, Samson, Shade, Solicitor General, Thomson, Vankoughnet, Werden—24.

" The amendment was lost by a majority of ten.

" In amendment to Mr. Samson's motion for the expulsion of W. L. Mackenzie, Esq., Mr. Duncombe moves, that after the word ' moves,' in the original motion, the whole be expunged, and the following be inserted, ' *Resolved*, That William Lyon Mackenzie, Esq., be called to the bar of this House, and that he be reprimanded by the Speaker. Yeas, 7. Nays, 31.

" On the original question the House divided, and the yeas and nays were as follows :—

" FOR EXPELLING MR. MACKENZIE.—Messrs. Attorney General, Berczy, Boulton, Brown, Burwell, Elliott, Fraser A., Fraser R., Ingersoll, Jones,

The majority had no idea of exercising their tyranny in an impartial manner. Their object was to sacrifice their opponents; not to deal out the same measure of punishment to their friends. Among those who would have been found guilty, if the inquiry had been pushed, were some of Mr. Mackenzie's accusers and judges. The vote for expulsion stood twenty-four against fifteen, and there were four absent members belonging to the official party, all of whom would, if present, have borne true allegiance on this occasion.

Attorney General Boulton, acting as prosecuting counsel on behalf of the majority, described the accused as a "reptile;" and Solicitor General Hagerman varied the description to "a spaniel dog." His accusers and judges affected to regard his censure as equivalent to praise; while taking the most extraordinary pains to prove by their acts that they believed precisely the contrary.

The Imperial Parliament has, times innumerable, punished individuals for libels upon either House. A libel upon an individual member has always been treated as a libel upon the whole body to which he belonged. Admitting the force of English precedent, Mr. Mackenzie, if guilty of libel upon the House, was liable to punishment. But the articles complained of as libellous, in his case, can hardly be said to have

Lewis, McMartin, McNab, Maçon, Morris, Mount, Robinson, Samson, Shade, Solicitor General, Thomson, Vankoughnet, Warren, Werden—24.

"AGAINST THE EXPULSION.—Messrs. Beardsley, Bidwell, Buell, Campbell, Clark, Cook, Duncombe, Howard, Ketchum, Lyons, McCall, Perry, Randal, Roblin, Shaver—15."

The *Courier*, an organ of the official party, announced that Messrs. Wilson, Cook, Chisholm, and Jarvis, who were absent, would, if present, have voted for the expulsion.

exceeded the legitimate bounds of discussion; and they were not nearly so bad as many others which the House thought it proper to overlook; and of which, indeed, some of the majority concerned in his con- demnation had been guilty. It is this gross partiality, this want of even-handed justice, which renders the proceedings against him so odious. Some of the libels which, in his defence, he showed had been levelled at particular members of the House, through the press, against other members, reflected upon a previous Parliament; but if English precedent be worth any thing, no right is clearer than that of one House to punish for libels upon a previous House. If the Assembly could punish for libel at all, it could punish for libels upon a previous Assembly. The punishment in Mr. Mackenzie's case, was altogether unusual. Deprivation of his seat was wholly unjusti- fiable.

The feeling excited in the unbiassed reader's own mind, as he goes over this recital, will be no safe indi- cation of the degree of public indignation aroused by this atrocious mockery of justice. During the week of the sham trial, petitions to the Lieutenant Governor were numerously signed, praying him to dismiss a House tainted with the worst vices of judicial par- tiality. For the result had been foreseen by the preliminary divisions. On the day of the expulsion, a deputation from the petitioners waited upon the Governor's private secretary, and informed him that next day, at two o'clock, a number of the petitioners would go to Government House in a body, to receive his Excellency's reply. At the appointed hour, nine

hundred and thirty persons proceeded to fulfil their
mission. They were received in the audience chamber;
and the petition having been presented, they were
dismissed with the studiously curt reply: "Gentlemen,
I have received the petition of the inhabitants."

But the precautions taken betrayed the fears of the
Government. "The Government House," says Mr.
Mackenzie, in a fragment of manuscript relating to
the event, "was protected with cannon, loaded, served,
and ready to be fired on the people; the regiment in
garrison was supplied with a double allowance of ball
cartridges, and a telegraph placed on the viceroyal
residence to command the services of the soldiers if
necessary." There were even then some who urged
an appeal to force; and the strange supposition seems
to have been entertained that the Scotch soldiers
would not fire upon them.* Mackenzie checked the
impetuosity of the more ardent spirits, who advised
violent measures. He had strong confidence in the
disposition of the new Reform ministry in England, to
do justice to the Province; and he inculcated the necessity of patience.

What his enemies intended to make the day of his
humiliation and ruin, proved the day of his triumph.
The violence exercised toward him by the dominant
faction won for him the sympathies of the people.
After the return of the petitioners from the Govern-
ment House, they proceeded to the residence of Mr.
Mackenzie, in Richmond street, largely reinforced.
The man rejected by the Assembly, as a libeller, was

* I find that even now some of the active men of those times are still of this
opinion; and speak in a tone of the greatest confidence.

carried through the streets amidst the acclamations of the populace, who took this emphatic way of testifying their approbation of his conduct, and of their determination to uphold the rights of a free press, which they felt had been outraged in his person. Among other places, the procession stopped at the Parliament House and cheered. They were cheers of triumph and defiance; telling how quickly the decision of the Assembly had been reversed by that public opinion, to which all elective bodies are ultimately accountable. At the office of the *Guardian* newspaper, then edited by the Rev. Egerton Ryerson, who had warmly espoused the cause of Mr. Mackenzie, the procession halted to give three cheers. From a window of the Sun Hotel, Mr. Mackenzie addressed the people; and cheers were given for the "Sailor King," and for Earl Grey and the Reform ministry. When Mr. Mackenzie had retired, the meeting was reorganized, and resolutions were passed, sustaining the course he had taken as a politician and a journalist; complaining of the reply of the Lieutenant Governor to the petitioners as unsatisfactory and insulting; asserting the propriety of petitioning the Sovereign to send to the Province, in future, civil instead of military Governors; and pledging the meeting, as a mark of their approbation of his conduct, to present Mr. Mackenzie with "a gold medal accompanied by an appropriate inscription and address."

At the same sitting at which the expulsion of Mr. Mackenzie had been decreed, the House had ordered the issue of a new writ for the election of a member in his place. The election was held at the Red Lion

Inn, Yonge street, on the 2nd of January. By what accident it is not necessary to determine, the election took place on the same day on which the town meetings were held throughout the county ; but in spite of this coincidence over two thousand persons were present. There was a show of opposition made to the re-election of Mr. Mackenzie; but any thing so pitiful had seldom been witnessed. Mr. Street was nominated by Mr. Edward Thomson, and supported by the influence of Mr. Washburn, a candidate at the previous election. Forty sleighs had come into town in the morning to escort Mr. Mackenzie to the polling place. An hour and a half after the poll opened, Mr. Street, having received only one vote, against one hundred and nineteen cast for Mr. Mackenzie, abandoned the hopeless contest.

After the close of the poll, came the presentation of the gold medal. It cost $250, and was accounted "a superb piece of workmanship." The medal and chain weighed one hundred and eighty-two dwts., or over nine ounces. On one side were the rose, the thistle, and the shamrock, encircled by the words, " His Majesty King William IV., the people's friend." On the reverse was the inscription : " Presented to William L. Mackenzie, Esq., by his constituents of the county of York, U. C., as a token of their approbation of his political career, January 2, 1832." The massive cable chain, attached to the medal, contained forty links of about one inch each in length.

CHAPTER XV.

Triumphal Entry into York—A Body of Electors force through the outer door
of the Legislative Building—Commotion in the Galleries, on a motion for
Re-expulsion being made—Solicitor General Hagerman prevails upon the
House to declare a Disability unknown to the Law—One hour for the Accused to make his Defence—The Abuse of Privilege—Specimen of a Solicitor General's powers of Vituperation—Mackenzie's Defence cut short by
the Speaker and the House—The Legislative Council call on the House to
afford it Reparation for an alleged Libel—Impassioned Appeal to the Electors of York—Re-election after the Second Expulsion—Proposed Address
for Dissolution—Bank Bills carried in Mackenzie's absence.

THE return to York was a triumphal procession.
An immense sleigh, belonging to Mr. Montgomery,
constructed with an upper story, carried, besides the
members elect, over twenty others, with a couple of
Scottish pipers. Over fifty sleighs joined the procession, which numbered over a thousand persons.
A small printing press, emblematic of the instrument
of victory, kept in order by the warmth of a fur-
nace, was throwing off impressions as the monster
sleigh moved along. Among the numerous flags
that surmounted the sleigh carrying the re-elected
member, one bore the device, "The Liberty of the
Press;" another, "Mackenzie and the People." As
Government House and the Parliament Building were
passed, the deafening cheers of the throng announced
the reversal of the decision of the House of Assem-

bly, by the freeholders of the county of York. Several soldiers of the 79th regiment went to the election,
and rode back on the sleighs. They appear to have
gone for the purpose of enjoying the excitement; and
as their presence was contrary to law, the government
papers strongly censured the commanding officer for
permitting them to attend.

When Mr. Mackenzie returned to the House, with
the unanimous approbation of his constituents, the
question of re-expulsion was immediately brought up.*

* " HOUSE OF ASSEMBLY. Tuesday, *January 3rd*, 1832.

" On the Speaker announcing to the House the return of WILLIAM LYON
MACKENZIE, Esquire, a member for the county of York—

" Mr. Vankoughnet, seconded by Mr. McNab, moved " That it be resolved,
that the entries on the Journals of the 12th December last, relating to the expulsion of William Lyon Mackenzie, Esq., be now read.

Mr. Vankoughnet also read to the House the two following resolutions,
which he declared to contain the object he had in view by moving the above
resolve :

" Mr. Vankoughnet, seconded by Mr. McNab, moves that William Lyon
Mackenzie, Esq., returned a member to represent the county of York in Provincial Parliament, having been expelled this House during this present
session for the publication of certain gross, scandalous, and malicious libels, intended and calculated to bring this House and the Government of the Province
into contempt, and excite groundless suspicion and distrust in the minds of the
inhabitants of the Province, as to the proceedings and motives of their Representatives ; and having made no reparation or atonement for his said offence,
but on the contrary, in the interval between his said expulsion and subsequent
re-election, having, in a certain newspaper called the *Colonial Advocate*, of
which he, the said William Lyon Mackenzie, has avowed himself the proprietor,
and responsible for the matter therein published, endeavored to justify and
maintain the said gross, scandalous, and malicious libels, in high contempt of
this House and its privileges ; he, the said William Lyon Mackenzie, is unfit
and unworthy to be a member of this House, and that his seat therein be therefore declared vacant.

" Mr. Vankoughnet, seconded by Mr. McNab, moves that it be resolved,
That the Speaker of this House do issue his Warrant to the Clerk of the Crown
in Chancery, for a new writ for the election of a member to serve in the present Parliament as Representative of the county of York, in the stead of the

29

While he stood at the bar of the House, waiting to be sworn in, Messrs. Vankoughnet and McNab raised the question, but the majority of the House seemed disinclined to incur the odium of a second expulsion; an amendment to proceed to the order of the day being carried by a vote of twenty-four against twenty. The motion was met by hisses below the bar, which were only suppressed by a threat to clear the House of strangers. The crowd of voters who had accompanied their re-elected representative to York, pushed their way into the House. An attempt was made to prevent their entering the lobby; but they forced through the outer door and got in.

The movers in the business had not put the case very skilfully. They had complained of alleged libels, as calculated to bring the government as well as the House into contempt; as if the House, in addition to being the guardian of its own privileges, had also been a constitutional screen for the protection of the government from censure. No new libel was charged;

said William Lyon Mackenzie, who has been declared unfit and unworthy to be a member of this House.'

"In amendment to Messrs. Vankoughnet and McNab's first resolution, Mr. Perry moved, in substance, that the House should proceed to the other ordinary business of the day, and drop all further proceedings in the libel case.

" In favor of dropping the proceedings, and against Mr. Vankoughnet's resolutions, voted Messrs. Attorney General, Beardsley, Bidwell, Buell, Campbell, Clark, Cook, Duncombe, Howard, Ingersoll, Ketchum, Lyons, McCall, McDonald, A., McDonald, D., Morris, Norton, Perry, Randal, Roblin, Samson, Shaver, Willson, W., and Warren—24.

For proceeding with Mr. Vankoughnet's resolutions for re-expelling Mr. Mackenzie, or rather of preventing him from taking his seat, and ordering a new election, (he having declared that step to be the object of his first resolve,) voted Messrs. Berczy, G. Boulton, Brown, Burwell, Crooks, Elliott, Fraser, A., Jarvis, Jones, McMartin, McNab, Maçon, Mount, Robinson, Shade, Solicitor General, Thomson, Chisholm, Vankoughnet, and Werden—20.

and the only offence that concerned the House consisted of an attempt to justify what the majority had
previously voted a libel and a breach of privilege.
The question raised was rather one of disability than
of any new offence. It was probably owing to the
fact that the majority saw this ground to be untenable
that they refused to sanction the motion. The House
had an undoubted right to expel any member for adequate cause; but it had no right to create a disability
unknown to the law.

Solicitor General Hagerman, who appears to have
known more of Parliamentary law than either Mr.
Vankoughnet or Mr. McNab, felt that it was necessary, in bringing up the question of the re-expulsion, to
go upon the ground of a new libel upon the House.
He therefore moved, January 6th, a resolution declaring certain matter which had appeared in the *Colonial
Advocate* of the previous day,* and of which Mr.

* The following are the only passages that reflect upon the House:—

"I have charged the present House of Assembly with sycophancy, in my capacity of a public journalist; I here before you and in the face of the world
reiterate that charge, as applied to the majority of its members.

"They have passed, at the request of the local Executive, and contrary to
British Constitutional principle, the everlasting salary bill; refusing at the
same time to limit its operation to the present reign; refusing to provide for
the independence of the judges on the Executive, while they secured to them
for ever the most extravagant incomes; refusing also to inquire into the
wasteful and dangerous system of applying the greater part of the revenue by
a power unknown to the constitution; refusing to exclude the judges from
seats in the Legislative and Executive Council; refusing to exclude bishops,
archdeacons, and gospel preachers from seats in the Executive Council; and
refusing to curtail the extravagance of the Council clerk, and the unjust
charges of the Crown officers, before these officers had voted themselves and
their successors, and the said clerk and his successors, incomes out of the taxes
for ever.

"They have imitated the Legislative Council in squandering your revenues

Mackenzie admitted himself to be the author, to be a false, scandalous, and malicious libel upon the House

under the head of contingencies ; they double and treble the incomes of some of their servants, grant the most extraordinary demands for services, carelessly examine accounts, and openly vote down, session after session, ordinary motions of inquiry into the items of expense which compose the thousands of pounds demanded in a lump from time to time as contingencies by the Legislative Council.   Adding together the probable incidental charges of the two Houses, from March last until March next, we shall have about £9,000.   And as the whole expense of their sittings, £25,000.   The Legislature of Vermont costs annually about half as many dollars, including the salary of Governor, judges, and all other charges ; yet the population of Vermont exceeds ours.

"They allowed the St. Lawrence to remain unimproved, although its being made navigable would have benefitted everybody ; and neglected further to encourage education, although the people cried out for it ; they put a negative in their first session upon the bill for distribution of intestate estate, although Upper Canada had but one voice in its favor ; they delayed and refused to pass the Clergy Reserve address in the same session, lest (as they said) the petitioners by Mr. Ryerson should profit by it ; and found, nevertheless, £50,000 to expend on Welland Canal, an unprofitable undertaking, *a job* prematurely gone into for the advantage of a few officers of this government, legislative counsellors, and speculators in waste lands.

"They neglected your numerous petitions, presented by myself and other friendly members, praying for the passage of many salutary enactments, or delivered them into the custody and safe keeping of placemen, by whom I had been personally insulted and defamed as a rebel and traitor ; and by this means prevented several useful bills being introduced into the House on your petitions.

"They passed the obnoxious York Market Bill in opposition to your petitions; and in defiance of the protestations of your members, they negatived and condemned the principle of voting by ballot ; they disapproved by their votes of the excellent principle of regulating by law the sales of all public or Crown lands, and preferred the present secret or corrupt system ; they refused to censure the Lieutenant Governor for keeping back this election twenty-one days instead of eight, in order that it might interfere with your town-meetings and delay my return ; they refused to inquire into the Tea Monopoly, by which you are so heavily taxed; they refused to remonstrate against the principle of the trade act of last April, so deeply affecting your interests ; they allow the important statements respecting extravagant pensions, salaries, fees, and law charges to slumber on their shelves, and thereby increase the incomes of attorneys, bailiffs, sheriffs, and other public functionaries at the expense of justice and good government; they neglect to inquire into the details of the many

of Assembly, and a high breach of its privileges; that
the author be expelled the House, and declared unworthy to hold a seat therein.* Mr. Hagerman had

thousands of pounds granted for road and bridge improvements; they neglect
to inquire into the whole provincial expenditure, and to provide due checks on
the revenue officers; they propose to double the power of the political bank at
this place, and they get rid of motions for inquiring into the state of its affairs
by motions for adjournment.

" They appoint committees on the state of the representation of the people
in their own House, and refuse to allow said committees to report.

" They get rid of bills for the general regulation of Banking; revenue inquiries; bank inquiries; inquiries into salaries, incomes, fees, and perquisites;
bills to amend the representation; inquiries into fines, forfeitures, seizures, and
the application of the same, and of your opposition to destructive monopolies, by
summarily expelling a member you sent to attend to these matters.

" They (the said majority) are chiefly placemen, during pleasure, such as
sheriffs, crown lawyers, postmasters, judges, registrars, custom-house officers,
military men on half pay or retired allowances, collectors of the customs elect,
&c., &c., who receive from the government six if not ten times the amount they
obtained from the people as legislators. They are the enemies of free discussion through the press, although such free discussion of the conduct of public
men is your best guarantee for the preservation of the rights of freemen."

* "JANUARY 6, 1832.—Mr. Solicitor General, seconded by Mr. Elliott,
moves that it be resolved, That William Lyon Mackenzie, Esq., a member
returned to represent the county of York, in Provincial Parliament, has been
expelled this House during the present session for the publication of certain
gross, scandalous, and malicious libels, intended and calculated to bring this
House and the Government of this Province into contempt, and to excite
groundless suspicion and distrust in the minds of the inhabitants of the Province as to the proceedings and motives of their representatives.

" That since his re-election, in a certain newspaper called the *Colonial Advocate*, dated 5th January, instant, in an article therein published, entitled,
'Articles of Impeachment, or public accusations read and submitted to the
consideration of the electors of the county of York, in County Court assembled, on Monday, January 2, 1832, by Mr. Mackenzie, their late member,
against the Lieutenant Governor and the advisers of the Crown,' of which he
has avowed himself the author, has, in high contempt of this House and its
privileges, not only re-asserted the said gross, scandalous, and malicious libel,
for which he, the said William Lyon Mackenzie, had been expelled; but hath
also in the said articles endeavored, by false, scandalous, and malicious representations, to cause His Majesty's subjects of this Province to believe that the

the prudence to leave out of view the general censures on the Executive Council, and the demand for the dismissal of himself and Attorney General Boulton, which were to be found in the article, part of which he brought forward as a ground for expelling the author from the House. It is not to be supposed, however, that he was insensible to these reflections; and the Imperial Goverment afterwards took the advice of Mr. Mackenzie to dismiss both these functionaries. One of the principal grounds of that dismissal was the part they took in the expulsion of a political opponent from the House, upon pretexts that were deemed to be constitutionally untenable.

Only one hour was given to Mr. Mackenzie to prepare his defence, during which the House adjourned. On its re-assembling, the clerk, at the request of the accused, read the whole of the article—part of which was complained of as a libel upon the House—extending to more than five newspaper columns.

majority of their Representatives should be held in execration and abhorrence by posterity, as enemies to the liberties of the people they represent—as persons who would, by violent and unconstitutional means, destroy the liberty of the press, and convert the fifty members of which the House is composed into tyrants in close and unholy alliance with trained bands of public robbers:— Wherefore, It is resolved that the said William Lyon Mackenzie be expelled this House, and declared unfit and unworthy to hold a seat therein.

"In amendment, Mr. McNab, seconded by Mr. Vankoughnet, moves, that after the word 'therein,' the following be added, 'during the present session of Parliament.'

"Debates ensued, and the House adjourned."

"SATURDAY, JANUARY 7, 1832.—Mr. Perry, seconded by Mr. Shaver, moves that so much of the order of the day as relates to the question of privilege be discharged. Lost—Yeas 17, Nays 22.

"Mr. McNab's amendment (see above, Jan. 6,) was then carried. Nays 19, Yeas 27.

"The final question, as thus amended, was then carried. Yeas 27, Nays 19.

Such an article would not now arrest the attention of the House; much less cause its author to be punished for libel, in any shape. Whether, technically speaking, it was libellous or not, it was far less so than many articles in other newspapers, some of them written by members of the Assembly, and of which the writers were neither prosecuted in the courts, nor expelled from the House.

Solicitor General Hagerman showed a disposition to carry the abuse of privilege as far as the most despotic sovereign had ever carried the abuse of prerogative. That he had no natural dislike of libels he clearly proved, by the profuse use he made of them under cover of that very privilege in the name of which he asked the expulsion of a fellow member.[*] He described Mr. Mackenzie as "the worst of slanderers," who "would govern by means of the knife, and walk over the bleeding bodies of his victims." Of the minority of the House, he said, if they continued there, they "would continue as slanderers, or supporters of slanderers." "Mr. Mackenzie," he said, when he had closed his defence, "cast a malignant and wicked glare across the House;" and that "at that moment, he left what was most virtuous within the walls, and took away what was the most vile and debased." When, in the course of his defence, Mr. Mackenzie read extracts from the speeches of Sir

---

[*] When the question of Mr. Mackenzie's first expulsion was before the House, Mr. Hagerman, after disclaiming all personal feeling in the premises, said, "he would now vote for Mr. Mackenzie's expulsion; but if he should be re-elected, he would be the first to receive him; he would not interfere with the elective franchise; he would leave to the people the free choice of their representatives."

Francis Burdett, Earl Grey, Lord Brougham, Mr. Macaulay, and others, the Solicitor General exclaimed that they were "base and diabolical." Here were libels a hundred times worse than that against which they were uttered. The difference was, that the Solicitor General, as a member of the House, was treated as a privileged libeller; though assuredly the use of language which from its violence strikes at the very existence of deliberative assemblies, by tending to render all discussion impossible, could hardly be in order.

Mr. Mackenzie attempted to convince the House of its error, by showing that it was setting itself in opposition to public opinion; and pointing in proof to the approbation of his constituents, as shown both by his re-election, and the gold medal that had been presented to him. He then took out of his pocket the massive gold medal, and by means of the enormous chain of the same material suspended it round his neck; declaring that he would wear it while he held his seat, if it were only for an hour. The alleged libel had been read by him at the hustings; and after the electors had heard it, only one person could be found to vote against him. This was pretty strong proof of public opinion, in the metropolitan county of the Province; and no doubt the result would have been the same if the appeal had been to any other populous county in the Province. The county of York had an unequal representation in the House; and the matter would be made worse by depriving it of one of its members. The constituency that had approved his conduct and sent him back was on its trial; and if he were expelled, the electors " would feel it their duty to come to the bar and defend their rights." The Solicitor General objected to the latitude taken by the accused; and the Speaker, being appealed to, declined to interfere; but he expressed a hope that "too great latitude would not be taken." After two or three other attempts on the part of the Solicitor General to stop the defence, on such grounds as that the reading of extracts from the English press to show the degree of liberty allowed there to criticisms upon Parliament, the Speaker declared Mr. Mackenzie out of order. Having appealed against the decision of the Speaker, whom the House sustained by a large majority, Mr. Mackenzie resolved to attempt no more. It was, he said, a farce and a mockery for the House to call on him to make his defence, and then prevent his proceeding. He disdained to attempt any further defence before such a tribunal. He then, according to the report of a journal violently opposed to him, tied up his papers, "after giving them a kick or two to put them in order, and walked out of the House amidst loud cries of 'order' from all sides."

The question was soon settled; the House voting the re-expulsion, by nine o'clock, the second day of the discussion, on a division of twenty-seven against nineteen.*

* YEAS—Messrs. Attorney General, Bercay, G. Boulton, Brown, Burwell, Chisholm, Crooks, Elliott, A. Fraser, Jarvis, Jones, Lewis, Maçon, McMartin, McNab, Morris, Mount, Robinson, Samson, Shade, Solicitor General, Thomson, Vankoughnet, Warren, John Willson, W. Wilson, and Werden—27.

NAYS—Messrs. Beardsley, Bidwell, Buell, Campbell, Clark, Cook, Duncombe, Howard, Ketchum, Lyons, McCall, A. McDonald, D. McDonald, Norton, Perry, Randal, Roblin, Shaver, and White—19. Mr. Ingersoll, who was out of the House, would have voted with the majority.

30

The resolution, forged in the mint of the Solicitor General, went much beyond a mere expulsion. It declared
the expelled member incapable of holding a seat in the
House during that Parliament; thus assuming that a
mere resolution of the House could create a disability
to which nothing short of a specific law could give legal
force.* If the object of Mr. Hagerman had been to
place the House in the wrong, he could not have succeeded more effectually.

On the day that this second expulsion was proposed,
the Legislative Council came to the aid of the Assembly. It complained of being libelled in the same article that had been arraigned in the other branch of the
Legislature ; and instead of addressing the Governor
to order a prosecution of the publisher for libel, it
sent to the Assembly resolutions, containing a "confident reliance" that the House "will view with just
indignation the efforts made by one of their members
for impairing the independence of the Legislative
Council, and diminishing the respect which is due to
them as a part of the constitution of this Province,
and that they will desire to afford reparation to the
Legislative Council for so unwarrantable a breach of
their privileges."† Supposing this complaint of libel to

---

* "If," says May, in his *Constitutional History of England*, "by a vote of the
House a disability, unknown to the law, could be created, any man who became obnoxious might, on some ground or other, be declared incapable. Incapacity would then be declared, not by the law of the land, but by the
arbitrary will of the Commons."

† On the 9th January the House resolved to send a message to the Legislative Council, in answer to its resolutions. "The Solicitor General, seconded
by Mr. Thomson, moves, That it be resolved that the Honorable the Legislative Council be informed that the resolutions of that honorable body of the

have been well-founded, the proper course would have been for the Council to address the Governor to order a prosecution, as was done by the House of Commons, in the case of Wilkes, who was only expelled after he had absconded to France. But there was a very substantial reason for avoiding this course. No conviction could have been obtained.

The alleged libel on the Legislative Council contained some plain truths which could not but grate harshly upon the ears of that Assembly. It also expressed some opinions, regarding which people differed at the time, and a few about which people still differ; but the number is less now than it was then. It was unhappily true that the Legislative Council was crowded with placemen and Executive dependents, and Mr. Mackenzie had the faculty of stating such unpleasant facts in a way calculated to create unpleasant sensations in those whom they affected; but in this case the greater part of the alleged libel consisted of a mere recital of bills rejected by the Second Cham-

6th instant were received at the time this House was engaged in the investigation of charges against the member named in those resolutions for an alleged breach of the privileges of the House of Assembly, which investigation has resulted in the expulsion of the said member as unfit and unworthy to hold a seat in this House, and therefore no further proceedings can be had on the complaint of the Honorable the Legislative Council. On which the House divided, as follows:—

"YEAS—Messrs. Bercsy, Boulton, Brown, Burwell, Chisholm, Crooks, Duncombe, Elliott, Fraser A., Ingersoll, Jarvis, Jones, Lewis, McMartin, McNab, Macon, Morris, Mount, Robinson, Samson, Shade, Solicitor General, Thomson, Warren, Werden, Wilson W.—26.

"NAYS—Messrs. Beardsley, Bidwell, Buell, Campbell, Clark, Cook, Howard, Ketchum, Lyons, McCall, McDonald A., McDonald D., Norton, Perry, Randal, Roblin, Shaver, and White—18.

"Question carried; majority eight."

ber.* Whether these measures were good or bad was a matter of opinion. Mr. Mackenzie thought they

* Here is the alleged libel:—"The Legislative Council is chiefly composed of persons dependent on the Executive government for their salaries, pensions, and fees of office, or who have been selected by that government, upon the principle on which the English Tories have selected peers and bishops for the last forty years, absolute and unlimited servility. It also contains naval and military half-pay officers, Roman Catholic and Protestant bishops, venerable archdeacons, excise officers, and bank directors, and its official organ is the chief criminal judge of the colony. From its very nature and composition it has scarce one feeling or sentiment in common with the country, being the mere breath of the Executive, and an expensive and cumbrous screen to shield that Executive from deserved odium.

"The Legislative Council rarely, if ever, originates any bills of general interest for the advancement of the public prosperity.

"It has, on innumerable occasions, rejected the most wise, salutary laws—laws earnestly desired by the people, and calculated to promote their welfare. Among the measures thus wantonly rejected by the Council since my entrance into the Legislature, I shall particularly enumerate bills for abolishing the law of primogeniture and dividing real estate more equally among the sons and daughters of land-owners who die intestate; for selling a part of the Clergy Reserves for the benefit of the country; for rendering sheriffs and their deputies ineligible to seats in Parliament for places within their jurisdiction; for appointing commissioners to meet commissioners already appointed by Lower Canada, to consider of the regulation of trade, customs' duties, and other matters of mutual interest; for appointing, first, the Hon. J. W. Willis, and, secondly, Mr. Speaker Papineau, to act as a judge in equity and reconsider the case of Mr. Randal's Chaudiere estate; for assigning yards to debtors incarcerated in prison; for facilitating the administration of justice, by removing the grounds on which frequent charges of partiality and corruption, or deep suspicion of corruption, have often been made against sheriffs and coroners for arbitrarily returning and impanelling juries; for excluding the judges from the Legislative and Executive Councils; for relieving Quakers, Mennonists, and Tunkards from the payment of fines for non-performance of militia duty in time of peace; for establishing, on a just and liberal principle, Upper Canada College in this town; for authorizing creditors to sue for debts against the Canada Company; for allowing persons who may be charged with felony, and unable to defend themselves, the benefit of full defence by counsel; for the better regulation of township meetings and the duties of town and township officers; for more fully securing the independence of town members, by granting them the same wages as county members; for stopping the payment of an Episcopalian chaplain when the Assembly no longer required his services; for allowing the people of Kingston to elect municipal officers instead of having

were good, and the expression of that opinion could hardly be considered libellous by any disinterested person in possession of his reason.

The appeal which Mr. Mackenzie now made to the electors of York was in his most impassioned style, and may be taken as a very fair sample of his powers of agitation. As such I subjoin a few extracts from a somewhat unequal, and what lawyers would probably call a seditious, document :—

their local affairs regulated by a few irresponsible individuals arbitrarily selected by the Executive government; for granting a small aid for a few years to the Academy incorporated in Grantham ; for incorporating a number of you as an association to hold your public store-house in York and store your grain ; for repealing the £2,500, or pension-fund act ; for amending the law of evidence and contracts ; for amending the law of libel ; for granting in 1829 £18,650 in aid of the roads ; and for authorizing the appointment of commissioners of roads and other officers for the management of highways by the township meetings. Also, for lessening the number of lawsuits and authorizing the appointment of arbitrators in certain cases, &c., &c.

" The Legislative Council is the cause of much waste of time and money in the House of Assembly, by continually rejecting bills much called for by the people, which causes great delay in the business of the Assembly each year, in again going through and discussing the same measures. The Gourlay Banishment Repeal Bill, the Prince Edward Division Bill, and several other bills of a general or local character, were often passed in the Lower House at a great expense to the colony, and finally assented to.

" The Legislative Council is opposed to a liberal system of banking, because its members are almost all deeply interested in the political and exclusive bank already established, as well from their profits as stockholders as from the influence they derive as placemen from the secret control of this dangerous institution.

" The Legislative Council have passed addresses in favor of particular church establishments, and are as much opposed to the independence of the judges on the Crown, as they were anxious to secure their independence of the people. They have no fear of the present judges lacking in pliability towards any administration.

" The Legislative Council grant the money arising from the taxes levied on you to their door-keepers and favorites for pretended extra services, and last spring grossly imposed upon the House of Assembly by representing a demand made to pay a door-keeper a douceur for some pretended service some years before, as being to pay contingencies of the then existing session."

"Canadians! You have seen a Gourlay unlawfully
banished; a Thorpe persecuted and degraded; a Randal cruelly oppressed; a Matthews hunted down even
to the gates of death; a Willis dragged from the
bench of justice, slandered, pursued even across the
Atlantic by envy and malice, and finally ruined in his
fame, fortune, and domestic happiness; you have seen
a thousand other less noted victims offered upon the
altar of political hatred and party revenge; sacrificed
for their adherence to the principles of the constitution; their love of liberty and justice; their ardent
desire to promote the happiness of your domestic fire-
sides. How many more sacrifices the shrine of unlaw-
ful power may require, none can tell. The destroyer
is made bold by your timidity, and the base and unprincipled triumph over your truest friends, because
they believe you will show a craven spirit, and put
up with every possible insult, however aggravated.
The hired presses style you the tag-rag and bob-tail
who assemble at town meetings, and in the Legislature your most faithful members are daily insulted
and abused as rebels in heart, and the factious abet-
tors of the libeller, the disaffected, and the disloyal.
* * * Had Charles X. profited by experience as
did his brother Louis XVIII., the elder branch of the
Bourbons had yet reigned in France. Louis was illu-
minated by his journey to Ghent, and stuck by the
charter ever after. But it is said that our great men
put their trust and confidence in the troops at Kingston and in this garrison. Do they expect to make
butchers of British soldiers, the soldiers of liberty,
the friends of freedom, the conquerors of the tyrant

of France, the gallant followers of the noble-hearted
Colonel Douglas? Are these the men they expect
to protect them should continued misrule bring upon
them the indignation of an injured, outraged, and
long-suffering community? Do they suppose that
men of honor would violate their obligation to their
country and their God, and imbrue their hands in the
blood of their kind and confiding brothers, to gratify
the bitter enemies of their noble King? Surely, the
champions of British liberty are unfit to perform the
drudgery of menial slaves! Surely, the men whom
our beloved Sovereign has sent here to protect us from
foreign aggression cannot desire to abridge our privileges. Their rights are ours—their history our history—their earliest recollections ours also! We acknowledge one common origin; our fathers worshipped
together in one temple. Does the infatuated junto,
who are now acting so foolishly, expect the bravest of
Scotland's sons to sabre their countrymen merely because they do not conform to the doctrines of prelacy
and follow the example of Archdeacon Strachan to
apostacy and worldly wealth? Do they believe there
is a soldier in Canada whose youthful heart ever
bounded with joy in days of yore, on old Scotland's
hills, while he sang the national air of 'Scots wha hae
wi' Wallace bled,' and whose manhood has been employed in repelling foreign aggression, who would disgrace his name and the regiment he belongs to by ·
increasing the widows and orphans of Canada? And
yet, if such are not the expectations of our rulers, why
do they trifle with the feelings of the people? What
would a handful of troops be to the natural aristo-

cracy of Canada, the hardy yeomanry who own the soil, even if the former were of the most ferocious class of human beings, instead of the manly and accomplished defenders of their country, covered with immortal honor and unstained laurels on many a victorious battle field? I disdain to hold out threats, but it is time to speak with plainness. * * *

"We come, at last, to the leading question, What is to be done? Meet together from all sections of the country, at York, on Thursday next, the nineteenth instant, in this town, on the area in front of the court house; let the farmer leave his husbandry, the mechanic his tools, and pour forth your gallant population animated by the pure spirit of liberty; be firm and collected—be determined—be united—never trifle with your rights; show by your conduct that you are fit for the management of your domestic affairs, ripe for freedom, the enlightened subjects of a constitutional Sovereign, and not the serfs of a Muscovite, or the counterpart of a European mob! Strive to strike corruption at its roots; to encourage a system calculated to promote peace and happiness; to secure as our inheritance the tranquil advantages of civil and religious freedom, general content, and easy independence. Such a connection as this with our parent state would prove long and mutually beneficial; but if the officials go much further they will drive the people mad."

To a certain extent, the majority of the Assembly had, by the injustice of which they had been guilty, gained their point. They had goaded their victim into the use of expressions which in his cooler moments he had never used. It must not be overlooked, however, that whatever there was of menace in his impassioned language, it was directed against the Provincial oligarchy. A marked distinction was made between them and the "noble King," whose "soldiers of freedom" were the "champions of British liberty." If he was indiscreet, we must not forget the galling provocation to which he had been subjected: in being not only expelled the Legislature for libels that others might print with impunity; but, with a view of preventing his re-election, the organs of the official party had represented that he was loaded with a disability unknown to the law, the creation of the arbitrary will of the House of Assembly. We shall see, as we proceed, that some members of the Family Compact shortly afterwards threatened to throw off their allegiance upon infinitely less provocation.

The election of a member, to represent the county of York, in the place of the expelled representative, commenced on the 30th January; Mr. Mackenzie being proposed, for the fourth time, by Mr. Joseph Shepherd. Two other candidates, besides Mr. Mackenzie—Mr. James E. Small, and Mr. Simon Washburn—presented themselves. Mr. Small stated from the hustings that "he did not come before the freeholders as approving of the conduct of the Assembly, in their repeated expulsions of Mr. Mackenzie; he considered their proceedings, in these cases, arbitrary and unconstitutional. But as they had declared Mr. Mackenzie disqualified, he had come forward, presuming that the electors would see the expediency of not electing a member who could not take

81

his seat. He opposed Mr. Washburn, not Mr. Mackenzie, who, he was satisfied, would have a majority of votes." Mr. Washburn, on the contrary, expressed his approval of the proceedings of the Assembly, in the expulsion of Mr. Mackenzie, of whom he spoke in terms of harshness, similar to those used by the more violent of the majority of the House. Mr. Washburn retired, on the second day of polling, much disgusted at having received only twenty-three votes. Mr. Mackenzie received six hundred and twenty-eight votes, and Mr. Small ninety-six.

Such a result might have been expected to convince the Assembly of the folly of their proceedings; but the truth is, the majority was entirely inaccessible to reason.

In the meantime, the Legislative session had been closed. Before the prorogation, Mr. Peter Perry moved to address the Lieutenant Governor to dissolve the House, in consequence of the excitement created in the country by the two expulsions of Mr. Mackenzie; for which motion he obtained eighteen votes against twenty-seven. The House, as if proud of its achievements, ordered two thousand copies of the proceedings on the privilege question to be printed.

In the absence of Mr. Mackenzie from the Assembly, the Bank of Upper Canada had been authorized to increase its stock to a very large extent, in spite of the refusal of its managers, on a previous occasion, to give to a committee of the House information on points of the first importance. The Bank was unpopular from the circumstance of the government holding stock in it, and appointing representatives of that stock at the Board of Direction. A large amount of stock was held by members of the Legislative Council; who, in enlarging the powers conferred by the charter, were legislating for their own individual interests. Under the rules to which the Assembly is now obliged to conform, members similarly situated would not be permitted to vote at all on the question. No other member of the House understood so well as Mr. Mackenzie the checks necessary to impose on banking corporations, for the security of the public; and his expulsion caused the suspicion to be expressed that the interested members of the House were not uninfluenced by the consideration that, in his absence, any bank scheme they might bring forward would be sure to succeed.* The bill was, however, vetoed in England, at the instance of Mr. Mackenzie, as based on unsound principles.

Frazer, a man of coarse manners and violent language, publicly threatened to horsewhip Mr. Mackenzie from his place in the Assembly during the mock trial; and it is said that within twenty-four hours he received from Sir John Colborne a promise of the collectorship of Brockville. The promise was faithfully fulfilled.

* It is proper to say that very few shares were held by members of the House. Mr. H. J. Boulton was interested as Solicitor to the Bank, and doubtless many other members expected favors from it. A Bank of U. C. return for 1831 showed that only fifty-seven shares were held by members of the House. 1,629 shares were held by members of the Legislative Council, and 1,402 by officers of the government; the government itself holding, on behalf of the Province, 2,000 shares. Other Provincial Banks were, at that time, conducted upon anything but correct principles. The whole capital stock of the Bank of Montreal, on the 15th November, 1830, was £250,000; and at the same time the Directors had borrowed from the bank £120,478, and were endorsers for others for £60,570 more! In short they had borrowed nearly three-fourths of the whole capital of the bank.

(♦)

CHAPTER XVI.

Popular Excitement and Sympathy for Mackenzie—Grievance Petitions—
Attempt to Assassinate Mackenzie—Trial and Conviction of Kerr for the
Outrage—Mackenzie Denounced by a Catholic Bishop—Disturbances in
York, and another Assassination Plot—Journey to England—Witnesses the
final reading of the Reform Bill—His Impressions of Earl Grey, O'Connell,
Rev. Mr. Irving, and Cobbett—Hume forwards his Objects—Interview with
Lord Goderich, Colonial Minister—Refuses the Postmaster Generalship of
Upper Canada—Lord Goderich's Dispatch and Concessions—The Legislative Council and Assembly on the Dispatch—Mackenzie procures the Dismissal of the Crown Officers in Upper Canada—The Tories threaten to
revolt—Hagerman restored to the Solicitor Generalship, and Boulton
appointed Chief Justice of Newfoundland—Post-office Policy and Revela-
tions—Disallowance of Bank Charters—Other Colonial Agents—Mackenzie's " Sketches of Canada and the United States"—Revisits Scotland—Returns to Canada—Declines public Dinners.

SIR WALTER SCOTT has stated somewhere that mankind feel more interest in the fortunes of two lovers
than in the fate of a nation. An interest scarcely inferior attaches to the career of an individual whom the
public regards as the victim of injustice, whose crime
consists of his having defended a popular right or
contended for a principle. The majority of the Assembly, in attempting to crush an opponent, had made
a martyr. The natural result followed. The expelled
member had crowds of sympathizers, in all parts of
the Province. Public meetings were held to denounce
this arbitrary stretch of privilege. Petitions to the

King and the Imperial Parliament for a redress of grievances, of which the expulsion of Mr. Mackenzie was one, were numerously signed. Of these petitions, it was already known, Mr. Mackenzie was to be the bearer to the Colonial office; where he would personally advocate the reforms for which they prayed.

A counter movement was set on foot by the official party. With the Reform ministry, in England, this party was not very sure of its standing. The petitions that had already been sent to the Colonial office, from Upper Canada, complaining of grievance and praying that they might be redressed, had produced an impression adverse to the official party in the Province. What might be the result of Mr. Mackenzie's visit, armed with numerous petitions, unless some antidote were applied, it would be impossible to tell. The prospect which this state of things held out enraged the official faction; and in more than one instance they resorted to violence, from which Mr. Mackenzie only escaped, by something little short of a miracle, with his life.

On the 19th of March, 1832, one of the meetings called by the government party was held at Hamilton. Mr. Mackenzie attended by special invitation. The meeting was a public one; and the opposition had determined to measure numbers with their opponents. Mr. Wm. B. Sheldon, of Barton, was proposed to be voted into the chair; and the Tories, fearing a defeat, assumed a tone of menace. Wm. J. Kerr, showing a more violent disposition than the rest, swore that no one but the Sheriff should preside. As too often happens where two political parties attempt to out-

number one another, at a public meeting, great confusion occurred. On a show of hands both parties
claimed the victory; but the Sheriff took the chair.
The other party—represented by a local paper as
being much the more numerous—retired to the Court
House Green; where an address to the King was
adopted.

After the meeting, Mr. Mackenzie had retired to
the house of a friend, Mr. Matthew Bailey, where he
dined, a few other friends being present. A rumor
had been circulated, in whispers, that a plan had been
formed, during the day, to take Mr. Mackenzie's life,
or at least to do him such bodily injury as would
render it impossible for him to make his contemplated
journey to England. Several of his friends apprised
him of this, and urged him strongly to leave town
before dark. Mr. Davis three several times attempted
to persuade him to go in his carriage to Wellington
Square. He declined all this advice, and all offers
of conveyance that would take him out of town before
dark; saying that he should prefer to start by the
stage at eleven o'clock. About nine o'clock that night,
when he was sitting in a parlor up stairs, with a
friend, writing, the door was suddenly opened without any premonition, and in stepped Kerr and one
George Petit. When asked to take seats, one of them,
Kerr, at first refused, but almost immediately after sat
down. He almost instantly rose again, and walking
up to the table and turning over the sheets Mr.
Mackenzie had been writing, remarked with much
apparent good humor: "Well, Mr. Mackenzie, have
you got all our grievances redressed at last?" Some-

thing more was said, when Kerr, asking Mr. Mackenzie to speak with him in private, was at once lighted
down stairs by the unsuspecting victim, by whom he
was followed. Kerr opened the street door; and,
while standing on the steps in front, introduced Mr.
Mackenzie to two or three accomplices,* remarking,
" This is your man," or " This is our man." All at
once, one of them seized him by one side of the coat
collar, while Kerr seized the other. The candle was
dashed to the ground, and they attempted to drag
their victim, in the dark, into an open space in front
of the house. Mr. Mackenzie, on whose mind the
terrible truth now flashed—the warnings he had received that a plan had been made to murder him, and
a threat made by Kerr some months before to take his
life, instantly coming to his recollection—grasped the
door, and struggling in the hands of the assassins,
shrieked, " Murder." One of the party now struck him
a terrible blow with a bludgeon, felling him down
upon the stone steps, whence he was dragged into the
square in front of the house; where he received repeated kicks and blows, and his life was only saved
by the opportune arrival of some neighbors, with Mr.
Bailey's brother; one of whom, named Peck, an Irish
laborer, caused Kerr to desist by approaching him
with an uplifted billet of wood. The villains took
to their heels, except Kerr who was upon the ground;

* It was stated in a local paper, at the time, the editor of which was present
with Mr. Mackenzie, in the House, that two of these were James Dennis and
Oliver Richie; and the statement was afterwards repeated in a work published
by Mr. Mackenzie, in London. There is, however, no judicial evidence of
the identity of Kerr's accomplices; as he was the only one brought to trial for
the outrage.

and when he rose, he resorted to the stratagem of
assuming not only the innocent man but the protector, saying, "Don't be afraid, Mr. Mackenzie; you
shan't be hurt, you shan't be hurt." He then scamp-
ered off as well as he could—for he was permanently
lame—after his accomplices; and next morning he
was heard boasting at the Burlington canal—a government work of which he was manager—that he had
saved Mackenzie's life from the attempt of a band of
ruffians! The victim was found to be bleeding profusely, disfigured in the face, injured in the head, and
hurt in the chest. "I was very unwell all next day,"
he said, "but able to sit up. I was a ghastly spectacle
to look upon; and for months after I felt the effects
of the blows and bruises."

Mrs. Bailey was so alarmed at the outrage enacted
in front of her husband's house, that she was seized
with convulsions, and was in such an alarming condition, during the greater part of the night, that it was
at one time feared she would lose her life or her reason. She gradually recovered towards morning.

It has been stated that Kerr and his friends met
next day, vowing to complete, at night, the work they
had begun; but, however this might be, Mr. Bailey's
house was too well guarded to render such an attempt
at all prudent, and it was not made.

Kerr was a magistrate, and had charge of a public
work. He was a man who might safely be looked to
to take his share of rough work, without any disappointment of expectations, as this outrage is sufficient
guarantee. He was brought to trial, for the part he
played in it, in August, 1832, at the Gore District As-

sizes; some person, unknown to Mr. Mackenzie, having laid the information. Mr. Macaulay was the presiding judge; and, considering the relations of all the parties, it is proper to say that he showed the greatest impartiality on the trial, though there might be a question about the adequacy of the punishment awarded. A fine of $100 is hardly felt by a man said to be worth £5,000 or £6,000. And the assault was of that aggravated nature which irresistibly carries with it the idea of serious premeditated injury, if not something more. The first blow would probably have proved fatal, had not the bludgeon come in contact with the lintel of the door. Solicitor General Hagerman appeared as prosecutor on the part of the Crown.

The name of Mr. McNab, as probable adviser of the outrage, has been freely used, both at the time and since; but as there is no evidence, beyond the fact that some of his friends were engaged in it, he must be acquitted. As the facts clearly show a conspiracy, it is strange that Kerr was the only one convicted. On what ground Petit could have been allowed to go scot-free, it is difficult to imagine; but he was admitted as a witness on the part of the defence, and he was permitted to evade answering the question whether he knew anything about a premeditated attack, by saying he himself had not gone to Bailey's to assault Mr. Mackenzie. His numerous evasions of the question, put in various shapes, could only lead to one conclusion, and that conclusion pointed to a conspiracy which no attempt was made to unravel.

The example of Hamilton was to be followed in York. Parties were pretty equally balanced at the

32

capital; and the official magnates were not always inclined to make a display of their tolerance at public
meetings. On the 6th of July, 1830, they had refused
to allow Mr. Mackenzie to be heard, at a public meeting called to organize an Agricultural Society, and
now they were emboldened by the measurable success of the Hamilton venture. The meeting having
been called for the 23d of March, the semi-official
organ* of the Government undertook to "caution the
faction against any attempt at deception," at the meeting, and threatening that, if the caution were not
heeded, "we most assuredly would not ensure the
leading revolutionary tools† a whole skin, or a whole
bone in their skins, for the space of fifteen minutes."
A sufficiently audacious threat! At the present time
we look back with astonishment at the insolent tone
of the semi-official journals of those days; but when
we scan the conduct, and read the language of Solicitor General Hagerman, in the Assembly, we cannot
doubt that they faithfully reflected the feelings of the
official party. No special constables were sworn in,
or any other precautions taken to preserve the peace.
The meeting having assembled at the Court House,
Dr. Dunlop, of the Canada Company, and Mr. Ketchum,
member for York county, were respectively proposed

---

* *The Upper Canada Courier.*

† The same paper, after the meeting, spoke of the farmers of Yonge street
as a herd of swine: "Every wheel of their well organized political machine
was set in motion to transmute country farmers into citizens of York. Accordingly, about nine in the morning, groups of tall, broad-shouldered, hulk-
ing fellows were seen arriving from Whitby, Pickering, and Scarborough,
some crowded in wagons, and others on horseback; and Hogg, the miller,
headed a herd of the swine of Yonge street, who made just as good votes at
the meeting as the best shop-keepers in York."

as chairman. As is usual, in such cases, both parties claimed the victory; but Dr. Dunlop took the chair, when the Reformers withdrew and organized an open air meeting, in front of the Court House, making use of a farmer's wagon for a platform. Mr. Ketchum being made chairman, Mr. Mackenzie, suffering considerably from the injuries he had received at Hamilton, began to address the meeting; stones and other missiles were thrown by the opposite party; close connections of some of the officials being engaged in the work. The riot soon assumed a serious aspect. A ruffian in the crowd drew a knife, with which he threatened the speaker. The wagon in which Mr. Ketchum and the speaker were standing was seized and drawn for some distance, amidst threats and imprecations. The Sheriff told Mr. Ketchum he was unable to preserve the peace, and begged him to bring the meeting to a close. Some one hit upon the expedient of advising the " friends of the Governor" to go up to Government House and cheer His Excellency. This being done, peace was restored, a new chairman appointed, and an address to the King resolved upon. After Mr. Mackenzie had addressed the meeting for about twenty minutes, those who had not signed the address went to his residence, at the corner of Church and Richmond streets, where, upon tables in the street, four hundred and thirty-eight names were added. While on his way, Mr. Mackenzie was seized hold of by Captain Fitzgibbon. On being questioned as to his intentions, Captain Fitzgibbon said he was going to take him to jail, to secure his protection from the mob. Mr. Mackenzie's friends, to whom his answer was given, replied that there was no necessity for this, as they would undertake to guarantee his safety; upon which Mr. Mackenzie went to his own residence. The disorderly mob, who had been to cheer the Governor, returned, bearing an effigy of Mackenzie, which they burnt, and then made an attack upon the office of *The Colonial Advocate*. They broke the windows and destroyed some of the type, and were only prevented from doing further mischief by the exertions of a few individuals, among whom was an apprentice in the printing office, named Falls, who fired a gun loaded with type,* over-awing the rioters. Captain Fitzgibbon did everything in his power to restore peace; and the Lieutenant Governor gave orders for seventy-five soldiers to be ready at a moment's notice, if required. Three or four magistrates remained at the police office all night, swearing in special constables; and a guard of citizens volunteered to protect Mr. Mackenzie's house and printing office. At midnight a mob surrounded the office, when Captain Fitzgerald ordered them to disperse, and threatened, if they did not obey, to call out the troops, which were kept under arms all night. This admonition had the desired effect, and the crowd, headed by a son of one of the Executive Councillors, moved off without venturing to execute the violence they had meditated. The house had to be guarded for three weeks, during which time Mr. Mackenzie remained in the country for safety; and the young man, who fired on the rioters, had to leave the city in consequence of his life being threatened.

A novel division of parties took place at this meet-

* *Christian Guardian.*

ing; the Roman Catholics going with the Family Compact. Mr. Mackenzie, who at all times made it a point
of respecting every man's honest religious convictions,
and quarreling with none on account of their particular views, had somehow managed to get at loggerheads
with Bishop McDonnell. It was stated on clerical
evidence that the latter had denounced him from the
altar.* The bishop received an annuity of some £500
sterling, and the Church something more, from the government; and these grants were objected to as invidious and unjust to other denominations. From one
party came the emolument; from the other the objections; a condition of things that might well be supposed to influence the political preference even of a
bishop, not otherwise burthened with wealth. But,
however it may be explained, the Roman Catholics
were, contrary to their usual habit, found in alliance
with the Family Compact, on this occasion. At the

* Dr. O'Grady, a Roman Catholic Priest, in his evidence before the
Grievance Committee, in 1835, stated that Bishop McDonnell "got up a petition
against Mr. Mackenzie, attended a public meeting in Mrs. Jordan's inn, and
harrangued the people; and by the use of the most inexcusable misrepresentations, obtained signatures to the said petition, inducing the signers to believe,
from altars dedicated to the service of religion, that the document to which
he invited them to affix their names was intended solely for the advancement
of the Catholic Church. Shortly after he left here (York) for Penetanguishine,
accompanied by the Rev. Messrs. Gordon and Crevier; and Mr. Gordon told me
that he stopped on his way to perform divine service in the Catholic Church of
the township of Toronto, and that he did, on that solemn occasion, instead of
preaching the morality of the gospel, inveigh in the most violent and unbe-
coming manner against William Lyon Mackenzie. He went from that [place]
to Adjula, where he parted from the Rev. Mr. Gordon, having given him
previous instructions to obtain signatures in the best manner he could to a
blank paper, which he left with him for that purpose. The Rev. Mr. Gordon
told me that he was shocked and scandalised at the manner in which this political crusade was conducted."

same time there appears to have been a good deal of political division among them; a meeting having immediately after been held in York, at which no decision was come to on the relative merits of the two political parties.

In April, 1832, Mr. Mackenzie started on his journey to England, as the bearer to the Imperial Government of petitions, which had, for the most part, been born of the excitement arising out of his expulsion from the Legislative Assembly. He expected to return in six months; but was delayed nearly a year and a half. During his absence, Mr. Randal Wixon took charge of *The Colonial Advocate.* The packet Ontario,* on which Mr. Mackenzie sailed, with his

* The following song, wishing God-speed to the agent, is one of several of the same kind, published about this time. It was dated Markham, April 10, 1832, and signed DIOGENES:

> Now Willie's awa' frae the field o' contention,
> Frae' the Land o' misrule, and the friends o' dissension;
> He's gane owre the waves, as an agent befittin';
> Our claims to support, in the councils o' Britain.

> Nae mair shall the *Soup-kitchen beggars** annoy him,
> Nor the *Hamilton murd'rers* attempt to destroy him;
> Nae dark deed o' bluid shall he dread their committin';
> He's safe frae their fangs, on his voyage to Britain.

> Blaw saftly ye breezes! nae turbulent motion
> Disturb, wi' rude billow, the breast o' the ocean;
> But zephyrs propitious, wi' breath unremittin',
> May waft him wi' speed, and wi' safety to Britain.

> There, there, the REFORMERS shall cordially meet him,
> An' there his great namesake, KING WILLIE, shall greet him;
> Our PATRIOT MONARCH, whase name shall be written,
> Wi' letters o' gowd in the Records o' Britain.

* This refers to some of the persons engaged in the York riot, on the 23d of March.

wife, had on board sixteen cabin and six steerage passengers. He described her as "a sort of Noah's ark,"
having on board pigs, poultry, turkeys, geese, and a
milch cow." The passage from New York to Ports-
mouth was made in twenty-nine days, commencing
on the first of May. Writing to Toronto, after he had
got on board at New York, he said: "I trust that the
good providence of that merciful Power who has protected and watched over your humble correspondent
until now, will continue to preserve him, direct all his
steps, and promote the object of his mission, in as far
as that object would be for the good of Canada and of
the English people."

The number of letters he wrote on board the vessel
attests that constitutional activity which always prevented his remaining idle; an activity which sometimes
took strange freaks, and of which an example may be
given in his going up to the mast-head, the first night

> Gae, Canada's Patriot, gae, strang in your mission,
> Gae bear to our Sov'reign, his subjects' Petition;
> Our Despots unmask—shaw the deeds they're committin',
> Pervertin' the blest Institutions o' Britain.
>
> An' dread na the Tories—they're toss'd frae their station,
> Thae tools that degraded and plundered the nation,
> The Bigots—the mitred, the titled are smitten
> To earth—and the Whigs are triumphant in Britain.
>
> Tho' here, we've a brood o' the Reptiles remainin',
> Like Vampyres, the vitals o' Canada drainin';
> Yet lax is their tenure, unstable their fittin',
> An' they'll soon be extinct like the Vermin o' Britain.
>
> Gae, Champion o' Freedom! fulfil your great mission;
> The cause you're engaged in defies opposition;
> An' Liberty's laurels, new glories emittin',
> Shall garland your brows when returnin' frae Britain.

in a storm, and only descending just before one of the sails was blown away.

The organs of the official party affected to be merry at the idea of a man who had twice been expelled from the Legislature, and declared incapable of sitting during that Parliament, taking a budget of grievances to Downing street, and expecting to obtain a hearing. But they had reckoned without their host, as the event proved.

He arrived in London in time to witness the third reading of the Reform Bill in the House of Lords:

"Having obtained the order of a member of the House of Lords for admission to the gallery on the eventful night of the third reading of the Reform Bill, I went as early as four o'clock, and obtained an excellent seat both for seeing and hearing in the front tier of seats immediately opposite the throne. It was well that I did so. Had I been a few minutes later, the order would have been of no avail, as the gallery holds only eighty persons, and each nobleman being entitled to give an order for the admission of one person, it was filled to overflowing almost immediately. At half past four but few of the peers had arrived; and perhaps a dozen members of the Commons' House were standing at the bar. They have either to stand or sit down on the matting, there being neither chairs nor benches placed for their accommodation."

With the appearance and bearing of Earl Grey he was in raptures:—

" Well does Earl Grey merit the high station and distinguished rank to which he has been called; truth and sincerity are stamped on his open, manly, Eng-

lish countenance; intelligence and uprightness in-
scribed on all his actions. You may read his speech
in *The Times* or *Chronicle;* you may imagine to yourself the noblest, happiest manner in which such sentiments might be delivered by a sincere and highly
gifted patriot; still your conception will fall far short
of the reality of the admirable address and manner
of the prime minister of Britain. His Lordship had
need of neither the peerage nor the post he fills to
point him out as one of the first among men; he was—
he is one of that aristocracy of nature which in any
free country are found among the pillars of its liberties, and in any despotism among the foremost to
break the tyrant's yoke, or perish in attempting it."
There was every thing to hope, Mr. Mackenzie wrote,
from the justice of Earl Grey. Upper Canada affairs,
he felt assured, would "be put to rights." He was
naturally of a sanguine disposition, and was also subject to severe fits of despondency.

His impression of O'Connell was also very favorable:—

"I have heard Mr. O'Connell, the great Irish agitator and champion of emancipation, address a meeting
of one of these [Trades' Political] Unions, not less
than eight hundred or one thousand members being
present. He has the most perfect self-command, and
an inexhaustible fund of genuine wit and broad humor;
is one of those speakers you can listen to for hours,
and yet regret when you cease to hear the sound of
his voice. There is a quaintness in his manner of expression which gives double effect to his jokes and
witticisms. Yet he can be lofty and majestic when he

pleases; and I rejoiced to perceive that his original and flowing eloquence, as he told in strong and emphatic language of the wrongs of Ireland, drew from an English audience the most enthusiastic, sympathetic cheers. I rarely ever witnessed a more successful speaker, in his popular character of an agitator, than Mr. O'Connell."

After he had been introduced to Mr. O'Connell, he writes under date, "19 Wakefret Street, Brunswick Square, London, July 28, 1832.

"Mr. O'Connel is a man of whom all Irishmen ought to be proud. In their cause, in Ireland's cause, in the cause of civil and religious freedom all over the globe, he is a powerful and consistent champion, and likely to be a successful one. He has also manifested the warmest attachment to the Canadas; and the kind manner in which he spoke to me of our affairs, and the interest he manifested on our behalf, entitles him to my lasting gratitude."

Having frequently gone to hear the celebrated Mr. Irving, who was then making a great sensation in London as a preacher, Mr. Mackenzie wrote:—

"Although I do not like the interruption from persons speaking, as if inspired, in an unknown tongue, yet there is something so noble, so honest, so captivating about this eloquent divine that I always leave the church more firmly determined to go back next Sunday, and always do so. There is such a power and energy in his discourses, such a simplicity in his manner, such convincing proofs of great judgment and sincere good-will towards men in his language and actions, that I cannot but feel the greatest regard for him as a minister. He preaches seventeen times a week, in doors and out, and his audiences frequently include the first families in the land."

Canadian affairs were accorded attention in social circles, where Mr. Mackenzie moved.* His estimate of Cobbett, formed from a personal acquaintance, does not exclude the defects of that remarkable man. In a letter, dated "September 20, 1832," he writes:—

"I am not sure that I mentioned to you that I dined on Sunday, last July, with the celebrated Mr. Cobbett, at his country-seat, Kensington. I was glad to accept an invitation which enabled me to see a man who has filled a large space in the public annals of Britain for the last forty years, at home. Mr. Cobbett is the centre of a party, formidable in numbers and not deficient in talent. He is a keen and unsparing critic, reviewing and animadverting upon the plans of other men with great severity and unquestioned skill. He is likely to succeed in being returned for the two hundred thousand inhabitants of Manchester to the new Parliament, which will give him great weight. His plans then will be exposed to the test of Legislative

---

* In his letter of the 28th July, from which an extract has already been made, he says:—" I was lately an invited guest at a dinner given in the White Conduit House, Pentonville, to the memory of Major Cartwright, an old and constant Reformer. Many distinguished friends of reform were present; Mr. Hume was chairman, supported by Sir John Scott Lillie, Deputy Lieutenant of Middlesex, the Editor of the *Westminster Review*, Colonel Evans, Mr. Babbage, etc. In the course of the evening, Mr. Hume gave as a toast, 'Reform in the Colonies,' and spoke at some length on the state of the Canadas. Of course, I returned thanks in a short speech. A Polish Professor from Warsaw spoke next, and gave a very interesting but melancholy account of the present state of Poland."

investigation, and we shall see how far he will be able to carry into practice his theory of an equitable adjustment of the national grievances, debts, bonds, and obligations.   Mr. Cobbett I consider a happy man. With the experience of threescore he possesses the vivacity of eighteen.   He is pleased with himself, with his plans, and his prospects.   Has a fine family, a comfortable fireside, and enjoys excellent health. He talks as much of trees, and flowers, and gardening, and agriculture, as of matters of government; and has evidently made farming his study to a great extent.   I should not be at all surprised if we find him not so great a democrat in the House of Commons as he is in the *Weekly Register*.   Mr. Cobbett is tall and well made, ruddy complexion and good-looking; his hair is as white as snow, and no sign of baldness.   He is evidently a man of an ardent temperament, of strong and powerful passions, and I believe his object is to increase the comforts and lessen the misery of the great body of the people; but it is evident he is not very scrupulous as to the means of bringing about this great good.   Mr. Noah, of New York, in his *Advocate*, and more recently in his *Enquirer*, and Mr. Cobbett, of Bolt Court, in his *Register*, appear to me to have adopted the maxim that 'all's fair in politics'— they both put forth, in a powerful strain of sarcasm or invective against political opponents, statements not always so correct as they might be.   Indeed, Mr. Cobbett has evidently acted towards both Whigs and Tories for many years as though he considered them an organized band of public plunderers, legalized by unjust statutes to oppress mankind, and of whom nothing could be said that would be 'too bad.' Mr. Cobbett's manner is kind and prepossessing, but I think he does not bear contradiction so well as some men of less genius and power of mind."

Cobbett noted down the heads of an article which he intended to write on Canada, but he does not appear to have carried his intention into effect.

Mr. Mackenzie made the acquaintance of Mr. Rintoul, editor of the *Spectator*, and Mr. Black, editor of the *Morning Chronicle*, which then held almost as important a position as *The Times*; and he was enabled to address to the British public, through these journals, any observations he had to make on the subject of Canada.

Of all the members of the House of Commons, Mr. Hume rendered the greatest assistance to Mr. Mackenzie. He was on the best terms of friendship with the Ministry, though he kept his seat on the opposition benches, and pursued that independent course which seemed to be the only one possible to him. When he laid before the House of Commons the petitions of which Mr. Mackenzie was bearer, he did so not only with the knowledge and consent of the government, but "he was happy to have the assurance of Viscount Goderich, [Secretary of State for the Colonies,] that his Lordship was busy inquiring into the grievances complained of with a view of affording relief." Mr. Mackenzie had, by this time, already had an interview with the Colonial minister, and, in company with Mr. Hume, Mr. Viger—who had gone to England on a similar mission, on behalf of Lower Canada—and Mr. George Ryerson—who had gone to England on behalf of the Methodist Conference—he was to have another interview, in a few days.

This first interview, at which all the four gentlemen named met Lord.Goderich, took place on the 2nd of July, 1832, at two o'clock, and lasted between two and three hours. The attempts made to lessen Mr. Mackenzie's influence, in the shape of attacks by political opponents in Canada, in the various forms they had taken, appeared to go for nothing with Viscount Goderich. Mr. Mackenzie could not trace the effect of such influence. "The conduct of the Colonial minister," he found to be "friendly and conciliatory; his language free from asperity; and I left him," adds Mr. Mackenzie, "with the impression strongly imprinted on my mind that he sincerely desired our happiness as a colony, and that it was his wish to act an impartial part." The agent of the Upper Canada petitioners explained at length his views of the state of Upper Canada. Viscount Goderich encouraged the deputation to lay the petitions before the House of Commons; and he appears to have recognized, from the first, the substantial nature of many of the grievances which were subject of complaint. If the ministry had shown a disposition to treat the petitions as of no great importance, Mr. Hume would have brought the whole subject of the political condition of Upper Canada before the House of Commons; and as he would have been warmly seconded by O'Connell and others, an effective demonstration would have been made. Although Mr. George Ryerson was present at this interview, he took no part in any of the questions discussed except those relating to religion and education, with which he had been specially charged.

On the 3d of August, Mr. Mackenzie, in company with Mr. Hume and Mr. Viger, had a second interview with Viscount Goderich, at the Colonial office, commencing at two o'clock and lasting about an hour and a half. "We left the Colonial office," Mr. Mackenzie wrote, "well satisfied that measures are about to be taken that will go a great way towards neutralizing the existing discontents."

These interviews were not obtained through the intercession of Mr. Hume, by whom the agent had first been introduced to members of the ministry, but at the request of Mr. Mackenzie, who desired that the three other gentlemen might be included with himself. He afterwards had several interviews with Lord Goderich, at which no third person was present. The Colonial Minister listened to Mr. Mackenzie's statements with the greatest attention, though he observed a decorous reticence as to his own views; and even when he had come to conclusions, he did not generally announce them till he put them into an official shape. In one of those interviews, Mr. Mackenzie complained that the revenue of the Post-office Department, in Upper Canada, was not accounted for; when Lord Goderich proposed to divide the management of the department in Canada, and give Mr. Mackenzie control of the western section, with all the accruing emoluments. Mr. Mackenzie replied by saying : "So far as I am concerned, the arrangement would be a very beneficial one, as I could not fail to be personally much benefited by it; but your Lordship must see," he added, "that the evil I complain of would be perpetuated instead of being remedied. I must therefore decline the offer." Mr. Mackenzie estimated the value of the office, undivided, at $15,000 a year ; one half of which he would have obtained if he had accepted Lord Goderich's offer. This was in strict accordance with the whole practice of his life. With every opportunity of acquiring competence, and even wealth, he lived a large portion of his life in poverty, and died under the pressure of pecuniary embarrassment.

Mr. Mackenzie was not received at the Colonial office in a representative character—he was delegated by the York " Central Committee of the Friends of Civil and Religious Liberty"—but as an individual having an interest in the affairs of the Province, and a member of the Legislature of Upper Canada. It was agreed that he should address what complaints he had to make to the Colonial Secretary in writing ;* and he addressed, among other documents, a lengthy " Me-

---

* He made the fullest use of this privilege; writing long documents on a great number of subjects in which Canadians were then interested. It was in the preparation of these papers that he performed the extraordinary feat referred to in a previous part of this work, of continuing to write six days and six nights, without ever going to bed, and only falling asleep occasionally, for a few minutes, at the desk. He ventured to predict that, unless the system of government, in Upper Canada, were ameliorated, the result must be civil war. "Against gloomy prophecies of this nature," Lord Glenelg, replied, "every man conversant with public business must learn to fortify his mind," adding, that he regarded them as the usual resource of those who wish to extort from the fears of governments conclusions in favor of which no adequate reasons can be offered.' Mr. Mackenzie often afterwards referred to this prediction ; and so far from having intended it as a threat, took credit for it as a warning of the inevitable results of the policy pursued, contending that, if it had been heeded, all the disasters that followed would have been averted.

moir" on the state of the Province, embracing a variety of topics. To this and some other documents
Lord Goderich replied at great length, on the 8th of
November, 1832, and in a tone and temper very different from those in which the local officials were accustomed to indulge.

Lord Goderich at first stated the number of names
to the petitions of which Mr. Mackenzie was the bearer
at twelve thousand and seventy-five; while he added
that there were other petitions signed by twenty-six
thousand eight hundred and fifty-four persons, "who
concur in expressing their cordial satisfaction in those
laws and institutions which the other sort of petitioners have impugned." At the instance of Mr.
Mackenzie, Lord Goderich afterwards caused the
names to be counted again, and it was found that instead of twelve thousand the number "far exceeded
twenty thousand."[*] While combating a great many
of the arguments adduced by Mr. Mackenzie, Lord
Goderich yielded to his views upon several points.
Hitherto no indemnity had been paid to members of
the Assembly representing town constituencies. The
effect, it was argued, was to confine the people in their
choice of town representatives to persons who could
afford to spend their time at the seat of the government during the legislative session, without a reim-
bursement of their expenses. Lord Goderich directed
the Governor not to oppose objection to any measure
that might be presented to his acceptance, "for placing

---

[*] Letter of Lord Howick to Mr. Mackenzie, January 22, 1833. Mr. Mackenzie (*Seventh Report on Grievances*) stated the number of signatures at about
24,500. Earl Ripon afterwards stated the number at 24,500.

the town and county representatives on the same footing in this respect." He agreed to place upon the
same footing as Quakers other religious bodies who
had a like objection to taking an oath. Another complaint Lord Goderich had anticipated. It was alleged
that the local Executive distributed the public lands
among their favorites without the authority of law;
and His Majesty, upon the advice of the Colonial
minister, interdicted the gratuitous disposal of public
lands, and requested that they should be made subject
to public competition, with a view "to the utter exclusion of any such favoritism as is thus deprecated."
He instructed the Lieutenant Governor to adopt all
constitutional means to procure a repeal of the law
which disqualified British subjects from voting at
elections, after their return from foreign countries;
also that "His Majesty expects and requires of you
neither to practice, nor to allow on the part of those
who are officially subordinate to you, any interference
with the right of His Majesty's subjects to the free
and unbiassed choice of their representatives." In
the name of His Majesty's Government, Lord Glenelg
disclaimed all responsibility for the opinion attributed
to Mr. Robinson, that the children of the yeomanry
ought to be consigned to ignorance lest knowledge
should render them independent in thought and
action; and he enlarged on the advantages of popular
education. "In the same spirit," he added, "His
Majesty now directs me to instruct you to forward to
the utmost extent of your lawful authority and influence, every scheme for the extension of education
amongst the youth of the Province, and especially the

poorest and most destitute among their number, which
may be suggested from any quarter, with a reasonable
prospect of promoting that design." It had been the
custom of the Lieutenant Governors to excuse themselves from laying a full statement of the revenue and
expenditure before the Legislature, by pleading the
restrictions imposed by their instructions. But Lord
Goderich rendered this excuse impossible in future,
by the averment that "if the Royal instructions are
supposed to forbid the most unreserved communication with the House of Assembly of the manner in
which the public money, from whatever source derived,
is expended, such a construction is foreign to His Majesty's design." "Nothing," it was added, "is to be
gained by concealment upon questions of this nature,
and a degree of suspicion and prejudice is naturally
excited, which, however ill-founded, often appears in
the result to be incurable." Coming to the question
of ecclesiastics holding seats in the Legislative Council, Lord Goderich said it was expected of the Bishop
and the Archdeacon, "that they should abstain from
interference in any secular matter that may be agitated
at that Board." But even under this restriction,
Lord Goderich added, "I have no solicitude for retain-
ing either the Bishop or the Archdeacon on the list of
Legislative Councillors; but, on the contrary, rather
predisposed to the opinion that, by resigning their
seats, they would best consult their own personal
comfort, and the success of their designs for the spiritual good of the people." But as their seats were
held for life, their resignations must be voluntary;
since, it was argued, there would be no justification

for degrading them from their positions, when no specific violation of duty had been imputed to them. If
the expense of elections was so inordinate as represented, the Lieutenant Governor was instructed to
" signify to the Legislative bodies that it is the earnest
desire of His Majesty, that every practical method
should be taken for correcting what would be so great
an evil, by reducing the cost " within the narrowest
possible limit." In reference to an independent judiciary, so strongly opposed by Mr. Stephens, counsel
to the Colonial office in 1828, Lord Goderich, antici-
pating the complaints now addressed to him, had directed the Lieutenant Governor to suggest the enactment of a bill for that purpose. Thus another point,
urged by Mr. Mackenzie and those who acted with
him, when they conceived that Judge Willis was
offered up a sacrifice to the displeasure of the local
Executive, had been gained.

Such are some of the concessions obtained by Mr.
Mackenzie, during his visit to England, from the Imperial Government. The dispatch of Lord Goderich
was intended for the public eye, and its style was
eminently diplomatic. On several points he differed
from Mr. Mackenzie; and sometimes he succeeded
in putting his correspondent in the wrong. Unfortunately, there were reasons, as afterwards appeared, for
doubting the sincerity of some of Lord Goderich's professions. In this very dispatch, he said: "With respect
to the charge of showing an undue preference to preachers
of religion belonging to the established churches of this
country, it is so utterly at variance with the whole
course of policy which it has been the object of my

dispatches to yourself to prescribe, that I cannot
pause to repel it in any formal manner." On the 5th
of April of the same year, he had written in reply to a
private dispatch of Sir John Colborne: "I quite concur with you in thinking that the greatest benefit to
the Church of England would be derived from applying a portion of the [Clergy Reserves] funds at least
under the control of the Executive Government, in
the building of rectories and churches; and I would add,
in preparing as far as may be for profitable occupation, that moderate portion of land which you propose
to assign in each township or parish for increasing the
future comfort, if not the complete maintenance, of the
rectors." This dispatch appears to have been marked
"private," when it was written; but the seal of privacy
was taken from it when it was published by order of
the House of Commons, some years after.

The reception which the dispatch of Lord Goderich met at the hands of the Family Compact, shows
better than almost any thing else the lengths to which
a Provincial faction, spoiled by a long course of un-
checked and irresponsible power, carried its insolence.
The Legislative Council, instead of placing it on their
journals, took the unusual course of returning it to
the Governor. Mr. Mackenzie's correspondence, to
which the Colonial Secretary had taken so much trouble
to reply, they assured the Lieutenant Governor they
viewed " with the most unqualified contempt ;" and the
dispatch of Lord Goderich, so far as it was a reply to
that correspondence, they could not " regard as calling
for the serious attention of the Legislative Council."
This branch of the Legislature felt a presentiment of

its impending doom. Its equanimity was seriously disturbed by the question of its being made elective having been raised. We can now look back with per- fect composure upon the party quarrels of those days ; but it is impossible for any impartial observer not to be struck with the fact that the Tories of those times were the real revolutionists. A Crown-nominated chamber, crowded with placemen and dependents upon the government, pursued a course of conduct that caused a demand to be made for an Elective Council; and to this circumstance we owe a revolution in that branch of the Legislature. Whether that change will eventually prove to be for evil or for good, it is impossible yet to say.

The Legislative Assembly discussed, at great length, the question of sending back this dispatch. Attorney General Boulton thought it ill became the Colonial Secretary to " sit down and answer all this rigmarole trash ;" and that " it would much less become the House to interfere with it," by giving it publicity. His whole speech was in a characteristic tone of su- preme contempt. ' Solicitor General Hagerman ob- jected to the printing of the papers.* Mr. Vankough- net, though belonging to the majority of the House, met such speakers as the Attorney and the Solicitor General by their own arguments. " If," he said, " you are opposed to Mr. Mackenzie, there can be no

* After his reinstatement in office, from which his dismissal will shortly be described, Mr. Hagerman found it necessary to declare his concurrence in the principles laid down in this dispatch. On the 5th of February, 1836, he voted for a resolution pledging the House to "advance and maintain the prin- ciples of government set forth in the dispatch," "of the Right Hon. the Earl of Ripon (previously Lord Goderich) of the 8th of November, 1832."

better mode, if his papers [sent with the dispatch]
contain such falsehood and fallacy as it is pretended
they do, to expose him than by publishing them." The
House, by a vote of twenty-one against twelve, resolved
not to allow the documents accompanying the dispatch,
and on which it was founded, to go upon the journals.
A subsequent House gave such portions of these documents as Mr. Mackenzie selected an enduring record,
in the famous *Seventh Report of the Committee on
Grievances*.

The newspaper advocates of the official party went
a little beyond the officials themselves. The principal
of them* described the dispatch of Lord Goderich as
"an elegant piece of fiddle-faddle," "full of clever
stupidity and condescending impertinence."

But the end was not yet. The repeated expulsions
of Mr. Mackenzie from the Legislative Assembly, in
which Crown officers had borne a conspicuous and discreditable part, had attracted the attention of the Imperial Government. The constitutional objections to
the proceeding had been brought before the attention
of the Lieutenant Governor, for the information of the
Crown law officers. The objections which the Colonial
Secretary entertained to these expulsions were early
communicated to Sir John Colborne; and they were
fully explained, in the summer of 1832, to the Crown
officers, Messrs. Hagerman and Boulton, and to
others "whose official situation placed them in a
confidential relation to the government."† The matter
was first brought before the attention of the Colonial

* *The Courier.*

† Letter of General Rowan to Mr. Mackenzie, November 30, 1888.

office by Mr. Hume; and the authorities sent instructions to Sir John Colborne to desire the officials by
whom he was surrounded not to be concerned in the
repetition of so objectionable a procedure. But notwithstanding this warning, they remained contuma-
cious. While absent, in England, Mr. Mackenzie had
again been expelled from the Legislative Assembly;
and the Attorney General, opposing his constitutional
law to that of the Imperial Government, argued for the
legality of the course pursued by the House. Both
the Crown officers voted for a motion to return the
dispatch and accompanying documents, and found
themselves in a minority.

The Solicitor General, who had obtained an odious
distinction for the virulence of his language, in urging
the previous expulsion of a political opponent, had
attempted to preserve his consistency by inducing a
majority of the Assembly to read Lord Goderich a
lecture for having, in his dispatch, noticed allegations
that "rested on no better testimony than that of an
individual who had been twice expelled this House,
and who, in consequence of his having fabricated and
reiterated libels of the grossest description, had been
declared unfit and unworthy of a seat in the Assembly during the present Parliament." Of what these
"libels" consisted we have already seen. The resolution of the House, that pretended to create an arbitrary disability unknown to the law, was the production of the Solicitor General, and to sustain his own
act he found it necessary to undertake to snub his
superiors. The dismissal of Attorney General Boul-

ton and Solicitor General Hagerman,* resolved upon
in March, 1833, was the result of the discreditable

* The subjoined correspondence, which took place at York, explains the
cause of these dismissals:—

"GOVERNMENT HOUSE, *April* 29, 1838.

"SIR:—I have the honor, by the direction of the Lieutenant Governor, to
transmit to you the accompanying copy of a dispatch from the Secretary of
State for the Colonies, in which His Excellency is interested, to inform you and
the Solicitor General, that His Majesty regrets he can no longer avail himself
of your services, and that you are to be relieved from the duties of your respective offices. I have, &c.,

"[Signed] WILLIAM ROWAN.

"Henry John Boulton, Esq., &c., &c., &c.

"No. 118. [COPY.]

"DOWNING STREET, *March* 6, 1833.

"SIR:—By the accounts I have lately received of the proceedings of the Legislature of Upper Canada, I have learned that the Attorney and Solicitor
General of that Province have, in their places in the Assembly, taken a part
directly opposed to the avowed policy of His Majesty's Government. As members of the Provincial Parliament, Mr. Boulton and Mr. Hagerman are, of
course, bound to act upon their own view of what is most for the interest of
their constituents, and of the Colony at large; but if, upon questions of great
political importance, they unfortunately differ in opinion from His Majesty's
Government, it is obvious that they cannot continue to hold confidential situations in His Majesty's service, without either betraying their duty as members
of the Legislature, or bringing the sincerity of the Government into question,
by their opposition to the policy which His Majesty has been advised to pursue.

"His Majesty can have no wish that Mr. Boulton and Mr. Hagerman should
adopt the first of these alternatives; but, on the other hand, he cannot allow
the measures of his Government to be impeded by the opposition of the Law
Officers of the Crown. In order, therefore, that these gentlemen may be at
full liberty, as members of the Legislature, to follow the dictates of their own
judgment, I have received His Majesty's commands to inform you that he
regrets that he can no longer avail himself of their services, and that from the
time of your receiving this dispatch, they are to be relieved from the duties
imposed upon them in their respective offices.

"You will transmit copies of this dispatch to Mr. Boulton and Mr. Hagerman. I have the honor, &c., &c.,

"[Signed] GODERICH.

"M. G. Sir John Colborne, K. C. B., &c., &c., &c.

"YORK, *April* 29, 1833.

"SIR:—Under the circumstances in which I find myself suddenly placed,
without any previous intimation from His Majesty's Government, and more

35

part they had taken in the repeated expulsion of Mr.
Mackenzie from the Legislature, as well as for having,
upon other questions, opposed the policy of the Imperial Government, and thus cast doubts upon the sincerity of its motives. Mr. Mackenzie had described
them to Lord Goderich as "the most active men in
the Province in their opposition to measures to which
your Lordship and the people are friendly;" and as
being backed in the Executive Council by their relatives, who, it was said, formed a majority of its members. "Without some change of men," added Mr.
Mackenzie, "what are considered good measures cannot be carried into effect. A Governor would stand
alone if he was to declare himself of your Lordship's
opinion. All his legal advisers would be found his
uncompromising opponents;" for which inconvenience,
one would suppose, a remedy would be found in their

especially in the absence of the Solicitor General, who is equally affected by
the measure with myself, I feel it due to him, as well as to myself, and to our
respective friends, to request, that His Excellency will have the kindness to
inform me for what breach of public duty His Majesty has been advised to remove us from office?   I have the honor, &c.,
                    "[Signed]   H. J. Boulton.
"To Lieutenant Colonel Rowan,
          "*Private Secretary to the Lieutenant Governor.*"

          "Government House, *April* 29, 1833.
"Sir:—I have the honor to acquaint you in reply to your letter of this day,
that the Lieutenant Governor understands, that the part of your political proceedings to which the dispatch of the Secretary of State particularly adverts, is
that you and the Solicitor General promoted the repeated expulsion of a member of the Assembly, although the constitutional objections to that course had
been conveyed to His Excellency by His Majesty's Government, and were, it
is concluded, communicated by him to you.
                    "I have the honor, &c., &c.,
                    "[Signed]   William Rowan.
"To H. J. Boulton, Esq., &c., &c., &c."

dismissal. Mr. Mackenzie enumerated a long list of questions, on which he assured Lord Goderich the Crown officers had opposed the wishes of the King's government. Among them were : A reform of the exclusive charter of King's College ; the monopoly by the Church of England of the Clergy Reserves ; eligibility of Quakers for election to the Legislature ; the disfranchising of British subjects for seven years after their return to Canada ; the indemnity of members of the Assembly representing town constituencies ; the expulsion, contrary to law, of a member of the Legislature, a second time for the same offence ; the independence of the judges ; and the naturalization of aliens.

The removal of Messrs. Boulton and Hagerman was made before these statements were reduced to writing. On the 7th of March, Mr. Mackenzie had a long interview with Lord Howick, under-Secretary of State for the Colonies, at the Colonial office ; and it was at the request of that official that he put his complaint against the Crown officers into writing. Next day, March 8, they assumed the required form ; and on the 10th, he had another interview with Lord Goderich, when, in reference to the Crown officers, the under-Secretary remarked : " They are removed." But it appears, by the date of Lord Goderich's letter, that their removal had been determined on four days before.

Mr. Jameson was appointed Attorney General, and Mr. Mackenzie said he had good reasons for believing that Dr. Rolph, whom he recommended, was made Solicitor General, but that Sir John Colborne and

Chief Justice Robinson prevented the appointment taking effect.

When the dispatch of Lord Goderich, ordering the removal of the Crown Law officers, reached Upper Canada, Mr. Hagerman had started for England, where, on the 6th of May, while going into the Colonial office, he met Mr. Mackenzie coming out. Mr. Boulton was at York, but soon followed. It is interesting to see how the official party, which had long claimed a monopoly of loyalty, bore this reverse. An article appeared in the *Upper Canada Courier*, attributed to the pen of the deprived Attorney General,. containing direct threats of rebellion. The removal of these two functionaries was described as being " as high handed and arbitrary a stretch of power as has been enacted before the face of high heaven, in any of the four quarters of this nether world, for many and many a long day." " The united factions of Mackenzie, Goderich, and the Yankee Methodists" were spoken of in the most contemptuous terms. The friends of Messrs. Boulton and Hagerman it was confessed, " instead of dwelling with delight and confidence upon their connection with the glorious empire of their sires, with a determination to support that connection, as many of them have already supported it, with their fortunes or their blood, their affections are already more than half alienated from the government of that country ; and in the apprehension that the same insulting and degrading course of policy towards them is likely to be continued, they already begin to ' cast about ' in ' their mind's eye,' for some new state of political existence, which shall effectually put the colony beyond the reach of injury and insult from any. and every ignoramus whom the political lottery of the day may chance to elevate to the chair of the Colonial office." The Colonial Secretary, it was added, by his course of liberality, had not only "alienated the affec tions" of the Boulton - Hagerman school of politicians; but had "produced the feelings of resentment, and views with regard to the future," which caused them to look for "some new state of political existence."

When Mr. Mackenzie came into possession of Lord Goderich's dispatch, he at once desired Mr. Hume to withdraw his intended petition to the House of Commons ; and he wrote to Canada, expressing a hope that no more petitions would be sent to England; since the Imperial Government had shown its anxiety to redress all the greivances that had been a subject of complaint. The dismissal of the Crown officers completed his satisfaction.

But affairs were soon to take another turn. Mr. Hagerman arrived in England about the time the dispatch ordering his removal reached Canada; and Mr. Boulton followed immediately on learning of his dismissal. Mr. Stanley, who succeeded Lord Goderich as Secretary for the Colonies, restored Mr. Hagerman to his official position, in the June following; within three months after his dismissal. It was afterwards officially stated that his restoration was the consequence of exculpatory evidence offered by Mr. Hagerman. Mr. Boulton at the same time obtained the office of Chief Justice of Newfoundland, where he soon embroiled himself with a large and influential

.section of the population. The Imperial Government, conceiving his usefulness to be destroyed, relieved him of that charge also.* He besieged the Colonial office for a pension or other compensation; but the Imperial Government, not feeling that he was entitled to the one or the other, turned a deaf ear to his demands. He never afterwards obtained any position to wipe out the stain of that dismissal.

Mr. Mackenzie, 'recently overjoyed at the success he had met, in obtaining the concessions contained in Lord Goderich's dispatch, and the dismissal of law officers of the Crown in Upper Canada,† was now plunged into despair by finding a portion of that success already neutralized. He addressed to Mr. Stanley a memorial, the object of which was to procure the cancelling of Mr. Hagerman's re-appointment. It was of course not successful; and it may well be questioned whether it was judicious to tell the Colonial Secretary that the re-appointment " would be a spoke in the wheel of another violent revolution in America." After recently expressing the greatest confidence in the justice of the Imperial Government, he now bit-

* In the report of the Privy Council, deciding upon Mr. Boulton's removal from the Chief Justiceship of Newfoundland, July 5, 1838, we find the members expressing regret " to be under the necessity of reporting that we have found, in some of the transactions brought under our consideration, so much of indiscretion in the conduct of the Chief Justice, and that he has permitted himself so much to participate in the strong feelings which appear unfortunately to have influenced the different parties in the Colony, (although we do not find that his judicial decisions have been affected thereby,) that we feel it our duty to state that we think it will be inexpedient that he should be continued in the office of Chief Justice of Newfoundland."

† On the 6th of May, he wrote: " Nothing can exceed the willingness I have of late found on the part of the government here, to do the people justice, in the North American Provinces."

terly exclaimed: "I am disappointed. The prospect
before us is indeed dark and gloomy."

The restoration of Mr. Hagerman seems to have
been due as much, if not more, to the change that had
taken place in the administration of the Colonial
office,* as to the exculpatory evidence he had offered.
Lord Goderich, so long as he retained the seals,
continued to court interviews with Mr. Mackenzie,
and to solicit information from him on the affairs of
Canada. Thus on the 27th of March, 1833, Lord
Howick wrote him: "I am desired by his Lordship
to acquaint you that he is disposed to think that much
advantage might be derived from a personal communication from yourself and Mr. Viger, either to this
place, the Postmaster General, or the Secretary of the
Post-office, on the questions which have been agitated
in Upper and Lower Canada, respecting the Post-

* "I am sorry to observe," wrote Mr. Hume to Mr. Mackenzie, under
date, 'Bryanston Square, June 24, 1833,' "by some of the proceedings of Mr.
Stanley, that he is rather disposed to promote than to punish the men who
have been removed from Upper Canada for improper conduct, and thereby
to encourage misgovernment on the part of the public officers of that Province
which Lord Goderich's late proceedings were calculated to prevent." "Indeed," Mr. Hume added, "the promotion of Mr. Boulton to a high judicial
office in Newfoundland, after the declaration of Lord Goderich of his conduct
and unfitness for office, I consider as an insult to the people of Upper Canada,
and to every lover of good government; and it may be taken as an earnest
that he will support the misgovernment which Lord Goderich had set himself
against." Lord Stanley consulted Earl Ripon (previously Lord Goderich) on
the appointment of Mr. Boulton to the Chief Justiceship of Newfoundland;
and the latter, though he had dismissed him from the Attorney Generalship
of Upper Canada, gave his entire concurrence in the new appointment. "I
am bound to add," says Earl Ripon, in a letter to Mr. Boulton, dated August 20, 1835, "that though the explanations which you gave on your return
to England did not, in my judgment, alter the facts upon which I had advised
a change in your situation, they did affect the inference which had been drawn
from those facts."

office, in those Provinces." If his known intention to leave London, in a few days, would prevent a
personal interview, Mr. Mackenzie was requested to
put any suggestions he might have to make into
writing. He thereupon drew up a scheme of Post-
office reform for the Province; supporting his recommendation by a number of documents, including
several reports on the subject by committees of the
Houses of Assembly, in Upper and Lower Canada.
The request for an interview, on the part of Lord
Goderich, was repeated; but when that gentleman was
about resigning the administration of the Colonial
office, he directed that the whole matter be left over
for the determination of Mr. Stanley. The new Colonial minister decided to send for Mr. Stayner, Deputy
Postmaster General at Quebec, to hear his explanation, before arriving at any conclusion; and Mr. Mackenzie left London the day on which Mr. Stayner
arrived there. The result of these movements of Mr.
Mackenzie was to bring out information regarding the
Post-office revenue, which had been persistently refused to the demands of the House of Assembly. A
return,* which Mr. Stayner was requested to make for

* This return formed a gauge of the circulation of the Canadian journals;
though of course the entire edition did not go by mail. The amount of postage
paid on the different papers in Canada, in 1830, was:

UPPER CANADA.—Christian Guardian (Sterling Money), £228 ; Colonial
Advocate, £57 ; Courier, £45 ; Watchman, £24 ; Upper Canada Gazette, £18 ;
Canadian Wesleyan, (commenced, 1831,) £18 ; Brockville Recorder, £16 ; Ham-
ilton Free Press, (commenced, 1831,) £11 ; Catholic, 0 ; Patriot, £6 ; Star, 0 ;
York Observer, £3 ; Kingston Chronicle, £10 ; Kingston Herald, £11 ; Brock-
ville Gazette, £6 ; Niagara Gleaner, and the Herald (together), £17 ; St.
Catharines Journal, £6 ; Perth Examiner, £10.

LOWER CANADA.—Quebec Gazette (thrice a week), £66 ; Montreal Gazette
(thrice a week), £57 ; Montreal Herald (twice a week), and New Gazette

the information of the House of Commons, showed him to be in possession of perquisites to several times the amount of his salary. With allowances, his salary was £811 a year; and he received in addition the whole of the postage of Colonial newspapers, amounting to £1,508, and a further sum derived from postage on United States papers, a percentage on United States letters, and other perquisites not stated in the return, but estimated altogether by Mr. Mackenzie— perhaps too highly—at £2,000.

In course of a long interview had with Mr. Stanley, at the Colonial office, in the month of May, during half an hour of which an archbishop was kept waiting, Mr. Mackenzie strongly urged the necessity of giving the Canadians the control of the Post-office revenue, as well as every other arising in the Province; as mismanagement must lead to discontent and estrange the colonist from the mother country. Mr. Stanley was " exceedingly kind and friendly;" and when Mr. Mackenzie was going away asked if there were any other matter about which he wished to speak; but he made no " admission that he was favorable to a change of the system condemned."

As has been already stated, Mr. Mackenzie successfully invoked the Royal veto against the bill, passed in his absence from the House occasioned by his

(weekly), £75; Montreal Vindicator (twice a week), £40; Montreal Minerve (twice a week), £50; Official Quebec Gazette, £56; Canadian Courant (twice a week), £46; Quebec Mercury (twice a week), £21.

Mr. Thomas Dalton, proprietor of the *Patriot* newspaper, being examined before the Grievance Committee of the House of Assembly, in 1835, stated that the official return of postage paid by him on that journal, in 1829, 1830, and 1831, was not correct. The whole amount given for the three years was £6; whereas the real amount paid was £70 or £80.

36

second expulsion, for increasing the capital stock of the Bank of Upper Canada. This result was obtained after the objections to the measure had been stated at length to Lord Goderich, and much correspondence with the Board of Trade. Among other things, the objections stated that the bank was in the habit of lending on the security of landed property; that the act contained no provision for winding up the affairs of the corporation, in case it became bankrupt; that only one-tenth of the proposed additional stock of £100,000 was required to be paid down, and that the act did not define what would constitute a fraudulent failure. At the same time, and for similar reasons, the Kingston Bank Act was disallowed.

It may strike the reader, at this time of day, as singular that an agent and leader of a Colonial party, which claimed to be the exponents of a liberal creed and the interpreters of popular opinion, should be so ready to invoke the interference of the Imperial Government, and the Royal veto, in the local affairs of the Province. To a certain extent the seeming anomaly admits of explanation. On many questions, the local Executive, acting through the Crown-nominated and dependent Legislative Council, thwarted the wishes of the people's representatives; and, under an irresponsible local administration, there was no effective appeal possible but to the Imperial Government. But, in some cases, interference against the decisions of the popular branch of the Legislature was invoked. Appeals of this nature, unless some plain and obvious principle were violated, could hardly be justified.

The Rev. Egerton Ryerson, arriving in England

while Mr. Mackenzie was there, was through him introduced to the Colonial office. Mr. Ryerson was delegated by the Canada Conference to submit a proposition for an union between the body it represented and the English Methodists. Without entering into the merits of the case, it will be sufficient to say that the course pursued by Mr. Ryerson, while in England and after his return to Canada, gave Mr. Mackenzie great offence, and he used often, to the last years of his life, to express regret that he had done any thing to secure Mr. Ryerson admittance to the Colonial office, which, in spite of the access which Mr. Mackenzie obtained, had for nearly eighteen months shut its doors in the face of Mr. Viger, who went as the delegate of the Lower Canada Assembly. And Mr. Baldwin, who afterwards visited London, was never able to obtain an audience of the Colonial minister. Mr. Viger was in London long before Mr. Mackenzie, whom he had vainly solicited to accompany him, offering to bear the charge of his expenses.

Early in 1833, Mr. Mackenzie published in London, an octavo volume of five hundred pages, under the title of *Sketches of Canada and the United States.* It treated of a great variety of subjects, having no necessary connection with one another, and little regard was paid to method in the arrangement. The greater part of the book consisted of notes taken by the author while travelling, at different times, in the United States and Canada; and if this had been explained, the intermingling of topics would not have appeared incongruous, as it did under the arrangement adopted. Political topics were not forgotten; and there was an agreeable seasoning of racy and remarkable anecdotes. Illinois, we learn from this source, had a model Governor, named Gilmer, whose salary was $500 a year; and who, uniting the business of tavern-keeper to the position of chief magistrate, boarded the members of the Legislature at the rate of $2 a week. A Brantford clergyman marries a couple in a stable; and when the ceremony is over, the bridegroom breaks the clergyman's table in revenge for the indignity put upon him. Politics form the serious part of the book. Any thing but an inviting picture is drawn of the irresponsible government with which Canada was then blessed. "The government of Upper Canada," we read, "is a despotism; a government legally existing independent of the will of the governed. Responsibility to the people from their rulers is in law," and practice too it might have been added, "merely nominal." The book is gossiping, disjointed, pleasant or censorious, according to the nature of the multiform subjects treated.

Before returning to Canada, Mr. Mackenzie revisited his native Scotland, in company with Mrs. Mackenzie, after making a tour of a large part of England. When he arrived in his native city of Dundee, he was struck with the changes that time had wrought. In a letter dated "Dundee, April 15, 1833," he says:

"After a long absence from a country, one of the most striking changes is that in the age of the people. I have been introduced to cousins I left in the cradle, who are now grown men and women—some of them married, some studying law, some at college, some clerks in banks, some learning mechanical occupa-

tions, and others farming. Many persons I knew as
heedless youths are heads of large families, sober,
staid, and prudent. Not a few I knew in active life
are now sunk into the vale of years and helplessness.
I have taken much pains to find out some of my old
school-fellows, but how altered they are! One of the
most active, spirited, intelligent youths I ever knew,
is married, has a large family, and toils in poverty as
laborer on a farm!"

In the churches the same changes are visible:—

" In the two Sundays spent here and in Strathmore
we have regularly gone to the Kirk, sometimes to the
Seceders, and sometimes to hear the established clergy.
The walls of the kirks, the seats, the pulpits, many
in the congregation I could remember from infancy,
but the ministers were, some of them, new to me.
There were enough, however, of old recollections to
make these last visits to Scottish places of worship
deeply interesting."

The reference to last visits was prophetic. About
two years before he died, he earnestly desired to re-
visit Scotland, but was unable to gratify that wish.

" Here," he says in another place, still speaking of
Dundee, " I was partly educated, and here I passed
some of my happiest days—the days of joyous youth
unencumbered with care." This was the bright side
of the picture, for he had elsewhere said: " Poverty
and adversity were my nurses, and in youth were
want and misery my familiar friends." But it is in
the nature of buoyant youth to enjoy gleams of happiness under the most discouraging circumstances.
" In the midst of our relations, friends, and acquaint-

ances of other years," he wrote from Dundee, "we are passing the time very agreeably."

There was one thing in Dundee that he did not like—the misery of its manufacturing population—and as his idea about large manufactories is opposed to the idea now prevalent in Canada, it may as well be given :—

"The number of mills for spinning flax into yarn in Dundee is now very numerous. The smoke of their steam-engines darkens the face of the heavens, and many a poor and miserable boy and girl eke out a wretched existence by long and incessant toil in these ever-to-be detested establishments—the graves of morality, and the parents of vice, deformity, pauperism; and crime. Long may Canada be free of all such pests ! Let our domestic manufactures be those which our children can easily carry on under the eyes and in the houses and homes of their fathers and mothers."

While in Dundee Mr. Mackenzie made a settlement with such of his creditors as he had been unable to pay, when he left Scotland for Canada, in 1820, with their consent. Mr. Edward Lesslie, who was perhaps his largest Scottish creditor, had long since emigrated to Canada, where his claim, amounting to about £70, was paid.

Partly satisfied with his success, though somewhat discouraged by the restoration of Solicitor General Hagerman to office, Mr. Mackenzie left England for Canada. The impression created on his mind by the latter act was that there was little reason to hope for a favorable change in the administration of the government of Upper Canada. He left London on the 25th of June, 1833, taking passage in the *Jordeson*, and arrived at Quebec on the 18th August, accompanied by Mrs. Mackenzie. Both in Quebec and Montreal he was pressed to accept of public dinners, but in both cases he declined, excusing himself on the ground of his long absence from Canada, and his desire to arrive at York as soon as possible.

To the last years of his life, Mr. Mackenzie was proud of the reforms which his journey to England was the means of effecting in the government of Upper Canada; and he ever continued to cherish a grateful remembrance of the aid rendered him by Mr. Ellice, Mr. Hume, and others, from whom he received assistance in the execution of his mission. Considering that he went to England in no official capacity; that he was probably opposed in the private communications of the military Governor; that attempts had been made by his enemies to disgrace him by thrice expelling him from the Legislative Assembly, it must be confessed that the success which he achieved was greater than that of any other man who ever went from Canada, in a non-official capacity, on a similar errand.

Of this journey the people's agent was left to bear the greater part of the expense. The actual disbursements were £676, of which he received £150. The balance remained unpaid all his life, and the country he had served with such disinterested devotion allowed him to go down to the grave in poverty. He despised the means by which many of his cotemporaries sought to obtain wealth, and held of greater value than stores of gold and silver a reputation unsullied by any stain of corruption.

CHAPTER XVII.

Mr. Mackenzie's Third Expulsion from the Legislative Assembly—Is re-
. elected by Acclamation—Refusal of the Commissioners to administer the
usual Oath—The House pretends that the Unanimous Election is no Election—Refuses to receive the Member Elect—Another Election by Acclamation—A Large Crowd of Electors accompany Mackenzie to the House—
Excitement in the crowded Galleries—The House cleared of Strangers—
Mackenzie Forcibly Ejected, while waiting to be Sworn in—A Stalwart
Highlander interposes—Mackenzie declared Expelled, without being permitted to take the Oath as a Member—The Attorney General decides that
the Oath must be Administered—The Commissioners apologize for not Administering it—Mr. Hume's "Baneful Domination" Letter—Produces great
Excitement—The Oath taken—Mackenzie walks into the House and takes
his Seat—Is Forcibly Ejected by the Sergeant-at-arms—Hissing in the Galleries—The House refuse to issue a Writ for a New Election—Mr. Stanley on
the Constitutionality of one Branch of the Legislature pretending to create
a Disability—Review of the Expulsions—The Proceedings Expunged from
the Journals of the House—Mr. McNab votes for the Erasure.

IT has already been stated that Mr. Mackenzie was
expelled, for the third time, from the House of Assembly, while he was absent in England. Some detail of this proceeding, which was clearly unconstitutional, must now be given. The third session of the
eleventh Provincial Parliament, of Upper Canada,
commenced on the 31st October, 1833. On the 2d
November, Mr. McNab, without waiting till the Governor's speech was answered, having found a seconder in Mr. J. S. Boulton, whom Mr. Mackenzie
had offended by giving him in the list of pages of the

Legislative Council, moved that the entries in the journals relative to the previous expulsion be read. Solicitor General Hagerman, who was then in possession of the constitutional objections urged by the Imperial Government against these proceedings, contended that though the county of York could elect whom they pleased, the House had the right, by a simple resolution, to determine the eligibility of whomsoever they might send; and thus, in fact, to create a disability not sanctioned by law. Very little argument was required to convince the majority that this monstrous stretch of privilege was equally proper and expedient. The resolution having been carried, on a division of fifteen against eight, all that remained to be done was to prove or assert the identity of the William Lyon Mackenzie, elected for York, with the William Lyon Mackenzie previously expelled by the House, and to declare him ineligible to sit or vote in the House. Mr. McNab and his faithful seconder thought it sufficient to assert the fact and the disability. They moved a second resolution to this effect.* Mr. Boulton assured the House that the fact was "notorious, and constituted a sufficient reason for the proposed re-expulsion." The second resolution hav-

* The resolution read: "That William Lyon Mackenzie, Esq., returned to serve in this Assembly as Knight Representative for the county of York, is the same William Lyon Mackenzie mentioned in the said entries, and twice expelled this House, and declared unworthy and unfit to hold a seat therein, during the present Parliament; that by reason thereof the said William Lyon Mackenzie cannot sit or vote in this House as a member thereof." For which voted: Messrs. Attorney General, (Boulton,) G. S. Boulton, Burwell, Chisholm, D. Fraser, Jarvis, McNab, Mount, Piney, Samson, Shade, Solicitor General Hagerman, Werden, J. Willson, W. Wilson. Against it voted: Messrs. Bidwell, Buell, Howard, Ketchum, McCall, Norton, Perry, Shaver.

ing been carried, on the same division as the first, the
third expulsion was decreed, for no other reason than
that there had been two others—a ground which Mr.
McNab himself afterwards admitted to be untenable.*
Already the question of visiting the county of York
with partial disfranchisement, for its persistence in
sending back a member whom the House had repeatedly expelled, was raised. Mr. Samson, who had
taken so prominent a part in the first expulsion, expressed the opinion, that no writ for a new election ought to issue till an act should be passed to
divide the county. But the Attorney General, not
wholly unmindful of the admonition of the Imperial
Government, hesitated to go to this length. Still he
argued that it would be the duty of the Returning
Officer to refuse any votes that might be offered for
Mr. Mackenzie.† Mr. Perry attempted to obtain from
the House a reconsideration of the expulsion, on the

* When the question of expunging these proceedings from the Journals
came before the House, on the 16th February, 1835, Mr. McNab admitted his
error, and voted for the motion. "He was willing to admit," he said, "that
the last words which went on to say that Mr. Mackenzie was expelled by reason of a former resolution were wrong, and we had no right to expel him on
account of a former expulsion." Mr. McLean, in noticing this remark, "saw
nothing in it which should influence the minds of honorable gentlemen."

† He said, "he would endeavor to show, that the causes of the disqualification of Wilkes and Mackenzie were the same. They were both expelled for
insults against the House of which they had been constituted members—the
difference being in their punishment, not their crime. Wilkes being declared
for ever unfit to become a candidate for the seat, the other only for the present
Parliament. Unless a candidate be ineligible, he cannot be prevented from
sitting in that House; but being ineligible, it is the duty of the Returning
Officer to refuse his votes and not receive any for him. He justified the proceedings of the House in this case, on the grounds of custom and expediency,
and would run the risk of any abuse of such precedent, whether the case should
happen on the side which he espoused or on the other."

ground that it had been affirmed when a large number
of the members were absent; but his proposition was
supported by only ten votes, in a House of twenty-nine
members.

In the absence of Mr. Mackenzie, his friends brought
his claims before the electors. The electors considered
their privileges invaded; and so strong was the feeling
that no one ventured to come forward and declare
himself the candidate of the official party. Mr. Mackenzie was therefore unanimously re-elected.

The Returning Officer had not acted upon the hint of
the Attorney General, and assumed that Mr. Mackenzie was incapable of being elected. There was no
opportunity of refusing votes, for the election took
place by acclamation; but if the Attorney General
was right in assuming that any votes given to Mr.
Mackenzie would be thrown away, he was incapable
of being returned by acclamation, because he would
have been incapable of election; and, on this view of
the matter, the Returning Officer should have reported
that no election had taken place. Mr. Fitzgibbon refused to administer to the member elect the usual
oaths. This time there was to be no expulsion. The
matter had assumed a new shape. It was contended
that there had been no election. Mr. Bidwell brought
the question to a vote. He moved, in substance, that
Mr. Mackenzie had been duly elected for the county
of York; that he was under no legal disability, and
was by the law and constitution a member of the
House; and that, upon taking the oath, which the
law made it the duty of the commissioner to administer, he would have a right to sit and vote in the

House. The motion was rejected on a vote of eighteen against seven.* The effect of this vote was to punish and disfranchise the county of York for having presumed to elect a candidate who was under no legal disability. Mr. McNab admitted Mr. Mackenzie's eligibility for election; but contended that, though the county of York might elect, the House had the right to refuse to receive the member elected. Mr. McNab had taken up an impossible position. He had voted that Mr. Mackenzie was incapable of holding a seat in the House during that Parliament; though he held that the electors had a right to elect him. When it was notorious that they would elect nobody else, the resolution of the House not to receive him could only keep up a perpetual contest, the practical effect of which was to disfranchise the county. Mr. Perry asked the House to affirm a principle, which is now held by the best authorities to embody sound constitutional law: that the House had no right without the concurrence of the other branches of the government, to disfranchise any elector, or to disqualify any person from being elected, when such elector or person elected is under no legal disability; but he was able to command only thirteen votes in a House of thirty-two members. On a vote of eighteen against fifteen, the House then repeated its resolution, that Mr. Mackenzie should not be permitted to take a seat or vote as a member during the session; after which,

* The division was: Yeas—Messrs. Bidwell, Campbell, Duncombe, Hornor, Howard, Ketchum, Shaver. Nays—Berczy, Boulton, Burwell, Chisholm, Elliott, A. Frazer, D. Frazer, Jarvis, Jones, McNab, McNeilledge, Morris, Robinson, Shade, Thompson, Werden, John Willson, W. Wilson.

a motion ordering a writ for a new election was carried by a bare majority of one; the minority being of opinion that Mr. Mackenzie, having been duly elected, was qualified to serve, and that in reality there was no vacancy.

Mr. Mackenzie went back to his constituents on the 16th of December, 1833, and was once more re-elected without opposition. It deserves to be noticed that, in his address to the electors, he declared " the grand defect in the Colonial Constitution" to be " the want of responsible government." The election being over, a series of resolutions were put to the meeting and carried unanimously. Among other things, they called for an inquiry into the conduct of Lieutenant Governor Sir John Colborne, whom it charged with interfering with the constitutional rights of the people. The intention of a large body of the electors to accompany Mr. Mackenzie to the House of Assembly, at York, being known, he entreated them to abstain from any acts of violence. They reached the House of Assembly soon after midday. The galleries were soon filled; some were admitted below the bar, and others remained in the lobbies, for want of room inside. The result was awaited with great anxiety by the large body of electors, who were becoming indignant at being defrauded of the franchise, by the repeated expulsion of one of their members from the House, or the refusal of the majority to receive him. Mr. Perry rose to present a petition against a repetition of the proceedings by which the county of York had been deprived of half its legal representation. Several members spoke against receiving it. Mr. McNab, in

opposing its reception, was hissed from the gallery.
It was now proposed to clear the gallery of the crowd
of strangers with which it was packed; and when the
operation had been partially completed, the Sergeant-
at-arms went up to Mr. Mackenzie, who was waiting
below the bar to be sworn in, and ordered him to
leave. He replied that, as had been stated by Mr.
Perry, he had been unanimously elected by the county
of York; and that the writ had been returned to the
Clerk of the Crown in Chancery, who was present in
the House. If leave were given, he would prove that
he had a right there. The Sergeant-at-arms—Mr. Mc-
Nab, father of the member—then seized him by the
collar, in a violent manner, saying, while he dragged
him towards the door, " You shall go out." A brawny
Highlander, one of the four or five who still remained
with Mr. Mackenzie, interposed either with a blow at
the officer of the House, or held him back. As soon
as the door was opened, the crowd, who had descended
from the gallery to the lobby, rushed forward; but
before they could get in, the door was bolted and bar-
ricaded with benches, members and officers pressing
towards the door to prevent it being forced. The galleries, which had only been partially cleared, were the
scene of great confusion. The excitement was extreme, and the business of the House was brought to
a stand. Many of the members were in a state of
violent agitation. Several of them went out, and ha-
rangued the people. The question of sending to
prison the stalwart Highlander, who had interfered
with the Sergeant-at-arms, was raised; but a bystander
remarked that " he feared it would be no easy matter

to find the jail, on such an errand." That official now returned to Mr. Mackenzie, asking him to give proof of his election. This having been done, the officer of the House informed the Speaker, from whom he received orders to clear the space below the bar of strangers, that Mr. Mackenzie claimed to remain as a member. The Speaker urged the commissioners to refuse to administer the oaths, and afterwards decided that Mr. Mackenzie was a stranger because he had not taken them. Mr. McNab (the member) said that to allow Mr. Mackenzie to remain below the bar would be a proof of pusillanimity in the House, in issuing an order which they had not the courage to enforce. Mr. Burwell said the scene recalled the tumult of the French National Convention. It was not till after a long debate, that the Speaker decided that Mr. Mackenzie was a stranger, and not entitled to remain below the bar.

The hissing that took place in the gallery was unjustifiable; it could but tend to put a stop to deliberation. Such a procedure is almost invariably the precursor of a revolutionary movement. But let us apportion the degree of censure due to the various parties. The electors of York had been defrauded of their elective rights, by the proceedings of the House, some of which were clearly unconstitutional. The endurance of the electors was well nigh exhausted; and while we cannot justify their interference with the deliberations of the House, by expressing their disapprobation in hisses, we must take into account the repeated provocations they had received. The conduct of the majority was revolutionary.

This will be a memorable day in Canada. There
were among the electors some who argued that, if their
member was forcibly ejected from the House, they too
would be justified in resorting to force in defence of
their violated rights. They had, they said to one another, some old rusty muskets which they might fur-
bish up for future use, if this sort of thing was to be
continued.

Next day, Mr. Morris, seconded by Mr. Donald
Fraser, moved that Mr. Mackenzie having libelled the
House on the 14th of December, 1831—more than two
years before—and made no reparation, a previous
resolution declaring him unworthy of a seat therein
ought to be adhered to ; to which Mr. McNab added,
by way of amendment, " and therefore the said William Lyon Mackenzie, again elected and returned to
represent the county of York in this present Parliament, is hereby expelled."* The resolution, as amend-

* Here is the official record : "Mr. Morris, seconded by Mr. Donald Fraser,
moves that it be *Resolved*, That this House on the 14th day of December, 1831,
in consequence of a false and scandalous libel published against a majority of
its members by William Lyon Mackenzie, Esq., one of the members then representing the county of York, of which he avowed himself the author and publisher, was induced to expel him, the said William Lyon Mackenzie, from this
House ; that notwithstanding the gross and scandalous nature of the said libel,
'this House, in the hope that the said William Lyon Mackenzie would abstain
from a continuance of the offensive conduct for which he had been expelled,
permitted him to take his seat on the 3rd day of January following as a member
for the county of York, after being re-elected ; that, in this hope, so important
to the deliberate transaction of public business, so essential to the respectability
of the Legislature and peace of the country, a few days' experience convinced
this House there was so little reason to rely, that on the 7th day of the same
month of January it was by a large majority again deemed necessary to expel
the said William Lyon Mackenzie for a repetition and aggravated reiteration
of the aforesaid false and scandalous libel ; and in doing so, this House, in
order to support the dignity which ought to belong to a Legislative body, con-

ed, was carried by a very narrow majority, the vote being twenty-two against eighteen. How a person, who was not a member, and who was not permitted to take the oaths or his seat, or even to be heard in his defence, could be expelled, is an enigma which it would have puzzled the actors in the affair to explain.

On the evening of the 17th December, Mr. Mackenzie addressed a communication to the Lieutenant Governor, stating what had occurred, and requesting to be permitted to take the oath before His Excellency, according to a provision of the constitutional Act; or that some other prompt and immediate relief might be afforded to him and his constituents. The question was referred to Attorney General Jameson, who reported that Mr. Mackenzie was entitled to take the oath, and that no person commissioned by the Go-

sidered it just and proper to declare the said William Lyon Mackenzie unfit and unworthy to hold a seat in this House during the continuance of the present Parliament; that as the said William Lyon Mackenzie has never made reparation to this House for the gross injuries he has attempted to inflict on its character and proceedings, there is no reason to depart from the Resolution of the said 7th day of January, 1882. Mr. McNab, seconded by Mr. Robinson (brother to the Chief Justice), moves in amendment, That the following words be added to the original resolution, 'and therefore he, the said William Lyon Mackenzie, again elected and returned to represent the county of York in this present Parliament, is hereby expelled.' Several motions to adjourn the debate were negatived, the House refusing to give Mr Ketchum an opportunity to reserve his objections till the following day, although it was then near eleven o'clock at night. The House then divided, and Mr. Morris's resolution, with McNab's amendment, was adopted by the following vote :

"YEAS—Messrs. Bercsy, Boulton, Brown, Burwell, Chisholm, Crooks, Elliott, Fraser, A., Fraser, R. D., Jarvis, Jones, McNab, McNeillege, Merrit, Morris, Robinson, Samson, Thomson, Vankoughnet, Werden, Willson, J., and Wilson, W.—22.

"NAYS—Messrs. Bidwell, Buell, Campbell, Clark, Cook, Duncombe, Fraser, D. Hornor, Howard, Ketchum, Lyon. McDonald, A., Norton, Perry, Randal, Roblin, Shaver and White—18."

38

vernor had a right to refuse, since his office was ministerial and not judicial. The Governor therefore directed Mr. Beikie, Clerk of the Executive Council, to administer the oath. Mr. Mackenzie did not go before the commissioner, Mr. Beikie, for this purpose till the 11th February; feeling no doubt that, as the House had declared him expelled, he would not be allowed to take his seat. He finally made the trial at the urgent request of his friends. But we must here pause to notice some events, and their consequence, that occurred in the interval.

The majority of the House were more than half afraid of the possible consequence of their own act. They were disturbed by a rumor that the Governor was in possession of instructions that would compel him to remonstrate with the House; and unless they changed their course, to resort to a dissolution. But the Governor was completely under the control of his irresponsible advisers. He firmly believed that the official party was the sole depositary of loyalty in the Province; and that the opposition, whose only object had been the reform of abuses, wished to deprive England of her remaining American possessions. The course he pursued tended to the realization of his fears, unfounded as they were when first entertained. In reply to representations made to him at a personal interview, by Messrs. Mackenzie, Mackintosh, Ketchum, and Shepard, the Lieutenant Governor, through Mr. Secretary Rowan, under date, December 27, 1833, recommended "that Mr. Mackenzie may offer to make the reparation which the House, by their late resolution seem to expect from him." A piece of advice

that was very unlikely to be taken. From the position taken by the Imperial Government, Sir John Colborne felt it necessary to say, that on these questions
of privilege, the House had decided "uninfluenced by
the Executive Government;" an assurance the value
of which could best be determined by an observation
of the course taken by such of the irresponsible advisers of the Governor as had seats in the House. In
their interview with Sir John Colborne, Mr. Mackenzie and the three gentlemen who accompanied him,
had complained of the refusal of Mr. S. P. Jarvis and
Mr. Joseph Fitzgibbon, commissioners appointed to
administer the oaths to members of the Assembly;
and along with Mr. Secretary Rowan's letter their
apology was sent. Mr. Jarvis pretended that he was
at first prevented from reporting Mr. Mackenzie's return, by the question of order that arose; and that
when he did so, "the Speaker declined leaving the
chair till the question of order had terminated;" that
he "did not leave the House till a few minutes before
six o'clock," and that no second application was made
to him on the subject. Mr. Mackenzie had been forcibly ejected from below the bar, in the meantime.
Fitzgibbon said he would have administered the oath,
if he had been asked, before the expulsion took place.

Petitions breathing defiance began to reach the
Lieutenant Governor. "Loyal as the inhabitants
of this country unquestionably are," said a petition
from Whitby, "your petitioners will not disguise from
your Excellency, that they consider longer endurance
under their present oppressions, neither a virtue nor
a duty. For though all mankind admit the claims of

good government to the respect and support of the governed, yet very different considerations are due to that which is regardless of public interests, wars with public inclinations and feelings, and only aids or connives at oppression." From Newmarket came a petition praying the House, since they would not allow the member so often elected to sit, in its wisdom to "nominate four fit, proper, competent and discreet persons,* to represent the county of York, who may be elected, pursuant to your choice, next general election.". When Mr. Ketchum discovered that this petition was a burlesque upon the House, he withdrew it. The Governor's reply to the deputation, already noticed, was criticized in petitions presented to him; the electors complained that laws were passed without their consent, and a dissolution of the Legislature was prayed for. A town meeting, in King, refused to appoint an assessor and collector of taxes, on the ground that they had no right to pay taxes, when the Assembly robbed them of half their representation.

Mr. Hume, removed from the influence of local feelings and prejudices, wrote from London to Mr. Mackenzie, giving his opinion that the events of the 16th and 17th of December—Mr. Mackenzie's unanimous re-election and his forcible ejection and re-expulsion—would hasten the crisis that would terminate in the independence of Canada.† But he was smart-

* An act had been passed dividing the county of York into four Ridings, each of which was, at the next general election, to send a member.

† This letter is dated "Bryanston Square, 29th of March, 1834," and contains some very strong language, "Your triumphant election," Mr. Hume says, "on the 16th, and ejection from the Assembly on the 17th, must hasten the crisis which is fast approaching in the affairs of Canada, and which will

ing under a sense of injury, in consequence of some
attack made upon him by the Rev. Egerton Ryerson;

terminate in independence and freedom from the baneful domination of the
mother country, and the tyrannical conduct of a small and despicable faction
in the colony." "I confidently trust," he added, "that the high-minded people of Canada will not, in these days, be overawed or cheated of their rights
and liberties by such men as Mr. Stanley and the Colonial compact. Your
cause is *their* cause; your defeat would be *their* subjugation. Go on, therefore,
I beseech you, and success—glorious success—must crown your joint efforts."
The subject of this letter was brought up in the City Council of Toronto, (late
York,) when Dr. Morrison moved an amendment to a resolution proposed by
Alderman Dennison: "That Mr. Hume justly regards such conduct [the
repeated expulsions of Mr. Mackenzie from the House] on the part of the
Legislature, countenanced as it was by the Crown officers, and other Executive functionaries in the Assembly, and unredressed by the Royal prerogative,
as evidence of baneful and tyrannical domination, in which conduct it is both
painful and injurious to find the Provincial officials systematically upheld by
the minister at home against the people." Mr. Hume accepted this as the
true explanation of his views. Proceeding to another topic, Mr. Hume said:
"I have lately seen, with mingled feelings of pity and contempt, the attacks
made by Mr. [Rev. Egerton] Ryerson against my public and private conduct."
"I never," he said, "knew a more worthless hypocrite or so base a man as
Mr. Ryerson has proved himself to be. I feel pity for him, for the sake of our
common nature, to think that such human depravity should exist in an enlightened society; and I fear the pangs of a guilty and self-condemning conscience must make his venal and corrupt breast a second hell, and ere long
render his existence truly miserable." Mr. Hume must have been severely
stung by the attacks made upon him or he could not have brought himself to
employ such terms of censure as these. Mr. Hume felt the more hurt because
he said he had paid a great deal of attention to Mr. Ryerson when the latter
was in England; regarding him as the "representative of a good cause and a
distant people," who were much in need of some influence being exerted in
their favor in London. After this letter had been made a subject of discussion
in the City Council, Mr Hume wrote another letter to Mr. Mackenzie, bearing
date 14th of June, 1834, in which he says of the oligarchical system that then
existed in Upper Canada: "To submit quietly to such domination would be
an acknowledgment of servitude of the most odious nature, as unworthy of
the people of Canada, as disgraceful and injurious to Great Britain." Con-
gratulating Mr. Mackenzie on his election as first Mayor of Toronto, he said:
"It is cheering to see the five times rejected by the selfish faction, elected the
first Justice of the Peace by the people, and placed in the post of authority
and honor."

and his letter is at once intemperate and indiscreet.* In speaking of the " baneful domination" of the mother country as a thing for Canada to rid itself of as soon as possible, he failed to make the proper distinction between the Colonial Oligarchy and the Imperial Government ; though the latter, with every desire to do justice, upheld a false system, and was not unfrequently misled by the prejudiced and interested statements of the knot of permanent and irresponsible officials by whom the Lieutenant Governor was surrounded.

The Methodist Conference, probably moved by Mr. Hume's attack on Mr. Ryerson, on the 20th of June, 1834, while in session at Kingston, unanimously adopted an address to Sir John Colborne, in which they " disclaim, with strong feelings of indignation, the recent avowal of revolutionary principles and purposes."†

---

* The language at which Mr. Hume took offence stated that he had "no influence as a religious man; has never been known to promote any religious measure, or object, as such, and has opposed every measure for the better observance of the Sabbath, and even introduced a motion to defeat the bill for the abolition of Colonial slavery."

† This address was signed by Gordon Grindrod, President, and James Richardson, Secretary. In September, 1831, Lieutenant Governor Maitland had replied in the most offensive terms to an address of this same body of Methodists. He told them that their preachers, whether from the United States or any other foreign country, would, "*while they act honestly*, and respect British institutions," enjoy the same protection as other Americans who had sought an asylum in the country. "But," he added, "you will readily admit, that the sober-minded of the Province are disgusted with the accounts of the disgraceful dissensions of the Episcopal Methodist Church and its separatists, recriminating memorials, and the warfare of one church upon another." With regard to the system of public education, of which the Methodists had complained, Sir John told them that it " would not be abandoned to suit the limited views of leaders of societies, who perhaps have neither experience nor judgment to appreciate the value or advantages of a liberal education."

The Colonial oligarchs, and their supporters in the
Assembly, were just as ready to complain of the domination exercised by Downing Street over the local affairs
of the Province as Mr. Hume himself, when their
interests were interfered with. The disallowance of
the bank charter acts, to which reference had already
been made, almost created a rebellion among the
Tories of Upper Canada. In March, 1834, the House
of Assembly passed an address to the King, protesting,
in the most energetic terms, against the exercise of the
Royal veto* in this case; laying down the general

* The following, which contains the substance of the address, will sufficiently show its spirit:—"We, Your Majesty's most dutiful and loyal subjects,
the Commons House of Assembly of Upper Canada in Provincial Parliament .
assembled, in full assurance of Your Majesty's earnest desire to promote the
welfare of your people, beg leave humbly to address ourselves to Your Majesty
upon a matter of the deepest interest to your faithful subjects in this Province.
* * * We humbly represent, that, although the disallowance of these acts
may appear to be authorized by the letter of the statute of the British Parliament, * * * yet it is contrary to its spirit and meaning, and to the principles
of a free government. We believe that this provision was made to remedy   .
the evil which might be occasioned by the Royal assent being given in the Colony to a Provincial Act that should be found incompatible with the rights and
interests of other portions of the Empire, but we cannot think it was intended
to give a power of interference with our internal affairs. Against such an interference we respectfully, but plainly and solemnly protest, as inconsistent
with those sacred constitutional principles which are essential to a free government; since it is manifest, that if Your Majesty's ministers, at a distance of
more than four thousand miles, and not at all controllable by, or accountable
to, Your Majesty's subjects here, and possessing necessarily a slight and imperfect knowledge of the circumstances of this country, the wants, and habits, and
feelings of the inhabitants, and the mode of transacting business among us, can
dictate a different course, in relation to measures affecting ourselves only, from
that which the people by their representatives, and with the concurrence of the
other branches of the Provincial Legislature, have chosen, we are reduced to
a state of mere dependence upon the will and pleasure of a ministry that are
irresponsible to us, and beyond the reach and operation of the public opinion of
the Province; and no one can rely upon our Provincial laws, although they may
be constitutionally and deliberately formed, but the most unhappy uncertainty

principle that, in all local affairs, the Provincial Legislature ought to be supreme. To have extorted assent
to such a declaration from a section of the Tories,* was
no small gain. There seems to be no question that
they did not comprehend the full force of a declaration
that was to make the Legislature supreme in local
matters. The truth is, the popular branch of the Legislature was a complete nullity. It had no control
over the Executive Council; and the second Chamber
constantly interposed between the representatives of
the people and the Family Compact of officials, to

and want of confidence will prevail and extend their disastrous influence over
all our business transactions. We respectfully claim the same right, in behalf of Your Majesty's subjects in this Province, to be consulted in the making of laws for their peace, welfare, and good government, which our fellow
subjects in Great Britain enjoy, in respect to laws to which their obedience is
required; and although, from the necessity of the case, power must be granted
to the Head of the Empire of preventing Colonial laws being adopted and enforced which are incompatible with treaties between Your Majesty's Government and foreign States, or with the just rights of any other of Your Majesty's
Colonies; yet, with these exceptions, we humbly submit that no laws ought to
be, or rightfully can be, dictated to, or imposed upon, the people of this Province, to which they do not freely give their consent, through the constitutional medium of representatives chosen by and accountable to themselves.
The force of our humble and dutiful remonstrance against the principle of an
interference of Your Majesty's ministers with our internal affairs, we are not
willing to diminish, by insisting upon the inconveniences and evils likely to
follow from the exercise of power which, &c. * * *

"We, therefore, respectfully and humbly pray that Your Majesty, taking
these matters into your favorable consideration, will be graciously pleased not
to disallow these Provincial Acts, and not to permit Your Majesty's ministers
to interfere with our internal affairs; but to leave the same entirely to the discretion and control of the Legislature of this Province."

* In a House of thirty members, six voted against that part of the Address
given in the previous note, five of whom were Tories. It was moved by Mr.
Bidwell, and seconded by Mr. Perry, in the shape of an amendment to another
address that had been proposed. Nine Tories voted for the amendment; and
thus affirmed principles mainly sound in themselves, but with which the whole
practice of their lives was in contradiction.

whose recommendations its members owed their Legislative position. The Tories in the House went the length of complaining of the interference of the ministry, in England, with its resolves, on the ground that it was not responsible to that Chamber; though they steadfastly supported a local ministry that could, at any time, set the Assembly at defiance, with impunity. Without intending it, the upholders of the oligarchy proved the necessity of having a responsible government in the Province.

The House, as we have seen, passed a resolution expelling Mr. Mackenzie, on the 17th of December, 1833. On the 11th of February, no new writ had been issued for a new election; and Mr. Mackenzie, at the request of his friends, went before the Clerk of the Executive Council and took the oath prescribed for members of the Legislature. The Clerk acted on the authority of the Governor's instructions, backed by the opinion of Attorney General Jameson. At three o'clock on the same day, Mr. Mackenzie walked into the House of Assembly, and took his seat among the members. The House was in Committee of the whole, Mr. Donald Macdonald in the Chair. He had not been long there when he received a visit from Mr. McNab, Sergeant-at-arms, who informed him that he was a stranger, and must retire. Mr. Mackenzie replied that he was a member of the House, legally elected and duly sworn; and he produced an attested copy of the oath. He was, he said, charged with no offence or irregularity that could disqualify him for sitting and voting. Before going to the House, he had given public notice that he should not leave his

39

seat unless violence were used; and he now told the
Sergeant-at-arms that, if he interfered, it would be at
his peril. This officer replied that he must use force.
Mr. Mackenzie was three times forcibly taken from
his seat; and when he appealed to the Speaker for
protection, that functionary replied that it was not
possible for the Sergeant-at-arms to have mistaken his
duty. Mr. McNab, the member, said he was ready to
vote to send Mr. Mackenzie to jail. Mr. Merritt, in
a passion, said he ought to be put out of the House,
and two men stationed at the door to prevent his return. A resolution in favor of his taking his seat was
lost on a vote of twenty-one against fifteen. Mr.
McNab attacked the Lieutenant Governor for having
instructed the Clerk of the Executive Council to administer the oath to Mr. Mackenzie; saying he " had
interfered very improperly, and in a manner no way
creditable to himself; and that he might find, like the
Vicar of Bray, by taking both sides of the question,
he might fall through between." Mr. W. Robinson
said Mr. Mackenzie would not have gone to the
House, if he had not had the Governor's sanction in
his pocket; and that the conduct of the head of the
government was entirely unjustifiable.

While these proceedings were going on, there was
a dense crowd in the gallery, whose general conduct
was orderly and decorous; Mr. Mackenzie having
previously cautioned them to remain " quiet and pas-
sive spectators." Once there was a hiss from the gallery. It was in response to a remark of Mr. Robinson that Mr. Mackenzie ought to be punished with
imprisonment and without being heard in his defence.

In giving his reasons for again making an attempt to take his seat, Mr. Mackenzie says he did so because he believed it to be his duty. In reference to the threats of imprisonment, he said : "I greatly desire personal liberty; but the fear of a prison, or of poverty, or of danger to life or limb, will not, I trust, make a coward of me in a good cause."

A few days after these arbitrary proceedings, on the part of the majority of the House, had taken place, Mr. Duncombe made a motion which was intended to bring about a new election for the county of York, by a side wind. Mr. Mackenzie's friends did not admit that his seat was legally vacant; and therefore they could not vote for the issuing of a writ for a new election. Mr. Duncombe's resolution instructed the Speaker to take the necessary steps to have any vacancy in the House forthwith supplied; but it was rejected, as was also a motion proposed by Mr. McNab for issuing a writ for the election of a member for York, in the place of Mr. Mackenzie expelled.*

* The vote for the issue of a writ for a new election would have been to as- sume that the expulsion had been legal, and had created a vacany. A case in point occurred about this time, in Lower Canada. The Lower Canada House of Assembly had assumed to disqualify Mr. Mondelet by resolution, on the occasion of his having taken office. The Governor-in-Chief, Lord Aylmer, refused to affix his name to a new writ for the election of a member for the county of Montreal, in the place of Mr. Mondelet. Mr. Stanley in a dispatch, communicated to the House on the 13th of January, 1834, expresses his entire approval of the conduct of the Governor. In that dispatch, the Colonial Se- cretary said the House of Commons, by their knowledge of the British consti- tution, and of what was due to the privileges of the other branch of the Legis- lature, had been preserved "from the fatal error of arrogating to themselves the monstrous right of giving to their resolutions the force of law." He added that the House of Commons "neither possesses, nor has ever claimed to pos- sess, any right, authority, or power without the consent of the Crown and the

To have ordered a new election would only have been to prepare the way for a fresh outrage in the shape of another expulsion. One result of these various proceedings against Mr. Mackenzie, was to deprive the county of York of one of its two members, during the term of nearly a whole Parliament.

Though some of the actors in this drama are still living, we are sufficiently removed from the time in which the events occurred, to be able to take a view of them unclouded by passion or prejudice. The recital of the facts will often create a feeling of honest indignation; but this feeling will be quite as strong in the mind of the reader fifty years hence. A brief review of the whole proceedings will give the best idea of the spirit in which they were conducted. At first, an attempt was made to expel the obnoxious member, because he had, at his own cost, distributed copies of the Journals of the House, without note or comment, unaccompanied by the appendix. A majority was ashamed to act upon so flimsy a pretext; but one object was gained: Mr. Mackenzie did not again tender for the printing of the Journals, and the work was a godsend to the partisans of the government. Next, a pretended libel, published in a newspaper, was made a ground of expulsion, and acted upon. Neither of the articles complained of was half so severe as arti-

House of Peers, to make laws relating either to the qualification or disqualification of electors or candidates, or rather to effect their object by resolutions only." And should the Speaker be called upon, in the exercise of his ministerial capacity, to issue a warrant for a new election, "in consequence of a member being unseated by an illegal resolution, the duty would devolve upon the Lord Chancellor to take notice of the cause of vacancy, as recited in the warrant, and on the ground of illegality to refuse to affix the great seal to the new writ."

cles that are now daily published without exciting attention. Then a new libel was discovered, and made
the cause of a second expulsion. This time the House
stretched the power of privilege to the monstrous extent of creating a disqualification unknown to the law.
The third time, the House contented itself with giving
force to this declared disability. Next time, a unanimous re-election was declared to be no election at all;
though the Returning Officer had returned Mr. Mackenzie as duly elected, and no candidate had appeared
to oppose him. The fifth time, he was declared expelled, though not allowed by the House to take the
oaths or his seat; and the same majority that now expelled him had declared, a short time before, that he
was not and could not be elected; they having assumed that he was incapable of being elected during
that Parliament. This last time he was, at first, forcibly ejected from the space below the bar, on a motion
to clear the House of strangers; because not having
taken the oaths, which the Speaker urged the commissioners not to administer, he must be treated as a
stranger; and then, after he had taken the oath, before a commissioner, instructed by the Lieutenant
Governor, on the advice of the Attorney General, to
administer it, he was again forcibly dragged from his
seat by the Sergeant-at-arms, condemned to silence
under the outrage, and threatened with imprisonment.
The frequency and the facility with which the majority
shifted their ground, showed that all they wanted was
a colorable pretext for carrying out a foregone conclusion, to rid themselves of the presence of an opponent
who gave them so much trouble.

As in the case of Wilkes, who was expelled from the House of Commons, the whole of the proceedings relating to these expulsions, were expunged from the Journals of the Assembly; being declared subversive of the rights of the whole body of electors of Upper Canada.* This was done in the first session

* Here is the resolution: "Mr. Mackenzie, seconded by Mr. McIntosh, moves, That it be resolved, that all the declarations, orders, and resolutions of this House, respecting the several elections of William Lyon Mackenzie, Esq., into Parliament for the county of York, as void elections, and the incapacity of William Lyon Mackenzie, Esq., to serve in the said Parliament, and for his expulsions therefrom, and disqualification by the mere force of a former vote or votes of expulsion, as also all orders, declarations, and resolutions, denying that the elections of William Lyon Mackenzie, Esq., were good, true, and valid, or affirming that the House having expelled and declared him unfit and unworthy to take a seat therein during the said Parliament, and that being convinced of the propriety of such expulsion and declaration, would not allow him to sit and vote, be expunged from the Journals of this House, as being subversive of the rights of the whole body of electors of this Province. Which was carried on a vote of twenty-eight against seven."

Mr. Mackenzie was not the first member of the Upper Canada Assembly who had been expelled for breach of privilege consisting of alleged libel. On the 4th of March, 1817, Mr. Durand, member for Wentworth, was declared guilty of a false, scandalous, and malicious libel, and ordered to be sent to the York jail during the session. Having placed himself out of the reach of the officer of that House; and for this "high contempt" of the authority of the House, and "flagrant breach" of its privileges, he was expelled. The libel arose out of an irregular suspension of the *Habeas Corpus* Act, by Sir Gordon Drummond, administrator of the Government of Upper Canada, during the latter part of the war of 1812. This act had been suspended during the former part of the war; and the House having refused to renew the suspension, Sir Gordon Drummond took it upon himself to declare the suspension by proclamation. In a newspaper called the *St. David's Spectator*, Mr. Durand alleged that great atrocities had been committed both by the regular troops and the militia, at the time when the administrator of the government assumed the exercise of a disputed power. The Assembly, in 1815, asked Sir Gordon Drummond for any papers he might have explaining the act; when he replied, in a style too much in fashion in those days among persons having authority in Colonial governments: "All measures of that nature were adopted by me, as commanding His Majesty's forces, and resulted from the exercise of my discretion." Mr. Durand's libel on the House appears to have consisted of a

of the next Provincial Parliament, on the 16th of July, 1835. Mr. McNab voted to expunge his own resolutions, and frankly admitted that the House was wrong in grounding its third expulsion on the fact of the second. He had copied the formula of the resolution, on that occasion, from one framed for the case of Mr. Christie, from the Journals of the Lower Canada Assembly. Among Mr. Mackenzie's notes I find a statement that Mr. Hagerman confessed, on this occasion, that he had, from the first, thought the whole of these expulsions inexpedient; but that, having been overruled by those with whom he acted, he had publicly supported them. But I find nothing of the kind in Mr. Hagerman's published speech. He did not defend the expulsions, it is true; he declared he would not stoop to inquire whether this act was right or wrong; it was sufficient for him that the House had done it. He objected to one Assembly, acting judicially, reversing the decision of a previous Assembly. From first to last, the proceedings against Mr. Mackenzie were conceived in a party spirit, and carried by party votes. No worse description or condemnation of them could be given; seeing that they were in their nature judicial.

statement of the alleged condition of things in the House, when the renewal of the *Habeas Corpus* suspension was proposed. "The House at this time," he said, "seemed agitated by prospects before them according to their various feelings—the tide of temptation, at this crisis, ran high—the terrors of the bill were on one hand, good contracts were on the other; and of course the man who opposed the President's will was for ever shut out."

CHAPTER XVIII.

York changed to Toronto—Was it the Site of the Indian Toronto?—Mr. Mackenzie elected First Mayor of the City—Mayor and Corporation borrow
£1000 for Municipal Purposes on their Individual Responsibility—3d. in the
£1 considered a monstrously oppressive Tax—Public Meeting called by the
Mayor to justify the 3d. Tax—Is adjourned and a Frightful Accident occurs by the giving way of a Balcony—The Cholera of 1834—How the Mayor
braved Disease and Death—Is attacked with Cholera—Formation of the
Canadian Alliance Society—Loss of his Infant Son—Resolution to abandon
the Press—Mackenzie as a Journalist.

On the 6th March, 1834, the town of York had its
limits extended, and it was erected into an incorporated city, under the name of Toronto.*   On the 15th

* Toronto is an Indian name, but that the Indians gave that name to the
place now called Toronto is more than doubtful.   All the evidence I have seen
is against the supposition.   Upon the early French maps the present site of
Toronto was designated Teiaigon or Teiaiagon.   In a *Carte du Canada ou de la
Nouvelle France*, by Del Isle, of the French Academy of Sciences, and first Geo-
grapher of the King, published at Paris, in 1803, it is called Teiaiagon.   In
the *Carte Generale du Canada*, of Baron Lahonton, in his *Nouveau Voyage dans
L'Amerique Septentrionale*, written at different times from 1683 to 1692, and published at the Hague, Penetanguishine Bay [mouth of the Severn] is set down as
Baye de Toronto ; and in another work, *Memoires de L'Amerique Septentrionale*,
the same traveller says of Lake Huron : "On voit au nord-est de cette Rivière
la Baye de Toronto qui a vingt ou vingt cinq lieuës de longueur et quinze
d'ouverture, il se décharge une Rivière que sort du petit lac du même nom,
[Lake Simcoe,] formant plusieurs cataractes impracticables, tout en descendant
qu'en montant.   De sa source on peut aller dans le lac de Frontenac [Ontario]
en faisant un portage jusqu'a la Rivière de Tonaouaté [the Don at the present
city of Toronto] que s'y décharge.   Vous pouvez remarquer au côté Meridional
de la Baye de Toronto le Fort supposé, dont je vous a fait mention dans ma

March, a proclamation was issued calling an election of Aldermen and Common Councilmen, for the 27th of that month. The Reformers in the new city were opposed to the act of incorporation on the ground of expense, because the assessment law was deemed objectionable, and Mr. Mackenzie expressed the opinion that it would not work well. The Reformers resolved, however, to profit by the circumstance, and having carried the elections, they selected Mr. Mackenzie for Mayor: the first Mayor not only of Toronto but in the Province. The event was looked upon as possessing some political significance, for Toronto was the seat of government and the headquarters of the Family Compact. And, as the sequel proved, it was prophetic of the result of the next Parliamentary election in the city.

Mr. Mackenzie gave his time gratuitously to the interests of the city; and discharged the duties of Mayor with the same vigor that he carried into every thing he undertook. Every thing had to be done. The whole frame-work of municipal government had to be constructed and set in motion. There was not a side-walk in the city; and those of planks were introduced by the first corporation. The city finances were in a condition that much increased the difficulty of the task. The value of all the rateable property in the

vingt troisième lettre." The English pronunciation of the name of the Don River at Toronto would be something like *Tonewatak*, from which Toronto could not have come as a corruption. Nor is it necessary to resort to any such hypothesis, since Toronto is certainly an Indian name. It is clear enough, from all the evidence, that the site of the city of Toronto was not known to the Indians by that name, but that there were a Bay, a Lake, and a River to the north called Toronto.

40

city was only £121,519; and there was a debt of £9,240, contracted on account of the market buildings, on which the interest was £550 a year. In anticipation of the taxes, it was necessary to borrow £1,000. The Bank of Upper Canada refused to advance the money; its president, the late Dr. Widmer, having unsuccessfully opposed Mr. Mackenzie in the ward election for Alderman. The advertisements of the bank were, at the same time, withdrawn from *The Colonial Advocate.* Application was next made to Truscotte of the Farmers' Bank. He asked what security would be given. The city charter was liable to be vetoed in England; and in this state of uncertainty personal security became necessary. The Mayor and other members of the corporation signed the note. To meet the demands on the city treasury, it was necessary to levy a rate of 3d. on the pound. This was regarded as a monstrous piece of fiscal oppression; almost sufficient to justify a small rebellion.* Fifteen times as much is now paid without a murmur. To such an extent was the public dissatisfaction carried at what was considered the exorbitant taxes, that the Mayor found it necessary to call a public meeting, to make an explanation.† This was felt to be the more necessary

---

* "There was," Mr. Mackenzie said, "a wonderful outcry raised in Toronto that the inequality of the taxes, and the burthensome extent to which they had been laid upon the citizens, were the acts of the corporation, and still more especially the doings of the Mayor. This unfounded statement induced many persons, not only to manifest an unwillingness to pay, but also to urge others to withhold payment, and gave the collectors a great deal of trouble; while some of the members of the council were daily met by complaints, to each of whom a long detail of facts had to be gone into, the whole appearing interminable."

† At this meeting, the Mayor proceeded to explain the system of assessments; the nature of the loan made for roads; the £1,000 assessed from the citizens to

because a small meeting, composed chiefly of officials
and their immediate friends and dependents, had
already passed a censure upon the Mayor for having,
as a journalist, published Mr. Hume's celebrated
"baneful domination" letter. The meeting, called by
the Mayor, took place on the 29th of July. After
Mr. Mackenzie had explained, at some length, the
necessity for the three penny tax, Mr. Sheriff Jarvis
interrupted, saying it was his intention to move a
censure on the conduct of the Mayor. There were
some two thousand persons present; and as the
majority were the friends of the Mayor, he met this
menace by a resolution pledging the citizens not to support, at the next Parliamentary election, a candidate
whose position as an office-holder made him dependent
on the government. The Sheriff felt the force of the
retort; and showing signs of impatience by taking out
his watch, his friends in the crowd raised a storm of
disapprobation, intended to drown the voice of the
Mayor. The confusion of voices, on both sides, rendered it impossible for any one to obtain a further
hearing; and the meeting was adjourned till next day.
The meeting had commenced at six o'clock in the
evening; and on the morning of the second day, the
opponents of the Mayor issued placards calling the
adjourned meeting at three o'clock in the afternoon—

be expended by the district magistrates: the legacy of 400L of city debt left by
the justices, and of £9,400 more for the market building; the "dreadful and
unbearable" condition of the streets; the complaints of the prisoners in jail;
the presentment of the grand jury, and the absolute refusal of the justices to
co-operate with the city council for a remedy; the expenses likely to be incurred in case the cholera were to spread, and the licence moneys withheld by
government.

an hour at which it would be very inconvenient for the mechanics and business men to attend. The Mayor, regarding this as a breach of faith, forbade the city bellman to cry the meeting for that hour, and resolved not to attend it himself. The market in which the meeting was held, was a parallelogram; and over the butchers' stalls was a balcony to accommodate spectators. While the Sheriff was addressing the meeting he said: "I care no more for Mackenzie than"—here he looked up and saw a crow flying over —"that crow," he added. This was deemed a great oratorical stroke, and it elicited a cheer. The crowd above, in stamping their feet, broke down the balcony; and in the descent some were impaled on the butchers' hooks, others broke their limbs or received some other injury. Seven or eight died of the injuries they received, and others were crippled for life.

The arms of the city of Toronto, with the motto "Industry, Intelligence, Integrity," were designed by Mr. Mackenzie.

During the term of Mr. Mackenzie's mayoralty, the cholera revisited the city, and swept away every twentieth inhabitant. During the whole of the time that it raged, the Mayor was at the post of duty and of danger. He sought out the helpless victims of the disease, and administered to their wants. He was constant in his attendance on the cholera hospital. In the height of the panic, occasioned by this terrible disease, when nobody else could be induced to take the cholera patients to the hospital, he visited the abodes of the victims, and placing them in the cholera cart, with whatever assistance he could get from the families of the plague-stricken, drove them to the hospital. On some days he made several visits of this kind to the pest-house. Day and night he gave himself no rest. At length worn out by fatigue, the disease, from which he had done so much to save others, overtook himself. The attack was not of an aggravated nature; and he was fortunate in obtaining the timely assistance of Dr. Widmer; for medical men were difficult to be obtained, and many persons without medical education or experience practised on the unfortunate sufferers.

The Mayor was assiduous in his attention at the Police Court, where he constantly sat to decide the cases that came up. He was frequently accompanied by Alderman Lesslie. At the Mayor's court, too, he presided. Here he had the assistance of juries. His magisterial decisions generally gave satisfaction; but he was much censured for putting into the stocks an abandoned creature, who had frequently been sent to jail without any beneficial effect, and who was, on this occasion, excessively abusive to the Mayor. But this species of punishment was not new. The stocks had till then formed a regular means of punishment. The error belonged to the times quite as much as to the individual. A little before that time, no criminal was allowed to have a counsel for his defence; and when this privilege was accorded, the Chief Justice expressed his doubts of the wisdom of the change. Mr. Bidwell, one day, made an eloquent speech in behalf of a negro charged with theft; and the Chief Justice thought the dangerous influence of such appeals was the best proof that could be given of the doubtful character of the new privilege accorded to persons accused of crime.

In the beginning of the year, before Toronto was incorporated, Mr. Mackenzie had been elected Town Warden, and, by a strange perversity of accidents, Church Warden also, Presbyterian as he was. Before the close of his mayoralty, he issued a circular, stating, his determination to decline to come forward again for the City Council; but when his friends complained that he had no right to desert the Reform cause, he, at the eleventh hour, permitted his name to be used by the parties who had insisted on nominating him for re-election. The Reformers—for the election was made a party question—were defeated; Mr Mackenzie being put out on a national cry raised by the friends of Mr. (afterwards Judge) Sullivan, the second Mayor of Toronto. The grounds of this cry consisted of a judicial investigation, arising out of an unpleasant occurrence at the dinner of the St. Patrick's Society, in which the Mayor unnecessarily, Mr. Sullivan contended, required the evidence of certain ladies.

On the 5th January, 1835, he received the unanimous thanks of a public meeting, "for the faithful discharge of his arduous duties during the period of his office."

While Mayor of Toronto, Mr. Mackenzie was elected to the Assembly by the Second Riding of York, this being the first election since the division of the county into four Ridings. His opponent, Mr. Edward Thomson, obtained one hundred and seventy-eight votes against three hundred and thirty-four. The general election took place in October, 1834; and in addition to the personal success of Mr. Mackenzie, the party with whom he acted secured a majority in the new House. Mr. Bidwell was elected Speaker, for the second time.

On the 9th December, 1834, the "Canadian Alliance Society" was formed at York. Mr. James Lesslie was President, and Mr. Mackenzie Corresponding Secretary. In the declaration of objects, formed upon resolutions drawn up and submitted by Mr. Mackenzie, for the attainment of which the society was formed, there were eighteen subjects of legislation, twelve of which have been acted upon.* In most cases these

---

* These are: Responsible Government; Abolition of the Crown-nominated Legislative Council; A more equal Taxation of Property; Abolition of the law of Primogeniture; Disunion of Church and State; Secularization of the Clergy Reserves; Provision for the gradual liquidation of the Public Debt; Discontinuance of undue interference of the Colonial Office in the local affairs of the Province; Cheap Postage; Amendment of the Libel Law; Amendment of Jury Laws; The Control of all the Provincial Revenue to be in the Representatives of the people. The other objects sought for, but which did not recommend themselves to the public reason, were: The prevention of a Legislative Union of Upper and Lower Canada, a Written Constitution, and the Ballot. The abolition of all licensed monopolies, and of all monopolizing land companies, is not accomplished; some may question how far our law system has been simplified and cheapened: two objects of the Alliance, in the latter of which much progress has been made. "To lessen the taxation on labor," and "increase the security of property," are such general propositions that different persons would dispute as to how far they had been carried into effect. The Alliance was to exercise the duties of a political vigilance committee, by watching the proceedings of the Legislature, and enforcing economy and retrenchment. The members were also to devote themselves to the political education of the people, by the "diffusion of sound political information by pamphlets and tracts." And they were to look beyond Upper Canada by "entering into close alliance with any similar association that may be formed in Lower Canada or the other colonies."

questions have been disposed of in the way recommended by the Alliance, and in others the deviation
therefrom is more or less marked. The objects of the
Society were denounced by the partisans of the government as revolutionary. Their tendency was certainly democratic; and the carrying out of many
of the objects of the Alliance shows how far we have
advanced in that direction. In making the Legislative Council elective, we have declared the impossi-
bility of realizing Pitt's idea of building up a Colonial
aristocracy. By the abolition of the laws of primogeniture, we have taken away the only foundation on
which a landed aristocracy could rest. And, in sev-
ering the connection of Church and State, we have
placed all denominations on a common level. But
we have stopped short of the aims of the Alliance.
We have not set up a written constitution, "embodying and declaring the original principles of government," nor applied the ballot to the election of Justices of the Peace. We do not select such officers by
popular election at all, except as an incident of municipal dignity. For the time, the tide of democracy
has been arrested by the civil war in the neighboring
Republic; and we may possibly remain at the point
of democratic advancement at which we have arrived.

On his return from England, Mr. Mackenzie had
announced his intention of giving up the publication of
a newspaper. The death of his infant, Joseph Hume
Mackenzie, occurring on the 26th of October, 1833,
had deeply affected him, and had much to do in bringing him to this determination. He seems to have
acted on the impulse of grief; for two days after that

on which the child died, this announcement was made. He would issue one or two irregular papers, and then stop the publication. He had commenced when Reform was less fashionable; and now there were other liberal journals, so that his own could be better spared. But the few fugitive sheets counted up to forty-eight, from October 28, when the announcement was made, to November 4, 1834, when the last number of *The Colonial Advocate* was published.

When he commenced the arduous, and in those days perilous, task of a Reform journalist, Mr. Mackenzie had no enemies among the official party. Setting out with Whig principles, he was driven by the course of events into the advocacy of Radical Reform. " I entered," he says, " the lists of opposition to the Executive, because I believed the system of government to be wretchedly bad, and was uninfluenced by any private feeling, or ill-will, or anger towards any human being whatever." He threw away much of the profits of his business by circulating, at his own expense, an immense number of political documents, intended to bring about an amelioration of the wretched system of government then in existence. " Gain," he truly says, " was with me a matter of comparatively small moment; nor do I regret my determination to risk all in the cause of Reform; I would do it again." He did afterwards risk all on the issue of Revolution, and lost the game. He had, he thought, in 1834, done with the Press for ever. The *Advocate* was incorporated with the *Correspondent*, a paper published by Dr. O'Grady, a Roman Catholic priest, who was at loggerheads with his bishop, under the name of the

41

Correspondent and Advocate; and Mr. Mackenzie expressed a wish that no one would withhold subscrip-
tions from any other paper, on the expectation that
he would ever again connect himself with the Press.

This will be a convenient place to make an estimate
of the subject of this biography as a journalist. His
writings show an uneven temper; but taking them in
the mass, and considering the abuses he had to assail,
and the virulence of opposition he met—foul slanders,
personal abuse, and even attempted assassination—we
have reason to be surprised with the moderation of his
tone. In mere personal invective he never dealt. He
built all his opposition on hard facts, collected
with industry, and subject to the usual amount of
error in the narration. Latterly, he had entirely
abandoned the practice of replying to the abusive
tirades of business competitors or political opponents.

" I part company," he said, " with the corps editorial in the best possible humor." With papers that
pursued him with abuse, he ceased to hold any communication ; refusing either to read or receive them.
He borrowed this metaphor to show how he might
have failed to come up to his original intentions :
"We begin to cross a strong river, with our eyes and
our resolution fixed on the point of the opposite shore
on which we propose to land ; but gradually giving
way to the torrent, we are glad by the aid perhaps of
branch and bush to extricate ourselves at some distant
and perhaps dangerous landing place, much farther
down the stream than that on which we had fixed our
intentions." He generally wrote in the first person ;
and his productions sometimes took the shape of letters

to important political personages. His articles were of every possible length, from the terse, compact paragraph to a full newspaper page. On whatever objects exerted, his industry was untiring; and the unceasing labors of the pen, consuming nights as well as days, prematurely wore out a naturally durable frame. Though possessed of a rich fund of humor, his work was too earnest and too serious to admit of his drawing largely upon it as a journalist. Of Robt. Randal, when his constituents had given him a new suit of clothes, he said: "He now moves among us literally clothed from head to foot with the approbation of his constituents." He sometimes kept note of time by printing at the head of his labors: "Midnight Selections and Reflections (half asleep)." Whatever he did, he did with an honest intention; and though freedom from errors cannot be claimed for him, it may truly be said that his very faults were the results of generous impulses, acted upon with insufficient reflection.

CHAPTER XIX.

Meeting of the new House—Discussion of Mr. Hume's "Baneful Domination"
Letter—Solicitor General Hagerman charged with threatening Physical
Force Resistance—The Grievance Committee—Epitome and Analysis of its
Contents—Read by the King—Meeting of the Legislature delayed till a
Reply to Grievance Report could be sent—Total Dependence of the Local
Government on Downing Street proscribed—Mr. Mackenzie appointed
Director of the Welland Canal—The Disclosures he makes—Career of Mr.
Hincks—Mackenzie visits Papineau and the other Popular Leaders of Lower
Canada—Letter to Mr. Hume.

THE new House met on the 15th of July, 1835. On
the first vote—that on the Speakership—the government was left in a minority of four.* The Solicitor
General branded Mr. Bidwell as a disloyal man, who
" wished to overturn the government and institutions
of the country." Mr. Mackenzie thought it necessary
to acquit Mr. Bidwell of the charge of being a member
of the Canadian Alliance Society.

The taunt of the Solicitor General was not forgotten
when the Lieutenant Governor's speech came up to be
answered. The resolutions on which the Address was
founded were moved by Mr. Perry, a member of the
opposition. The letters of Mr. Hume to Mr. Mackenzie had been denounced by the official party as rank
treason. Referring to this circumstance, the Address

* The vote was thirty-one against twenty-seven.

in reply to the Lieutenant Governor's speech expressed satisfaction that "His Majesty has received, through your Excellency, from the people of this Province, fresh proofs of their devoted loyalty and of their sincere and earnest desire to maintain and perpetuate the connection with the great Empire of which they form so important a part;" proofs which would "serve to correct any misrepresentations intended to impress His Majesty with the belief that those who desire the reform of many public abuses in the Province are not well affected towards His Majesty's person and government." It also deprecated the spirit in which honest differences of opinion had been treated by persons in office, who, on that account, had impeached the loyalty, integrity, and patriotism of their opponents, as calculated "to alienate the affections of His Majesty's loyal people and render them dissatisfied with the administration." "But," the Address concluded, "should the government be administered agreeably to the intent, meaning, and spirit of our glorious constitution, the just wishes and constitutional rights of the people duly respected, the honors and patronage of His Majesty indiscriminately bestowed on persons of worth and talent, who enjoy the confidence of the people, without regard to their political or religious opinions, and your Excellency's councils filled with moderate, wise, and discreet individuals, who are understood to respect, and to be influenced by, the public voice; we have not the slightest apprehension but the connection between this Province and the Parent State may long continue to exist, and be a blessing mutually advantageous to both."

A majority of the House—the vote was twenty-nine against twenty-four—rejected an amendment indirectly censuring Mr. Hume's "baneful domination" letter; on which the Solicitor General remarked that the majority avoided the opportunity of "condemning treasonable sentiments." "If," he added in allusion to Mr. Hume's letter, "there be an honorable member of this House who is bound to identify himself with treason; who will stand up and sustain him* who says you are to keep in continual view the revolution of the United States and its results; and that a crisis is fast approaching in the affairs of Canada which will terminate in its independence from the baneful domination of the mother country, I would pronounce such a man to be deeply disloyal indeed." At the same time, Mr. Hagerman found it necessary to defend himself from an insinuation that he was the author of a declaration which, on behalf of the Tories, had threatened to look out for a new state of political existence.

During this debate, Mr. Mackenzie sat silent; though it was against him, as the correspondent of Mr. Hume, that the thunder of the Solicitor General was launched. But the aim, not being direct, left nothing to be parried.

But the matter was not to rest here. On a future day—January 30th—Mr. Gowan brought up the question of Mr. Hume's letter, but without naming it. Having no love for the Family Compact, he included in his resolution of censure the "public declaration of Christopher Alexander Hagerman, Esq.,

* Mr. Hume.

His Majesty's Solicitor General for Upper Canada,
that he would resist, by physical force, a law passed
by the constituted authorities of the land, and upon
the especial recommendation of the King's Government." The Solicitor General's explanation was that
he had said he would not pay a capitation tax on
emigrants—though it was very clear he could not be
asked, since he was not an immigrant—but would
rather be sent to prison. Mr. Mackenzie saw that
"this proceeding was intended as a shot at him over
the head of Mr. Hume;" as the publisher of the letter,
the resolution must affect him even more than the
writer. "Mr. Hume had said the affairs of the
Canadas were coming to a crisis; and had he not the
best authority for saying so? The Governor-in-chief
had said, in one of his dispatches, that Lower Canada
was fast going into a state of confusion." "As for
himself," Mr. Mackenzie added, "his loyalty was not
suspected either in this country or in England."

In the early part of the session, (January 26,) Mr.
Mackenzie moved for and obtained the since celebrated Select Committee on Grievances, whose report,
Lord Glenelg stated, was carefully examined by the
King, was replied to at great length by the Colonial
minister, and was taken by Sir Francis Bond Head
—so he said—for his guide, but was certainly not
followed by him. As we approach the threshold of
an armed insurrection, it is necessary to obtain from
those engaged in it their view of the grievances which
existed. For this purpose an analysis of the famous
Seventh Report of the Committee on Grievances will
be necessary.

Soon after, in addressing the Assembly, Mr. Mackenzie said:—"I would impress upon the House the
importance of two things: the necessity of getting
control of the revenue raised in this country, and a
control over the men sent out here to govern us, by
placing them under the direction of responsible advisers." The House, about the same time, addressed
the Lieutenant Governor for information "in respect to
the powers, duties, and responsibilities of the Executive Council; how far that body is responsible for the
acts of the Executive Government, and how far the
Lieutenant Governor is authorized by His Majesty to
act with or against their advice." The Lieutenant
Governor replied that the Executive Council had no
powers but such as were conferred on them by "the
express provisions of British or Colonial statutes,"
about which the House knows as much as he knew.
However, he condescended to proceed to particulars.
" It was necessary," he said, " that they should concur with the Lieutenant Governor, in deciding upon
applications for lands, and making regulations relative to the Crown Lands Department." And as if
there was a peculiar necessity for contradicting his
first statement, he said these duties were additional to
those imposed by statute. " It was, also," His Excellency proceeded to state, "the duty of the Executive
Council to afford their advice to the Lieutenant Governor upon all public matters referred to them for
their consideration." He himself, as well as his council, was responsible to the Imperial Government and
removable at the pleasure of the King. Where by
statute the concurrence of the Executive Council was

required to any act of the government it could not be dispensed with, and in such case the Executive Council must share the responsibility of the particular act. But the Lieutenant Governor claimed the right to exercise "his judgment in regard to demanding the assistance and advice of the Executive Council, except he is confined to a certain course by the instructions of His Majesty."

The Lieutenant Governor fairly expressed the official view of ministerial responsibility, as was afterwards shown by Sir Francis Bond Head's instructions, on his appointment to the Lieutenant Governorship of Upper Canada.

In order to understand what were, at this time, the subjects of complaint by the popular party in Upper Canada, the contents of the Grievance Report must be examined. And to discover the spirit in which these complaints were met in England, the reply of Lord Glenelg, then Secretary of State for the Colonies, must be consulted. We are not entitled to pass over, as of no interest, these complaints which proved to be the seeds of insurrection, and the prompt response to which would have prevented the catastrophe that followed, in less than three years after.

To the Select Committee on Grievances was referred a number of documents, including the celebrated dispatch of Lord Goderich, and the accompanying documents, written by Mr. Mackenzie while in England; the answer of the Lieutenant Governor in reply to an address of the House of Assembly for information regarding the dismissal of the Crown officers, the reappointment of one of them, and the selection of Mr. Jame-

42

son as Attorney General; together with petitions, vice-regal messages, and other documents. The committee examined witnesses as well as documents, and their Report, with documents and evidence, makes a thick octavo volume.

"The almost unlimited extent of the patronage of the Crown, or rather of the Colonial minister for the time being," the Report declared, was the chief source of Colonial discontent. "Such," it added, "is the patronage of the Colonial office, that the granting or the withholding of supplies is of no political importance, unless as an indication of the opinion of the country concerning the character of the government." Mr. Stanley, while in communication with Dr. Baldwin, as chairman of a public meeting in York, some years before, had pointed to the constitutional remedies of " addressing for the removal of the advisers of the Crown, and refusing supplies." The former remedy had been twice tried, but without producing any good effect, and almost without eliciting a civil reply. The second was hereafter to be resorted to. When the Province first came under the dominion of the British Crown, certain taxes were imposed by Imperial statute for the support of the local government. In time, as the House of Assembly acquired some importance and had attracted some able men, the control of these revenues became an object of jealousy and desire. Before there had been any serious agitation on the subject, in Upper Canada, these revenues were surrendered in exchange for a permanent Civil List. An opportune moment was chosen for effecting this change. Neither of the two previous Houses would have assented to the arrangement, nor would that which had now come into existence, so long as there were no other constitutional means of bringing the administration to account than that which might have been obtained by a control of the purse-strings. The granting of a permanent Civil List had looked to the Reformers like throwing away the only means of control over the administration. Indirectly the Executive controlled what was, properly speaking, the municipal expenditure. Magistrates appointed by the Crown met in Quarter Session to dispose of the local taxes. The bench of Magistrates in the Eastern District had, that very session, refused to render the House an account of their expenditure. This was, somewhat illogically, held to be proof that the mode of their appointment was vicious. Considered as dispensers of local taxes, the objection was good; but if it extended to their magisterial duties, it was bad. This distinction was overlooked by the committee. The old objections to the Post-office being under the control of the Imperial Government were reiterated. The patronage of the Crown was stated to cover £50,000 a year, in the shape of salaries and other payments, exclusive of the Clergy Reserve revenue; the whole of the money being raised within the Province. The £4,472, which had annually come from England for the Church of England, had been withdrawn in 1834. Considering the poverty of the Province, the scale of salaries were relatively much higher than at present. Ten persons were in receipt of $4,000 a year each for their public services. The mode of treating the salaries received by the public functionaries, pursued in this report, is not free from objection. The bare statement that "the Hon. John H. Dunn has received £11,534 of public money since 1827," proved nothing; yet the aggregate sum was calculated to create the impression that there was something wrong about it. Some salaries and fees were undoubtedly excessive. Mr. Ruttan received, in fees, as Sheriff of the Newcastle District, in 1834, £1,040, and in the previous year, £1,180. Pensions had been pretty freely dispensed out of the Crown revenue.

Under the head of pensions, £30,500 is set down as having been paid to eleven individuals, within eight years; but we hardly think the payment to Bishop McDonnell should have come under that designation. While the Church of England received the proceeds of the Clergy Reserves, annual payments were made by the government to several other denominations.* Profuse professions of loyalty sometimes accompanied applications for such payments; and there seemed to be no shame in confessing something like an equivalent in political support. The Church of England managed to get the lion's share; and this naturally brought down on her the envy and jealousy of other denominations. Of twenty-three thousand nine hundred and five acres of public lands set apart as glebes,

---

* Archdeacon (afterwards Bishop) Strachan, when called before the committee, said : "There should be, in every Christian country, an established religion; otherwise it is not a Christian, but an infidel country." The Roman Catholics, under the treaty between England and France, by which they were guaranteed all their accustomed rights and dues, at the conquest of the country, collected tithes from their own people in Glengary and Essex, the two parts of the Upper Province where the Catholics were numerous. The tithe, as it was called, extended to only a twenty-sixth part of the tithable produce.

between 1789 and 1833, the Church of England had obtained twenty-two thousand three hundred and forty-five acres.

It was complained that much of the money granted for general purposes was very imperfectly accounted for. "The remedy," said the Report, "would be a Board of Audit, the proceedings of which should be regulated by a well considered statute, under a responsible government." In due time, both these things came; Mr. Mackenzie having, in these as in numberless other instances, been in advance of the times.

Justices of the Peace, it was complained, had been selected almost entirely from one political party.

The necessity of a responsible administration to any effectual reform of abuse had been frequently insisted on by Mr. Mackenzie. "One great excellence of the English Constitution," says this Report, "consists in the limits it imposes on the will of a King, by requiring responsible men to give effect to it. In Upper Canada no such responsibility can exist. The Lieutenant Governor and the British ministry hold in their hands the whole patronage of the Province; they hold the sole dominion of the country, and leave the representative branch of the Legislature powerless and dependent." English statesmen were far from realizing the necessity of making the Colonial government responsible; and for some years after the official idea continued to be that such a system was incompatible with Colonial independence. Mr. Stanley had been one of the few who thought that "something might be done, with great advantage, to give a really responsible character to the Executive Council, which at

present is a perfectly anomalous body, hardly recognized by the Constitution, and chiefly effective as a
source of patronage." Only a few years before, Attorney
General Robinson had denied the existence of a ministry in Upper Canada, and claimed the right to act
solely upon his own individual responsibility in the
House, and without reference to any supposed necessity for agreement with his colleagues. And Lord
Goderich held that the Colonial Governors were alone
responsible. He complained that the Legislative
Councils had been used " as instruments for relieving
Governors from the responsibility they ought to have
borne for the rejection of measures which have been
proposed by the other branch of the Legislature, and
have not seldom involved them in dissensions which
it would have been more prudent to decline. The
effect of the institution therefore," he added, " is too
often to induce a collision between the different
branches of the Legislature, to exempt the Governor
from a due sense of responsibility, and to deprive the
representative body of some of its most useful members." The Executive Council had scarcely any recognized duties beyond those which were merely ministerial. The Lieutenant Governor did not at all feel
bound to ask the advice of his councillors, or to act
upon it when given. In appointments to office, they
were, as a rule, not consulted. The giving or withholding of the Royal assent to bills passed by the
Legislature was a matter entirely in the hands of the
Lieutenant Governor. Yet the Executive Council was
recognized by the Constitutional Act; and cases were
specially mentioned in which the Governor was re-

quired to act upon their advice. The Lieutenant Governor, coming a stranger to the Province, could not
act without advice ; and he was lucky if he escaped
the toils of some designing favorite, who had access
to his presence, and could determine his general
course. The vicious habit of sending out military
governors, who were wholly unsuited for civil administration, was in vogue. The only excuse for pursuing
this course was that a Lieutenant Governorship was
not a sufficient prize to attract men of first rate abilities. There was great diversity of opinion as to the
possible success of responsible government. It had
never been tried in any of the old colonies. Mr. Mackenzie had, while in England, endeavored to convince
Lord Goderich that, with some modifications, it might
be made the means of improving the Colonial Government. The sum of the whole matter is that the
system made the Lieutenant Governor responsible, in
the absence of responsible advisers by whom he might
have been personally relieved ; and he, in turn, was
only too glad to make the Legislative Council perform
the functions which, on questions of legislation, naturally belonged to a responsible administration. He
had them under his control.

The Committee, insisting on the necessity of entire
confidence between the Executive and the House of
Assembly, tracing it to the material progress of the Province ; thereby admitting by implication that, in the
early states of colonial existence, the want of a responsible administration had not been recognized. "This
confidence," it was truly added, "cannot exist while
those who have long and deservedly lost the esteem

of the country are continued in the public offices and councils. Under such a state of things," it was added, "distrust is unavoidable; however much it is to be deplored as incompatible with the satisfactory discharge of the public business." Sir John Colborne had admitted* that, "composed as the Legislative Council is at present, the Province had a right to complain of the great influence of the Executive Government in it." In 1829, it comprised seventeen members, exclusive of the Bishop of Quebec, not more than fifteen of whom ever attended; and of these six were members of the Executive Council, and four more held offices under the government. It was no easy matter, in the then state of the Province, to find persons qualified to fill the situation of Legislative Councillor; and that circumstance had doubtless something to do in determining its character. In 1834, the Council contained an additional member;† but he drew an annual salary from the government, and did not therefore, by his presence, tend to increase its independence of the Executive. While Sir John Colborne professed to be desirous of seeing the Legislative Council rendered less dependent upon the Crown, it was in evidence that the Executive was in the habit of coercing the members whom it could control. Instances of remarkably sudden changes of opinion, effected by this means, were given. A disseverance of judicial and legislative functions had been frequently asked by the Legislative Assembly; but the Chief Justice still continued Speaker of the Legislative Council. From

* Dispatch to Sir George Murray, February 16, 1829.
† Bishop McDonnell.

the facts before them, the committee concluded that
the second branch of the Legislature had failed to
answer the purpose of its institution, and could "never
be made to answer the end for which it was created;"
and that "the restoration of Legislative harmony and
good government requires its reconstruction on the
elective principle."

Although many may think this an erroneous opinion, it cannot be matter of surprise that it should
have found expression. The Legislative Council,
owing its creation to the Crown, and its members
being appointed for life, found itself in constant collision with the Representative Chamber. This collision created irritation; and the people naturally took
the part of their representatives in the contest. If
there had been an Executive Council to bear the responsibility that was thrown on this branch of the
Legislature, a change of ministry would have obviated
the desire for a change of system. The Legislative
Council would have been modified by having additions
made to its numbers, as was done after the inauguration
of responsible government; and the second Chamber,
being kept in harmony with the popular will, would
not have been attacked in its constitution. The
opinion that the Council ought to be made elective was
not confined to Canada; it had been shared by several
English statesmen, including Sir James Mackintosh,
Mr. Stanley, and Mr. Labouchere.

Instances were adverted to by the committee, in
which the members of the local Executive had prevented the good intentions of the Imperial Government being carried into effect. Three members of the

Executive Council, Messrs. Markland, Strachan, and
P. Robinson, refused to answer several of the questions put to them by the committee. This un-English
habit had been encouraged by Lieutenant Governor
Maitland, who, in 1828, in a dispatch to the Secretary
of State for the Colonies, said : " If the Assembly can,
without communicating with the Lieutenant Governor,
summon the Receiver General or the Inspector General of Public Accounts, or any of their clerks, to attend
a Select Committee, and compel their attendance at
the peril of imprisonment, the government here has
no longer any discretion to exercise."

Such was the famous Report of the Committee of
Grievances.* It elicited from the Secretary of State
for the Colonies a reply, which we must now proceed
to consider. But before the reply came, Lord Glenelg,
October 20, 1835, conveyed to Canada the assurance
that the King, having had the Report before him, had
" been pleased to devote as much of his time and
attention, as has been compatible with the shortness
of the period which has elapsed since the arrival in
this country" of the dispatch enclosing the document.

---

* Whether from oversight or whatever cause, the Grievance Report had not
been adopted by the House; though two thousand copies had been ordered to
be printed in an unusual form, and had been distributed. On the 6th of February, 1836, however, the Assembly resolved, by a vote of twenty-four against
fifteen, "that the facts and opinions embodied in that report continue to receive the full and deliberate sanction and confirmation of the House and the
people whom it represents; and that it is our earnest desire that the many important measures of reform recommended in that report may be speedily carried into effect by an administration deservedly possessing the public confidence." A copy of this resolution was ordered to be sent to the Secretary of
State for the Colonies. It was passed a week after Lord Glenelg's dispatch
had been laid before the Legislature.

In the ordinary course of things, the Upper Canada Legislature would have met in November; but so im-portant was it deemed that the report should be re-sponded to, that Major-General Colborne was directed to delay the calling of the House till the ensuing January—a delay of three months. At the same time, an assurance was conveyed that the House would find, in the promised communications, "conclusive proof of the desire and fixed purpose of the King to redress every real grievance, affecting any class of His Ma-jesty's subjects in Upper Canada, which has been brought to His Majesty's notice by their representa-tives in Provincial Parliament assembled." A belief was at the same time expressed, that the Assembly "would not propose any measure incompatible with the great fundamental principles of the constitution," which, in point of fact, had been systematically vio-lated by the ruling party.

The promised reply of Lord Glenelg was dated De-cember 15, 1835. It took the shape of instructions to Sir Francis Bond Head,* on his appointment to the Lieutenant Governorship of Upper Canada. The hope was expressed that, unless in an extreme emer-gency, the House would not carry out the menaced refusal of supplies. But Lord Glenelg must have

---

* Sir F. B. Head, who had been instructed to communicate the substance of these instructions to the Legislature, laid the entire dispatch before the two Houses; a proceeding for which he incurred the disapprobation of the Colo-nial office, and of the British public. He admitted that he was aware the proceeding would embarrass Lord Glenelg; but he excused himself by al-leging that the original draft of the dispatch authorized him to communicate a copy of it; and the King had made the alteration with his own hand; as if the original intention of the Colonial minister ought to supersede the final de-cision of the minister and the Sovereign.

seen that the House must be the judge of what constituted such an emergency as would justify a resort
to this extreme measure. The patronage at the disposal of the Crown, which had been so much complained of, had been swelled by the practice of confiding to the government or its officers the prosecution
of all offences. But this circumstance was declared to
be no proof of any peculiar avidity on the part of the
Executive for the exercise of such power. The transfer of the patronage to any popular body was objected
to as tending to make public officers virtually irresponsible, and to the destruction of the " discipline
and subordination which connect together, in one un-
broken chain, the King and his Representative, in the
Province, down to the lowest functionary to whom any
portion of the powers of the state may be confided."
The selection of public officers, it was laid down, must
for the most part be entrusted to the head of the local
government ; but there were cases in which the anal-
ogy of English practice would permit a transference
of patronage from the Lieutenant Governor to others.
Whatever was necessary to ensure subordination to
the head of the government was to be retained ; every
thing beyond this was at once to be abandoned. Subordinate public functionaries were to continue to hold
their offices at the pleasure of the Crown. They incurred no danger of dismissal except for misconduct ;
and great evils would result from making them independent of their superior. The new Lieutenant Governor was instructed to enter upon a review of the
offices in the gift of the Crown, with a view of ascertaining to what extent it would be possible to reduce

them without impairing the efficiency of the public
service, and to report the result of his investigation
to the Colonial Secretary. He might make a reduc-
tion of offices either by abolition or consolidation;
but any appointment made under those circumstances
would be provisional and subject to the final decision
of the Imperial Government. In case of abolition,
the deprived official was to receive a reasonable compensation. What share of the patronage of the Crown
or the local government could be transferred to other
hands was to be reported. A comparison of claims or
personal qualifications was to be the sole rule for appointments to office. As a general rule no person not
a native or settled resident was to be selected for
public employment. In case of any peculiar art or
science, of which no local candidate had a competent
knowledge, an exception was to be made. In selecting
the officers attached to his own person, the Lieutenant
Governor was to be under no restriction. Appointments to all offices of the value of over £200 a year
were to be only provisionally made by the Lieutenant
Governor, with a distinct intimation to the persons
accepting them that their confirmation must depend
upon the approbation of the Imperial Government,
which required to be furnished with the grounds and
motives on which each appointment had been made.

If this shows a disposition to treat the colonists
with consideration, it was the sort of consideration which
we bestow upon infants, and persons wholly incapable
of managing their own affairs.

To any measure of retrenchment, compatible with
the just claims of the public officers and the efficient

performance of the public duties, the King would
cheerfully assent. The Assembly might appoint a
commission to fix a scale of public salaries. The pensions already granted and made payable out of the
Crown revenues were held to constitute a debt, to the
payment of which the honor of the King was pledged;
and on no consideration would His Majesty "assent
to the violation of any engagement lawfully and ad-
visedly entered into by himself or any of his Royal
predecessors." At the same time, the law might fix,
at a reasonable limit, the amount of future pensions;
and to any such measure the Lieutenant Governor
was instructed to give the assent of the Crown. The
Assembly was anxious to dispose of the Clergy Reserves, and place the proceeds at the control of the
Legislature. The other chamber objected; and Lord
Glenelg urged strong constitutional reasons against
the Imperial Parliament exercising the interference
which the Assembly had invoked. And it must be
confessed that, in this respect, the Assembly was not
consistent with its general principles or with those
contended for by the popular party. It was easy to
put the Assembly in the wrong; and Lord Glenelg
made the most of the opportunity. But with strange
inconsistency, the Imperial Government, in 1840, assumed, at the dictation of the Bishops, a trust which
five years before they had refused to accept at the so-
licitation of the Canadian Assembly, on the ground
of its unconstitutionality. Lord Glenelg admitted
that the time might arrive, if the two branches of the
Canadian Legislature continued to disagree on the
subject, when the interposition of the Imperial Parlia-.

ment might become necessary; but the time selected for interference was when the two branches of the local Legislature had for the first time come to an agreement, and sent to England a bill for the settlement of the question.

On the question of King's College and the principles on which it should be conducted, the two Houses displayed an obstinate difference of opinion, and the Lieutenant Governor was instructed, on behalf of the King, to mediate between them. The basis of the mediation included a study of Theology; and it was impossible satisfactorily, in a mixed community, to do this with a hope of giving general satisfaction. This college question having once been placed under the control of the local Legislature, Lord Glenelg could not recommend its withdrawal at the instance of one of the two Houses.

The suggestion for establishing a Board of Audit was concurred in. As a fear had been expressed that the Legislative Council would oppose a bill for such a purpose, the Lieutenant Governor was authorized to establish a Board of Audit provisionally, till the two Houses could agree upon a law for the regulation of the Board. Lord Glenelg objected to the enactment of a statute requiring that the accounts of the public revenue should be laid before the Legislature, at a particular time, and by persons to be named; since this would confer on them the right to " exercise a control over all the functions of the Executive Government," and give them a right of inspecting the records of all public offices to such an extent as would leave "His Majesty's representative and all other public functionaries little more than a dependent and subordinate authority." Besides, it was assumed they would be virtually irresponsible and independent. At the same time, the Lieutenant Governor was to be prepared at all times to give such information as the House might require respecting the public revenue, except in some extreme case where a great public interest would be endangered by compliance.

Rules were even laid down for the regulation of the personal intercourse of the Lieutenant Governor with the House. He was to receive their addresses with the most studious courtesy and attention, and frankly and cheerfully to concede to their wishes, as far as his duty to the King would permit. Should he ever find it necessary to differ from them, he was to explain the reasons for his conduct in the most conciliatory terms. The celebrated dispatch of Lord Goderich, written in consequence of the representations made by Mr. Mackenzie, while in England, was to be a rule for the guidance of the conduct of Sir Francis Bond Head. Magistrates who might be appointed were to be selected from persons of undoubted loyalty, without reference to political considerations.

On the great question of Executive responsibility Lord Glenelg totally failed to meet the expectations expressed in the Grievance Report to which he was replying. He did more; he assumed that "the administration of public affairs, in Canada, is by no means exempt from the control of a sufficient practical responsibility. To His Majesty and to Parliament," it was added, "the Governor of Upper Canada is at all times most fully responsible for his official acts."

Under this system the Lieutenant Governor might wield all the powers of the government, and was even bound to do so, since he was the only one who could be called to account. The House of Assembly, if they had any grounds of complaint against the Executive, were told that they must seek redress, not by demanding a removal of the Executive Council, but by addressing the Sovereign against the acts of his representative. Every Executive councillor was to depend for the tenure of his office, not on the will of the Legislative Assembly, but on the pleasure of the Crown. And in this way responsibility to the central authority in Downing street, of all the public affairs in the Province, was to be enforced. The members of the local government might or might not have seats in the Legislature. Any member holding a seat in the Legislature was required blindly to obey the behests of the Lieutenant Governor, on pain of instant dismissal. By this means it was hoped to preserve the head of the government from the imputation of insincerity, and conduct the administration with firmness and decision.

These instructions embody principles which might have been successfully worked out by a Governor and Council. But they were inapplicable in the presence of a Legislature. There was no pretence that the system was constitutional, and the elective chamber must be a nullity when the Crown-nominated Legislative Council could at any time be successfully played off against it. As for responsibility to the Canadian people, through their representatives, there was none. All the powers of the government were centralized in

44

Downing street, and all the Colonial officers, from the highest to the lowest, were puppets in the hands of the Secretary of State for the Colonies. At the same time, the outward trappings of a constitutional system, intended to amuse the colonists, served no other end than to irritate and exasperate men who had penetration enough to detect the mockery and whose self-respect made them abhor the sham.

On the 6th of March, 1835, Mr. Mackenzie was appointed by the House of Assembly Director of the Welland Canal Company, in respect of the stock owned by the Province. He entered into a searching investigation of the manner in which the affairs of the company had been conducted; and if he showed a somewhat too eager anxiety to discover faults, and made some charges against the officers and managers of the company that might be deemed frivolous, he also made startling disclosures of worse than mismanagement. With the impatience of an enthusiast, he published his discoveries before the time came for making his official report; sending them forth in a newspaper-looking sheet, entitled *The Welland Canal*, three numbers of which were printed. A libel suit, in which he was cast in damages to the amount of two shillings, resulted from this publication; and Mr. Merritt, President of the company, in the ensuing session of the Legislature, moved for a committee to investigate the charge brought against directors and officers of this company. It was a bold stroke on the part of the President; but, unfortunately for the canal management, the committee attested the discovery of large defalcations on the part of the company's officers.

Accounts sworn to by the Secretary of the company, and laid before the Legislature, were proved to be incorrect.* Large sums—one amount was £2,500— of the company's money had been borrowed by its own officers, without the authority of the Board. Improvident contracts were shamefully performed. The president, directors, and agents of the company leased water powers to themselves. The company sold, on

---

* In a letter to Mr Mackenzie, dated Toronto, September 16th, 1836, Mr. Francis Hincks, than whom there was no better judge of accounts, said: "As to the Welland Canal books, I have already said, and I now publicly repeat and am willing to stake my character on the truth of it, that for several years they are full of false and fictitious entries, so much so that if I was on oath I could hardly say whether I believe there are more true or false ones. I am persuaded it is impossible for an accountant who desires to arrive at truth to investigate them with any satisfaction, particularly as the vouchers are of such a character as to be of little or no service. With respect to the charges against the Welland Canal officers, the press and the public seem to have predetermined that unless Mr. Merritt and others were proved guilty of an extent of fraud that would have justly subjected them to a criminal prosecution, they were to be absolved from all blame, and to escape censure for the numerous charges which have been clearly proved. The conduct of the press, and indeed, the House of Assembly, on this subject, has been such as to encourage a similar system of managing the money of the people, and, most assuredly, to deter any individual from even attempting to expose similar abuses. It has been clearly proved that large sums of money have been lost to the Company, and, of course, to the Province, which, if the present directors do their duty, can, in great part, be recovered; yet you, the person who have discovered these losses, and what is still better, have exposed the system, have been abused in the most virulent manner from one end of the Province to the other, and have not obtained the slightest remuneration for your services. At the same time it is never asked, in any of the public prints, whether Mr. Merritt, who was twice paid, (as is admitted even by himself, although as he states, 'by mistake,') about $1,000 of salary several years ago, has refunded this money, or whether any steps have been taken to rectify errors already proved."

Mr. Mackenzie met a shower of abuse from the men whose misconduct he had exposed. On the floor of the Legislative Assembly they and their partisans treated him as an enemy to the canal and to the country; deserving, for what he had done, only the worst epithets they could heap upon him.

a credit of ten years, over fifteen thousand acres of lands, together with water privileges, for £25,000, to Mr. Alexander McDonnell, in trust for an alien of the name of Yates; allowing him to keep two hundred acres, forming the town plots of Port Colborne and Allanburg. A quarter acre sold at the latter place for $100. They repurchased the remainder, for which the company's bonds for £17,000 were given to Yates; though all they had received from him was eighteen months' interest, the greater part of which he had got back in bonuses and alleged damages said to have arisen from the absence of water power. If such a transaction were to occur in private life, the committee averred that it "would not only be deemed ruinous, but the result of insanity." Mr. George Keefer, while a director, became connected with a contract for the locks. A large number of original estimates, receipts, and other important documents were missing; and no satisfactory account of what had become of them could be obtained. The books were kept in the most slovenly and discreditable manner, being blurred with blunders, suspicious alterations, and erasures. The length of the canal was unnecessarily extended; but if the company suffered from this cause, individuals profited by the operation. Improvident expenditures, all the worse in a company cramped for means, were proved to have been made. One Oliver Phelps owed the company a debt of $30,000 covered by mortgage, which was released by the Board without other satisfaction than a deed of some land worth about $2,000. It was not a case of writing off a bad debt, because the property covered by the mortgage was good for the amount. Over \$5,000 worth of timber purchased by the company and not used was parted with without equivalent. Some of it was stolen, some used by Phelps who was not charged with it, and some purchased by a member of the Assembly, Mr. Gilbert M'Micking, in such a way that the company derived no advantage from the sale.

The difference between Mr. Mackenzie and the Committee of the House was this: he suspected the worst, in every case of unfavorable appearances; they were willing to make many allowances for irregularities, where positive fraud could not be proved. The committee carried their leniency further than they were warranted by the facts. In the same sentence in which they acquitted the directors of any intentional abuse of the powers vested in them, they confessed themselves unable to explain the Phelps transaction.

The ludicrous part of this investigation consists of numerous items charged to the contingent account by Mr. Merritt, President of the Company. A few samples may be given. "Play, 3s. 9d.;" "Barber, 7½s.;" "Repairing my watch, 7s. 6d;" "Segars and Snack." "Club for gin, 3s. 1½d. Club for segars, 1s.;" "Paid doctor for attendance, 10s." There were whole columns of such figures as these, amounting to about \$400, duly audited and passed by the Board. But it must be admitted that even this petty larceny showed method and exactness; and if the amount had been charged as travelling expenses, without a ridiculous detail, it would probably not have been challenged. Certainly it would not have excited ridicule.

In this investigation, there was employed as

accountant, a young man of whose abilities Mr. Mackenzie conceived a very high opinion ; so much so that he remarked to him, that he should be glad to see him Inspector General of Public Accounts for Upper Canada. But he added with sleepless suspicion, " The only question with me is, whether you would be proof against the temptations of the position." That accountant was Francis Hincks. He was afterwards Inspector General for United Canada, and leader of the government; then Governor of the Windward Islands, and is now Governor of British Guiana, with a salary of £5,000 a year, and £2,000 for contingencies. He has fully justified the prevision of Mr. Mackenzie, and risen by the force of his talents to a higher position than the latter had ventured to assign to him. ·

Mr. Mackenzie spent several months in this investigation at St. Catharine's, the head-quarters of the company. In 1836, a committee of the House recommended a compensation of $1,000 for his services ; but, as the regular supplies were not granted that year, the money was not paid. The Canadian insurrection, occurring towards the close of 1837, led to his exile for several years, in the United States ; and as he was the last of the exiles to whom the Royal clemency was extended, he was not paid the $1,000 till 1851, and then without interest.

In November, 1835, Mr. Mackenzie visited Quebec, in company with Dr. O'Grady. They went as a deputation from leading and influential Reformers, in Upper Canada, to bring about a closer alliance between the Reformers in the two Provinces. In the Lower Province affairs were more rapidly approaching a crisis than in the West. The difficulties arising out of the control of the revenue had led to the refusal of the supplies by the Lower Canada Assembly; and in 1834, £31,000 sterling had been taken out of the military chest, by the orders of the Imperial Government, to pay the salaries and contingencies of the judges and the other public officers of the Crown, under the hope that, when the difficulties were accommodated, the Assembly would reimburse the amount. But the difficulties, instead of meeting a solution, continued to increase. As the grievances of which the majority in the two Provinces complained had much in common, the respective leaders began to make common cause. The Provinces had had their causes of differences, arising out of the distribution of the revenue collected at Quebec. But the political sympathies of the popular party, in each Province, were becoming stronger than the prejudices engendered by the fiscal difficulties, and which had acted as a mutual repulsion. Mr. Mackenzie and his co-delegate met a cordial and affectionate welcome. "All the liberal members" of the Lower Canada Assembly " flocked around them to testify the sincere interest they took in the progress of good government in Upper Canada, and to tender them their hearty co-operation."* This expression of sympathy, extending to all classes of Reformers, was expected to prove to the authorities, both in Canada and England, "that the tide is setting in with such irresistible force against bad government, that if they do not yield to it before long, it will shortly overwhelm them in its rapid and onward progress." Mr. Mackenzie was on good terms

* *Montreal Vindicator.*

with Papineau, whose word was law in the Assembly
of Lower Canada, of which he was Speaker, but who,
in Committee of the Whole, used the greatest freedom
of debate. This visit resulted in establishing a better
understanding between the Reformers of the two Provinces.* Mr. Mackenzie has left it on record that
"changes were then in contemplation, which would in
a certain degree have affected individuals," if generally known; but as this statement was shortly afterwards published, it cannot be taken to have reference
to that armed insurrection which ultimately followed.
To a very late period, Mackenzie and those who acted
with him continued to hope that the reforms for which
they contended would be peaceably granted.

In December, 1835, he addressed a long letter to
Mr. Hume—which was published just before the elections of the next year took place—on the condition of
the Province. Its principal complaints were: that
jury trials were in the hands of sheriffs, who held
office during the pleasure of the King; that an extensive domain had been improvidently ceded to the

---

* In the session of the Upper Canada Legislature for 1836, Mr. Mackenzie
carried the following resolution by a large majority:—"That it is the desire
of this House to cultivate a good understanding with Lower Canada, and that
a select committee be appointed to draft a bill to this House, for the appointment of commissioners to meet any commissioners that may be appointed by
the Legislature of Lower Canada, to consider of matters of mutual importance
to both Provinces, especially the questions of boundaries, trade, emigration,
customs' duties, and revenue." This resolution was in the spirit of one of the
declared objects of the "Canadian Alliance Society." This year, Mr. Papineau, the Speaker of the Lower Canada Assembly, sent a long letter to Mr.
Speaker Bidwell, of the Upper Canada Assembly; in which the principles of
Colonial Government laid down in Lord Glenelg's dispatch in reply to the
"Grievance Report" were denounced, and a responsible government and an
elective Legislative Council declared to be necessary.

Canada Company; that the Legislative Council continued to reject the bills passed by the Assembly; that the administration of justice was in the hands of a party forming among themselves a Family Compact; that, owing to these circumstances, property and liberty were held by a very precarious tenure; that the administration of the government was in the hands of men, in whom neither the people nor their representatives had any confidence; that, as a consequence of this state of things, there was little immigration,* and many residents were thinking of quitting the Province; that the idea of successive Colonial Secretaries had been to govern the Province by orders sent from Downing Street, to be executed by agents selected there; that there was no means of exacting strict accountability for the public moneys; that the Reformers of both Provinces directed their exertions mainly to the accomplishment of four objects: an elective Legislative Council, an Executive Council responsible to public opinion, the control of the whole Provincial revenues, and a cessation of interference on the part of the Colonial office—"not one of which," he said, "I believe will be conceded till it is too late."† The prediction proved correct; but all these changes have been effected since the insurrection of 1837. He ten-

* In 1835, the immigration to Upper Canada had fallen off two-thirds as compared with the average of former years.

† Though all these objects have now been carried into effect, Sir Francis Bond Head regarded their advocacy as proof of treasonable designs. In a dispatch to Lord Glenelg, dated June 22, 1836, after quoting the above passage, he says: "As the Republicans in the Canadas generally mask their designs by professions of attachment to the mother country, I think it important to record this admission on the part of Mackenzie of the traitorous object which the Reformers in this Province have in view."

45

dered his thanks to Mr. Hume for his exertions on behalf of Canada in these words:

"On behalf of thousands whom you have benefited, on behalf of the country so far as it has had confidence in me, I do most sincerely thank you for the kind and considerate interest you have taken in the welfare of a distant people. To your generous exertions it is owing that tens of thousands of our citizens are not at this day branded as rebels and aliens; and to you alone it is owing that our petitions have sometimes been treated with ordinary courtesy at the Colonial office.

"We have wearied you with our complaints, and occupied many of those valuable hours which you would have otherwise given to the people of England. But the time may come when Canada, relieved from her shackles, will be in a situation to prove that her children are not ungrateful to those who are now, in time of need, their disinterested benefactors."

A shadowy idea of independence appears already to have been floating in men's minds; and it found expression in such terms as are employed in his letter about Canada being relieved of her shackles.

CHAPTER XX.

Sir Francis Bond Head arrives in Upper Canada—His Speech on opening the
Legislature—Mackenzie tries to remove the Restrictions on the Trade of
the Province—The House snub the Lieutenant Governor in their Reply to
the Address—Why were Members of the Government supported in a Departure from Lord Goderich's Dispatch?—Sir F. B. Head affects a Readiness to redress all Grievances—He appoints three new Executive Councillors
from the Liberal Party—Resignation of the new Council because they were
not consulted on the Affairs of the Province—They are sustained by the
House, and the Lieutenant Governor sharply censured—Responsible Government and Separation from England—The Lieutenant Governor and
the "Industrious Classes"—Four new Executive Councillors—The House
of Assembly address the Lieutenant Governor to dismiss them—He refuses
—Question of Popular Colonial Councils—Sir F. B. Head boasts of having
provoked a Disturbance at a Public Meeting—Stoppage of Supplies and Reservation of Money Bills—Dissolution of the House—Unconstitutional and
violent Means resorted to by the Lieutenant Governor for carrying the
Elections—He instructs the Colonial Office how to act—Opposes the Surrender of the Crown Revenues and denounces the Project of a Responsible
Administration—"Let them come if they dare"—Practical Joke on the
Lieutenant Governor—His strange Doings and his Contumacy—Mackenzie,
Bidwell, and Perry lose their Elections—Excitement at Mackenzie's Election—The Influences arrayed against him—He weeps over his Defeat—Is
attacked with a dangerous Illness—His Protest not allowed to go to an Election Committee—Proof of the Lieutenant Governor's Unconstitutional Interference in the Elections—He was required to put in his Defence.

ON the 14th January, 1836, Sir Francis Bond Head,
who had just arrived in the Province as Lieutenant
Governor,* opened the session of the Upper Canada

*Sir Francis Bond Head afterwards admitted, with admirable candor, that
he "was really grossly ignorant of every thing that in any way related to the

Legislature. The Royal speech, in referring to the dissensions that had taken place in Lower Canada, and to the labors of the Imperial commissioners appointed to inquire into the grievances complained of, assured the House that, whatever recommendations might be made, as the result of this inquiry, the constitution of the Provinces would be firmly maintained. As the constitution of the Legislative Council was one of the subjects of inquiry, this information could not be very consolatory to the Reformers.

During the session, Mr. Mackenzie carried an Address to the King on the subject of the restraints imposed upon the Province by the commercial legislation of the mother country. British goods could not pass through the United States, on their way to Canada, without being subjected to the American duty; and the Address prayed that the Sovereign would negotiate with the Washington Government, for the free passage of such goods. The facility of transport thus asked for was fully secured by the United States Bonding Act passed ten years after. For the purpose of upholding the monopoly of the East India Com-

government of our colonies." He was somehow connected with paupers and poor laws in England when he was appointed; and was totally unfitted by experience and temperament to be Lieutenant Governor of an important dependency of the British Crown. How Lord Glenelg could have stumbled upon so much incapacity is as great a mystery to the Canadians, at this day, as it was to Sir Francis when, at his lodgings at Romney, in the County of Kent, his servant, with a tallow candle in one hand, and a letter brought by a King's officer in the other, enabled him to make the discovery that he had been offered the Lieutenant Governorship of Upper Canada. He was in a sound sleep when the servant arrived; and if other men have found themselves famous when they woke of a morning, Sir Francis Bond Head found himself suddenly roused up to be informed that he was on the way to enforced greatness.

pany, not an ounce of tea could be imported into
Canada by way of the United States. The abolition
of this monopoly was demanded. Canadian lumber
and wheat were heavily taxed—25 cents a bushel on
the latter—on their admission into the United States:
the same articles coming thence into the Province were
free of duty. Mr. Mackenzie anticipated by eighteen
years the Reciprocity Treaty of 1854. The Address
prayed " that His Majesty would cause such representations to be made to the Government of the United
States as might have a tendency to place this interesting branch of Canadian commerce on a footing of reciprocity between the two countries." Nor did he
stop here. He thought it right that this principle of
reciprocity should be extended to all articles admitted
by Canada free of duty from the United States.

In those days, the Address in answer to the Royal
Speech was no mere echo of the statements and recommendations contained in that document. The occasion was frequently seized upon as a favorable one
for an exposition of public grievances. On a number
of points, the Address, on this occasion, differed from
the Speech to which it was an answer. It went so far
as directly to rebuke the Lieutenant Governor for the
reference he had made to Lower Canada. "We
deeply regret," said the Address, " that your Excellency has been advised to animadvert upon the affairs
of the sister Province, which has been engaged in a
long and arduous struggle for an indispensable amelioration in their institutions and the manner of their
administration. We respectfully, but firmly, express
our respect for their patriotic exertions; and we do

acquit them of being the cause of any embarrassment and dissensions in the country."

It was a subject of frequent complaint, in both the Canadas, that the good intentions of the Imperial Government were thwarted by the agents selected to execute the Royal wishes. Mr. Mackenzie introduced a series of resolutions making a complaint of this nature; and after it had been verbally amended, on motion of Mr. Perry, acting, no doubt, under the suggestion of Mr. Speaker Bidwell, an Address to the Lieutenant Governor was founded upon it. The Address asked for any dispatches that might serve to explain the contradiction between the Royal instructions relative to the dismissal of public officers when they cease to give a conscientious support to the measures of the government, and the retention of persons —Mr. Hagerman was mentioned in the original resolution—as legal advisers of the Crown and members of the Executive Council, in spite of their opposition to many of the Reforms sanctioned by the Earl of Ripon, as Colonial Secretary. The case of Mr. Hagerman, whose name was not mentioned, was described as glaring in the extreme; since he had desired to send back the famous dispatch of Lord Goderich, afterwards Earl Ripon. The Solicitor General, during the debate, denied that he had gone to this length; but the House, by a majority of ten, refused to accept his statement as correct. "We cannot reconcile with the principles of our Constitution," the Address reads, "the appointment and continuance in office of persons, as counsellors and advisers of the government, who are known to stand opposed to the wishes of the people and the recommendations of His Majesty, on great leading questions of Reform, and who do not possess the confidence of the people, and acquiesce in their general political views and policy, as expressed through their representatives." The appointment of Mr. William Morris, whose name was struck out of the amended resolutions, to a seat in the Legislative Council, after he had, as a member of the other branch of the Legislature, violently denounced the dispatch of Lord Goderich, was condemned as contrary to the recommendations of the Canada Committee of the House of Commons, in 1828, and the declared principles of the Imperial Government; and as calculated to increase the obstacles to Reform. The union of legislative and judicial powers in the Chief Justice, who continued to be Speaker of the Legislative Council, and the presence in that branch of the Legislature of the Bishop of Regiopolis and the Archdeacon of York, were spoken of in terms of censure. Mr. Mackenzie accepted the amendment, and declared it preferable to his own resolution.

In the course of the debate on this Address, Solicitor General Hagerman professed to give a cordial assent to the principles of Lord Goderich's dispatch, which, when laid before the House he had denounced in unmeasured terms; and he still charged his opponents with revolutionary designs because they demanded the application of the principles laid down in that state document.

Sir Francis Bond Head, unused to government, had been instructed by the Colonial Secretary in the rules of official etiquette and courtesy which he was to observe. And in answering this Address he did not assume that objectionable tone which shortly afterwards marked his utter unfitness for the position to which he had been appointed. In regard to the removal of the Crown officers there was a dispatch marked " confidential," and which for that reason he did not produce. He had no means of explaining the continuance in office of Solicitor General Hagerman, further than that his reinstatement was the result of exculpatory evidence offered by that person, while in England. The Lieutenant Governor could require, and, if necessary, insist on the resignation of officials who might openly or covertly oppose the measures of his government; but he would not take a retrospective view of their conduct, or question the wisdom of what had been done by his predecessors, in this respect. The same rule he applied to appointments made to the Legislative Council; as he could not undertake to judge of the principles that guided his predecessor. Lord Ripon, he considered, in giving his opinion of the presence of the Roman Catholic Bishop and the Anglican Archdeacon in the Legislative Council, had expressed no intention in reference to them. Sir Francis confessed, with maladroitness, to the existence of dispatches which he did not feel at liberty to communicate; besides that already mentioned, another dated Sept. 12, 1835, and containing observations on the Grievance Report. He asked from the House the consideration due to a stranger to the Province, unconnected with the differences of party, entrusted by his Sovereign with instructions

" to correct, cautiously, yet effectually, all real grievances," while maintaining the Constitution inviolate.

During this session an event occurred which, though
Mr. Mackenzie was not directly connected with it, had
an important bearing on the general course of affairs
that was to lead to the armed insurrection, in which
he was a prominent actor. It is necessary to a clear
comprehension of all the circumstances which produced this crisis, that the event should be briefly related.

On the 20th of February, 1836, Sir F. Bond Head
called three new members to the Executive Council ;*
Messrs. John Henry Dunn, Robert Baldwin, and John
Rolph.† The two latter were prominent members of

---

* Sir F. B. Head was pressed by one of the old members of the Council to
appoint some additional members. The number, as it stood, was only sufficient
for a quorum, and if one fell sick no business could be done. Besides, Mr.
Peter Robinson had charge of the public lands, and, as an Executive Councillor,
was placed in the invidious position of having to audit his own accounts.
When Sir F. B. Head arrived, it was believed that he was going to reform the
abuses complained of, and effect the desired changes in the government. Handbills, on his arrival, were foolishly placed on the walls of the city, describing
the new Lieutenant Governor as a "tried Reformer." The Tories were shy
and distrustful. They petitioned the King against the first act of his administration. Had they not taken up this hostile position, he afterwards declared,
he never would have gone to the other party for material to enlarge his
Council ; and he would have appointed neither Mr. Baldwin nor Dr. Rolph.
But he soon threw himself completely into the arms of the Family Compact ;
adopted their designs, echoed their opinions of their opponents, and repeated
their worst calumnies, in official dispatches and other state documents.

† Sir Francis Bond Head, in An Address to the House of Lords against the
Bill before Parliament for the Union of the Canadas, in 1840, says that when he
offered office to Mr. Baldwin, the latter replied that "he considered as abso-
lutely necessary the assistance of Dr. Rolph and of Mr. Bidwell ;" and if this
statement be correct, the matter was compromised by one being taken and the
other left. Rolph became a member of the Executive Council, and Bidwell
was left out.
46

the Liberal party, and Mr. Dunn had long held the office of Receiver General. Their appointment was hailed as the dawn of a new and better order of things, and the Lieutenant Governor professed, with what sincerity will hereafter appear, a desire to reform all real abuses. But it was not long before this hope was disappointed. On the 4th March these gentlemen, with the other three members of the Executive Council,* resigned. They complained that they had incurred the odium of being held accountable for measures they had never advised, and for a policy to which they were strangers. It shows the irresistible force which the popular demand put forward by Mr. Mackenzie and others for a responsible administration carried with it, that the three Tory members of the Council should have joined in the resignation. The current was too strong to leave a reasonable hope of their being able to make way against it. But what they shrunk from undertaking, Sir Francis Bond Head was to try, by the aid of more supple instruments, to accomplish. The six councillors, on tendering their resignations, insisted on the constitutional right of being consulted on the affairs of the Province generally, and resorted to some elaboration of argument to prove that their claim had an immovable foundation in the Provincial charter.

The Lieutenant Governor, on the other hand, contended that he alone was responsible, being liable to removal and impeachment for misconduct, and that he was at liberty to have recourse to their advice only when he required it; but that to consult them on all

* Messrs. Peter Robinson, George H. Markland, and Joseph Wells.

the questions that he was called upon to decide would
be "utterly impossible." He, too, attempted to establish his position by reference to the constitutional
charter and other instruments; but the House charged
him with garbling and misquoting. His political
theory was very simple. "The Lieutenant Governor
maintains," he said, "that responsibility to the people, who are already represented in the House of Assembly, is unconstitutional; that it is the duty of the
Council to serve him, not them." A doctrine that
was soon to meet a practical rebuke from his official
superiors in England.

The answer of His Excellency was sent to a select
committee of the House, who made an elaborate Report, in which the Lieutenant Governor's treatment
of his Council was censured in no measured terms.
The increasing dissatisfaction which had been produced by the maladministration of Lieutenant Governors Gore, Maitland, and Colborne, was said to have
become general. The new appointments to the Executive Council of liberal men, made by Sir Francis
Bond Head, were stigmatized as "a deceitful manœu-
vre to gain credit with the country for liberal feelings
and intentions when none existed;" and it was declared
to be matter of notoriety that His Excellency had
"given his confidence to, and was acting under, the
influence of secret and unsworn advisers." "If," they
said, "all the odium which has been poured upon the
old Executive Council had been charged, as His Excellency proposes, upon the Lieutenant Governors, their
residence [in the Province] would not have been very
tolerable, and their authority would become weakened

or destroyed." The authority of Lieutenant Governor Simcoe, whose appointment followed close after the passing of the constitutional Act of 1791, was adduced to show that "the very image and transcript" of the British constitution had been given to Canada. The Lieutenant Governor was charged with having "assumed the government with most unhappy prejudices against the country," and with acting "with the temerity of a stranger and the assurance of an old inhabitant." Much warmth of feeling was shown throughout the entire Report, and the committee gave it as their opinion that the House had no alternative left "but to abandon their privileges and honor, and to betray their duties and the rights of the people, or to withhold the supplies."* "All we have done will otherwise," it was added, "be deemed idle bravado, contemptible in itself, and disgraceful to the House."

The House adopted the Report of the committee, on a vote of thirty-two against twenty-one; and thus committed itself to the extreme measure of a refusal of the supplies. To the resolution adopting the Report a declaration was added that a responsible government was constitutionally established in the Province.

In the debate on question of adopting the Report, the Tories took the ground that responsible govern-

* The object of the Assembly, in stopping, or rather restricting, the supplies, was to embarrass the government. They did not go to the extent of refusing all money votes, but granted different sums for roads, war losses, the Post-office, schools, and the improvement of navigation. Twelve of these bills Sir Francis B. Head reserved, in the hope that he would be enabled to embarrass the machinery of the Legislature, if they were vetoed in England. But, much to his disgust, they were assented to by his Sovereign. When he received the dispatch containing the assent to these bills, he at first thought of suppressing it, but on sober second thought he transmitted it to the Legislature.

ment meant separation from England. "The moment," said Mr. McLean, "we establish the doctrine
in practice, we are free from the mother country."
Assuming that the Imperial Government would take
this view of the matter, Solicitor General Hagerman
covertly threatened the majority of the House with
the vengeance of "more than one hundred and fifty
thousand men, loyal and true." The temper of both
parties was violent, for already were generating those
turbulent passions of which civil war was to be the
final expression.

In times of excitement the slightest incident may
add fuel to the flames; and men, rendered keenly sensitive by the endurance of wrongs, readily re-
sent the most distant approach to insult. Sir Francis
B. Head, having received an Address, adopted at a
public meeting of the citizens of Toronto, assured
them that he should feel it his duty to reply with as
much attention as if it had proceeded from either
branch of the Legislature; but that he should express
himself "in plainer and more homely language."
This was regarded as a slight to the inferior capacity
of the "many-headed monster," and was resented
with a bitterness which twenty years were too short to
eradicate. The manner of the Lieutenant Governor
gave as much offence as his words. He met the deputation, surrounded by a crowd of military officers;
and the members fancied that he pried impudently
into their faces, as if he regarded them with the sort
of curiosity that one would look upon a collection of
orang outangs.

They left the Vice-regal residence, inspired by a

common feeling of indignation, at what they conceived
to be intentional slights put upon them. It was soon
resolved to repay the official insolence with a rejoinder.
Drs. Rolph and O'Grady prepared the document.
Instead of being drawn up in the slip-shod style of
the Report of the House Committee, its biting sarcasm
betrayed a master hand. "We thank Your Excellency," said the opening sentence, "for replying to our
Address, 'principally from the industrious classes of
the city,' with as much attention as if it had proceeded
from either branch of the Legislature; and we are
duly sensible in receiving Your Excellency's reply, of
your great condescension, in endeavoring to express
yourself in plainer and more homely language, presumed by Your Excellency to be thereby brought
down to the lower level of our plainer and more
homely understandings." They then pretended to
explain the deplorable neglect of their education by
the maladministration of former governments of the
endowment of King's College University, and the
many attempts of the Representative Chamber, baffled by the Crown-nominated Legislative Council, to
apply three millions of acres of Clergy Reserves to
the purposes of general education. "It is," they
added, "because we have been thus maltreated, neglected, and despised, in our education and interests,
under the system of government that has hitherto
prevailed, that we are now driven to insist upon a
change that cannot be for the worse." The change
they desired to 'bring about was "cheap, honest, and
responsible government." The responsibility of the
Lieutenant Governor to a government four thousand

miles distant, " and guarded by a system of secret dispatches, like a system of espionage," which kept in
" utter darkness the very guilt, the disclosure of which
could alone consummate real and practical responsibility," had never, they declared, "saved a single
martyr to Executive displeasure." Robert Gourlay
still lived in the public sympathy, "ruined in his fortune, and overwhelmed in his mind, by official injustice and persecution; and the late Capt. Matthews, a
faithful servant of the public, broken down in spirit,
narrowly escaped being another victim. The learned
Mr. Justice Willis struggled in vain to vindicate himself and the wounded justice of the country; and the
ashes of Francis Collins and Robert Randal lie entombed in a country in whose service they suffered
heart-rending persecution and accelerated death. And
even Your Excellency has disclosed a secret dispatch
to the minister, in Downing Street (the very alleged
tribunal of justice), containing most libellous matter
against William Lyon Mackenzie, Esq., M. P. P., a
gentleman known chiefly for his untiring services for
his adopted and grateful country. We will not wait,"
they plainly told the Lieutenant Governor, "for the
immolation of any other of our public men, sacrificed
to a nominal responsibility, which we blush we have
so long endured to the ruin of so many of His Majesty's dutiful and loyal subjects." After an elaborate
argument, to prove the necessity of a responsible administration, the rejoinder concluded by what Mr.
Mackenzie, in a manuscript note he has left, calls the
first low murmur of insurrection. " If Your Excellency," the menace ran, " will not govern us upon

these principles, you will exercise arbitrary sway, you will violate our charter, virtually abrogate our law, and justly forfeit our submission to your authority." There was not yet, however, the most distant idea that the final issue would be open insurrection.

The rejoinder being ready,* the next question was how it was to be delivered. Such a document was quite irregular in official correspondence, and a violation of official etiquette. It was arranged that Mr. James Lesslie and Mr. Ketchum should drive in a carriage drawn by a noble Arabian horse to Government House, deliver the document, and retire before there was time for any questions to be asked. They did so, simply saying they came from the deputation of citizens.

Sir F. Bond Head did not even know who were the bearers of the unwelcome missile. He sent it, in a passion, to Mr. George Ridout, on the speculation that he had been concerned in the delivery. Mr. Ridout sent it back. It was in type before being dispatched, and scarcely had it reached the Governor when a printed copy of it was in the hands of every member of the House. The Lieutenant Governor was puzzled, half stupefied, and well nigh distracted.

On the 14th March, four new Executive Councillors were appointed, consisting of Messrs. Robert Baldwin Sullivan, William Allan, Augustus Baldwin, and John Elmsley. The latter had resigned

---

* It was signed by Jesse Ketchum, James H. Price, James Lesslie, Andrew McGlashan, James Shannon, Robert McKay, M. McLellan, Timothy Parsons, William Lesslie, John Mills, E. T. Henderson, John Doel, John E. Tims, William J. O'Grady.

his seat in the Executive Council some years before, on the ground that he could not continue to
hold it and act independently as a Legislative Councillor, though the principle of dependence had never
before been pushed to the same extent as now. Three
days after these appointments were announced, the
House declared its "entire want of confidence," in
the men whom Sir Francis had called to council.*
The vote was thirty-two against eighteen. An Address to the Lieutenant Governor embodying this
declaration of non-confidence, and expressing regret
that His Excellency should have caused the previous
Council to tender their resignation, while he declared
his continued esteem for their talents and integrity,
was subsequently passed on a division of thirty-two
against nineteen. The Address requested His Excellency to take immediate steps to remove the obnoxious Council. In reply he said he felt guiltless of
having caused the excited state of public feeling in
the Province, and was not at all disposed to listen to

* While these proceedings were going on, the people were not idle spectators. A petition came from Pickering township, complaining that the Lieutenant Governor had "resolved to hold the powers entrusted to him by his
Sovereign, to reduce British subjects to a state of vassalage," and praying the
House to address His Excellency to remove his councillors. As soon as the
Executive Council resigned, Sir Francis Bond Head wrote to Lord Glenelg,
under date, Toronto, 22d March, 1836, "Mr. Mackenzie and his party, at an
immense expense, forwarded to every part of the Province" copies of a circular, to which was annexed "a printed petition to the House of Assembly,
which only required the insertion of the name of the township and of the
subscribers." This is probably correct, but the authority of Sir Francis Bond
Head is never reliable when he is speaking of persons whom he considered
it his sacred duty to revile. It is certain a number of petitions of the same
purport as that from Pickering were presented to the House.

47

the advice of the House, on whose good sense he, at the same time, affected to be ready to rely.

The popular party had unintentionally given an incidental sanction to the assumptions of the Lieutenant Governor, founded on the dispatch of Lord Glenelg, on the dismissal of the Crown officers, in 1833. Their removal was the result of their opposition, in the Legislature, to the expressed wishes of the Imperial Government. In procuring the annulment of the bank charters, Mr. Mackenzie was not sustained by the party with whom he acted, and by whom the dismissal of the Crown officers was gratefully accepted. It was the misfortune of Sir Francis Bond Head to be required to carry out the principle of complete subordination of all the officers of the local government to the Downing Street authorities, at a time when the disposition of the colonists to repudiate that system and to insist on the responsibility of the Executive Council to the Legislative Assembly, had become irresistible. But he showed the greatest reluctance to deviate from this course after he received a confidential dispatch from Lord Glenelg,* laying it down as a principle that in the British American Provinces the Executive Councils should be composed of individuals possessing the confidence of the people. Every Canadian who had advocated this principle had been set down by Sir Francis as a republican and a traitor, and the principle itself he had denounced as unconstitutional.

Sir Francis Bond Head conceived his mission to be to fight and conquer what he called the " low-bred

* Dated September 30, 1836.

antagonist democracy." He thought the battle was
to be won by steadily opposing "the fatal policy of
concession," keeping the Tories in office, and putting
down the party which he indifferently designated
Reformers, Radicals, and Republicans. He thought
himself entitled to claim credit for having by his
reply to "the industrial classes of Toronto," caused a
scene of violence at a public meeting, at which, he
relates to Lord Glenelg with much satisfaction, "Mr.
Mackenzie totally failed in gaining attention," and
Dr. Morrison, who was then Mayor of Toronto, "was
collared and severely shaken." "The whole affair,"
he adds, "was so completely stifled by the indignation
of the people, that the meeting was dissolved without
the passing of a single resolution."

The Lieutenant Governor, who had completely
thrown himself into the hands of the Family Compact, had other schemes for influencing the constituencies in favor of one party and against another; for
he was not long in resolving to dissolve a House that
voted only such supplies as would subserve the purposes of the majority, while it withheld others of
which the want tended to embarrass the machinery of
the government.* The avowed object of reserving
the twelve money bills was to deprive the majority of
the House of what might be so distributed as to conduce to their re-election. On motion of Mr. Perry the
House had adopted the vicious principle of making
the members of the Legislature a committee for ex-
pending the £50,000 road money granted; and there
was some point in the observation of Sir F. B. Head

* The dissolution took place on the 28th May, 1886.

that this member's name appeared too often in connection with such expenditures. But although the reservation of these money bills did not lead to their being vetoed, the effect on the constituencies was the same. The elections were over before it was known that the Royal assent had been given, in opposition to the recommendation of the Lieutenant Governor, who takes care to make it understood that, on this question, he had the concurrence of his Council. Before the elections were announced, steps, of which Sir Francis B. Head appears to have been cognizant, were taken for procuring petitions in favor of a dissolution of the House. Perhaps they were suggested by himself or his Council. Certain it is that he had timely warning of petitions in process of being signed, some time before they were presented. The Tory press divided the country into two parties: one of whom was represented to be in favor of maintaining the supremacy of the British Crown in the Province, and the other as being composed of traitors and republicans. This representation was transferred from partisan newspapers to official dispatches and replies to admiring addresses. Timid persons were awed into inactivity; not thinking it prudent to appear at the polls, where their presence would have caused them to be branded as revolutionists. The Tories subscribed largely for election purposes; votes were manufactured and violence resorted to.*

---

* "The circumstances under which they (the members of the House) were elected, were such as to render them peculiarly objects of suspicion and reproach to a large number of their countrymen. They are accused of having violated their pledges at the election." "In a number of instances, too, the

By such means was Sir F. B. Head enabled to boast of the perilous success he had achieved. He had done everything upon his own responsibility; having never consulted the Imperial Government, to whose direc- tions he professed to feel it his duty to pay implicit obedience. He had written to Lord Glenelg, inform- ing him that it was his intention to dissolve the House; and instructing him—as if he were the superior—to send him no orders on the subject. Nor was this the only occasion on which he undertook to transmit his orders to Downing Street. When, in the spring of 1836, Mr. Robert Baldwin, one of his late councillors, started for England, Sir F. B. Head described him to Lord Glenelg as an agent of the revolutionary party, and expressed a wish that he might not be received at the Colonial Office; adding a suggestion that if he should make any application he should be effectually snubbed in a letter in reply, which should be trans- mitted to Canada for publication. He denounced to the Colonial Minister the project of surrendering to the control of the Canadian Legislature the casual and territorial revenues; being desirous of keeping the Executive, as far as possible, financially independent of the popular branch of the Legislature. He quar- relled with the Commission of Inquiry, which had been sent to Canada, headed by Lord Gosford, for re-

elections were carried by the unscrupulous exercise of the influence of the go- vernment, and by a display of violence on the part of the Tories, who were emboldened by the countenance afforded to them by the government; that such facts and such impressions produced in the country an exasperation and a despair of good government, which extended far beyond those who had actu- ally been defeated at the poll."—*Earl Durham's Report on the Affairs of British North America.*

commending that the Executive Council should be made accountable to public opinion; and assured the Imperial Government that the project was pregnant with every species of danger. When he received a confidential dispatch from Lord Glenelg, acquainting him that this course had been determined on, he became half frantic; and on the publication of a dispatch from Sir Archibald Campbell, Lieutenant Governor of New Brunswick, directing him to increase the number of his councillors, and to select them from persons possessing the confidence of the people, he vented his disappointment by declaring that " the triumph which the loyal inhabitants of our North American colonies had gained over the demands of the Republicans was not only proved to be temporary, but was completely destroyed." He carried his indiscretion to an inconceivable extent. The Province, he openly declared, was threatened with invasion from a foreign enemy; and he proceeded to throw out a defiant challenge to this imaginary foe. " In the name of every regiment of militia in Upper Canada," he said, " I publicly promulgate, let them come if they dare." This piece of audacious folly made him the subject of a remarkable practical joke. A deputation, headed by Mr. Hincks, waited on him to inquire from what point the attack was expected; the inference being that they desired to know in order that they might be prepared to repel the invaders.* If the Lieutenant

---

* " We, the undersigned electors of the City of Toronto," the address ran, "having read in your Excellency's answer to the address of certain electors of the Home District the following language :—' They (the people of Toronto) are perfectly aware that there exist in the Lower Province, one or two indi-

Governor did not see that he was quizzed, he felt thrust into a corner; and his face crimsoned with indignation at the impertinent inconvenience of the inquiry. His dispatches contain a mixture of insolent dictation, intended for advice, and a craven fear of the disapproval of his superiors.

The fate of British dominion in America, he assured the Colonial Minister, depended upon his ruinous advice being taken, and his mad acts sustained. Several times it was necessary to curb him; and once he made an inferential rather than a direct tender of his resignation. He dismissed Mr. George Ridout from the offices of Colonel of the Militia, Judge of the District Court of Niagara, and Justice of the Peace, on the pretence that he was an active member of the Alliance Society, who had issued an address on the subject of the resignation of the late Executive Council, which contained words personally offensive to the Lieutenant Governor;* and when this charge was

viduals who inculcate the idea that this Province is about to be disturbed by the interference of foreigners whose powers and whose numbers will prove invincible. In the name of every Regiment of Militia in Upper Canada, I publicly promulgate, '*Let them come if they dare.*' We do not doubt the readiness with which would be answered upon any emergency your appeal to the Militia, which appeal we are satisfied would not have been made without adequate cause. In a matter so seriously affecting the peace and tranquillity of the country and the security of its commerce, we beg to learn from your Excellency from what quarter the invasion is alleged to be threatened."

* The document, to which exception was taken, is subjoined; the particular words deemed most offensive being in those in italics:—"The difference between Sir Francis Bond Head and the House of Assembly, growing out of the resignation of the late Executive Council, has led to a dissolution of Parliament. The unanimous representation of the late Executive Council, severally signed by the Hon. Peter Robinson, Hon. G. H. Markland, Hon. Joseph Wells, Hon. J. H. Dunn, and Robert Baldwin and John Rolph, Esquires,

proved to the satisfaction of Lord Glenelg to be groundless, he refused to obey the order of the Colonial Minister to restore Mr. Ridout to office. When the only
charge made against Mr. Ridout had been disproved,
he trumped up seven others—none of which had been
communicated to Mr. Ridout for explanation—taking
the ground that he neither deemed an inquiry necessary, nor that the person dismissed should be made
acquainted with the grounds of his dismissal.   On
both these points the Lieutenant Governor met the
opposition of Lord Glenelg.*   He refused to obey the
instructions of the Colonial Secretary to appoint Mr.
Marshall Spring Bidwell to a judgeship in the Court

we declare to be moderate, just, and constitutional. The refusal of Sir F. B.
Head to allow the Executive Council to discharge the duties obviously belonging to their office, and imposed by their oath, of advising the Lieutenant Governor upon our public affairs, preparatory to his final and discretionary action
upon those affairs, betrays a disposition as a stranger to conduct the government in an arbitrary, unsafe, and unconstitutional manner, which the House
of Assembly, unless traitors to us, could not sanction or grant supplies to uphold.   The fifty-seven Rectories could not by law have been established without the advice and consent of the Executive Council of the Province; and
their recent establishment and endowment with their exclusive ecclesiastical
and spiritual rights and privileges, is a practical and melancholy proof of the
indispensable necessity of a good and honest Executive Council, alike possessing the confidence of the King and the people. *It is our duty solemnly to assure you, that the conduct of Sir Francis Bond Head has been alike a disregard of
constitutional government and of candor and truth in his statements to you.* We
therefore appeal to you most earnestly not to abandon your faithful Representatives at the approaching contest, but by your manly conduct prove yourselves
worthy of good government and honest public servants." So far from Mr.
Ridout being a member of the Alliance Society, he had opposed its establishment, when Mr. Mackenzie proposed the resolutions on which it was based.

    * "I am unaware," wrote Lord Glenelg to Sir F. B. Head, April 5, 1837,
"of so much as a single instance in which a public officer has been dismissed
as a punishment, and on the ground of misconduct, without the most explicit
disclosure to him of the reasons by which his superior vindicated such an exercise of authority.

of Queen's Bench; and when he had done his best to drive men into rebellion he claimed credit for his foresight in having pointed out their traitorous intentions.

Messrs. Mackenzie, Bidwell, and Perry, were among the members of the popular party who failed to secure a re-election. It was the first election at which the county of York had been divided into Ridings. Mr. Mackenzie stood for the Second Riding, having for opponent, Mr. Edward Thompson, a negative sort of man, without decision enough to make him a very decided partisan.* As he had not energy enough to be bitter, many timid voters, alarmed by the cries of revolution raised by the Lieutenant Governor and the Family Compact, thought that if they voted at all, it would be safest, if not best, to vote for him. He obtained four hundred and eighty-nine votes; Mackenzie, three hundred and eighty-nine. Just before the election, there had been a sale of lots by the Government, at the mouth of the River Credit. They were mostly divided into quarter acres, and were sold for $32 each. Some of the patents were issued during the election; others only a few days before. But this did not turn the scale of the election; for in the list of voters, I find only four who voted for Mr. Thompson on lots at Port Credit. About an equal number of votes offered for Mr. Mackenzie were turned away on what appear to be frivolous grounds. If such great pains had not been taken by Mr. Thompson's friends to prevent a scrutiny, there might, looking at the disparity in the number of votes received by the two

* He passed for a modified Liberal at the election, which was a great advantage to him; and acted with the Family Compact when he got into the House.

48

candidates, have been some reason for concluding that Mr. Mackenzie was beaten by a majority of legal votes. Nothing but a scrutiny could have settled the point in dispute. There was said to have been a suspiciously large increase in the number of voters.

The unscrupulous influence of the Government in the election, attested by the Earl of Durham's Report, is beyond question. Streetsville was the polling place for the Second Riding of York; and violence was apprehended on the day of nomination. A procession of Orangemen, an organization with whom Mr. Mackenzie was on ill terms, took place; the "Boyne Water," "Protestant Boys," and "Croppies Lie Down," being played by the band. They afterwards drew up in line at a point where it was necessary for Mackenzie to pass. Several were provided with loaded fire-arms, on both sides. One Switzer, a man of enormous muscular power, led the way through the lines; and Mr. Mackenzie followed unharmed. He delivered a speech much more calculated to excite than to soothe the hostile crowd, and which shows that the idea of the possibility of England losing the Province by misgovernment was floating in his mind.*

---

* From this speech, delivered on the 27th June, I give an extract: "When I last met you here I told you the causes of our difficulties, and showed you how far they might be removed by the concessions or interposition of the British Government. I regret to say that all the efforts of the Reformers during the last two years have only gone to show that the Government is above all law; that a person, living in one of the streets of London is the autocrat of Upper Canada; and that the people's representatives have neither power nor influence to promote education, encourage trade, redress grievances, secure economy, or amend your laws and institutions. I have been diligent in the Legislature; every proposition calculated to make you happier I have supported; and whatever appeared to me to be against popular government and

It was said that he was opposed by Bank as well as
Government influence; and this seems not improbable,
since he had procured the disallowance of two bank
charter bills, when he was in England.* Complaints

the permanent interests of the many I have opposed, please or offend whom it
might. The result is against you. You are nearer having saddled on you a
dominant priesthood; your public and private debt is greater; the public improvements made by Government are of small moment; the chartered Banks
and the Canada Company have you more and more under their control; the
priests of the leading denominations have swallowed bribes like a sweet morsel;
the revenues of your country are applied without your consent; the principle
that the Executive should be responsible to public opinion and acceptable to
the people is denied to your use, both by the Governor here, and by his employers elsewhere; the means to corrupt our elections are in the hands of the
adversaries of popular institutions, and they are using them; and although an
agent has been sent with the petitions of the House of Assembly to the King
and House of Commons, I dare not conceal from you my fears that the power
that has oppressed Ireland for centuries will never extend its sympathies to
you. It will seek to elevate the few, who are suitable instruments for your
subjugation, in order that (like the Canada Company, Thomas Clark's £100,000
estate, John McGill's £50,000, and I might add, Colonel Talbot's vast accumulation) such men may will, or take their wealth elsewhere, to impoverish you.
Look into the history of our race:—'Ages pass, and leave the poor herd, the
mass of men, eternally the same—hewers of wood and drawers of water.' I
have taken less pains to be elected by you this time than I ever did before, and
the reason is, I do not feel that lively hope to be able to be useful to you which
I once felt. On this subject I spoke my mind with great frankness at Cooks-
ville, when I told you that the country was beginning to lose all hope from
Reform majorities under this government, and that I feared the result of the
elections would show that it was so. We are, of course, to wait for the answer
to our petitions to England. If it be favorable, it will be our duty to uphold
the system of monarchical government, modified, of course, by the removal of
that wretched playhouse, the Legislative Council, together with the mounte-
banks who exhibit on its boards. If the reply be unfavorable, as I am appre-
hensive it will, for the Whigs and Tories are alike dishonest, contending factions of men who wish to live in idleness upon the labors of honest industry,
then the Crown will have forfeited one claim upon British freemen in Upper
Canada, and the result it is not difficult to foresee."

* One of these related to the Commercial Bank of the Midland District; and
the story told is that, about a month previous to the election, the managers of
the branch of this bank, at Toronto, sent for Attorney General Hagerman,

of bribery were also made; and if they were well
founded, it is reasonable to suppose that the money
formed part of the official election fund subscribed in
Toronto. After the desperate policy resorted to for
the purpose of ejecting Mr. Mackenzie from a previous
Legislature, it is not to be supposed that any effort
would be spared to prevent his return. There can be
no doubt that the improper use of official influence
was the main cause of the election resulting as it did.
Besides the intimidation so generally practised, at
these elections, the sheriff of the county, Mr. Jarvis,
was at Streetsville, interfering in a manner that had
been strongly condemned years before by Lord Goderich. He insisted on swearing Mr. Mackenzie to his
qualification, a second time, till the Returning Officer,
Mr. Hepburn, who was a strong partisan of the Family
Compact, was obliged to interfere, and declare that the
qualification had already been sufficiently attested. I
do not wish to repeat a possible calumny; and I should
not have ventured to give new currency to the statement that the Lieutenant Governor had thrown out
hints that a worse thing than a riot might happen, had
he not, in his official communications with the Colonial Office, already taken credit for having aroused a
feeling that produced violence at a public meeting.

took him into the bank parlor, and Mr. John Ross the cashier, in presence of
the others, handed him a large number of notes due to the bank by persons
living in this constituency, and gave him distinct and positive instructions to
be very lenient with every debtor who would pledge himself to vote against
Mackenzie, but "to put the screws on" every one of them who refused to
pledge himself. It was said that a like policy was pursued by the Bank of
Upper Canada, whose amended charter Mr. Mackenzie had caused to be vetoed in England. But stories of this kind must always be received with some
degree of allowance.

He himself rode out to the polling place during the election. A clergymen offered a vote, to the validity of which he refused to make oath;* and the voters were sharply questioned on both sides.

Mr. Mackenzie's mortification at a result which he

* The following scene occurred: The Reverend Thomas Phillips, D.D., Rector of Etobicoke, Chaplain to the House of Assembly, late Professor in King's College, Toronto, presented himself and offered to vote. After his property had been described and entered on the poll-book, the following inquiry was made:

Mr. Mackenzie.—"I think I saw your reverence standing in the rain the other day, up to the ankles in mud, waiting to edge in a non-resident vote for Mr. Draper, I dare say you have been going the rounds of the county, since, to uphold 'the Constitution,' and as it is probable you have your deed about you, I wish you would produce it.

Dr. Phillips.—(Producing his deed.)—"I have a good title, or I would not have taken the pains to come here.

Mr. Mackenzie.—"I find that you have bought this half or quarter acre of a sand bank for £8, a year's interest on which is eight shillings Are there any buildings?

Dr. Phillips.—"There are none.

Mr. Mackenzie.—"No buildings! How then is your income obtained?

Dr. Phillips.—"I rented the property last year for a dollar; but, this year, the times are so bad that I have left the woman have it for nothing.

Mr. Mackenzie.—"You have been paid for teaching others what the English Constitution is for a number of years; you have known what a 40s. freeholder means for these forty years back at least; you belong to an order who live sumptuously at the expense of the community, and enjoy fat rectories, the value of which is enhanced by the farmer's labor, and you are here to-day to uphold your order by voting me out of the House. I shall make your own conscience the umpire between us—the inward monitor shall decide. Did you, when you came here, for one moment believe you had a right to vote? Did you not rather hope to edge in a bad vote on account of the respectability of your personal appearance? If you think you are an elector of this Riding, take the constitutional oath as such, and then you may vote; but remember I'll look carefully into the matter next session.

Returning Officer.—"The oath is as follows:—

Dr. Phillips.—"Stop, stop, I won't swear to my freehold. Really, Mr. Mackenzie, you are too sharp upon me." And the reverend gentleman, who was brother-in-law of the Sheriff of the Home District, gathered up his papers, slunk down stairs, and deferred the oath and his vote till another occasion.

believed to have been brought about by improper means, was extreme. He retired with a few of his supporters to the house of Mr. Graham, in Streetsville, and wept like a child. Such was the power of sympathy, that several of the friends who were present, wept with him.

About the time of the commencement of the first Legislative session, which took place on the eighth of November, 1836, after the House had been elected, Mr. Mackenzie was taken dangerously ill of inflammatory fever, followed by inflammation of the lungs and pleura, brought on by his taking cold. It says much for his constitution that he was enabled to escape with his life from the hands of four doctors, Barclay, of the garrison, Widmer, Rolph, and Telfer, who dosed him with seventy or eighty grains of calomel; but it must be admitted that they were all men of repute in their profession. On the 23d of November, he was pronounced convalescent; but his ultimate recovery was slow.

Petitions against the return of any member, whose seat it is intended to contest, are required to be presented within fourteen days of the commencement of the session. On the 13th December—one month and five days after the session had commenced—Dr. Morrison, on producing medical certificates of Mr. Mackenzie's illness, obtained an extension of the time for presenting a petition against Mr. Thompson's return. Seven days were allowed. The regulation set aside was not one of law, but was simply a rule of the House. When the allegations in the petition had become known to the House, the majority evinced extreme anxiety to avoid inquiry. Mr. Mackenzie, continuing to collect evidence and increase his list of witnesses, refrained from completing his recognizances as security for costs, till nearly the expiration of the time required: fourteen days after the presentation of the petition. New facts continued to come in, and, before handing in his list of witnesses, he wished to make it as complete as possible. But, by an entirely new construction of the law, he was held to have exceeded the time. Dr. Rolph showed the untenableness of the position which a partisan majority was ready to assume; but without avail. The petition was introduced on the 20th of December. It then, as required by law, lay on the table two days before being read; which last act, it was contended, completed the series which made up the presentation.* The House had

* On the 20th of January, 1887, a motion having been made for allowing one week to petition against the return of Mr. Charles Richardson from the town of Niagara, Dr. Rolph, seconded by Dr. Morrison, moved to add the following words:—"And that the above relief be also extended in like manner to such freeholders of the Second Riding of the county of York, as may within the same time desire to make their complaint of any wrongs to their elective franchise at the late general election; because, as the late petition of W. L. Mackenzie, complaining of the undue election and return of the sitting member for that Riding (Edward W. Thompson, Esq.) was in the terms of the forty-first rule of this House only 'brought in' on the 20th, and not 'read' till the 22nd of December, it could not till then be considered as fully presented; and because the Provincial Act, 4th Geo. IV., ch. 4, copied from the English Act 25th, George III., requires that 'whenever a petition complaining of an undue election or return of a member or members to serve in Parliament shall be presented to the House of Assembly, a day and hour shall, by the said House of Assembly, be appointed for taking the same into consideration, and notice thereof in writing shall be forthwith given by the Speaker to the petitioner or his agent;' according to which Act, in the invariable practice of the British House of Commons, the bringing up readily, and acting on such petition, and the giving of the said notice forthwith by the Speaker to the peti-

always acted on this construction; and it could not have one rule for itself and another for petitioners. The petition must therefore be considered as having been presented on the 22nd; and the fourteen days

tioner, are always immediately consecutive; and as this House have by their own practice put such a construction on the said Act, as not to consider such a petition presented, so as to require them to appoint a day and hour for taking the same into consideration, and giving forthwith the said notice to the petitioner, till the reading thereof on the second day after it is brought up, so the exigency of the said statute ought to be considered as satisfied by the said petitioner, by his computing his fourteen days from the said reading of the petition, as properly the time of the full Parliamentary presentation thereof; for the same construction by which the House is governed should, in justice and good faith, be applied to the petitioner, and not one construction be adopted for the House, and another construction for the people praying them for relief; from which it follows, that as the petition of Mr. Mackenzie was brought up on the 20th, and not read and acted on by the House till the 22nd, the petitioner's fourteen days reckoned from the 22nd, for entering into recognizances as security for costs, did not elapse till the 5th of January inclusive, although this House discharged the matter from the order of the day on the fourth, thereby giving the petitioner only twelve instead of fourteen days: and because the Speaker, in behalf of the House, did not, according to the exigency of the said Statute, give notice to the petitioner 'forthwith' on the 22nd, but omitted to do so till the 30th of December, thereby abridging the time of the notice, which would otherwise have put the petitioner and his attorney on their guard; and this House having themselves been therein guilty of laches, ought not rigidly to hold the said petitioner unexcused, even had he been guilty of laches too: and because this House adjourned from the 22nd of December till the 2nd of January, which interval, as the Speaker was not in attendance in his room at the House, ought not to be counted against the petitioner, who should have the benefit of fourteen sitting days, and not pursue the Speaker, as possibly might be needed in a future case, to his country seat, a distance of several hundred miles: and because Mr. Mackenzie had gathered from William Patrick, Esq., the Senior Clerk of this House, an officer of eighteen years' experience, that the computation of his fourteen days would be from the reading of the said petition: and because an investigation into grave charges affecting the freedom of election, and the invasion thereof by the Executive Government, and consequently affecting the constitution and character of this House, ought not to be lightly arrested, when the injured parties are willing and anxious to prosecute it, but should, on the contrary, be openly, fully, and honorably facilitated."

for completing the recognizances would not end till
the 5th of January, though the order had improperly
been discharged on the 4th ; by which the time allowed
by law had illegally been abridged.   The Speaker
was required, on the 22nd, to have given notice to the
petitioner of the day fixed for taking the petition into
consideration; but he failed to give it till the 30th,
and for his default, the House, not the petitioner, was
responsible.   This argument was conclusive; but the
vote was hostile, being thirty-two against fifteen.

It may seem strange that the presentation of a petition should include its reading—fixed by law at two
days after its introduction—but the House must be
judged by its own practice ; and this is stated to have
been uniformly different, on all previous occasions,
from the course now taken.   Mr. Jonas Jones, by
whom the act relating to contested elections was
brought in, did Mr. Mackenzie full justice on this
occasion ; and the fact deserves to be noted 'the more,
since he was a political opponent of the petitioner.
" He considered that Mr. Mackenzie had a right to
count fourteen days from the time his memorial was
read, and that he had neglected no requirement of the
law ;" and, on this ground, Mr. Jones voted against an
amendment declaring that the order relating to the
petition had been legally discharged, and that therefore it ought not to be restored.   And Mr. Gowan, another political opponent of the petitioner, showed that,
in the previous Parliament, he had been placed in precisely the same position as Mr. Mackenzie with respect
to time ; and that not a single member of the House,
a large majority of whom were opposed to him in

politics, raised an objection. One thing is very clear
—and it must be regarded as a circumstance of suspicion—the Government party was seriously anxious to
avoid an investigation. If they had nothing to fear
from a scrutiny, it is difficult to conceive what motive
they could have had for departing from the uniform
practice in order to avoid an investigation. The delay
on the part of the petitioner arose entirely from the
supposition that the time would not expire till the
5th of January.

He had the authority of the senior clerk of the
House for believing that this was the uniform practice, and on the 22d December, the day on which it
was contended the presentation of the petition was
completed, Mr. McNab obtained fourteen days for the
sitting member to prepare his list of witnesses—an
implied confession that the fourteen days after which
the petition would be acted upon commenced on that
day. An amendment was added to this motion giving Mr. Mackenzie the same time to prepare the list
of his witnesses, and yet the majority afterwards refused to give, for completing his recognizances, the
time they had thus agreed upon. The motion to discharge the order for taking the petition into consideration was made by Mr. J. S. Boulton, who had taken
an active part in the expulsion of Mackenzie from a
former House, and of whose brother the petitioner
had some years before obtained the dismissal from
the Attorney Generalship.

There was the more reason for the inquiry, because
the allegations in the petition included even the head
of the government in charges of undue interference;

by making inflammatory replies to addresses, with a view of influencing the election;* by the issue of land-

* Here are a few specimens of the partisan and inflammatory replies given by Sir Francis Bond Head to addresses, and published with a view of influencing the elections generally. The following language was used in his reply to the Electors of Toronto:—

"GENTLEMEN:—No one can be more sensible than I am, that the stoppage of the supplies has caused a general stagnation of business, which will probably end in the ruin of many of the inhabitants of this city; and in proportion as the Metropolis of the Province is impoverished, the farmers' market must be lowered; for how can he possibly receive money, when those who should consume his produce are seen flying in all directions from a land from which industry has been publicly repelled?

"In the flourishing Continent of North America, the Province of Upper Canada now stands like a healthy young tree that has been girdled, its drooping branches mournfully betraying that its natural nourishment has been deliberately cut off."

Still dwelling with affected lamentation over the universal devastation caused by the withholding of his supplies, (the whole amount of which was less than £10,000,) he thus attempts to work the electors up to the highest pitch:—

"GENTLEMEN:—I have no hesitation in saying that another such a victory would ruin this country. But this opinion is hourly gaining ground; the good sense of the country has been aroused; the yeoman has caught a glimpse of his real enemy; the farmer begins to see who is his best friend: in short, people of all denominations, of all religions, and of different politics, rallying round the British Flag, are now loudly calling upon me to grant them constitutional redress.

"When the verdict of the country shall have been sufficiently declared, I will promptly communicate my decision."

Denouncing the Reformers as agitators, he says:—

"GENTLEMEN:—My plans and projects are all contained and published in the instructions which I received from the King. They desire me to correct, without partiality, the grievances of this country; and it is because the agitators see I am determined to do so, that they are endeavoring to obstruct me by every artifice in their power. They declare me to be their enemy, and the truth is, I really am."

But his Address to the Electors of Newcastle District, if possible, transcends the rest, and would alone, Dr. Rolph declared on the floor of the Legislature, have formed a solid foundation for his impeachment:—

"As your district has now the important duty to perform of electing representatives for a new Parliament, I think it may practically assist, if I clearly lay before you what is the conduct I intend inflexibly to pursue, in order that

patents to persons known to be hostile to the petitioner, without exacting a compliance with the conditions of purchase; besides, gross partiality on the part
of the Returning Officer, and bribery on the part of
the sitting member.* It would have been far better
that these grave charges had been subjected to the
test of a rigid scrutiny; because, if they were not
well-founded, their refutation could most easily and
most effectually have been made in this way. But
by the choice of your new members, you may resolve either to support me or
oppose me, as you may think proper.

"I consider that my character and your interests are embarked in one and
the same boat. If by my administration I increase your wealth, I shall
claim for myself credit, which it will be totally out of your power to withhold from me; if I diminish your wealth, I feel it would be hopeless for any
one to shield me from blame.

"As we have, therefore, one common object in view, the plain question for
us to consider is, which of us has the greatest power to do good to Upper Canada? or, in other words, can you do as much good for yourselves as I can do
for you?

"It is my opinion that you cannot! It is my opinion that if you choose to
dispute with me, and live on bad terms with the Mother Country, you will, to
use a homely phrase, only quarrel with your own 'bread and butter.' If you
like to try the experiment by electing members, who will again stop the supplies, do so, for I can have no objection whatever; on the other hand, if you
choose fearlessly to embark your interests with my character, depend upon it
I will take paternal care of them both.

"If I am allowed I will, by reason and mild conduct, begin first of all by
tranquilizing the country, and as soon as that object shall be gained, I will use
all my influence with His Majesty's Government to make such alteration in
the land granting departments, as shall attract into Upper Canada the redun-
dant wealth and population of the Mother Country. Men! women, and money are what you want, and if you will send to Parliament members of moderate politics, who will cordially and devoid of self-interest assist me, depend
upon it you will gain more than you possibly can do by hopelessly trying to
insult me; for let your conduct be what it may, I am quite determined, so long
as I may occupy the station I now do, neither to give offence, nor to take it."

The reference to "bread and butter," in this Address, caused the House,
elected in 1836, to be called the "Bread and Butter Parliament."

* See Appendix C.

this is the strongest evidence that many of them were true.

The decision of the House can scarcely excite surprise ; for in a case of that peculiar nature, where either side of the case could be sustained by plausible arguments, a partisan majority, so violently opposed as they were to the petitioner, were not likely to be very scrupulous in their decision. Rightly or wrongly the petitioner was firmly convinced that he had been defrauded of his seat, and unfairly and illegally denied the liberty of proving how it had been done, and recovering what had been unwarrantably taken from him. He had a keen sense of personal injury, and when wrong done to him was also done to the public, he was slow to forget, and not too ready to forgive.

Dr. Duncombe, a member of the Liberal party in Upper Canada, who had held a seat in the Legislative Assembly, brought to the notice of the Colonial Secretary, Lord Glenelg, the complaints made against the Lieutenant Governor, in connection with this election, as well as against his general policy, and Sir Francis Bond Head was required to put in his defence.

CHAPTER XXI.

Mackenzie commences the Publication of *The Constitution* newspaper— Revolutionary Literature—Mock Trial of Sir Francis Bond Head, by a Committee of the House of Assembly—A Verdict of Acquittal did not allay
the Public Discontent—Samuel Lount—The Fatal Resolution—Personal Insult added to Political Wrong—The Session of 1836–7—The House shows
its Fear of an Appeal to the People by repealing the Act by which the
Death of the King effected a Dissolution—Recklessness in Money Votes—
The House sanctions the Creation of the Rectories—Turbulent Close of the
Session—A Trade Appeal to Washington—Mr. Mackenzie goes to New York
and purchases largely at the Trade Sales of Books.

ON the 4th July—a significant date—Mr. Mackenzie
published the first number of *The Constitution* newspaper, the last issue of which appeared on the 29th
November, 1837. The first and fourth page of the
number for December 6th were printed, when at this
stage it was brought to a violent close by the break-
ing out of the insurrection. The forms of type were
broken up by the loyalist mob. When he brought
The Colonial Advocate to a close, he was anxious to bid
adieu to the harassing cares of Canadian journalism
forever; but his political friends had, by their urgent
entreaties, succeeded in inducing him to re-enter a
career to which he had previously bid a final adieu.
As editor of *The Constitution*, he became the organ of
increasing discontent, and might easily be mistaken
for the promoter of it. But, as always happens, the

press reflected public opinion with more or less accuracy, and already the Liberal portion of it had begun to speak in no muffled or ambiguous accents.*

We are entering upon the period of revolutionary ideas, expressed in speeches and rhymes, in newspapers and more solemn documents. Sir Francis Bond Head may be said to have produced the first specimens in inflammatory replies to addresses. What nearly always happens, on such occasions, happened on this. People found themselves committed to revolutionary ideas without the least suspicion of the extent to which they had gone, much less of what was to follow. Dr. Duncombe's letter to Lord Glenelg, charging the head of the Provincial Government with crimes which deserve impeachment, was referred to a committee of the House of Assembly. Every one knew in advance what the decision would be; but the proceeding was in the nature of an impeachment against Sir Francis Bond Head. For if he were found guilty, what was to be done? A Colonial Governor who misconducts himself, can only be tried in England; and unless there were a foregone conclusion to exculpate him from the charges made against him there could be no object in referring them

* As an example, the following verse from "Rhymes for the People," which appeared in the St. Thomas *Liberal*, in August, may be cited:—

"Up then! for Liberty—for Right,
Strike home! the tyrants falter;
Be firm—be brave, let all unite,
And despots' schemes must alter.
Our King—our Government and laws,
While just, we aye shall love them,
But Freedom's Heaven-born, holier cause
We hold supreme above them."

to a committee. Dr. Rolph, assuming a serio-comic air, ridiculed the proceeding in a speech that will ever be memorable in Canadian history.*

* Dr. Rolph thus opened his battery on the miscalled treasury benches: "Perhaps never did a day, wearing a more lowering aspect than this, dawn upon a British Colony! The glory of Provincial Monarchy, subjected ignominiously to these proceedings, is sullied beyond the power of your acquittal to redeem. Kings are sometimes tried. But nations are their judges. And when a people, goaded by injury, rise in their majesty to occupy the judgment seat, grand is the spectacle and vast the result! Popular sympathy generally mingles with the royal fate, and interest is transmitted with the very block which is dyed with their blood. But Kings even in Europe would dwindle into shadows, were they arraigned and tried before subordinate tribunals. Only imagine it; King William the Fourth tried by a select committee of the House of Commons! The proposition, Sir, shocks you. * * Impeachment, did I say? Oh no. They have doomed their illustrious personage to drink the cup of humiliation to the very dregs. The trial has not been conducted even before the Legislative Council, our Provincial House of Peers, who would, perhaps, regard a guilty participation little less than petit treason! It has not even been conducted before this honorable House, while the chair, Sir, was occupied by the Speaker, in whom is embodied, besides his Parliamentary phylacteries, the aggregate dignity of the Assembly, with the Mace, surmounted with a Crown, lying massively on the table, and defended by the Sergeant-at-Arms, girded with a sword and glowing with a chivalrous spirit. Such inquisitorial proceedings even over Royalty have, when clothed with stateliness and wrapt up in form, an imposing effect upon the eyes of the multitude, who are therefore the less likely to have their habitual reverence seriously impaired. But as if there were a conspiracy to bring His Excellency to the very dust, to shadow his dignity, mortify his pride, and republicanize the people, the investigation was repudiated by the House, and insultingly transferred to an ordinary committee! * * What will the British Government say to this impolitic proceeding? You who ought to be the first to keep within, at least, the bounds of impeachment in the Mother Country, have assumed to try, and either condemn or acquit the representative of the King! The Governor has been charged with interfering, to an alarming degree, with the purity and freedom of the late general elections. It is a charge of treason against the people. You are this day teaching them a lesson they will not easily forget. They find themselves, through the persons of their representatives, bringing under the ordeal of this inquiry the head of the Executive Government. If it is thought expedient to exempt him from civil and criminal responsibilities in the courts of justice, by what law do you now assume a jurisdiction, of which even the King's Bench is

The report, as every body had foreseen, was a verdict of acquittal; and a special verdict, it must be
remarked, since it declared that the country owed the
Vice Regal defendant a debt of gratitude for his patriotism and other inestimable qualities. But if Sir
Francis Bond Head was pronounced a model Governor, by a partisan committee,* the public was not
convinced, and the discontents were not allayed.

A considerable portion of Dr. Duncombe's letter,
containing the charge against the Lieutenant Governor,
on which the committee had pronounced, related to
the Second Riding of York election, on which a committee had illegally been refused to Mr. Mackenzie.
Nor was he allowed to produce before the committee,
that pretended to inquire into these charges, the
evidence which he was prepared to produce in support of them.

The case of Mr. Mackenzie, though perhaps not
exactly like any other, cannot be regarded as having
stood alone. The improper means taken by the Executive to influence the elections, did not affect him
alone. Sir Francis Bond Head openly proclaimed

ousted? If found guilty, will you put him into the custody of the Sergeant-
at-Arms? Will you as it were dethrone him—or bring him to the block?
You may have an authority from the British Ministry to exercise this inquisitorial function; but I cannot even then acknowledge its wisdom. When you
familiarise the people with these summary proceedings against Kingly functionaries, you make them compare their own strength and importance with
that of their rulers. * * By the adoption of this report you acquit, and by
the rejection of it, you convict Sir Francis Bond Head of the high crimes and
misdemeanors brought against him."

* The committee first sat on the 25th of November, composed of Messrs.
McNab, Draper, Parke, Sherwood, and Woodruff. On the first of December
Messrs. Jones and Norton were added. And on the 22d, Mr. Draper retired
and was succeeded by Messrs. Prince and Burwell.

50

himself the enemy of the Reformers; and he brought
all the weight of his position to bear against them as
a party. It was the general conviction of the popular
party, that if Mr. Mackenzie's complaints of the undue return of Mr. Thompson had gone before a committee of the House, he could not have hoped to obtain
justice; a conviction which prevented others from
seeking to reclaim seats out of which they believed
they had been fraudulently cajoled. This was the
case of Mr. Samuel Lount, who was goaded into rebellion and hanged for high treason.*

The sense of injustice engendered by these means
rankled in men's minds; and it tended to beget a fatal
resolution to seek redress by a resort to physical force.

---

* "On the 15th of February, 1837," Mr. Mackenzie related, "Mr. Samuel
Lount, the late upright and patriotic member for Simcoe, called at my house,
accompanied by Mr. Thrift Meldrum, Merchant and Innkeeper in Barrie,
and I mentioned to them that I was collecting evidence for a pamphlet to
expose the Government, as the Executive influence had cheated me out of my
right to do so through an election contest for the Second Riding. Mr. Lount
took out his pocket memorandum book, and stated that Mr. Meldrum had
been requested to open his tavern for Robinson and Wickens, at the time of
the late election, and that he did so; that since the election he (Meldrum) had
informed him (Lount) that on one occasion, he (Meldrum) accompanied Mr.
Wellesley Ritchey, the Government Agent, from Toronto to the Upper Settlement; that Mr. Ritchey called him (Meldrum) to one side at Crew's tavern,
where the stage stopped, and told him that Sir Francis had employed him
(Ritchey) to give the deeds to the settlers in Simcoe, and that he (Ritchey)
wanted him (Meldrum) to assist in turning Lount out. Meldrum agreed to
do his best, opened his house, and says that Wickens paid him faithfully for
his liquor, &c. When Mr. Lount had read the above from his memorandum,
I asked Mr. Meldrum if he could swear to these facts, he said he could, for
they were perfectly correct. I then asked Mr. Lount, who gave me a number
of important facts, why he did not contest the election, and he told me it
would have been throwing £100 away, and losing time, for that no one
who knew who the members were, could for a moment expect justice from
them."

This resolution, which did not assume a positive shape
for some time afterwards, was a capital error, and
one which some were to expiate with their lives, others
with sufferings and privations and contumely scarcely
preferable to death.

It was not sufficient for Sir F. B. Head and his
friends to pursue one of the two parties into which the
country was divided with injustice; they were not less
ready to assail them with personal calumny. The
Tory press asked, "Who is Wm. Lyon Mackenzie?"
And then they proceeded to give their own answer.
The Celtic blood boiling in his veins, at the personal
insults offered, Mr. Mackenzie replied in terms that
cannot be characterized as either temperate or discreet.* The fiery words, he used under the excitement, can hardly be held to express more than the
exasperation of the moment; and if they did not fall
harmless, it was because the government of Sir F. B.
Head had inclined the people to listen to desperate
counsels.

---

* "Small cause indeed," he said, "have Highlanders and the descendants
of Highlanders to feel a friendship for the Guelphic family. If the Stuarts
had their faults, they never enforced loyalty in the glens and valleys of the
north by banishing and extirpating the people; it was reserved for the Bruns-
wickers to give, as a sequel to the massacre of Glencoe, the cruel order for de-
population. I am proud of my descent from a rebel race; who held borrowed chieftains, a scrip nobility, rag money, and national debt in abomina-
tion. And notwithstanding the doctors' late operations with the lancet, this
rebel blood of mine will always be uppermost. Words cannot express my
contempt at witnessing the servile, crouching attitude of the country of my
choice. If the people felt as I feel, there is never a Grant or Glenelg who
crossed the Tay and Tweed to exchange high-born Highland poverty for substantial Lowland wealth, who would dare to insult Upper Canada with the official presence, as its ruler, of such an equivocal character as this Mr. what do
they call him —— Francis Bond Head."

In the session of 1836–7, which closed on the 4th
of March, Sir F. B. Head's " Bread and Butter " Assembly was very far from realizing his election promises of Reform.* But it is not probable that any
section of the public was disappointed, for they were
not promises that any one expected to see fulfilled.
The fear of a legal and inevitable dissolution, which
seemed to be impending, weighed heavily upon the
" Bread and Butter " Parliament. King William IV.
would probably not live four years ; and on the demise
of the Sovereign the Legislative Assembly legally
ceased to exist. Sir F. B. Head was not likely to fare
so well in a second election as he had in the first. A
bill was therefore passed, taking away the effect of the
Sovereign's death, of dissolving the House. Of the
majority, who passed this act, Mr. Mackenzie said,
" They tremble and shake for fear of the just retribu-
tion their covetousness has provoked ; and at Head's
nod vote themselves fit to outlive kings and emperors,
though utterly unfit to face their injured country."
The Lieutenant Governor was greatly scandalized at
a vote of £50,000 for roads, in the previous session ;

---

* In one of his electioneering replies to addresses, Sir F. B. Head said:
" Upper Canada has been so cruelly deceived by false statements, that the
farmers' interests are neglected, while the agitators of the Province have been
reaping a rich harvest.

" Gentlemen, I was sent here by His Majesty on purpose to correct the grievances of the country. I see quite clearly who are its enemies; and I declare
to you, that if the farmers will assist me, I will assist them.

" It is quite certain that I can render this Province powerful assistance ; and
it is equally certain that I have been ordered by His Majesty so to do."

. And in another: "Gentlemen, I need hardly assure you that I myself am
an advocate for reform, because if you will but take the trouble to read my
instructions, they will show you, that I was sent to Upper Canada by our
Gracious Sovereign for the express purpose of carrying reform into effect."

but now ten times that amount was voted for the same
purpose. The bill authorized the government to appoint commissioners to expend the money. If there
were grave objections to allowing members of the
House to perform this duty, the matter was not likely
to be made much better by investing an irresponsible
administration with the entire control of the expenditure, through agents of its selection. The money
bills, passed this session, show an extraordinary
degree of recklessness, on the part of the House,
in incurring debt. The Welland Canal debt was
increased to nearly a million of dollars. Authority
was given to borrow on the credit of the Province
over three quarters of a million (£300,000) more,
on account of a projected railroad from Hamilton
to Sandwich; to lend $400,000 to the Toronto and
Lake Huron Railway Company; for a loan of £77,000
for the improvement of the Trent Navigation. A
large number of other loans to companies connected
with harbors, canals, and navigation, was authorized.
The entire amount voted must have been about five
millions of dollars; bearing a larger proportion to
the revenue than a hundred millions would at present.
The establishment of fifty-seven Rectories by Sir J.
Colborne, before he left the government, which had
given great offence to a large majority of the population,* received the approval of the Assembly.

The session closed in one of those hurricanes of pas-

---

* When Sir F. B. Head undertook to manage the elections, he found the
Rectory question one of his difficulties. "The feeling which the endowment
of these Rectories created through the Province," he admitted in a dispatch to
the Colonial Secretary, " was one of the many difficulties I had to contend
against, during the late elections."

sion which often precede a violent revolutionary movement. The question of a Union of Upper and Lower Canada had been before the House during the session, and resolutions had been passed condemning the project. At twelve o'clock on the last day of the session—the prorogation was to take place at three—Messrs. Sherwood and Jones asked the concurrence of the House in an address to the Crown founded on the resolutions. Dr. Rolph moved an amendment, the object of which was to prevent a decision on the question in the absence of many members who had already gone home. He was followed by two other speakers on the same side, and as time was running rapidly against them, and Black· Rod would soon make his appearance, the Tories began to show signs of impatience—moving about, whispering in little knots together, and calling " question" and " order." Then, at the instance of Messrs. Jones and Draper, the Speaker called Dr. Rolph to order, laying down the rule that the question of Union could not be discussed on the amendment, but that it was only permissible to argue from the absence of members. Trying what he could do within these narrow limits, Dr. Rolph proceeded :—

" Our geographical situation," he said, " is singular. To the South we are barred from the Atlantic coast by the American Republics ; to the North and North-West you pass through barren lands to mountains covered with everlasting snows, and among Indian tribes unknown ; and to the East we are intercepted by the sister Province, the very Province with which it is proposed to unite us." Here he paused amidst

a scene of wild confusion. Three members were con-
ferring with the Speaker, and others of the majority
were consulting together in clusters, when the Speaker,
addressing Dr. Rolph, told him he must confine himself to the question. "Most logically, sir," was the
reply, "nothing but the gossipping about you prevented
you from comprehending the bearing of my remarks,"
Mr. Jones, in an undertone: "This is indecent." Dr.
Rolph: "The honorable and learned member says,
'This is indecent.'" Mr. Jones: "I only said so to
you, not to the House." Dr. Rolph: "What is said
to me is said to the House. Indecent to discuss the
question of Union introduced by himself!" The
Speaker interposes: "That, sir, is beside the question." Dr. Rolph: "Do, sir, then your duty by pro-
tecting the minority against the majority." There
was now a scene of complete confusion and disorder;
members moving about, whistling and talking, amid
cries of "Chair." The Speaker again interposed:
"Really the time must not be thus consumed; we
shall soon have to wait upon the Lieutenant Governor
with some joint address." Dr. Rolph: "Then post-
pone the discussion till next session; surely want of
time is attributable to those who now bring on the
question at the eleventh hour, not to this side of the
House, who are forced into it." After a further alter-
cation, the amendment was put and lost, and just
as the Speaker was about to put the main motion, Dr.
Rolph rose, saying: "Mr. Speaker, I have another
amendment to propose, notwithstanding your high-
handed method of putting me down." Mr. Sherwood: "Order! order! chair." Several voices: "Pro-

tect the chair." The Speaker made some remark that was not audible below the bar. Dr. Rolph: "Bear it; yes, it is but little of what is deserved." He then moved that the sense of the country on the subject of a Union of the Province would be best ascertained by dissolution, as a means of appealing to the country. Having thus obtained the right to enter on a wider range of discussion, he went on amid the same confusion as before, and when he was uttering the words, " The evil of our inland situation is admitted; what is the remedy?"—the Speaker announced: " The time has arrived—half-past one—to wait on the Lieutenant Governor with some joint address." And the scene was abruptly brought to a close.

Thus ended the last regular session of the Upper Canada Legislature preceding the outbreak of 1837, though an extraordinary session was to intervene. Several such scenes had occurred during the first session of the " Bread and Butter" Parliament.*

In the last session of the previous Parliament, Mr.

---

* The Montreal *Gazette*, a Tory paper, was greatly scandalized at the " scenes of an unseemly character that have lately been enacted in the Commons House of Assembly of our sister Province of Upper Canada. We particularly allude," it said, " to the disorderly, and, we must add, disgraceful manner in which important questions were discussed during the late session. Why, we ask, on any question, however much it may involve the interests of the public, or excite the feelings of contending and opposite parties, should the present House of Assembly of Upper Canada, of all others, so far forget what was due to itself, to the dignity of its deliberations, to the welfare of its constituency, to the prosperity of the Province, and the fair fame and honor of its character, as to permit itself for an instant to break loose like so many Bedlamites into those scenes of riotous disorder to which we have alluded, and which, it is admitted on all hands, reflect but little credit on the best and wisest among them."

Mackenzie, as has already been noticed, had carried an address to the King, praying that the Imperial Government would, by the use of its diplomatic instrumentalities, endeavor to procure for Canadians transit of goods through the United States free from import duties. But as it had not brought about the desired result, a large number of Canadians petitioned the Federal authorities, at Washington, to grant a drawback of duties on Canadian imports passing *in transitu* through the United States. And it was alleged that the petition received more attention than was paid to the address sent to England, though it appears to me that the facts hardly bore out the statement.

This spring Mr. Mackenzie went to New York, arriving there about the end of March. At the trade sales, then going on, he purchased several thousand volumes of books, and made large additions to his printing establishment. About two years before he had added a large book-store to his other business, and his present purchases furnished decisive proof that, at this time, the idea of risking every thing upon an armed insurrection had not entered into his calculations.

51